Somewhere
more simple

omewhere more simple is Marion Molteno's third novel. Her earlier
ovels have both won prizes: *A Shield of Coolest Air* won the David
Thomas fiction prize. *If You Can Walk, You Can Dance* won the
Commonwealth Writers Award for the best book in the Africa region
was selected in the top 20 books of the year for the Women's Book
val in New Zealand. Her volume of short stories, *A Language in*
ion, has been translated into five languages.

n Molteno grew up in South Africa, spent some years in Zambia
ince 1976 has lived in Britain. She has pioneered educational
cts with multi-ethnic communities and is now an advisor on
en's rights in Save the Children, supporting projects with
vantaged children in over 50 countries. She has two grown up
ters and is an enthusiastic grandmother.

Marion Molteno

Somewhere more simple

Longstone
BOOKS
—
LONDON

This story is entirely fictional. None of the characters
or incidents relates to any real individual.

Somewhere more simple
first published in 2007 by
Longstone Books, 33 Theatre Street, London SW11 5ND

copyright © Marion Molteno 2007

cover design by Andrew Corbett
set by Long House Publishing Services, Cumbria
printed and bound by Biddles Ltd, King's Lynn, Norfolk

distributed by Central Books
99 Wallis Road, London E9 5LN
All rights reserved

A catalogue record for this book
is available from the British Library

ISBN 10: 0-9554373-0-X
ISBN 13: 978-0-9554373-0-4

for May
who wanted an island story

One

In the beginning there was the barge, and the child woke each morning to the stillness of river and forest. For a few moments she lay watching the doll-sized curtains above her lift and move as the wind found its way through some not-quite-fitting corner. Then quietly, not to disturb her sleeping sister, she knelt up to lift the curtains and peer out, to see the bank of the river beginning to come to life. Ducks waddling about, leaves stirring with unseen creatures, and beyond, the towering trees.

Her sister, three years younger, had only the vaguest memories of that time. 'The little cupboards under the bed,' Cari pressed, urgent for her sister to recover this world they had shared so intimately. 'And the copper pipe, you *must* remember that?' The pipe had led off from the woodburner at the far end of the living space and ran the length of the barge. Extra-ordinary to think that they had lived through the northern winters with only that burner and the copper pipe for heat, but she didn't remember being seriously cold. Wet, yes. They had to strip off their clothes when they came in and drape them over that pipe. Then they would be wrapped up in something warm and sit on cushions on the floor, and fight over who got the one with little mirrors in it, while their mother cooked and the whole place fugged up with the steam.

The world she had come to consciousness in, defining still the shape of safety. A small space, warmed by their own breath.

Her father became restless, and rivers too tame. The vision now was a boat he could take on the ocean. Energy sprang from inside him like a natural force. He required no stimulus from outside, in fact was impervious to it. When an idea was on him there was nothing the rest of them could do except go with it, for the plans were always 'we'. They were essential to his vision – she, her sister, their mother. So that was how it was, her father building an ocean yacht in all the hours he wasn't logging, and her mother trying to keep two young children from falling into the river and all of them fed and dry. As for Cari, she learnt early on to avoid having any visions of her own, there being no room for any one else's in a place as crowded as a boat.

Early spring, and with snow still lying among the trees the yacht was done. They packed it up with provisions, handed the barge over to someone else, and sailed off down to where the river joined the ocean. Then out, just beyond the waves, and turning so that they were going the same way as the coast. The sun rose over the land in pinks and silver, and in the afternoon became a deep red ball that sank slowly into the sea. She kept her head down as the boom came over, eyes watching to see the sail above balloon out with new wind. She took the wheel on straight stretches. When the wind was high her father barked instructions and she learnt instant obedience, nimble movement. It did not occur to her to be proud of her skills for she had no idea they were unusual for an eight-year-old.

Her father was always calculating distance and wind and weather, and pushing them on. The sun burned hotter, more relentless. They turned in to a canal choked with large ships, and out the other end. They looked in on islands that were lush and green, where small brown children gathered to stare at them. Now they turned again, north, and instead of the sun sinking into the sea each evening it rose out of the sea in the morning, golden, firing the heaving world of water with magic light.

The coast slipped endlessly past, the sails billowed out above her head. The wind pushed them on through the water, further, further. The names of places they were passing blew lightly over her head, to waft back again years later in fragments of over-heard conversation, from diaries, from maps. Land was always in sight but out of reach until her father decided. There were bays they could not put in to because the swamps were treacherous, he said; others they could not get to because the currents went the wrong way. She played mind games to get there on her own, reached out her arm as far as it could go and closed her eyes to slits so she could see the faraway tips of her fingers touching the beguiling curve of the coast. Or she became a seagull, perched on the railing of the yacht, choosing the perfect moment to take off and wing her way with steady powerful beating towards the land. She watched her bird self, invisible to other eyes, touch down, strut about, explore; then lift again into the air and wing her way back to the yacht that she never let out of her sight.

They put in at a little fishing town. Her father began over-hauling the boat. A pause. She knew it couldn't last but she savoured it while it did. She watched the children who lived in houses, and thought, it must be lovely going to sleep in the same place every night and know what you'll see when you wake.

Her father and mother had talked about getting back home. At first she had hardly listened, for home had no meaning, it had always been wherever they happened to be. But now while her father fixed up the boat and studied the weather with a new intensity, it began to penetrate that what they were about to do was something on a different scale from what had gone before.

The vision was, they were going to sail back to England. Two adults and two children, crossing the Atlantic.

Day after day stuck on the boat, sea wherever she looked. Nowhere to move, forbidden ever to run. She had read all her books and there was never anything different to eat, just the same boring food out of tins. And she was so tired of waves, this heaving mass of nothingness surrounding them in every direction.

Now the sheer awfulness of the thing began to get into her soul. She dreamed at night of trees and rocks and the shape of a land horizon, but secretly she had begun to be afraid that the memory of these things was itself a dream, that there would never again be anything but this vast, impersonal circle of water. And she was anxious all the time, about her sister. Perhaps her father had said, 'Make sure she doesn't fall in.' But it was equally possible that no one said it and she just took it on herself. It hardly mattered now, the thing was done – the constant fear that harm would come to her sister, that it would be *her* fault. She was amazed in after years that the photographs showed none of the tension, just two children with life belts clambering around the deck, laughing, her mother coming up from below holding a mug of coffee, her father with his hair long and his chest bare, brown to the waist. The sea always calm. Of course, for on the other days no one had time to think of the camera. But she had pictures that came from another domain, so detailed she knew she could not have imagined them. She saw the sails straining against the wind, the rain lashing at her father as he struggled to get them down and shouted at her to get below. Then the light was suddenly gone from the world, and she and her sister lay huddled in their bunk while the boat heaved terrifyingly and adult voices shouted tensely above, and the anger of the storm became personal now, punishing them all, sweeping her mother and father off the deck, leaving the children at the mercy of the sea. And through it all she heard her own voice, telling her sister stories so she wouldn't be afraid.

A day when the sea was calm, the air clear and magical. Birds wheeled around them, wings lifted against the sky. Her father called them over to look through his binoculars. At first all she could see was a minute black thing that kept changing shape as the waves moved around it. Nothing you could take seriously. But the excitement had begun to squirm within her, and every little while they took turns to look again. Now the black blob had grown into a rock sticking out above the water. Now they were near enough to see the lighthouse pinnacled on it. It was miraculous, something a child might draw, with steps for the lighthouse keeper to climb up by, and windows all the way up the sides. Did he live there alone? How did he get there? Sailing past, and now the sea around them was dotted with rocks and her father was calling out instructions and her mother constantly checking their position on the charts. The rocks got larger, craggier, some tall as cliffs, others mere boulders scattered by mistake. Slipping by on either side of them now, while thousands of seabirds circled and mewed, in and out from their nests in the clifftops that no human being had ever disturbed. Past them, and now the first real island, with patches of green land and one tree, windblown and gaunt against the sky. Another lighthouse, this one dumpy and domesticated, and huddled round it on this small piece of earth, a cluster of whitewashed houses.

The excitement was by now out of control. 'Can't we stop?' they pleaded, but her father only laughed. 'There's better than that to come,' he said, and steered them round the end of the island, to see another looming ahead, looking as big as all the land she had ever longed for.

≈≈

Cari Lawrence, twenty-three, sat over a breakfast coffee and the Education Jobs pages of the newspaper, trying to summon up the energy to face the beginning of another term. Her third year as a teacher in an inner-city school. The start of her seventh term, and it had to be the last. She did not want still to be here past Christmas.

A small entry – 'Temporary English Teacher, six months maternity cover' – and then that word, *island,* standing out as if in darker type. She stared, not quite knowing what she was reacting to. Temporary, yes, that would suit, marking time till Andrew finished his thesis. She'd have to be ready to move again anyway once he got a job, no sense getting too attached to a place. But that wasn't it. It was the *island*.

At first she didn't take in that this might be her island. The name was there, but oddly she had never called it by name, it was simply The Island. 'Twenty-eight miles west of the mainland', said the ad – but she had never bothered much with where things were on maps. 'The Atlantic', it said – and now something began to twitch at the back of her consciousness. 'The school serves the five inhabited islands', it said – and suddenly it got through.

She went through to Andrew in the living room, getting himself set up for the day. Table spread with papers covered with equations and scribbles incomprehensible to Cari. Luckily he had not actually started, so she had a chance of getting his attention. She said casually, as if mentioning a thing of minor importance, 'I think I might have found something.'

He lifted up a pile of papers, looked at it in a puzzled way as if it were not what he had expected. 'Hmm?'

'Could you cope with an island?'

'An island?' he repeated, but still absently.

8

'My island.'

A pause. He straightened up now and looked directly at her. 'The one you – your dad?'

She nodded.

'It has a *school*?'

'Apparently. With a job I could do. Starting January.'

'*January*, Caroline?' His incredulity coming out in mock imitation of her dad. 'Out in the Atlantic on three foot square of earth, and nothing between us and America?'

His tone triggered a counter reaction. For the first time she began to take the possibility seriously. 'We've got to be *somewhere* in January. You said you could be anywhere. And they grow daffodils in winter, it must be warm.'

Andrew looked at her, assessing. He wasn't used to her being so definite. He liked it and felt desire stirring. She turned and went back to the kitchen, tore out the page with the ad, and went to rinse out her mug. He put down the papers and followed to stand in the doorway, watching each movement – her long hair falling over her slim shoulders as she stood at the sink, then as she turned, her grey-green eyes alive with the excitement of her idea. He knew that look of absorption in an idea but it was usually others who evoked it, the children she taught, people she watched. A look that both attracted and excluded him, not deliberately but because he was momentarily irrelevant. Yet here it was, and for something they might do together.

He thought about suggesting they go back to bed. There would be just time, before she had to leave for work. But they'd never done it by day and he felt awkward about proposing it. Why? He had no reason to think Cari would think it odd. It was some earlier voice inside him that could not conceive of anything being done outside its appropriate time.

The island was out there, a place of the imagination, cut off from land, out of the range of other voices. The picture rose before him of making love by day to the sound of waves crashing, of Cari wandering around the house naked, all embarrassment dissolved.

She said, fully clothed, 'And there'll be no distractions.'

Walking the city pavements to work she felt different from her yesterday self. Lighter, from just having glimpsed that distant possibility of getting away. And free, almost, as if heading for the school was something she did voluntarily. Gone that sense of having to gear herself up to face the day. Silly that she should so often feel that. Once she was there and the children in front of her it was always OK, but she lost faith each morning and had to find it again. Becoming a teacher had been not so much a decision as avoiding the need for one. It was the easiest thing to do – she knew what happened in schools and had no idea what happened in other jobs. She had opted, without quite knowing why, to teach younger children. Middle school, or at most the first years of secondary. Old enough not to need mothering but before rebellion stirred. The age she had been on the island.

For two months of that childhood summer she had woken each morning to the gently bobbing boats in the island harbour. While her dad fixed up the yacht and her mother made forays to the shops, Cari and her sister Robyn learnt the island. A bus did a round-the-island run. The bus driver greeted them like friends as they got on and waved to them as they got off, two small girls setting out on a path or along a headland walk, to find the inlets that nestled at the border of land and sea. They buried secret hordes of shells and collected stones that the sea had formed into smooth oval shapes, each with its own unique colouring. To each bay and inlet they gave their own names, and

10

when later they discovered that officially they had others, they were mildly insulted. They were the only children who didn't have adults somewhere in tow, but on land Cari felt no nervousness. The island was so obviously a place without danger. They kept their distance from the children of the holiday families, who behaved in what seemed to them strange ways, constantly running to their parents for small things they could far better have sorted out alone. At their end of the beach Cari invented for Robyn stories about the ships that had been wrecked here, the lives violently slashed across by storms, then saved at the last minute by the discovery of the island ...

An interlude of safety, dangled before her at one critical moment of childhood, then gone. A place forever lost in the middle of an ocean. It had never occurred to her that she might return to it as an adult.

Year 1, thirty-two eleven-year-olds milling about.

'Can't find my book, miss.'

'Miss, she's taken my pencil.'

They have the concentration of butterflies, Cari thought, but then so have I. Attention so easily caught by anything that moved past her. She stood now waiting for them to calm down, and eventually a sort of order asserted itself. She got them started, all the time watching to see how each child found its own way into the task. They interested her deeply, being both so like how she had until quite recently been, and so unlike. They were tough and streetwise, which she had never been, but also vulnerable, alternately needing to be noticed and to be left alone. And there was no sham about them, none of that need to pretend to go along with things that she remembered so painfully from her awkward years. If someone got in their way they said, 'Shift your arse.' If they were bored they said, 'Miss,

11

do we have to do this?' If she managed to catch their imagination they were suddenly open to her, impulsive and warm.

Bending over a table to help one of the groups, she felt a silent presence at her side. She turned. Lisa, waiting to tell her something. A shy child with a lisp, she never called out from her desk the way the others did. The only conversations Lisa did were intimate. Now Cari saw that the child was holding a flower out to her.

The other children had seen, were distracted. The comments began.

'She's soft on you, Miss.'

'Where d'ye nick that flower from, Lisa?'

'Piss off, Charlie, didn't your mum ever teach you to do nice things?'

A boy mimicking, falsetto voice: 'Oh Mith, you tell thuch good thtorieth.'

The girl let the carping of the crowd pass over her as if she had not heard, and thrust the flower towards Cari. Cari took it and said, to her alone, 'Thank you, Lisa, it's beautiful.'

Lisa lent confidentially closer, to whisper, 'It'th cauth you thaid you liked flowerth.'

Cari was touched, beyond the receiving of a flower. She felt a compassion, for all the years of shyness this child had still ahead of her. And she felt known, for who she was.

'Yes, I do like flowers.'

She had told them once, on an afternoon when their restlessness seemed curable only by being told a story, of the island of her childhood, and the flowers that lit her memory of it with a thousand small specks of colour. A constantly unfolding secret, hardly impinging on those who walked past, but she and Robyn were down at flower level, time spreading endlessly.

12

They noted colour and shape, the thickness and texture of leaves. They described the qualities of personality of the bloom – shy, curious, determined. They had been taught no countryside lore and had no idea that anyone before them had ever classified or described. They made their own connections, in this place that was to them a world entire, a miracle of nourishing land defying the endless sea.

Andrew was working late again, banging away on his typewriter. Nothing unusual in that, but tonight she was restless with her new idea and felt the lack of company. She knew better than to try and disturb his concentration. Normally she would just have curled up with a novel, but tonight – Odd that you can be in a couple and still be lonely, she thought; then pushed the thought aside.

She unplugged the phone from the living room and took it through to the socket in the bedroom, climbed onto the bed to sit cross-legged under the blankets, and dialled.

'Hiya.' Robyn's voice. Her little sister, little no longer.

'It's me,' Cari said.

'Hello me. How's things?'

'It's months since we talked. I can't think why I let things drift so.'

'Life's busy, that's why.'

'No it's not most of the time. I just get stuck doing the things that are in front of me.'

'Doesn't matter anyway. I don't know that I'd like regular phone calls. Like, it's Wednesday, better phone Cari.'

Cari laughed, pulling the blanket up higher around her, snuggling into familiarity. 'Something's happened. You'll never guess.'

'Andrew's finished his thesis?'

'Don't be ridiculous. I've seen a job ad, on our island.'

A shocked silence. Very gratifying.

Robyn said, 'You're sure?'

'Yep.'

Another silence. Then, almost a long breath rather than a word, 'Wow.'

'D'you think I should apply?'

'You wouldn't be telling me if you hadn't already decided.'

No hesitations about Robyn. Why can't I be like that?

'What's Andrew think?'

'You can't say he's noticed. But you could pick him up and dump him on the moon, as long as he had his box files and his typewriter with him.'

'I've never understood what keeps you two together.'

'Nor do I. But it works OK.' She thought of Andrew, deep in work in the other room, and felt affectionate. 'He's got nice eyes.'

She fell asleep unusually early, and dreamt she and Robyn were still at home together, paging through an album of family photos. The official history of their childhood – two confident small girls in orange life-jackets while the wind filled the sails behind them.

'It's a lie,' Cari said, 'that's not what it was like.'

But Robyn didn't seem to hear her, just went on turning the pages, saying, 'Look, remember that?'

She stirred into half-wakefulness, to pictures of that house in Southampton that they had learnt to call home after they had been taken away from the island. And out at the back, where she and Robyn had played their Island Game. They had dug a huge area in the yard behind the garage, and their dad had filled it with sand, and in it they created bays with rocks and shells that they got on Sundays hanging about the harbour where their dad kept his boat.

'It could be that beach Dad took us to last week,' Robyn suggested once, being more fickle in her attachments. Cari was shocked. 'That wouldn't be *any* good for the Game.' Mainland beaches drifted miscellaneously to east and to west, with roads coming in from all directions and off again, with different people every time you went, all strangers to each other. Such a beach offered nothing to the imagination, none of the sense of shelter or unspoken stories.

'The thing about an island,' she said to Robyn, 'is it has *edges*, so you know exactly where you are.'

Could their island really still be there, as it had been in her mind all those years, untouched by complexity? Somewhere forever more simple than the life she had arrived at in adolescence, the inner confusions that seemed to overtake her? She lay now in the adult dark, vulnerable to memories of that time ... Passivity, weighing her down. Her life moving forward by some mechanism that had nothing to do with her, as if she were in a play scripted by someone else, and the only thing she could do was to learn the lines and move where she was required to by the larger plan. The unreality of it, pressing on her, a feeling she could not begin to explain, even to herself. She was not part of the teenage world her school friends explored with such intense involvement, nor any longer comfortable going along with the things her parents liked to do. She was easily able to do what was required of her at school to get by, but nothing in it sparked her off. In the hours when she could escape the demands of parents, teachers, friends, she would lose herself in novels – *other* people's reality, a different fiction in exchange for the one she seemed destined to live.

Her dad said, 'Caroline, you can't spend your life reading.'

Her mum said, 'Leave the girl, there's no point chasing her.'

Robyn said, 'I'm going to do a speed-reading test on you,' and they discovered it was 450 words a minute, with almost total recall.

Her dad said, 'Well *that's* a talent. What are you going to do with it?'

'Nothing,' Cari said –

She stiffened, suddenly completely awake.

Something. She was finally going to do something of her own choosing. She was going back to the island.

Andrew crept into the room. God knows what time.

'You still awake?' he said in surprise; but it didn't occur to him to ask why.

Do I want him to? she wondered. She supposed she did, otherwise why did she feel miffed? She turned over to watch him undress, get into his pyjamas. I could do with a cuddle, she thought. He climbed in next to her, instantly ready for sleep. She wound herself around him, willing him to stay awake and respond.

'I'm full of strange feelings,' she said.

'Tell me in the morning,' he mumbled. And was off.

≈≈

It was all a lot simpler than she could have imagined. By morning Andrew was focusing, and gratifyingly amenable. 'I dare say we could give it a try. I'd have to come back a couple of times to see my supervisor, but it could be done.'

She laboured over her job application as if life itself depended on it, but all the while unable to shed the feeling that it was make-believe. When the letter came inviting her for an interview she stared at it in amazement, then went dancing and yodelling round the flat. She was interviewed in an office in Cornwall — still the island was beyond, over the waters, unreachable. The panel seemed to make it easy for her, as if they had already decided she would do. Maybe they hadn't had any other applicants — who could tell? The next day the call came. The job was hers.

December. Nearing the end of term, saying goodbye to the children, whom she would miss, to Birmingham, which she wouldn't. Packing up one life, not yet able to imagine another.

A phone call from Robyn, 'Have you heard what's happened at Greenham Common?'

'Where's Greenham Common?'

'Cari, don't you listen to the news? It's a missile base. American Cruise missiles. And a group of women just broke in. Phenomenal!'

Phenomenal. Yes, of course it was. She tried to react, but she was gone already in her mind, off to another dimension.

Possessions packed in boxes, at least half of them Andrew's papers. Flat locked up, keys handed over. Back home for Christmas, to her parents. Robyn there too. Cari thinking, this will be my last Christmas with them all before — before what?

Something, something significant.

Christmas over. Hugging them all goodbye. Her mum saying, 'Make sure you phone.' Her dad saying, 'Tell me if that sail-making place is still there.' Robyn saying, 'Don't forget to find our special cove.'

Train to Penzance. One night in a bed-and-breakfast. Morning, and now it really was irrevocable, standing high on the deck of a ship, watching the land slip away. Going, going, gone.

Cari stared down while the ship ploughed lumpily across the

waves. Miles and miles of sea, but way down there, with this hulk of metal lifting her clear out of them. She *knew* waves, she realised, knew them not as her dad did, a force of nature to be watched with a scientist's eye lest they get the better of you. She knew them as shape, movement, the clarity of the colour changes. Up here she had just the distance from them that she needed.

Scraps of land began to appear on the horizon, so low it seemed incredible that the sea didn't just wash them away. Nearer, till she could see the outlines of bays. Nothing looked quite familiar, coming at it this way, and she began to be afraid that it was not her island after all. Closer. Boulders growing, scraps of beach slipping by, till they were moving slowly past a greensward with the foundations of a stone age village where she and Robyn used to make up stories about the people who once long ago lived there – and she became almost rigid with recognition.

≈≈

The Island of St Martin's, June 1982
The long white sands stretched into the distance, washed firm by the retreating tide. Against the low line of dunes held in place by wiry grasses a woman lay, eyes closed, completely still. A group of holiday makers coming over the dunes onto the beach stopped as they saw her – something odd about her. A woman in middle age, fully clothed and definitely not sunbathing. Her body, spreading slightly to flab under a long skirt and unflattering blouse, lay so still it was like something abandoned. Her arms were at her sides but awkwardly, as if she had not the energy to rearrange them.

The watchers shifted, uncomfortable. They moved off and

were soon wading out into the shallow water, calling and laughing, letting the sun glinting on the sand and the cold water on their feet wipe away the picture of the misery of another human creature, so naked it felt wrong to have seen it.

Anna Feldman opened her eyes. She sat up, to look out at the sea. The light reflecting off the white sand blinded her. She lowered her eyes, voluntarily confining her attention to the small circle of what immediately surrounded her. She lifted a handful of sand and watched as she let it dribble down through her fingers. Finely crushed sea shells, the life in them lost in eons past.

Her hair was falling over her eyes. She wanted to push it out of the way but the cut-glass grains of wet sand were clinging to her hands and she didn't want them in her eyes. She flicked her head instead, and felt a stab of pain in her neck and shoulder. Damn, now she had a ricked shoulder, on top of everything else.

Her hair, Anna reflected, was the one part of her body that showed no signs of stress. It was thick and unmanageable as it had always been, and no trace of grey even though she was heading for fifty six. The rest of her didn't bear thinking about. She had put on weight again — small wonder since for almost two months she had hardly been able to find the energy to move herself through the day. Her body ached, every limb and joint stiff when she woke, and barely loosening in the sun. The physical symptoms were real enough but she had not the energy to attend to them, knowing they were simply another expression of her unshiftable misery.

There seemed no point considering the matter further. She lay back, closed her eyes, and tried not to think.

She lived for her first weeks on the island — was it weeks?

months? she hardly knew — in her cousin Bella's farmhouse. 'Come in,' Bella had said when she had arrived with her one small suitcase and her face that could not hide her misery. Come in, as if they were back in the Liverpool of the thirties, living down the road from each other, knowing all the kids in the streets around and moving in and out of each other's houses.

She came in, to a croft with a few small bulbfields attached, barely sheltered from the sea by the dunes. The walls were stones lifted from the land by people long since forgotten. In the blank hours Anna found herself staring at the stones. They announced their own kind of history, a succession of plant life that had attached itself, surviving the salt spray and the battering winds; lichen, and the tiny starshaped flowers of stonecrop. Survive, they said. Flatten yourself against the stone, make yourself small and invulnerable. On the inner walls hung a clutter of pots blackened with use and tools whose function she could hardly guess at. Work never ends, said the walls.

There was little to the house. A kitchen, a living room, a bedroom for Bella and Thomas, a small box-shaped room for their daughter Yvonne, a fourteen-year-old and away all week at school on St Mary's, the largest of the islands. So young and gone already, Anna thought as she unpacked her bag in the girl's room, and tried to close off the sounds of the holiday children floating up from the beach.

They sat at the kitchen table with mugs of tea and looked out through the open door at the clouds that threatened. Thomas said, 'Must get on,' and disappeared out into his fields. Bella went back to her sink and cooker, leaving Anna alone. It was not tact, simple necessity. The work was relentless. The sand never stopped blowing over the bulbfields that year, threatening to engulf everything Thomas's labour had created. Anna watched him out there in all weathers shovelling the sand away and shoring up the stone windbreaks, and felt the centuries of struggle that lay behind the survival of this man, last son of his family. Just a daughter to follow him, but would she? The face in the framed photo on the living room wall was red-cheeked from the wind, but the girl's eyes were on a future far from the islands. Would Thomas grow old watching his fields lie unattended, reclaimed by the heath?

And Bella, what did she make of this life she had married into so late but learnt so thoroughly to make her own? Anna watched the small daily interactions that spoke the quality of Bella's acceptance. Thomas was large and heavy; a warm smile around the eyes, but he said nothing beyond the practical. We're going to need a new washer on that tap. The wind's up again today. What's for dinner? The Bella whom Anna had known in childhood had had a sense of fun, they had giggled together, made up silly songs – did she still do that, married to Thomas?

As for Anna's own state, Bella did not probe. When Anna talked, as she did compulsively at first, Bella accepted it, letting it flow while she continued working, making occasional small comments. When the pendulum swung and Anna retreated, Bella accepted that too. She accepts *me*, Anna thought, simply because I am her cousin. It seemed too limited a reason; but gradually she gave up fighting against what she so badly needed. She let herself be held in this small space, hedged about by the routine of their daily lives, held against the inner chaos that hovered, constantly threatening.

Friday, and Yvonne was due back on the afternoon boat. Anna heard Bella sing in the kitchen as she baked for the weekend, and thought, so that *is* still there. She tidied her few possessions compulsively out of sight, but she need hardly have bothered. Yvonne slept on the sofa without appearing to notice the loss of her room, and was out all the hours of daylight finding her friends. Periodically she would reappear in the kitchen with a younger child in tow, an eager boy of ten or eleven. 'David's dad says he'll take us out sailing. Can I?'

'When your homework's done.'

'I've only got the maths left. *Please* Mum.'

'Well remember Hugh's got work to do like your father. Don't you keep pleading to stay out longer.'

Yvonne didn't wait to discuss details. Anna and Bella stood at the door watching the children hurtle down the path. 'So much life in her,' Bella said, 'I can't bear to pin her down.'

Anna turned away, not able to watch the imbalance of need.

Another week with the children gone, the house quiet. Another weekend, young life back in it again. Another week ...

'You need to get out,' Bella said. 'A change might lift your spirits.' Anna knew it would not but to get out of Bella's hair she made herself go on the boats that ferried holiday-makers on day trips to the other islands. She went first to St Mary's, the only island big enough to have what passed for a town. 'How was it?' asked Bella when she got back. What to say? By the standards of the mainland it was a toy-town but in her fragile state even that had felt more than she could handle. She had walked the few streets aimlessly, watching the people who all looked too normal to be real. They drifted about in shorts licking ice-creams, and children called to each other as they played on the beach. She had spoken to no one and no one had spoken to her. The whole experience left her exhausted.

'Try St Agnes,' said Bella. 'It's good for birds.' Birds there were in plenty but they felt alien to Anna, wheeling about so free, white and screeching. And now she was bothered by the absence of people – the only buildings were a pub, a lighthouse and a strangling line of houses. She felt lost and came back early.

Bella tried again. 'Tresco will suit you better. The gardens, so peaceful.' But peace starts within. Anna stared at the architecture of trees against the sky, at the exotic plants that defied geography to flourish here behind windbreaks, thousands of miles from where nature had intended them to be. None of it seemed to penetrate the layers of non-feeling. Only extremes made sense. Complete dark, white light, blanking out detail.

'Bryher,' said Bella, but without much conviction. Yet it was Bryer that first stirred in her something approaching real feeling. It was the furthest west island with even fewer houses than St Agnes. A fine misty rain began to descend and there was nowhere to shelter, so she just walked, ignoring it, following a path up a windswept headland of heather and stoney outcrops until at the highest point she found herself looking down onto the massive rocks of Hell Bay. Atlantic waves crashed on the rocks, shooting white spray hundreds of feet into the air to wet her face where she stood high above. The thunder of waves was deafening, blotting out thought. For the first time in months she felt comforted. Submit, said the swirling torrent. Feel the onslaught. Become part of the void.

And standing there alone, feeling strangely emptied by the violence below that crashed so near yet could not touch her, she felt at last some clarity about what she should do.

'I have decided I am staying on the islands.'
Bella looked steadily at her, saying nothing.
'There's no point pretending I can go back.'
Bella nodded. 'Yes. I see that.'
'I'll find my own place, of course.'
Bella said, 'You're welcome to stay longer, you know that.'
'I can't,' said Anna. 'This is your and Thomas's life. I have to

23

work out my own.' And then, belatedly, like a child remembering her manners, 'But thank you.'

Bella brushed it aside. 'Where will you go?'

'St Mary's. I have to learn to face people again.'

'That's right,' said Bella calmly, as if it were all quite normal.

≈≈

A small stone cottage in Old Town, a collection of houses
overlooking the old harbour on the eastern side of St Mary's.
She saw it first in the morning with light slanting down over
upturned, sleeping boats. It was the light that did it. She gave
the inside of the cottage the most cursory look and then stood
in the doorway looking out, at the light touching the stone
church across the bay, the churchyard still in shadow, the sleep
of centuries of past lives. She came back that afternoon and
stood this time inside the living room, looking out of the
window at the same view. Light coming now from the other side
of the harbour. A blue-grey light, almost. Or was it?

The cottage was unfurnished; whitewashed walls and
echoing spaces which she was in no hurry to fill. It was part of
a row, sharing a complete wall with its neighbour on the
downhill side, but on the uphill side it had a jutting-out corner.
Whoever had built it had understood the importance of light
and used those few feet of exposed east wall to fit in an extra
window. Anna put a piece of cheap foam down in the upstairs
room with the extra east window, and left it uncurtained so she
would be woken by first light and know it was day by some
means other than a clock. For downstairs she bought one chair
to sit on, one small table. For the kitchen, one cooking pot, one
wooden spoon, one sharp knife, a fork and spoon to eat with. At
first she did not think about these things, it was simply an

instinct to reduce life to its essentials so she could discover what they were. But gradually it formed into a rule: she could not buy anything until she knew for sure that she wanted it, and what for.

Unbidden, her needs began to state themselves. First she realised she needed a bicycle, to help shift the aches in her limbs, and so she could get herself to all corners of the island and see the light from all angles. The hours of staring gave birth to a tentative attempt to record the emphemeral, and she bought a block of sketching paper, then an easel – all before she had bought any more knives and forks. All of this was a surprise. She had not painted since she left school.

She set up her easel in the room that had light coming in from two sides. As the winter settled in and she was driven in more often by rain, it was this room she came to, and thought about how the angle of the light affected colours, and through them her perception of shapes. It didn't matter, she discovered, that she was not actually seeing the things her mind was working over; just a short spell of stimulus from nature would carry on working its way through her, blanking out her sense of time.

Bella visited, bringing Yvonne to see Aunt Anna's still half-empty white house. When they got to the room with the easel Bella said, 'Well Anna, you've got a real little studio here,' naming her new life to help it along. Anna pushed the word away, brusquely. Far too soon to be caught by a new set of categories.

'It's all water-colours,' Yvonne said. 'Don't you like oils?'

No she did not like oils. Oil was the slick left on the surface of the sea after an accident. Oil weighed you down, sank slowly, horribly. She could smell the thick paint still on hands that had come in from painting boats, and she was urgent to free herself from it. This was something from another element altogether.

She had given herself up to the mysteries of water, of light washes of colour created from the very substance that filtered the colour of the world outside. Water vapour hovering always in the air, blown in from the sea. Water that marked the edge of the land she looked out on, slapping angrily against it when the wind was up, lapping gently when the air was quiet. Water, air, earth, wind. You start with a blank white space and this is what you find – the elements. Our origin and our end.

Bella and Yvonne left. She was aware that they thought her a little mad, as perhaps she was. That Bella was sad about it, and Yvonne perhaps embarrassed. But affectionate at the same time, tolerant of this aunt who couldn't help how she was.

≈≈

St Mary's, January 1984
The arrival of the new young couple was noticed, of course. The entire population of the island in winter was hardly more than one and a half thousand, and this was not a time for new faces. They were noticed in the bread shop, in the Co-op, in the pub where they thought they were listening to the locals, unobserved. The woman who ran the bed-and-breakfast could tell her friends that the young woman had come to do Janet Ross's maternity cover and the young man was going to finish a thesis, something mathematical. The woman in the information office who kept the list of self-catering cottages could provide details about the couple's preferences. The husband hadn't cared what they got as long as it had a desk and shelving for his papers. The wife wanted to be up at the north end, furthest from the town. The taxi driver who transported them and their possessions to Mrs Tremain's farm – two miles – had his own bit to add. The girl had eyes in her head, he told his wife that

evening, but her young man seemed pretty useless. One of those thin towny types. Book clever, maybe, but he came from West Bromwich and didn't know a thing about football.

'What brought them?' the woman in the Co-op asked the wife of the taxi driver.

She didn't know, but the bed-and-breakfast woman did. 'She was here once as a child.'

'Ah, the usual,' they smiled knowingly. 'The islands in summer.' And they waited to see how long this latest set of newcomers would last.

The farm grew narcissi in winter, holiday rooms in summer. Mrs Tremain worked the farm alone, she told them, 'With a couple of lads helping at busy times. Not that there are unbusy times.' They stood in her kitchen that first day as she searched for the cottage key amidst piles of ironing waiting to be done, bottles stacked perilously, coils of string with papers on top of them. 'Narcissus time,' she said, 'cutting the flowers and tying them. It's addling my brain. They say you can always tell a flower-tyer because their eyes are glazed.' Now she was searching for the bus timetable. 'I know it's somewhere here,' she said, and wouldn't give up though she had just told them the bus wouldn't start its rounds again until Easter.

One of the lads appeared. 'Oh that's not them, that's my Ollie.' Ollie wandered through the kitchen mumbling a hello, and then out into the yard, 'My youngest,' Mrs Tremain said. 'Can't get rid of him. Thinks life owes him something, that's the young these days. But he's got a job on the ferry now, starting Monday. Let's see how long he keeps that one.'

She found the key and showed them around. It was an outhouse of stone, only just converted. The walls were cold, waiting for an imprint of personality to turn the spaces between them into something one could possibly call home. It was small but it had what they needed, a place to sleep, a room for Andrew and his papers, a living space with a sofa just big enough for two. Everything fitted as neatly as on a barge.

'If the plumbing goes wrong, ask one of the lads. If you can find them.' And she was off, to the next task. After that they saw her each day but fleetingly, always heading somewhere, into the fields or back inside, mud on her wellies, tools in her hands, hassle in the air. No time to stop for more than a hello.

It was blowing great guns their first night. Cari couldn't sleep, alert to the storm as if she had to monitor its intensity. She pulled the still new-smelling blankets closer around her, burrowing away from strangeness. When she slept it was fitful. Once when she woke she thought she had felt Robyn's small hands touching her face, waking her to tell her stories so she wouldn't hear the menace in the storm. Then she woke in reality, to Andrew's hands moving tentatively over her. Already the hands had become shy because she wasn't responding quickly enough; by the time she had worked out where she was, they had removed themselves. By then she was longing for his arms around her to take away the pressure of Robyn's fear revisiting her after so many years.

But Andrew was moving to get up, brisk and practical.

Out – finding her bearings – here, *now*. No longer a place of long summer days, wandering around in flip-flops, legs coated with sand. Now the winds blow in from the Atlantic and the beaches are deserted by all except the seagulls. In the small harbour the yachts are moored and covered with canvas, tossing drunkenly one day, sleeping another. The town itself seems half packed away, and so vulnerable, huddling on its narrow neck of land between the harbour and the sandy bay.

A cargo boat docks twice a week. The tall cranes swivel and dip to lift out the containers that bring from the mainland every item the islanders need to keep life going, but no more than a handful of people come down the gangplank. The streets are quiet. Each person passing seems an event.

The nights are long and there is little to do. The wind howls in the chimney and the rain beats against the windows. It is hard not to feel trapped, almost as if they are on a boat, nowhere to go while the storm rages, just lie low hoping it will pass. On calmer evenings she and Andrew sometimes go down to the town and spend an hour or two in the pub near the pier – two young outsiders, faces fresh and unmarked by life, the look of mainland cities still in their clothes. They sit in a smoky corner, listening as the island men tell stories – the drama of high waves whipping up against the Western Rocks, the week no one could land food for the lighthouse keeper on Bishop's Rock, the year the storm smashed boats in the harbour. It is the sea that holds sway in their imaginations, that challenges them to make forays out to life, to danger. Life on land features only in the stories of rivalries between the groups of boatmen, clans defending their honour. The island is a place to recoup, to gather shoulder to shoulder in the closed-in night and down another pint and cap each other's stories, until the adrenalin builds up again to a level that demands action.

Cari listens, absorbed but having to defend herself against the fear they disdain to feel. Their bodies exude maleness, thick thighs, hands tough and calloused, arm muscles that can haul wet ropes against the pull of a galeforce wind. Sudden bursts of laughter over their beer. Men who were born on the islands and have grown up with boats, who have gone away for years perhaps but been drawn back by that indefinable pull of a place so extreme. Surely they must once have been small boys who were afraid of the whining of the wind on a dark night? But all trace of that is buried, things they once tried to forget and now can't remember.

A postcard to Robyn. What to say? 'It's amazing being here. Still can't quite believe it.' And then? 'Everything looks smaller, but even more beautiful.' True, but it misses the point. No way to say what it is evoking in her, the sense of long-buried things being opened up, anything-might-happen.

≈≈

It was January 1984, halfway through Anna Feldman's second year on St Mary's, when she first sighted the girl. That was how she thought of it, like observing a rare bird that had been blown off course, buffeted by sea winds to land on the island. The girl could not possibly be a holiday-maker, arriving as she had in mid-winter. Nor could she be the daughter of an island family, returning. Something too concentrated about her gaze, an intensity about her relationship to where she was, altogether unusual. Otherwise her face gave off little, being rather unformed, as if she hadn't yet become the person she was intended to be. But then the young all seemed so much younger these days.

Anna was out on her bike and had paused halfway up the rise that would eventually take her back down to Old Town bay. The incipient arthritis in her hip had baulked at the first indication of having to pedal up a hill. She stood astride her bike, pushing back from her face the strands of hair that had worked their way out of the clasp, and waited a few moments for the pain to settle down. And there was the girl, standing a little way ahead on the other side of the road, having stopped to look over a low windbreak hedge. There was a remarkable stillness about her as she stood, looking – at what? Anna followed her gaze. A field of winter narcissi waiting to be cut. Colour hardly visible, heads still tight closed, glory hidden till they would be bought in markets on the mainland, to open out on kitchen tables and remind people that spring would eventually come.

The girl didn't notice Anna pushing her bike uphill past her. Too absorbed.

At the second sighting the roles were reversed. It was mid-afternoon, just getting dark. Anna was cycling back from her weekly visit to a place where she was certain to see no one, and was therefore still in a solitary state of mind. She had stopped near the turn-off to Porth Hellick, the point at which the sea was suddenly visible, and was looking out at the pile-up of clouds over the sea. She was wondering about the relationship between their density and the light, and whether if she mixed just a touch of green into the grey she might get something of that ominous quality. Then she looked up to see the same girl passing on the other side of the road, walking downhill – and something about the movement of the head told Anna that she had been observed.

Anna wasn't sure that she liked the idea. In fact, she was quite sure she didn't. Absurd, she told herself, what harm is there? And if I can watch her, why not she me?

Now Anna began to watch out for her whenever she was out on her bike. She began to observe a pattern. If she saw her in the early morning the girl would be walking down from the north of the island; in the afternoons, back up again. Then for several weeks there was no sign of her, and Anna began to think she must have been a visitor after all.

But the girl suddenly reappeared, this time on the far side of the island. Mid-afternoon it was and the days just beginning to lengthen. Anna came cycling round the corner and there the girl was at the bottom of the downhill stretch, walking up towards her. The wheels carried Anna down towards the slim walking figure but the world around her seemed to have gone into slow motion, and in those few hyper-alert seconds she noted each quality of the girl's body, almost as if it might be a clue to something in her own life. How she moved, limbs lithe and easy. The hair, shoulder length. Last time it had been tied behind her head, today it hung loose. Anorak a little too big. The girl looked lost in it, so little bulk to her, pushing against the wind.

Closer, slowing down, almost about to pass each other. She could see the girl's face now. Their eyes met for a second. Anna almost decided to stop but then the impulse failed her and she pedalled on down the hill. The wind tugged at her hair, pulling it out from the clasp. She freewheeled into the white clouds that sailed ahead of her.

≈≈

The school was a two-storey modern block overlooking the harbour. It could have been a secondary school anywhere, except that it was so small. The first time Cari walked into it she was suddenly shy as a new girl. She had come in, as arranged, a few days before term started, and the building was empty. Her footsteps echoed alarmingly in the corridor.

The head teacher found her before she found his office. He came walking along the corridor to greet her, a man in his fifties, grey hair, spare build, intelligent eyes. 'Caroline Lawrence? Welcome to the islands. I'm Neville Hill. I hope you'll be happy with us.'

'Thank you,' she said. Then, to get it straight from the start, 'Actually, I'm Cari.'

'Ah, Caroline was just for ticking you off, was it?'

She nodded, and in her dad's deep voice, 'You've got to get serious about life, Caroline.'

His eyes were laughing. 'I'll avoid it at all costs.'

You're OK, she thought. You passed the first test.

Into his office, to talk through what she was taking on. English with each year group, form tutor to the fourth years. He handed over a large ring binder. 'Janet Ross's work records, registers, last term's reports. Fortunately she's a most systematic person. There's not much you need to know that isn't in there, but she's happy to come in for an hour or two if you want to talk through any of it.' He looked at her speculatively. 'After Birmingham this will seem easy. Small classes, no discipline problem worth speaking about. But there are challenges you don't find in a city school.'

'Like?'

He got up and went to stand at the window, looking out. 'Come over here,' he said. She moved over to stand next to him. The small harbour, boats covered and rocking gently. The sea beyond, stretching out past smaller islands that dotted the wide disk of water, to disappear eventually into a haze that was neither sea nor sky.

'It's a small piece of earth we're on,' he said. 'Two and a half miles at its widest, under nine miles all the way round. An environment that takes your breath away every time you stop and look. Still does that to me, after twenty-five years. Safe. No traffic, no crime, everyone knows everyone. You couldn't find anything more ideal for the younger children. But for the older ones – too little stimulus for growing minds. No challenge. They settle too easily for the average.' He turned to look at her. 'Tell me why you're here.'

It was a real question, and she knew he would listen properly to the answer. She said, 'When I was eight I had a couple of months of exactly what you describe for the younger children. I never forgot it.'

He nodded. 'Just remember, this will be something different. Keep your eyes open, watch what's going on for these young people, now.' Then, brisk, 'Come, let's go to the staffroom. There are a couple of the others in, I can introduce you.'

The familiar staffroom look, armchairs round the walls, low tables in the middle with piles of books, a rack of wooden pigeon-holes for messages. Two teachers over by the kettle, talking while they waited for it to boil. The man in his late thirties maybe, jeans and loose pullover, a mop of fair hair, engaging manner – talking energetically, hands gesticulating; the woman younger, in a long skirt that didn't flatter her, and tense body language. Unimpressed by her colleague's enthusiasm; heard it all before.

Neville said, 'Here's Cari Lawrence, our replacement for Janet. Paul Cooper, history, tireless organiser of school trips to the mainland. Fran Norton, maths. Fran does primary liaison, three small schools on the off-islands, as well as the one on St Mary's.'

Paul said, 'Reinforcements from the mainland – we can do with some of that.'

The first Monday – get in early to watch the boats come chugging in across the shallow but treacherous waters, each with its handful of children from the smaller islands who will board at the school during the week. Cari imagines them seeing this island as she first did, not as a small place but a big one.

Inside, the familiar push of young bodies in the corridors, the start-of-term calling to friends. Into each class for the first time, a sea of faces, gradually over the first week sifting themselves out to become known people. She watches the teenagers, remembering what Neville said. They have less of the talking-big of city kids, more practical confidence. They have all known each other since they can remember. One in particular she notices, a girl called Yvonne from St Martin's, who seems to take motherly charge of the younger boarders. Just turned sixteen, hovering on the edge of adulthood. Sure of her place in a world small enough to comprehend.

In the staff room the chat is pleasant, but contact with the other teachers after school does not seem on offer. The school itself is an island where she knows what's expected, knows she can do it. Once outside she is thrown back on herself, on the questions about why she is here. She is just Cari, someone washed ashore unexpectedly, and conscious all the time that she is an outsider.

February already. The weeks slipping by, everything losing the sense of newness. Andrew working alone on his thesis up in their cottage, Cari down at the other end of the island, becoming daily more absorbed. Stepping out each morning to a world new-created, stretching to where thin sun glints on distant rocks. Choosing her route as a reflection of mood, partly her own, partly that of earth and sky. The paths curve with the island's shape, around promontories and inlets. If she loses the sea on one side it reappears on another, framed by a familiar landmark that has suddenly come at her from a surprising direction, and she stops, caught again by the wonder.

Andrew's approach to his new environment is intellectual. He buys books of island history, of island geology. In the evenings he drapes his lanky body over the sofa and reads out bits. The rock is chiefly granite, he tells her. There is little evidence of neolithic settlement but a remarkable number of

35

Bronze Age remains. Cari lets him instruct her, but only the surface of her mind is listening.

Cari – coming out of the school with a shoulder-bag of essays to mark. Chatting to Paul Cooper, history teacher, tireless organiser of school trips. 'See you tomorrow,' as they each set off their different ways. Turning towards town, to do a bit of shopping before going home. On the road along the seafront a car comes towards her. She waves. It's the taxi driver who first took them up to the cottage. She passes the Yachtsman's Friend where once her dad bought tackle for his boat, and there is Brad Tointon from her fourth year class, standing outside the shop door, hands in his jeans pockets. A man appears at the door to summon him in. His father.

Andrew – up in the cottage, speaking to no one all day, and rather liking it that way.

Cari – walking back home, delighting at the wild flowers that have started coming up along the roadside. She coaxes Andrew out to admire them. He does it with a good enough grace, taking the flower book along so at least she can start giving them names. And then says, 'This wind is really unpleasant. Let's get back in.'

Even the people Cari doesn't know are familiar now, faces she keeps seeing. She entertains herself by giving them imaginary lives. That tired looking young woman has a husband she has learnt to settle for but has never loved. The two middle-aged women who have stopped on the pavement to chat have children on the mainland whom they seldom see. The older the inhabitants, the more evocative. That bent old man sitting on the bench that looks out over the harbour, he's been planting trees for windbreaks since early in the century, and can remember shipwrecks that washed up onto the beach, and the islanders scrabbling to salvage the only wealth the sea ever offered.

And there's the woman on the bike again. For her Cari cannot find a story that satisfies. So often out cycling, but not going anywhere obvious. Posture consciously poised, as if cultivating inner calm. Her hair twisted up behind, inadequately held in place by a large leather clasp – hair that might once have been free-flowing and does not take well to middle age. She is certain only that the woman lives alone, and that aloneness is necessary to her. She is careful not to let her curious eyes intrude on that fragile privacy. She waits until the bike has passed before she turns to watch the upright back, the firm rounded arms, the skirt pulled by the wind.

'I bet she's not an islander,' Cari decides. But all she has to base this on is the intent way the woman looks at what she is passing.

Such a quiet, slow start it all had, those first few months before everything started winging out of control.

≈≈

March 1984
The first sign was a sudden deterioration in the weather. There were gale warnings out at sea and the children from the off-islands couldn't get in to school, too dangerous for the small boats to set out. The talk in the staffroom was of remembered disasters, the freak storm that two years ago had smashed a yacht against the rocks, drowning three young men

Then as suddenly as the clouds had come, they blew past, leaving behind them fragments of sunny days.

Andrew stood by the window watching as Cari set off into the misty morning, and welcomed the knowledge that for the next eight hours he would be alone. He went in to the kitchen to make his ritual start-the-day coffee. While he waited for it to brew he spread his papers. Within minutes of settling down he was off, pen scribbling, mind working at speed, coffee half-finished and forgotten.

Hours later he noticed that his body was stiff from sitting, realised with surprise that it was almost three and he was ravenous. He came out to get something to eat and saw a letter on the floor at the front door. Letters didn't happen often. He picked it up, opened it. From Karl, a Swedish mathematician he had met at a conference two years ago and corresponded with occasionally. 'Eva and I will be holidaying in Britain for a couple of weeks around Easter. Your island sounds interesting. Can we come and visit you?'

He liked Karl, it would be good to have someone he could really talk to; but that was Karl alone. This was 'Eva and I'. He'd never even heard there was an Eva in Karl's life. A trapped feeling began to come over him. He looked around the cottage. Definitely too small for four people. Where would they sleep? The awful realisation hit him. Cari, Karl and Eva, all of them would assume there was an obvious answer – his study. A whole week with no place to be alone and get on with his work.

On the last stretch home the skies opened. Cari arrived back, soaked.

Andrew said, 'Why didn't you get a taxi?'

'It came on suddenly. Anyway, it doesn't matter.' Inside she was saying, 'I don't care about getting wet, that walk is what *makes* being on the island for me.' But she kept it to herself – it seemed unfair that each day should be a delight to her, while Andrew merely tolerated the place.

'You do like it here, don't you?' she checked.

'Come on,' he said, 'don't start on that again.' His tone was half joking, but only half. He wished she would just let him be. She gave him a hug, or rather put herself up against him asking for one. Her need for reassurance felt a pressure and he moved away as soon as he decently could. 'I'm going to watch the news. A war could break out and we'd be the last to know.'

Cari joined him on the sofa but he knew it was just for the cuddle. Things happening on the mainland seemed to her to have lost reality. Island vision, he called it privately, like tunnel vision but leading nowhere. He shifted to free himself from her snuggling body, to stop himself from being drawn down into her cosy, myopic space.

Cari got up, suddenly cross and not knowing why. The news was finished and Andrew was letting the TV drone on, some game-show with a lot of pseudy people. He knew she had books to mark and there was no way she could do it with that inane laughter going on. She went into the bedroom, picked up a novel. Later, lying on the bed and already well into chapter six, she heard the noise of the TV click off and became suddenly aware – all those essays still to mark.

She went back into the living room and started spreading her papers on the table. Andrew said, 'It's ten-thirty, you can't start marking *now*.'

'I have to.'

But of course he was right, it was crazy to lie around reading all evening and only get started now. No he's *not* right, she told herself, suddenly obstinate. He just can't accept a disturbance of routine. His life works on routines, a system that runs itself with no apparent need for maintenance but he can't tolerate spontaneous variation. Well, I'm different. I've been adjusting to his rhythms for three years and I'm not going to go on doing it –

But she said only, 'I have to, they've got to be in tomorrow.' And turned her back, to get started.

Andrew went off to bed without saying goodnight. He had been meaning to tell her about Karl and Eva, but in their mutual irritation he forgot.

It took a few minutes for Cari to free herself from the awareness of his huffy shoulders. Then gradually her attention returned to the task, lighting on each girl or boy in turn. They paraded before her, absorbing yet conveniently confined to words on paper, a relief from emotions she did not understand.

Hours later she went quietly into the bedroom to get her pyjamas. She looked detachedly at Andrew's sleeping body. What would it be like to be here without him? Not to have to think, Have I been out too long, maybe I should get back?

She woke next morning feeling guilty for her disloyalty, however private. Our lives are too separate, she thought, that's the trouble. With daylight coming in at the window it seemed easily possible to take a positive approach.

Andrew woke. She cuddled up against him. 'Sorry I was cross last night.'

'Oh, don't worry.'

For some reason that made her feel less like cuddling. She thought, you were cross too, you could also say sorry.

Andrew said, 'I forgot to tell you, Karl and Eva want to come and stay.'

She sat up, stared. 'Who are Karl and Eva?'

Easter, and the holiday season getting underway. The passenger ferry arrives daily from Penzance. On the headland the sound of the helicopter arriving and taking off throbs noisily. The bed-and-breakfasts begin to buzz, the coffee shops are piled with fresh cakes. In the high street people amble by, peering into shops. Children carry buckets and spades, teenagers buy postcards and trinkets. Down at the pier there are queues each morning waiting for the boats that do the run between the islands. The population of the island has doubled in the space of a few weeks. Cari watches, one of the islanders now, observing the invasion.

Saturday morning, and they are down at the pier, waiting. Bright light, no rain, but the sea high. Andrew says, 'I'm not sure I'll recognise Karl. That conference was two years ago.' Cari doesn't hear, she has been looking out over the bay where the anchored boats lurch about. Then something nearer by catches her attention. A few feet in front of her is the woman whose story she is still trying to puzzle out, the woman on the bike. No bike today, for the woman too is waiting for someone to arrive, her attention firmly on the steamer that is now slowly docking. Her face is strained, a look akin to − hunger, thinks Cari, and feels a stab of compassion, knowing, without knowing how she knows, that this woman needs too much from the person she is waiting for. A lover? No, she must be fifty at least. A grown son, more likely. A son who leaves her too long between phone calls. I hope to God he comes.

The first passengers are moving down the gangplank. Anoraks of blue and green, toddlers in yellow Christopher Robin rainhats, a group of teenage girls giggling. Within minutes the pier is crowded, the excited pushing of people arriving on holiday. The woman Cari is watching starts forward, her face breaking into life − towards a young woman with a two small children. So much for the errant son. She bends down to draw the children into her arms, her body warm and enfolding, but when she stands up again there is a painful awkwardness between the two women, a hug that is all angles. Cari knows she shouldn't be watching but she can't stop herself. The children wait for the adult ritual to be got out of the way so they can get on with the holiday…

Andrew yanking at her hand, 'That's him!' and calling out, 'Karl!'

Two people walking towards them, both tall and Nordic, exactly the same rather square cast of face and sandy-coloured hair, the same long-stride, arm-swinging walk. 'Eva and I' were no couple afterall, but unmistakably brother and sister. Two beds needed, not one.

Introductions, continental kisses on both cheeks, and they set off to walk back along the pier. Andrew and Karl in front, she and Eva behind. 'This is amazing,' Eva turned her head to take in the harbour, the boats bobbing, the green headland beyond. 'And all those little islands we passed, so enticing!' Chattering on about the journey on the ferry, not the slightest shyness at being with someone she didn't know. Cari listened, enjoying her easy enthusiasm, responding; and at the same time watching in a detached way the swing of the arms of the man ahead of her. The tilt of his head. He was letting Andrew do all the talking, his head inclined as he listened or made the occasional response. Once Andrew stopped walking and turned to him to make a point, hands jabbing the air in emphasis. Karl's face turned towards him, a small appreciative nod, eyes half-smiling. Something about him she found immediately attractive, a confidence that required no stating, no unnecessary push.

They took the bus and arrived at the cottage. Carried the bags in, showed Karl and Eva around.

'You get settled,' she said. 'I'll get a salad together for lunch.'

Eva said, 'Let me help you,' and followed her to the kitchen. Andrew took Karl off to his study and was already showing him the article his supervisor had sent him, someone else working on his PhD question. He'd talked about nothing else for days, and Cari was relieved for him to have another audience for it, and one infinitely better able to understand.

In the kitchen Cari and Eva washed and chopped companionably. Cari saw it now, she was short of female company. Three months they had been here, plenty of small friendly encounters but still no one who seemed a candidate for a friend.

Karl appeared at the door. Eva said, 'Cari's a teacher and it's her holidays. Isn't that good? She can come around with us.'

Cari had not thought of it, had assumed they would want to go off on their own – but that was when she had thought of them as strangers, and a couple. Now everything was different. 'Sure I'll come.'

They carried the food through to the living room.

Karl said, 'Have you a favourite island?'

'They're all different. It depends on what you want.'

'Everything,' said Eva, and they laughed, all three of them, high already on their own pleasure.

Andrew came in. 'What's the joke?'

'No joke,' Karl said, 'these are serious decisions. Which island to go to.'

'Where's the best beach?' Eva asked.

'St Martin's,' Cari said, 'but it needs a perfect day.'

She got out the map and was tracing her finger to show them the strip of white that ran the length of the island. Karl leaned over to follow. She felt oddly shy, aware of the closeness of his body, his breath touching the back of her neck. 'See, south-facing beach with a bank of grass behind. It's like being in a glass house, all the sun reflects up at you, and this huge sky, and the birds wheeling about, and the sea disappearing for miles as the tide goes out.'

So simple, people to share her pleasure. That was all that had been amiss, she and Andrew each experiencing life so differently. She understood it now from the contrast, the lightness in her spirit at their responding enthusiasm. For so long she had been waiting for Andrew's thesis to be out of the way so that other things in life could begin. 'All I need,' he had said three years ago when they first got together, 'is six months without distractions, and I can finish it.' But even here where life was set up so he had nothing else to do, there seemed no sign of it coming to an end. When they made love she felt he was only half there, his body operating on autopilot while his mind was preoccupied with equations. Once in their early days together he had tried to explain the question he was investigating but the words had no meaning she could connect with, just these disembodied mathematical concepts that moved around each other in a bizarre mental dance. Nothing to do, she had decided eventually, but give up and come to an accommodation with reality; or rather with the two realities that didn't intersect, hers and his.

Now with Karl and Eva here she felt something shifting. She *wanted* him to be part of their planning, their pleasure. She turned to draw him in. 'Where do you think? For tomorrow?' – but realised immediately that her voice sounded too solicitous, as if she were encouraging a child. And knew for sure Andrew would not like that.

He did not. 'It's up to all of you.' It wasn't just the words, his tone put deliberate distance between them.

'You're not coming with us?' Eva said.

'I can't. I've just been showing Karl what I'm up against.'

Karl, trying to smooth the awkwardness, 'He's just found out someone else is working on his PhD question.'

'That's a good reason to take a break,' said Eva. 'Get your mind fresh before you start again.'

Wow, thought Cari. Now why can't I do that? No tension,

just refusing to take his self-imposed pressure seriously. But Andrew just said again, 'I can't, really. It's pushed me back months. I've got all his stuff to work through now.'

Well, do what you like then, Cari thought petulantly. None of his notes would go away if he left them for a few days. He was losing perspective, living so alone, and she had been colluding in that. All it had taken was someone else walking into their lives to make her see that. To the others she said, 'PhDs are the pits, don't ever get trapped by one.'

Andrew got up and walked to the kitchen, leaving behind him an embarrassment that no one knew how to dissipate.

It was Karl who broke the silence. 'You hadn't finished showing us the maps.'

They bent over them again, but the elan had gone. Andrew came back in with a tray of mugs of coffee. They each took theirs, steering carefully past the tension, talking of neutral things. Cari battled against an undertow of misery. Andrew avoided looking in her direction. Then he took himself off early to bed.

She did the washing up, refusing Eva and Karl's offer to help. 'Not on your first night,' she said, and left them with a pile of guidebooks. Alone with the dishes she was caught in a litany of self blame. She wished she had not herself consented so readily to go with them next day. But impossible now to cry off.

≈≈

Anna opened the low gate, and watched as her grandchildren ran up the path, racing each other. Gail was next to her, the daugher she had waited so long to introduce to this place.

At the door the children stopped, waiting for the adults to catch up.

45

'You can go in,' Anna said. 'Just push - it's not locked.'

'You don't lock?' Gail asked.

'No need.'

The children were in already, running around like excited puppies, exploring. Gail stopped a few feet inside the door, taking it in. A small awkward silence.

Anna said, 'Come, let me take you up to where you'll be sleeping.'

Gail looked around the upstairs room, took in the easel stacked out of the way to one side, the light coming in the east window. She turned to her mother. 'This place is beautiful. I mean, what you've done with it.'

'I'm glad you like it.'

Their words were glosses, over so many things unsaid. Extraordinary to have them here, connecting the unconnectable bits of their lives. Keep to the practical, she told herself firmly. 'It's a bit of a squeeze. I hope you'll manage.'

'We'll be fine. But where will you sleep?'

'The floor downstairs. I've got a piece of foam.'

'Oh Mum, don't be ridiculous. Let me. You keep your bed.'

Anna said firmly, 'You're sleeping here, near the children.' And then, half apologetic, 'I'm a bit of an isolate these days. It'll be better for me having a bit of space to myself downstairs at night.'

'Are you telling me you don't sleep well?'

'Not through the night. That's a talent you lose as you get older.' She kept her voice light, determined not to allow Gail to be anxious. 'It doesn't signify. I potter about till I'm ready to sleep again.'

Noel came up the stairs. 'Mama, come see, there are stools in the kitchen, with three legs!'

They followed, and watched with shared pleasure as the

46

children experimented. Anna said, 'There's a story to those stools.'

'Oh?'

'They were the first luxury I allowed myself.' Cautiously testing the edges of her self-imposed rules ... visualising a bit of coloured fabric there, in that corner ... watching it take on shape and become a comfortable chair, covered in woven cloth ... cycling to the small town to ask if there was anyone on the island who made furniture ... She had found him, a mono-syllabic young man with a workshop in a shed. She had been about to ask for the cheapest wood, the simplest design, just a strong frame to hold the padding that she would cover with the fabric that was in her mind's eye. Then she had seen the loving touch he had with wood, the way his eye picked out the grain and his hand moved with it. And suddenly she could visualise quite clearly stools made of that wood, for the children. She tried to think herself back into the mind of a child. What kind of stool would please them? She had seen too little of them, could only guess what they would be like now. Three tall legs, she saw, and the children's legs dangling. She knew it was a risk to attach the feeling for particular people to any object, that every day now as she came into the kitchen and saw the stools her inner eye would watch the children climb up onto them and then the pleasure would turn to longing as the months went by and Gail did not bring them.

But she was here now.

Gail gave her a hug, the first real one. 'It's good to see you, Mum.' Then, pulling away quickly, 'Don't know why, but I was scared.'

'I know. Maybe we both were. A lot's happened.'

Out with the children to the beach that lay just below their front door, on the bus around the island to Pelistry, to the butterfly centre. Ice cream cones, buckets, spades, sand in their sandals, in their hair, little piles of stones and shells collecting on the window ledge. The getting of meals and the clearing-up, the setting-out of toys and packing them away again, the doing-up of shoelaces and wiping-up of messes.

She was absurdly unprepared. She'd forgotten how she would be aware all the time of how Gail was dealing with the minute-by-minute demanding-ness of it all, anxious about the toll it would take on this young woman she loved so fiercely and whose temper had never been even. Had not thought how it would be to have the children around her, their urgency nourishing a part of her that she had kept so deeply under wraps she had almost forgotten it was there. Climbing up onto her lap for a cuddle, pulling her over to show her things on the beach. She had meant to hold back a little, knowing they would so soon be gone, but they had not been there a day before she realised that she had lost the ability.

Now it all came flooding back as she sat digging in the sand with the two-year-old Penny, while Noel, two years older, set off to explore the beach beyond. She and Gail watched as he picked up shells, this little boy whom she had held in the first days of his life, feeling his small fingers cling to hers, primate survival instinct ... outings to the park, back among the mums and pushchairs ... being there to distract him when Penny was born, reading him stories when his mum and dad were too tired ...

'How's Stan?' Anna asked.

'Fine,' said Gail. 'But really busy. He wanted to come too, but no way.'

Anna didn't say, 'It's nice just to have you.' There were things she and Gail had shared that Stan had no part in, and she was grateful to have this small space alone to try to connect with them again.

Gail suddenly jerked into action – 'Noel, *wait* for me, don't go in the water till I get there.'

The day drifted on, at the pace of the tide. Anna had a nap on the sand with the gentle spring sunshine touching her face. When she woke Gail was off in the distance with the children. She watched them, there but needing nothing from her … And began to see pictures of an earlier Gail. Gail in Chichester, a schoolgirl of thirteen or fourteen, so close yet so prickly, and confused about the model her mother held up to her. Remembering Wednesday afternoons when Gail would detour on her way back from school, to appear at the well-woman clinic where Anna was doing her weekly session. 'Your daughter, Doctor,' the receptionist would say with a smile, popping her head round the door in the gap between patients. Anna would come out and she and Gail would greet like mature friends, relaxed and calm together, and would chat for a few minutes about the day at school. Until Anna would have to say, 'I'd better get back, darling,' and Gail would set off home, having got what she had come for – to see her mother in this world of work, through the eyes of the receptionist, the women who waited to be seen and who came out to make the next appointment saying, 'Can it be with Dr Feldman again?'

Then home. Max arriving back, tired and uncommunicative, the commuter train from London late again. And over the so called family meal all the old, destructive patterns would resurface. Max cross-questioning Gail in a way he meant as fatherly interest, and she received as criticism. Anna trying to conciliate, to explain them to each other, and only making things worse. Max saying, 'I don't need you to tell me how to talk to my own daughter. And if you were at home more she'd never have got so unruly.' Anna not answering, for what answer was there? She was trapped by the need to smooth things down, to stay connected to a husband whose values and instincts seemed ever more at odds with her own. Trying to change the subject, to find something they could all be pleasant about. Max drinking more wine than was good for him, his tone becoming aggressive – 'You and those banner waving friends of yours.' Anna wondering if the trains *were* always late, or if there was someone in London he was spending time with before he came home. Gail taking herself off to her room, shoulders hunched against both her ridiculous parents. But particularly, Anna knew, against her. Max was Max, a given they all had to find a way to deal with. It was her mother she blamed, for not remaining herself in the face of it.

'Why do you let him *say* those things to you?' she would accuse, when Anna appeared in her room. 'I can't understand why you don't stand up to him.' Gail angry, rejecting, refusing to be hugged …

Another picture floated into her mind, from a time after the girl had left home. Anna had been up to London for a meeting and was coming out of Guys Hospital, heading for a train back home. In the concourse at London Bridge station she saw ahead of her a slim young girl in too-tight jeans hurtling across the space and throwing her arms around a young man. She watched, struck by the life in the girl, and by the way the young man just stood and received her adoration as if it were his due. Not knowing who she was looking at, Anna was rivetted by the body language, by all it said about women and men, and what might lie ahead for this young girl who held nothing back. Then the young girl turned – and Anna realised it was her daughter …

Later still – how long after, she could not remember – Gail arriving home unexpectedly. They had not heard from her for months, had tried to learn the patience of parents who need more than they are needed. And now suddenly Gail appeared, but not alone. With this same young man at her side, his hands in his jeans pocket, elbows jutting in embarrassment. They looked like two waifs, uncomfortable at finding themselves stranded in this too-spacious, too-gracious livingroom, once the home that Gail had grown up in but no longer a place where she belonged. Gail's face, trying to act cool, wanting so much for it to be easy.

'This is Stan,' she said. 'Stan Waites.'

Anna welcomed him, thinking, you look so *young,* both of you. Max gave a perfunctory 'Hello' and then ignored Stan, turning to Gail. 'And where have you been all this time, young lady?'

'Dad, don't let's go through all that again.' But she could see already that Max was several glasses of good wine beyond the recommended limit.

'Still working in the cheese shop? Your brilliant career?'

'*Dad.*'

Max turned to Stan. 'And what do you do?'

'I lay carpets.'

'Lay carpets?'

'It's just what I'm doing for now. I gave up college last month. Didn't like the course.'

'Another one,' Max said. 'The pair of you. Honestly, I don't know what you people think the world is like. You going to lay carpets forever?'

Anna said, 'Max, stop it.' And to Stan, in deep embarrassment, 'You're very welcome.'

Too late. Gail had taken Stan's hand, was standing a little closer, their bodies a statement. She said, 'Let's go.' And they went ...

All the pictures, all those times. And through it all she felt that she, Anna, was the passive watcher. Loving her daughter, seeing what she was going through, wanting to be there for her, but having to learn not to be the one to *do,* but to wait for the girl to be ready. It was Gail who had always determined how they could be together, the ease, or the prickliness.

And now, was it any different? Gail at twenty-seven, a mother; and so much that had passed between them. But still Anna did not know how to talk to her about the things that most needed saying. She heard Gail's voice in the letter she had written when Anna had first come here – resisting the incomprehensible – 'I wish you hadn't put yourself there on that island, miles from anywhere.' But that was the Gail who missed her, who felt abandoned; and Anna knew that another lurked beneath the words, a Gail who couldn't have handled her if she had stayed.

I wish you hadn't put yourself there –

What could Anna say? That coming here had hardly been a matter of choice? That it had been decided by what had overtaken them all? But she knew already how Gail would reply – 'Mum you've got to stop *dwelling* so.'

Dwelling. Living in the past, Gail meant. But *to dwell* means simply to live in a place. 'It is to be where you belong,' she said to Gail, who for so long wouldn't come. To be where your life is cast. This is where I dwell now. That's my way, my only way.

And now Gail had finally come to see her, making peace.

≈≈

It was a gift of a day, a sudden break in the wind and only short light bursts of rain. Eva kept stopping to notice the spring flowers that were everywhere, purple fumitory scrambling over stone walls, bright blue eyes of speedwell on the edges of the path. Cari picked some hairy leaves of storksbill, crushed them, and gave them to Eva. 'Smell.' Musky.

Karl strode ahead, eyes taking in the whole vista of coastline and sea. Once he turned and asked Cari, 'How did you *find* this place?' as if it were a treasure she personally had unearthed. Most of the time he said little but his silence was alive. His eyes moved to some thought of their own and she felt that given the right circumstances he might open up and communicate all sorts of things. *That* was what she missed in Andrew, that sense of unexpected possibilities. All his life force went into his mathematics. Karl had a mind too, he must have, even to understand what Andrew was on about, but not that all absorbing, one-directional focus.

'That's Old Town we're coming to,' she said. 'The cafe does great milkshakes.' The cafe looked out over the bay, the natural harbour that had served the island for centuries before the pier was built on the other, deeper side. After their milkshakes they walked to the church on the far side of the bay and up through the churchyard that climbed the hill behind. They sat on the stone steps, looking down to the sand way below, where children dug and parents chatted.

'Look, those kids were on the boat with us,' Eva pointed as they set off to walk back. 'Remember? Those ones with the yellow buckets.'

They followed her line of sight — two children and two women sitting on the sand. The older woman was packing up, the younger one encouraging the children up the harbour wall steps and onto the path that overlooked the bay. The little group was about thirty yards ahead of them now, the children scrambling to test out garden walls, the mother and grandmother walking behind, not talking much. Cari moved slightly to one side so she could catch their profiles. Then something made her look up, to see Karl watching her. Her pulse surged, taking her by surprise. Stop it, she told herself, there's nothing in that look except curiosity.

'Do you know her?' Karl had come a little closer so their voices wouldn't carry. She sensed his arm right next to her, the hair on it almost brushing against her.

'No, but I keep seeing her, going about on her bike.'

Eva came closer too, to listen in.

'And I think,' said Cari, 'it's the children's first visit.'

'How can you know *that*?'

'They were excited when they arrived but neither of them was saying, look, remember that?'

Eva said, 'You should be writing stories.'

'Guessing real ones is more interesting.'

The group ahead turned in at a small white-painted gate and disappeared into one of the cottages. As they came up to it they saw a board at the gate, angled so people would see it as they came up the hill – 'Paintings for sale.'

Eva said, 'So now you know something else about her.'

Up on the headland beyond the last cottage the thrift was out, the first pink flowers waving above their springy tufts of green. Then that airy sense at the top, land under one's feet but all around space, the cliff dropping away, nothing but sea and sky. Cari and Eva stopped to take it in. Karl kept going for a few paces, then he too came to a halt on a rise ahead of them. Cari watched his tall body outlined against the sky. He turned to say, 'The colours are incredible. If I lived here I'd take to painting too.'

When they came in Andrew was uncommunicative. Cari felt a pang of guilt, but it had been such a glorious day that nothing could pull her down again to the tension of the previous night. He's fine, she told herself. He's been doing what he would have been doing anyway, and now he's got Karl to sit drinking beer with him and talk work. Company, of a kind she couldn't supply.

In bed that night she said, 'I was stupid to say that about your thesis. I only meant it would be nice if you came too. It's ages since we took time off together.'

'You made it sound as if I can *choose* not to work.'

And of course that was what she had meant. She understood with belated clarity that the thesis wasn't just his work, it was a wall he had erected against having to grow up and begin life for real. She felt sorry now for what she had said, properly sorry, out of compassion. But she knew she could feel that because she had had a wonderful day, and was going to keep having wonderful days, all week. Walking free, walking into the wind.

Into the wind. But what had happened to dull her antennae, she who was usually over-alert to danger? Looking back it seemed that everything had conspired to lull her into a state of childlike acceptance of the present as the only thing that mattered. The island had never been more beautiful. Each rock and headland stood out sharper, more crystalline. The clouds swept more majestically across the bay, by turns angry and gentle. The spray leapt higher, its drops shimmering in the air. Out with these friends in the place that she loved, it was enough to hear their laughter as they all clambered into the boat that would chop its way slowly across the basin of sea to Bryer. Enough to watch the wind lifting Karl's straight sand-coloured hair while he stood outlined against a wild sky on a high point of land, while hundreds of feet below the western sea crashed against slabs of black rock.

Karl hardly talked, most of the time it was she and Eva. He

listened to their chatter, every so often adding a question, a laconic comment, smiling at something they were laughing at. Yet his presence heightened everything. His quiet humour — amused, sharing it, but not angling for a reaction. How he moved, how he walked, how he sat on a rock, long legs dangling. How he bent to examine some spearwort in a wet patch along the nature trail, or lay on his back on the sands at Pelistry, or ran for shelter when the clouds he had been watching suddenly let loose their weight of water.

She could hide no longer from the knowledge that she was measuring his proximity at every moment. She watched and waited for any small accident that might bring them in contact, an arm flung carelessly as they walked, hand brushing against hand as they each reached for something across a table in a tea room. It never happened. And now she thought, we are so close together all day that it *not* happening seems pointed. Was Karl deliberately avoiding it? Which could only mean that he was conscious of . . .

How could he not be? Something so palpable.

But he couldn't be, or surely there would be some sign?

She was caught up in feelings so unlooked for, so outside anything she had known in all the three years with Andrew that they blotted out the voice of caution. The hyper-awareness to Karl did not leave her even when they returned each evening to Andrew, it just became further complicated by the return of guilt. Guilt clear enough to work away like an internal barometer, looking for signs of squalls to come, but not apparently enough to give her the clarity to adjust course.

Being near Andrew began to feel a burden. The only way to free herself from confusion was to be out of his presence. When finally she shut the door as they left each morning, she thought he was probably relieved to have her gone.

≈≈

Friday, their last day. As if it were making a statement, the sun rose in a sky washed clear by the night's rain, not a scrap of cloud to disturb its china blue.

'That's weather no one could quarrel with,' Karl said at breakfast. 'Is it St Martin's, then?'

'Come on Andrew,' Eva said, 'today you *have* to join us.'

Andrew smiled but shook his head. 'I've done St Martin's.'

'But not in weather like this,' said Cari, and then wondered why she hadn't stayed quiet. Just leave him, if he wants to be like that.

So the three of them it was who joined the queue of twenty or thirty people climbing down the stone steps of the pier into the waiting boat, and were carried out across a sea so calm they seemed the only thing moving.

'This boat's going back at three-fifteen,' the boatman said as he gave them each a hand to climb out onto the small strip of concrete that did for a pier on St Martin's. 'There's another at four. You miss that one, you sleep on the beach.' They all laughed. The standard boatman joke.

Within minutes the island had absorbed them as if they were no more than a passing flock of birds.

The beach seemed whiter and longer even than Cari had remembered. Their eyes blinked as a million glass-edged grains reflected the sun. White sand stretched out ahead of them till it narrowed in the distance and seemed almost to touch the island beyond. If they turned back east, the morning sun glinted on a sea dotted with craggy rocks, inhabited only by birds. Ahead they looked out across a calm basin fringed by islands.

For a time that seemed timeless they sat watching the seagulls dip and rise over the water that moved further away from them with each backwards-trickling wave. Eventually Eva lay down, letting the sun absolve her from all need to be active. Her voice came through sand and the slight wind in the grass bank behind. 'Do what you like, I'm not moving. Who knows when I'll find a beach like this again?'

Karl stood up, bending to wipe the sand from his legs. 'I'm going to walk out after the tide. See how long it takes to get to that rock.'

Was that a statement or an invitation?

He was standing looking down at Cari. 'What about you?'

She was up instantly, and they were walking out past the small children digging in the firm wet sand, out past the bigger children splashing where the water had collected in small dips, out past the last figures bent over, collecting shells. And still the sea bed stretched ahead of them, wet and glistening, out to where there was no one else, nothing but the sand in their toes and the seabirds wheeling and the rock still tantalising out there, beyond, lapped by the retreating waves –

Then he turned to walk back. She followed.

They ate their sandwiches. 'What's the other side of the island like?' Karl asked.

'Smaller beaches. A wilder sea.'

'Two hours till the boat goes. Can we do it?'

'Sure.'

Climb the grass bank and onto a little path past hedged bulbfields, now lying fallow. They leant over a gate, idly surveying the fields. A man came out of the stone farmhouse heading in the opposite direction. Cari watched him go, knowing she had seen him before. Where? Parents' evening, that was it — father of Yvonne Penruth. She remembered him because he was so much older, out of place among the other dads ... Cari looked up, to see Karl's eyes, absorbed in her absorption. Just for a fragment of time, then his eyes moved to take in the path ahead, and she couldn't be sure it had happened.

Up over the top of the heath, down to a cove on the northern side. Less sun but no people, so it had its own charm. Then it was time to head back for the boat so they climbed back up to the heath and headed off in what Cari hoped was the right direction — it looked slightly different from what she remembered. But it was all so small-scale, they'd find it all right.

'The weather's giving up on us,' Eva said. 'Look.'

They turned, to see rolling in from the west an ominously low cloud.

'Out of a totally clear sky,' said Karl. 'It's hard to believe.'

'That's the Atlantic for you,' Cari said. 'It's not to be trusted. Not even for an hour, let alone a day.'

The clouds were after them now, blocking out the sun, turning everything a weird green-grey light. She was even less sure of their direction now, all the paths on the heath looked the same. And they were having to push the pace to get back in time.

Karl's eyes caught hers. Same thought, same moment. The boat — but she was also thinking, If we miss it we'll have to spend the night on St Martin's and then we'll be too late for them to get the ship back to the mainland in the morning. And there isn't one on Sunday so they'll have to stay till Monday.

Eva was saying, 'I thought this was a small island but it goes on forever.' She stopped. 'Look, that bush with the strange shaped branch, I've seen that before. We're going round in circles.'

Cari caught the change in her voice. She's beginning to be afraid, like everything's slipping out of control. Instantly she was alert. It wasn't the boat Eva was worried about but the fear of being at the mercy of the elements. The wind had got going now and they were having to push against it. They gave up talking, it took too much breath. The heath was flat and open, not a sign of anything to shelter under. Cari scanned ahead and found a slight lift in the land ahead and to the left, that looked as if it might drop down on the other side. Against the rising of the wind she called, 'Make for that rise.'

They turned direction, pushing towards it. She looked up again to check the sky. God, it was about to break. The others were a few feet away, bodies bent forward, hoods of their anoraks pulled tight around their heads. She yelled to them, 'It's coming, lie down.'

They swivelled round, Karl's face questioning, Eva's really afraid now. 'Lie face down,' she yelled, 'so you're not giving any resistance.' She waited till she saw them both obey, then dropped down herself just as the rain hit, driving at them and sweeping over them, battering, deafening. And cold beyond belief.

It lasted maybe five minutes but it felt like eternity. Then the wind dropped slightly and the rain settled into a good hard rhythm, but the worst of the violence had gone from it. She crawled over to where they were lying – 'Come' – and they were up again and heading for the rise ahead, pushing against the rain in their faces. Once Eva stumbled and Karl waited for her to catch up and put his arm around her to help her move forward. They got to the small crest of land and could see now that it did drop very suddenly on the other side, into a basin-shaped dip in the land, like something left by a meteor crashing into the earth. They huddled up against the rim, pressed close together.

A lull in the rain, the dense curtain lifting slightly. Karl stood up, shook each leg in turn and waved his arms about. Eva and Cari stayed holding on to each other. They were laughing, camaraderie taking over now the need for fear was past.

'You were great,' Eva said.

'Don't be silly,' Cari said.

'But you knew what to do. I completely panicked.'

Karl had walked a few steps over to look down into the crater hole. 'Come and see.' They got up to join him. In the deep scoop below them was a graveyard of filled black dustbin bags, piled on top of each other, torn, and the rotting contents spilling out. Karl said, 'It makes you grateful for a good clean storm.'

A sudden fierce gust of wind, and the rain was pushing at them again. They fled, back to the semi-shelter beneath the rim.

Eva started sneezing. 'All I want is to be warm.'

Cari pulled her tighter into the huddle. Karl had his arms around them both, rubbing Eva's back. It felt right, natural, as if there had never been a time when touch was taboo.

≈≈

A storm blowing up out of nowhere always made Anna nervous. They were inside when it came, dry, safe – but still. She couldn't stop herself from watching it lash against the windows, tossing the boats in the harbour as if they were no sturdier than driftwood. Then she became aware of her daughter watching her, and felt another kind of anxiety. She didn't want Gail to worry. About anything. But now her own inability to let go was making Gail anxious. Only the children were oblivious.

Gail said, 'Tell me a bit about your days, when we're not here. You were always so busy, I can't imagine you with nothing to do.'

'I've got plenty. It's just a different kind of pace. And much better for me.'

Gail looked sceptical. 'What about friends?'

'It takes a while in any new place.'

'It doesn't have to. Do you try?'

Anna smiled. 'It's nice having you nagging me again.'

'But *do* you?'

Do I?

'Painting's great,' Gail said, 'but you need people too.'

Do I? She found it difficult to keep concentrating in this kind of conversation. But Gail had pressed some kind of button, for she was remembering back to her first months on St Mary's when she had gone through most days hardly speaking to anyone. She hadn't wanted to, wasn't ready. It was enough, she had told herself, to see other people around her, to begin to pick out who might be the islanders, there week after week among the holiday-makers who came and went like shoals of fish. To see, but not connect. But she remembered now that she had found the *silence* difficult, never speaking, never being spoken to, just listening in distantly to other people's sounds. Finding little devices to fulfil that minimal need ...

Like buying a ticket for a concert of the local choir so she could sit in the audience among holiday-makers, safe that no one knew her but needing them all the same. The singing started, and caught her in some place she had been trying desperately to close off, and she had to fight to keep the tears back. During the interval she went outside, stood alone in the autumn air, and almost did not go back in. But the draw of that sound was too strong. She waited for the interval to be over, hovered in the porch, listened to the buzz of voices inside. She studied the notice board with fixed attention. Flower rota for the church. Choral Society Practice Tuesday Evenings, All Welcome.

And she had arrived, not the next Tuesday but three weeks after, having thought about it, decided, cancelled her decision, and thought again. Finally the reason she went was that it was absurd to have become such a recluse that she was nervous simply to walk in and say hello to people she did not know.

They were standing about talking to each other as she came in. Some faces she now recognised. Someone coming to speak to her.

'Neville Hill,' he put out his hand. A man around her age. 'I'm the musical director. You coming to join us?'

She did not say, 'I know, I saw your name in the programme notes. And I also know you're the head at the school, I've heard my cousin Bella talk of you.' She assumed he needed his privacy as she needed hers. She said simply, 'I'm Anna Feldman.'

'I thought so. Yvonne Penruth's aunt.'

So much for privacy. She was instantly nervous. If he knew Bella and Thomas, he would know her story. They probably all did. The place was too small, she should have put herself in a city.

'What do you sing?'

No sign of pity, or any other kind of knowing.

'Contralto,' she said.

'That's good, we're short of contraltos.' Then to the assembled company, 'Meet Anna, our new contralto.'

Anna, our new contralto. Anna, Yvonne Penruth's aunt. Her anxiety calmed down. They were safe enough ways to be known.

She sang, almost surprised that she could still read music, as if that too might have been lost in the flood. She gave herself to the familiar sensation of standing with people close by her, arms touching, all facing forwards, shared concentration. At coffee-break her defences were up again. She held herself on the edges, wary as she had been of Neville. But no one said anything remotely personal. If they knew, they were leaving her undisturbed. They seemed settled, conventional people; if they had their own storms beneath the calm, they gave no sign of it. At the end of the evening she watched Neville set off with his arm linked through his wife's, and knew that this too was a reason she had chosen to put herself here, a place where middle-aged couples walked home like that, and the most exciting thing in the week was the choral society practice ...

'Mum.'

Gail's voice, coming at her from some way off.

'Mum, you've gone off somewhere of your own again.'

Anna came back, suddenly clear, present, and definite. 'I sing,' she said firmly, 'that's one of the things I do. I sing. I paint. I look, I listen. I feel the sand under my bare feet and the rain on my face. I watch all life going on around me, and it grounds me.'

Gail stared. 'OK, I get the message.'

Through the open door to the kitchen the children were experimenting with the stools. 'Mine's a boat,' Noel said, stool upturned – bottom in the boat, legs dangling out. Penny turned hers too but climbed into it, feet first.

'That's all they need,' Anna said, 'they keep busy for hours with an upturned stool.'

Gail – voice edgy – 'Are you trying to tell me that I spoil them?'

The ease broken again. I am *tired*, Anna thought. It doesn't matter what I do or say today, it's wrong. A sharp pain each time that happened, and Gail too quick not to know.

'Mum,' Gail said, as if to a difficult child, 'I wish you wouldn't *over-react* so. I feel like I can hardly move without hurting you.'

The girl was right. She was allowing herself to need things

64

again, and it was a burden. Anna said, she hoped lightly, 'Just pay no attention to me, it doesn't mean anything.'

But they both knew it did.

Gail said, 'Do you know what I've just remembered? That time when I was little and you went off without Dad, without me.'

'Went off? Never.'

'You did. For ages. Or I thought it was. You left me with Dad and he had to take me to school in the mornings and he was always cross because he thought it would make him late for his train. And Debbie's mum collected me after school and I stayed there till Dad came home. And the worst was, he had to put me to bed and he didn't know how to do it the way you did. He'd never even watched.'

'I remember now, it was the time I took your grandpa back to where he'd grown up.'

'Yes, and I said why couldn't I come too, and you said, you can't miss school.'

'It was the only time I ever gave your grandpa proper time after I left home. My own dad. And he died a year later.'

Gail paused, following that thought. 'Grandpa came at Christmas sometimes, didn't he? He used to speak differently from other people. And he had some funny words.'

'Liverpool was far away, we didn't get there often.'

'I remember asking him to read me a story, and he said he couldn't. I thought he was just being mean, you had to explain to me he'd never learnt to read. It was the first time I realised that grown-ups couldn't do everything. And I remember thinking, Mum wants him here but Dad doesn't.'

'My God Gail, was there nothing you missed?'

'A bit scary, isn't it?' she grinned. Then serious, 'I wonder sometimes what Noel and Penny see.'

Anna waited, curious, but apparently there was nothing more coming on that one.

'Where was it you took Grandpa?'

'An island called St Kilda's. Off the coast of Scotland. It's where he was born, where he grew up till he was a young man. Then he had to leave. When he was older he started thinking about it again and wanted to see it.'

'Why did he leave?'

'It's too barren to sustain life. Just bare windswept cliffs and seabirds.'

And the journey there, across the wildest sea – seeing it now as if it were something she were painting. Her young-woman self standing with her father on the deck of the ship that chopped for hours over rough sea. His face, weatherbeaten from a lifetime of working out in all weathers, on the docks, on building sites, shimmying up and down scaffolding as in his boyhood he had scaled down cliffs – his eyes watching those cliffs appear again out of the water, distant, getting closer – till eventually they reached the island that for thirty years now had been uninhabited.

Gail had got up and was moving around the room, looking at a painting, touching the fabric of a chair cover. 'I love the way you've kept this place so simple. So uncluttered.'

Anna smiled. 'A bit of a contrast, you mean?' – to the house Gail had grown up in. The furnishings. The paintings. The antiques. The car, new every year, shining status. The yacht down at the harbour for weekends. Possessions. Investment. Leisure. Pleasure.

Shut up, she told her spinning mind. Shut it back down again.

But Gail's antennae had tuned in. 'So the way we lived was Dad's style, not yours?'

Anna answered carefully. 'That wouldn't be fair. It was our

style, what I let myself go along with it. But it was he who thought that was the way to be happy. I'd never had any of those things before I met him, I was never the one who came up with the idea.'

'Just the one who went out and bought it, and arranged it, and kept it immaculate, and felt responsible.'

Anna said wryly, 'There's not much you didn't see.'

Claim the house, Anna's friends had said when everything fell apart. It's your home, you've put all the work into it. He owes you. But she couldn't begin to think what she would do in it alone, or with any of the possessions if she walked off with them. She had left with one suitcase, and acquired this unexpected freedom.

Gail said, 'His new place is gross. Myra doesn't have your flair.'

Myra, the new wife. Anna was long used to that thought, but now hearing Gail talk of her she was facing another – the picture of Myra in Gail's life, more often than she, Anna, could be. Carefully she asked, 'So you go there? That's new, isn't it?'

'A couple of times a year.' Then, 'Do you want to hear?'

'Why not?' It was ancient history, nothing that could still hurt her.

Gail paused, as if wondering what was safe to offer. 'Myra's kind. She tries. But she's – different.' She paused, then got into her stride. 'And Dad buys the kids lots of presents, the kind you'd hate. Plastic, glaring colours, noisy. The kids love them.'

They laughed. Anna said, 'OK, what's new?'

'I'll tell you what's new. He's a surprisingly good grand-father.'

'Not so surprising,' Anna said.

'Oh?'

Anna shrugged. 'He was different when we first got together,

67

from the way you remember him, your growing-up years. Those things must still be in him somewhere.'

'Which things?'

'He was fun. He made things happen. He enjoyed introducing me to all the things I'd never had.'

'As long as *you* joined in *his* things. I don't remember it ever happening the other way.'

'True. But affection came easily to him. As long as it didn't get in the way of what he wanted to do. He couldn't stand anything being required of him.' She stopped, drawn back by all those pictures.

Gail was watching her, considering. 'So was it good between you, before I was born?'

'It was. But don't get it into your head that you had anything to do with what went wrong.'

'Was that why you held on so long?'

'I suppose so. And you.'

'Me?'

'I didn't want you to have a divided life. Which was ridiculous, because you had one anyway.'

'Stop worrying, Mum. It's long ago.'

'I'm not worrying.'

'Oh yeah?' Then, 'I have to say, I find Myra really painful. She's just like Dad about spending money, but with him at least you feel – I don't know, he actually gets *enthusiastic* about each new thing. With Myra it's just status, show. She's so – *Ugh*.'

Anna smiled, despite herself.

Gail was getting into her stride. 'And she tries so bloody hard, ingratiating just isn't in it. It makes me want to back away a million miles. And what *really* gets my goat is seeing Dad being so much nicer with her than he ever was with you.'

Anna laughed, softly at first, caught by surprise at this picture of Gail being at her prickliest with this woman Anna had never met. It was not funny, of course it wasn't, so why was she laughing? But she was, louder all the time, hand to her mouth to try to stem the flow – then abandoning all attempt at restraint, she whooped and rocked, as if nothing in life had ever been so hilarious.

Gail stared at her. 'Mu-um?' Then she too started, a tentative giggle of shock, then they were both of them holding on to each other, eyes watering, breath gasping.

'Oh, oh –' Anna managed to stop. 'That's too awful.'

Gail said, 'About time we found something to laugh about.' Then, wiping her eyes she said, voice resolute, 'And what I think about Dad is, it's a pity it took something so *mega* to shock him into learning how to be with people.'

≈≈

St Martin's, almost dusk. Three bedraggled people pushing through the now steady rain, lifting tired feet over uneven ground. Visibility very low.

Something loomed ahead of them, something bulky. Cari said, 'A house – it must be.' Nearer – a rough stone building emerging, isolated against the heath. A couple of straggling fields beyond.

They knocked, timid because of the aura of the place but made bold by their need. 'I hope they like strangers,' Eva said.

A man opened the door. Rather heavily built, rough farm clothes. Clearly an isolate like his house. He stared at them, anoraks dripping, hair plastering their faces. Then his face relaxed into a slow grin. 'Well, you certainly copped it. Welcome to St Martin's, the island in the sun.'

They stepped inside, to a room musty with clobber and

windows that weren't often opened. He opened drawers of an old wooden dresser, rustled among piles of things stashed in a corner and eventually came up with towels and extra clothes. While they got themselves dry he cut slices of bread and put hot mugs of tea in their hands, and even produced a hanky for Eva's streaming nose. They were overcome at being taken care of, effusive in their gratitude. They sat huddled in his old jerseys in a kitchen smelling of wood smoke and tractor oil, at a bare board table that looked as if he had made it himself, the tree still visible in its grainy surface. Cari watched the movements of his body as he lifted the heavy lids on the stove. It was extraordinary, the intimacy they had stumbled on, here in this warm enclosed space with a stranger. Already his presence felt familiar, his earth-clogged fingernails on the tough workman's hands that reached up to search a high shelf, opening one biscuit tin after another, hopefully, as if he had no idea what he might find in them. He handled them with surprising lightness. The tins were painted like the kettles of the canal boat people, flowers like those children draw because adults have shown them, this is how you draw a flower; colours bright and unreal.

Karl was asking the man – Hugh he said his name was – about the deep hollow and the rubbish bags. Hugh said, 'A year ago that was one of the most beautiful spots on the island.'

'That's just a year's dumping?' Karl asked.

'Since the new self-catering cottages went up.'

'What do the rest of you do? With your refuse?'

'What people have done since life began. We compost what's good for the earth, burn what can be burnt to make good clean ash, and bury the rest. But the townies who come for a week just tie up the whole lot in a bag and don't give a thought to how it's going to be got rid of. And the man who rents them the cottages supplies the bags and then goes and dumps them. The cottagers never even know, you can walk on the heath for hours and never see it. So the rent keeps rolling in and so does that foul dump of plastic that's never going to decay.' He gave a short laugh. 'You probably noticed, you touched a raw nerve.'

Karl said, 'And on an island if you have differences with your neighbours, you don't easily get away from each other!'

Cari was listening more to the tone of the exchange than the words, Hugh's intensity, Karl's calm, that way some men have of turning something personally felt into a detached non-fiction topic. But Hugh wasn't letting it stay there. 'There are one or two people here who'd like to throw me off because I'm not letting them just cover up what's going on.'

Eva's mind was on more immediate things. 'Do you know any way we can get back?'

'In my boat,' Hugh said, as if the matter had been decided some time before.

Of course, Cari thought; and she could see him holding the tiller, assessing the wind.

Karl began to make a little speech of thanks. Hugh interrupted, smiling drily, 'It's a choice between that or having you for the night. And I'm a few beds short. But I'll let you pay me for the fuel if you like.'

'Yes,' said Eva and Karl, together.

They all laughed.

Hugh said, 'I don't like asking but you have to make your living in bits and pieces around here.' Then, 'And there's no knowing if that wind has settled. I think we should get moving.'

Out again, into a world washed clean, the air deceptively still. Walking down a long track till it crossed a path that led to the quay, but he led them straight over, towards a bank of sand with

71

grass waving, and then dropped over the edge to land on a strip of beach and a boat dragged up high on the sand. Climbing in, pushing out, the diminishing light over the sea that kept St Martin's here, St Mary's there, that made of each a world in itself, with the water heaving and shifting between them, enticing, treacherous. Eva sat hugging herself. Karl was up at the prow, back straight, looking out towards the open sea. All Cari could see was his outline, no details, but it was enough.

St Mary's looming now, getting more solid. The lights of the town, on the harbour pier. The yachts dancing quietly in the harbour, peaceful as if there had been no storm.

Almost dark when they landed. Karl pulled out a roll of notes. Hugh said, 'That's over the top.' Karl said, 'It couldn't be, for what you've given us.'

Cari looked at the darkening waters and then at Hugh. 'Will you be all right going back?'

He laughed at that. 'I've done that run more times than I could count, in all lights, all weathers.' And was gone.

Eva said, 'I'm cold, I want to get home.'

Karl put an arm around each of them. 'Come, sing, that'll warm us,' and they walked down the pier, bundled together in their borrowed jerseys. Cari taught them *What shall we do with a drunken sailor*. Eva joined in between sneezes and Karl sang in a deep baritone, all the way down the high street where the evening pub-goers were just settling in.

And that was how Anna saw them, carousing down the road, arms round each other. It was a jolt to encounter her nameless young woman in this transformed state – not alone, and the three of them flaunting their exuberant youth. Anna knew she was staring, knew she should stop. Gail said, 'Come on, Mum,' and they turned into the fish shop.

That was it; nothing else happened.

But something nagged at the edges of consciousness and eventually it took on shape and colour while she watched Gail trying, too patiently, to get the children to decide if they wanted salt on their chips. There was something else she had seen apart from three young people singing with their arms around each other. It was what the young woman was wearing. A jersey. A jersey of grey chunky wool with a poloneck. An unremarkable jersey, except that Anna knew it. She had seen it twice before, and each time on a different person.

≈≈

It felt to Cari as if they had been away a month. In fact they were only a couple of hours' late. Andrew had been working and had scarcely noticed the storm, nor their absence. They were all bubbling to share their drama; Andrew listened but he couldn't rise to it. Cari thought, how pathetic, hasn't he *any* sense of what we're feeling? She could see he was thinking, OK, they got caught by the rain, so what? She wanted to say, this was *different* Andrew, this was really scary. But she was too removed from him that night to bother.

Eva's nose was streaming non-stop. Cari said, 'You're a candidate for Lemsip and an early night.' She fussed over her till she was settled, enjoying having someone in the house who would let her do it.

Andrew said, 'I'm for bed too,' and he too took himself off. The door closed behind him. Cari turned, almost expecting Karl to – what? She did not know. Whatever it was, he didn't. He was settling himself with a book in an armchair, one leg stretched out, the other draped over one side. The same as always, needing nothing from anyone.

She went into the kitchen to tidy up, fighting off a feeling of unreality about all of this coming to an end. Just ten hours and she and Andrew would be standing on the pier again, seeing them off. Then back. The house to themselves. She and Andrew. What *was* she going to do with herself when they were gone? What had life been like before? She could hardly remember. She was afraid, a kind of fear she had never experienced before, afraid of herself, of not knowing who she was, what she wanted, what she should do. She didn't want to cope with all this having happened, and yet nothing. The same her, left just where she had started, but totally disturbed.

She went back into the living room, sat on the sofa, picking up a book as camouflage. Every sense was hyper-aware, her eyes seeing Karl's body opposite hers though she did not look up from her book, her nose receiving the smell that came off the borrowed jerseys they both still wore, wood smoke and tractor oil, linking them to that other place, that easy intimacy. The urgency to touch seemed to be taking her over. We *have* touched, she thought, we have sat with our arms around each other sheltering against the elements. More intimate than that you could hardly get, while you have your clothes on. How come we can't do it now, just for ourselves? It's absurd, two adults, both of us know what's going on between us and neither of us can move to make it happen.

She put down her book. She made herself look at him, willing him to do the same. She was amazed at her brazenness. What if I'm wrong? she thought. I'm about to make a complete fool of myself –

Karl looked up, looking at her without smiling. That's the first time, she realised. The first time he has let himself be serious.

'So,' he said, quietly.

So. Then nothing. Just that quiet, straight look.

'So finally we have a little time alone.'

She went very still, waiting.

Karl said, 'You have wanted to know if I have been feeling it too.'

She nodded, incapable of speech. They stared at each other across the space of that acknowledgement, neither of them moving. He said, even more quietly, 'I do. But what to do? Andrew is my friend. And we are gone tomorrow.'

She could say nothing. There was nothing to say. She was finding it difficult to think, her pulse was taking over like a wave.

He said, 'It is obvious that all is not easy between you. But when you drop in on someone else's life you see only that moment, and every couple has low times.'

She could deny none of his words but they were the wrong ones for all that they were true. She could sit no longer opposite him, so many feet separating them. Abruptly she got up from the sofa and went to sit on the floor at his feet, head leaning against his legs. A momentary shock, like plunging into water, then floating, physical relief so intense that it hardly mattered that his words kept saying, we can't, we can't, for his firm thigh accepting her cheek said, Yes.

After a while she realised he must have stopped talking some time ago. She had gone into a blank state, retreating to where she could simply hold on to that physical presence, to the comfort of having had desire recognised even if he would do nothing about it. His hand was caressing her hair, a small movement but so infinitely better than nothing.

Eventually Karl shifted his legs. Putting both hands under her armpits he lifted her as he stood up. Then he dropped his hands and made no move to hug her. She knew he was waiting for her to go so that he could spread out his sleeping bag and sleep.

With a slightly old-world movement of the head, as if searching in his repertoire for something that would have served in a simpler age, he said, 'I think maybe we both need some rest.'

≈≈

'Come again, darlings, anytime,' Anna said as the children hugged her passionately on the pier, though she knew it would probably be a year at least. Between now and when she saw them again Grandma's island would settle into the realm of the mythical in their imaginations. The place where you got ice creams everyday, where the beach was waiting for you each morning when you woke, a short run down the hill. Where butterflies sat on your hand and the man with the beard let you lift up one of his lobster pots to see if it was heavy.

She let herself back into her house. Despite all her mental fortifications against this moment the emptiness screamed at her. The very walls had become barren. How would she learn to accept the silence again, the knowledge that no one but she breathed between these walls? Just her and her growing stacks of paintings. She had produced far more than anyone would ever buy, that was the truth of it, two winters' worth of compulsive effort, driven by a need to get right this one thing at least. When they were finished they occasionally gave her pleasure; mostly all she could see was what she had failed to convey. They sat stacked against the wall, more fragments of life, abandoned.

On the quayside today, she and Gail – Well, they had managed. What more could one say? There had been things they hadn't said all week, that they both knew ought to have been spoken about. But it hadn't happened and now was too late, with people all around them and the children excited about getting onto the ship again. They exchanged no easy words about writing soon, for Gail seldom got time; or phoning, for Anna had no phone. Once Gail had said, 'I was thinking –' but then changed her mind.

Anna took refuge in chatting with the children. Gail seemed to like that, so it ended well.

Better without them. Better to face up to being alone.

For most of the next week Anna painted compulsively. She hardly went out, her mind so full of stimulus that what she needed most was the solitude to absorb it, and then to let whatever had become of those feelings take form through streaks of coloured water applied to paper. A bizarre process but she had no need to analyse or explain. It worked and she was grateful to have discovered it.

The first paintings were of the children. Nothing more than small blobs of colour on the sand but suggesting constant movement, and that was the trick. She discovered how to capture that almost by accident and excitedly washed colour over colour, till it became almost too simple and the paintings began to lose their life. Then she discovered there was something else inside her waiting to emerge, waiting until the skipping and clambering youngsters had moved out of the way and she could touch again the settled sadness that the pleasure in their vivid small lives had temporarily obscured.

She did not know what she was going to paint but she knew before she started that it would need a larger than usual sheet of paper. She prepared it carefully, pasted it onto the easel, adjusted the angle to get the light, and waited to see.

The pier, people gathered. The passenger steamer arriving. Or departing. It was the same thing. No it wasn't. She could see it now, it was definitely arriving. It was the steamer that had brought them all the first time they had come to the islands, so they were all there on deck, those streaks of colour that to the unknown person who would eventually buy the painting would simply be splodges of red and green. But it was them, Max and her, Gail and Jason. Jason, whose name she and Gail had managed not to mention once in a whole week together. Jason was there in her painting, quietly refusing to be left out. She saw him so clearly, still a boy who had not yet begun to put on adult height, standing a little apart from the rest of them as he always did, hands on the railing, nose sniffing the spray. Eyes like his grandfather's, staring out to the islands that hovered on the edge of the sea.

Two

Chichester, summer 1975

Afterwards Anna could not remember why a family holiday on a remote island had seemed a good idea. An attempt to patch up something that had already gone irrevocably wrong, she supposed. And her cousin Bella, pressing her to come and see where she now lived.

What she remembered mainly was a painful sense of holding-on. To the closeness she had once had with Max, that had been eaten away, she hardly knew how, by an accumulation of unresolved tensions. By his ambition, his immersion in his work, that reduced her and the children to extras. If they could just get away, all of them together. Holding on to Gail, seventeen and about to go off to college, to those moments of mother-daughter companionship, still there but increasingly rare. To Jason, thirteen, escaping into some place of his own, somewhere more simple where the tensions between his parents couldn't harm him. 'Going over to Craig's,' he would say. Or Ivan's. But they never came over to Jason's. In a way she was glad for him that his centre of gravity had shifted. But she was losing her son long before she needed to, and it was their doing, hers and Max's.

And then another letter arrived from Bella with some photos of the island. She stared at them. The small stone house. The low, almost treeless land. The colours of the wildflowers. The sea stretching beyond. So simple a beauty, life pared to its essentials. Wholesome. *That* was what she wanted.

Max, as usual, left everything to her. '*Make* him help, Mum,' Gail said, with that easy clarity of youth. 'Why should *you* always do it?' But there was no way to make him. He just said,

'Yes, yes, that sounds fine, you fix it,' and was off again, till finally she had to virtually airlift him out of the board meeting that had suddenly been scheduled for the day they had to leave. Then tiredness from all the pressure caught up with him, and he slumped in a semi-comatose state the entire length of the road, Chichester to Penzance. Anna driving.

'Our one holiday of the year,' Gail said to the back of her father's unresponding head , 'and you couldn't even get back on time. Mum's done *all* the packing, and you don't even *know.*'

Please, Gail, Anna urged, a wordless plea, leave him, don't spoil it, let's just try and pretend we're a normal family. But there seemed no way to distract the girl. Anna tried to concentrate on driving. Max had slumped back into sleep. She hoped he would stay that way a while. In the back seat next to his sister Jason watched the world passing by the window, saying nothing. Disconnected.

In Penzance Max suddenly moved into action. Being in the hotel trip-switched him back into chief executive mode. Surveying the dining room he told the waiter, 'We need a table with a view of the sea,' while Gail hissed in agonised embarrassment, '*Dad,* can't you see, there aren't any free.' Max paid no attention. To the waiter he was all charm but made it absolutely clear that the matter wasn't up for discussion. The waiter recognised the tone. 'If you would just care to have a drink in the lounge, sir. In about fifteen minutes, sir, I'm sure we can oblige.' And Max, having got his way (the seaview, an excellent dish of grilled seabass and a quite acceptable wine) was in an expansive mood. As he got up from the table he said to Jason, 'Let's go look at the boats.' Through the hotel window Anna and Gail watched them stride out along the seafront in the still-light evening, father and son, with the spray from the waves flinging high over the sea wall.

And Anna thought, '*That's* how he can be when he tries.'

But as soon as they got to St Martin's the whole thing backfired. How could she have been so feeble-minded as to think that everything would come right if they were all thrust together for weeks in a place where it was almost impossible to get away from each other? The rented cottage was far smaller than the brochure indicated. The bedrooms were just big enough for the beds, and the livingroom-cum-kitchen seemed ludicrously small for a man Max's size, and their four so different sets of energies. She had forgotten that the simple life would mean only one bathroom. Jason always seemed to need the loo just when Gail had settled into the bath. The shower (Max didn't like baths) was a hand-held attachment that dripped ineffectually and had only two temperatures, tepid or scalding. Max was incensed – she had to hold him back from making a scene with the owner, who happened to be Bella's brother-in-law. He acquiesced, reluctantly, but made her pay for her victory by retreating into reading the papers, and complaining because they arrived a day late. (Brought in by helicopter to St Mary's, then by launch from St Mary's to St Martin's, but no charm in that to Max, simply a sign of inefficiency.) Then suddenly he would rouse himself to a pacing-up-and-down energy, saying, 'Isn't anyone coming out to one of the other islands? What do you think we paid all this money to get you all here for?' Jason was usually gone by the time this happened – he had taken to disappearing each morning after breakfast. Anna had no idea where he went to or what he did, except that it almost certainly had something to do with boats. Gail came with them on the outings, but with an adolescent air of 'I'm only doing this because there's nothing else to do.'

They visited Bella and Thomas, of course. Bella exclaimed over the now-almost-grown children whose photos she had received with every year's Christmas card but only ever seen once, years ago, at Anna's father's funeral. Gail and Jason sat awkwardly on the sofa next to Max, wishing this duty visit were over and they could escape from the 'And what are you planning to do when you finish school?' kind of questions. Yvonne, seven years old, squeezed in next to her mother in the big old armchair, a little in awe of these so-grown-up cousins. Anna tried to draw Thomas out about his Penruth family history, 'It's one of the oldest families on the island,' she told Max. If she had hoped that might create something for the men to talk about, she was disappointed. Max's boredom was distressingly obvious. I have nothing in common with these people, his body language said. But it wasn't just him – Anna saw Gail's eyes doing a tour of the china ornaments on the mantlepiece, the over-patterned carpet, the Coronation mugs in the dresser. She's embarrassed, Anna realised, to have an aunt who actually chooses these things. Afterwards Bella said all the expected things, what nice-looking young people they were, and Anna just felt sad. She and Bella belonged together from a time that had nothing to do with Max and the children. Alone, she could have slipped back into being with Bella as once they had been, to a life when having a bathroom would have seemed the height of luxury and the china ornaments an expression of fine taste. She felt sad that all that had happened to her since then had cut her off from a closeness she had taken for granted, and never bothered to nurture. And sad that her children could not see beyond the surface of things. They had grown up so differently, it was unrealistic to expect them to – but she wished they could have been just a bit more open, accepting.

Next morning Gail said, 'I'm going over to St Mary's to have a look at the shops.' At first Anna thought it was an invitation – Come with me, Mum – but then saw Gail's eyes, needing escape. Of course, she was after company her own age. Anna said, 'Have a good time.' After Gail had gone she hung about, waiting to see what Max's mood would require of her. By late morning there was still no sign that they would do anything other than feel trapped by each other. She finally said, 'I'm going to see Bella.' And do what you like, she announced to the air outside, wishing she had the gumption to say it directly to Max.

No question of talking to Bella about what was going on in the cottage. She sat at the kitchen table and helped Bella peel potatoes. Yvonne trotted in with a small stubby boy in tow, maybe three years old, and then out again to play in the yard. Children's voices floated in on the late afternoon air. The normality of Bella's daily routine worked quietly through to Anna, calming her. They talked about the Liverpool of their childhood – the long lines of small houses facing each other, door-window, door-window, too crowded to contain the children who spilled out of them into the narrow street. About how it had all changed now. So far away, in time, in place, in what seemed possible to think and feel, that it seemed safe now, stable and contented, as it never was at the time.

'Do you remember,' Anna started saying – but a neighbour had arrived. A man of thirty or so, ruggedly built for an outdoor life.

'Hugh Stanford,' Bella introduced. 'This is Anna, my favourite cousin.'

'Favourite cousin.' Hugh seemed amused. 'Now what did you do to earn that?'

'We stuck together when the older ones were leaving us out.'

'She was the clever one,' Bella said. 'She used to do my arithmetic homework for me so I wouldn't get into trouble.'

Hugh grinned, 'Does Yvonne know that story?'

'No she doesn't, and don't you tell her.' Then, to Anna, 'Hugh's the father of Yvonne's little friend.'

'Time I took the runaway home,' Hugh said.

'They're out at the back,' Bella said.

But he seemed in no hurry, and propped himself against the sink, over-filling Bella's small kitchen. The chat was easy, the kind you have with people you know well and see most days. Island matters, them talking, Anna listening. Not a real local like Thomas, she thought, a trace of the north in his accent. But he looked the part, those big shoulders in that grey jersey, polo neck, very nautical. For some reason that she could not immediately track, the jersey seemed familiar. Then he shifted his weight, pressing his hands back against the sink in a movement that reminded her of her father, and she knew. Her father had had a jersey not unlike it, knitted by her grandma, and he had worn it on that last journey he and Anna had made together, crossing the turbulent northern sea to the island that had been abandoned by human beings. An odd group they must have been, travelling on that trawler. Her father in his sixties but an old man already, bent from years of too-hard physical labour, heaving with his asthmatic cough, but still looking tough as they come. And sharp, sharp eyes that missed nothing in the sea around them. She a woman of thirty-seven, temporarily leaving a world of professional work and spacious houses and going-to-concerts and carefully prepared meals, to expose herself to the elements so that her father could connect again with the lost island of his youth. And the child Jason, a three-year-old, too small to be left behind with his father as she had left Gail – but also too small to bring on such an expedition she realised now, holding onto him tightly as the ship lurched and tossed, fearful every minute that he might hurtle himself over the edge. And then they had landed, and she could let the child run on the windswept headlands where his grandfather's childhood had been spent ...

She came to, back to the prosaic present of Bella's kitchen. To Bella chatting to her neighbour, the man whose hands had evoked her father. Powerful hands, encrusted with grime, earth that never gets out from under the finger nails, grease from delving about inside tractor engines. A scar where he must have burnt himself, welding or something. And so utterly unlike Max's hands, that were always scrubbed and immaculate, as he expected his shirts to be. Hard to reconcile that the owners of the two pairs of hands were part of the same species.

Something disturbing about this man, she decided, an almost palpable sense of a restless mind, suppressed energy. She felt a flash of protectiveness for the quiet Thomas. I hope he doesn't come in now and see this man leaning back against his sink, making himself at home.

Hugh said, 'I'd better get moving. Sylvie will be scolding me for not getting the boy back for bedtime.'

They all three got up to go and find the children.

The view hit her as they emerged, the land that ended so suddenly hardly three hundred yards from where they stood; the sky enormous, the sea stretching forever. Hardly a human sound, for the boats had taken the day-trippers back to St Mary's and the island was resting in the last gentle hours of light. I could be happy living in this place, she thought, to her own surprise. Even if things kept going wrong between the people, there would always be this to come out to, a more fundamental level of connectedness.

A few yards from where she stood Hugh had got down on his haunches to be with the children, and they were telling him excitedly about what they had been doing. His little boy had climbed onto his knee and had his hand up to hold the polo neck of his father's chunky grey jersey as he stammered in his eagerness to get it all out. And in the man's face was such obvious pleasure in the boy's existence that Anna couldn't stand there watching any more because she felt stabbed with loss.

That once. And then she had seen the same jersey again five years later, on Jason. In circumstances too painful to allow herself to think about.

≈≈

St Martin's, late March 1984
The spring storm that had landed three drenched strangers on Hugh Stanford's doorstep had caught him at a particularly low time. He had spent the day brooding resentfully over his grievance with his ex-wife Sylvie, a mood he had been unable to shake off for a week, since her letter had arrived.

It had come on a Saturday, the day Yvonne helped out at the Post Office Stores. Earlier that morning he had caught sight of her when he had been up in the top field, from where he had a view down to the quay. He had watched the boat from St Mary's slip quietly in alongside the quay and the line of day trippers trail up the road. Now the skipper had climbed out and was handing something over to a young girl. The girl's head tilted as she laughed at something the boatman was saying. Yes, Yvonne for sure – she had had that way with her head ever since the first time she had sat with him and David in his dinghy and he had put a rope into her small hands and said, 'Keep your head down when that boom comes over.'

He watched her set off up the path, all the way to the top where he lost sight of her behind the hedges. He was a slow reactor, he knew, but he found it hard to take in the change in her from the small creature who only a few years ago he used to swing about, to this almost young-woman whose T-shirt showed all too clearly the round lift of her breasts. At least David was still a kid. Or had been, when he last saw him. Just turned twelve now — did boys' voices begin breaking when they were twelve? He couldn't remember. He remembered other rites of passage, the embarrassment of waking up with the bed wet and not knowing what the hell had happened. And then when he had worked it out, years of making it happen for himself, having taken the precaution of shoving his gym shorts into the bed before he turned the light out, so there would be nothing to show on the sheets. And by day watching the girls at school take on shape, and every now and then catching a whiff of that underarm smell that was completely different in girls and heady beyond belief. The girls pushing past in the corridors and the dinner queue just as they had when they were kids, but they were certainly kids no longer. Their breasts bounced as they ran, their thighs were firm and shapely under their short skirts. The nearness of what their presence flaunted made concentration on anything else impossible.

God, what a performance growing up was. And David had all that before him still, poor kid.

He turned back to his ploughing. Up, turn, back, turn, up. The rhythm of the furrows. Two weeks till David's back, said the rhythm. Two weeks ... Two weeks in April, three in the summer, a week in October, all so finely rationed. 'A straight split between us,' Sylvie had said, always with the words ready to rationalise what she had decided to do. But she had David all through the term, why did he only get half the holidays? When David was back everything was transformed. The pace of life, companionship, laughter, energy. Noise, cheerful disorder. The house lit with activity, not just David's but the young of the island trooping in and out with him, to fetch gear, to grab something to eat, to say, 'Hugh, can you take us out?' But then so soon the weeks were gone and he stood again with the boy next to him on the deck of the ship that would carry them across twenty-eight miles of sea, where he would give David one last hug and hand him over to his mother; then cross the sea back again, to return to a house that the life had gone out of. And with David gone the other youngsters disappeared, back to school on St Mary's, and at weekends moving in and out of each others' homes but never so much as passing his, for it was not on a path to anywhere.

He finished the field he was ploughing, came in, had a wash. He needed a couple of things from the Stores – if he got them today, he could have a word with Yvonne, let her know about David.

In the shop Yvonne was chatting to a couple of new arrivals at the self-catering cottages, telling them about the bread days. 'Three times a week,' she said, 'fresh baked on St Mary's. You need to order it a day in advance.' He picked up the things he needed from the shelves and waited to pay for them. In his mind he was already saying to her, 'David's coming in two weeks.' But the couple from the cottage had an interminable string of questions, and then there were others waiting. All Yvonne fitted in was a smile and a '£3.45' in his direction, and then as she gave him his change, 'You're the lucky one today, you've got a letter.'

The sight of the handwriting was enough to put him out of sorts. It occurred to him as he walked back up the hill that the fact that someone chooses to write to you does not mean you are obliged to read it. There was nothing to stop him sticking this letter on the pile of rubbish to be burned as soon as he got back. But curiosity is stronger even than a dislike of being shat on, it seemed. He compromised by sitting on the step outside the kitchen door to read it. At least he didn't have to let her back into the house.

'I'm sorry but there's been a change of plans,' she wrote, voice civilised and lethal. 'The school choir is going to Austria at Easter and one of the boys has dropped out so they've offered the place to David. I told him I was sure you wouldn't want him to turn up a chance like this. Perhaps he can come for longer in the summer instead.'

Perhaps. And then again, perhaps not, because some other bloody thing would be happening then.

He shoved the letter in the bin for burning. Could David not have written himself? Did he even *want* to go to Austria, when it meant missing his time on the island? Ah, stop thrashing about. Get back to your ploughing. Thank God for work that needed doing, hard physical work.

On the day of the storm he had been fixing the fence of the chicken run, and was driven in by the sudden onslaught. He hated to leave a job half done but he wasn't sorry to be shut in. He was tired, exhausted in fact, from a week of feelings he couldn't seem to shift. The storm suited his mood. He bolted the windows against the wind and lit the fire. For an hour or so it was like a winter night – the storm blotting out all light, everything tight closed against the elements, no possibility of human contact.

It was the isolation of the house that had been its appeal when he had first found it. It had been half falling apart then, a farm old people had died in. He had felt challenged at the sight of it, at the work that he knew he could do to make the house sound again and the land productive. And the space. He had heard visitors say St Martin's was beautiful but too small to live in. Not for him – he had felt far more shut in in cities. Here the sky expanded forever around him, and the sea, space to move in,

91

space beyond measure. Each day he worked his small corner of earth, absorbed in detail, what it could grow, what it needed to nurture it, but he had only to lift his eyes and there was that other element of life, the vast untamable, unknowable sea. There were weeks when the wind blew and the fields turned to sand, burying everything that was trying to grow. Then the weather would lift as suddenly as it had blown in and he would wake to a morning when he knew that work or no work he was taking the dinghy out, and the restlessness from those weeks cooped up would be blown away with the wind that filled his sails, carrying him out to islands that only the birds inhabited.

Before Sylvie had joined him, being alone had never been a problem. Now that she and David were gone, everything seemed harder. With only one pair of hands the farm was hardly viable. The nights had seemed longer this last winter, the days heavier, the joy gone out of the work, with no future to it. He felt so betrayed by Sylvie that there was now no question of wanting her back, but the hostility gnawed destructively inside him. Alone and in silence he vented his anger, but the target was several hundred miles away and not listening; *he* was the one it damaged.

Through the noise of the wind and rain some unfamiliar sound reached him. Repetitive, like a bird hammering its beak on a shell. Nearby, short, regular sounds. Someone knocking? Impossible. In the middle a storm who could be so crazy? But there it was again. He moved to the door, thinking, Is the sound even real? Is it me that's crazy? Opened the door – stared stupidly. Three drenched bodies stood on his doorstep, dripping anorak hoods hiding their faces. Stood silent, waiting for him to do something.

Reason switched on and he took them in. Now he was suddenly hyper-alert, aware of his life being exposed to these outside eyes. Of how neglected he had let the place become this last year, how grubby the towels were, how tatty the jerseys he offered them. How he had to root around in the disorganised kitchen to find enough mugs. But their presence and laughter got past the obsessive self absorption into which he too often allowed himself to lapse these days, whenever he wasn't physically active.

When he got back from taking them over to St Mary's he sat quietly staring at the fire. The fight of earlier in the day had gone out of him, shifted, finally, calmed simply by having people around him. He let the remembered sound of their voices sift around him, the sense of their presence, and he savoured a pleasure that had become regrettably rare, of having met someone else's needs. Needs so simple. Just to be dry, to hold a steaming mug in hands that had become stiff from exposure to inhuman elements. To come inside, to warmth.

≈≈

Cari and Andrew spent the evening as they had spent most evenings before Karl and Eva came. He cooked, they ate, she cleared up, he turned on the news. The miners' strike, more violence on the picket lines. Then a chat show, and the sound of inane laughter following her as she put things away in the kitchen. When she had finished she curled up in an armchair with a novel, her back to the telly, trying to shut out the noise. She had already read the novel but it was comforting knowing she could trust the author to end it the right way.

Andrew turned the telly off. 'I'm heading for bed.' It meant, 'We're heading for bed.' She made a vague noise but didn't follow.

As soon as she was alone the pictures of Karl came flooding

back. Standing on the pier, watching as Karl and Eva walked away from them. Karl's long strides taking him up the gang-plank, onto the deck, Cari holding on to each movement of that already distanced body, feeling bleak with misery. She forced her eyes to let go, to move over the ship that would carry them away from the islands, pushing through the sea that lay between here and wherever it was people went when they left. An unfathomable distance, a setting-off into nothingness. Sea to the horizon, sea swelling and dipping, giving no clues.

The last people were on board, the gangplank being lifted. Her eyes searched the deck, desperate now to find him, to hold on – and found instead the young woman with the two children they had seen on the beach, holding one of them up to wave goodbye. No sign of Karl or Eva. A mournful hoot, signalling the point of no return. Slowly the huge whale-bulk of ship moved away from the quayside, slowly swung its prow out into the harbour, slowly edged its way round the end of the pier.

She turned. Next to her stood Andrew, and all the pushed-aside guilt of the week rushed back.

Andrew said, 'Let's go.'

All the way back along the pier she waited for him to speak but he didn't. She did not try to break the silence. What would she say? 'Andrew, I need to tell you something that happened,' when nothing had? Or, 'Andrew, I've changed. If we're to go on being real with each other, you need to know'? Or should she continue to say nothing, and let a vast space grow up between them ...

What was happening to them? In three years with Andrew it had not occurred to her to want anything else. He had followed her to this place that she had needed to find again, and now look what she was doing to him. She seemed driven by something to which she couldn't even give a name.

He must be asleep by now. She tiptoed into the bedroom to get her pyjamas. All she could see of him was a hump on the bed — so still and defenceless she felt compassion surging, for him, for them both, for what was going wrong between them. It isn't anything he's done, she thought, it's me. I'm changing and I don't know why or where it's going to lead.

The second week of the holidays and nothing much to do with it. Cari lay around reading, went for the occasional walk down to a beach, collected shells and bits of sea weed. I must take those jerseys back to the guy on St Martin's, she thought. But her period had started and she couldn't summon the energy. A postcard from Robyn – 'Spring's got into me, I'm restless. Taking a month off to travel. No idea yet where. Expect a card from somewhere exciting.' Robyn's life moving, hers stuck.

Then the weather was back in full power, a fierce wind blowing up in the night, rattling the window panes and howling in the chimney. Cari could not sleep, she never could when the wind was strong. She thought of Robyn. I hope she's inside somewhere, and safe. She thought of Karl, back in the life he lived in Stockholm that she knew nothing about, putting the incident on the islands behind him. She thought of the man on St Martin's who had brought them back in his boat. I hope he's not out in this, she thought.

Andrew stirred in his sleep. She moved closer, put her arm around him, knowing he was only half awake but not able to stop herself saying, 'Andrew I'm scared. There may be people out in boats.' Andrew half-surfaced long enough to say, 'Who would be so crazy?' But her dad had been so crazy and there were plenty like him.

Andrew was asleep again, heavy breathing.

Eventually she drifted off, but into a bizarre dream. She was with Robyn, somewhere familiar but she couldn't quite place it. Robyn was saying, half curious, half challenging. 'Getting *married?* Why?'

'Because we're living together anyway, so why not?'

'That's no answer. Have you *read* the service? Are you really going to promise to obey?'

'It's just words. It wouldn't occur to Andrew to tell me what to do.'

'It's so banal. Why don't you at least write your own?'

'I like it that way. It's what people have said for ages. The same words, but different because now it'll be us saying them.'

Robyn said, 'Well, go for it, if that's what you want' …

She woke, rigid with unexpressed tension. Andrew was in a dead sleep next to her.

If that's what you want … But she didn't know, she never did.

She slipped quietly out of bed and went through to the kitchen. She needed to be alone, needed it with an intensity that frightened her. She made a cup of tea and sat cradling her hands around its warmth … The first year she was with Andrew she had felt a definite need to keep him separate. She still went back home for Christmas, birthdays, weekend visits, but always without Andrew. To her parents she was always Cari the child; it was warm and safe but it didn't fit with being with Andrew, and she didn't want him seeing her that way. Had marrying been a way of finally announcing to them, I have changed?

Andrew had come a week before the wedding to meet them. Robyn was travelling, this time Thailand, but had promised to cut it short to get back for the wedding. Her mum was preoccupied, hundreds of things to get ready. Her dad was being her dad, full of energy, the magnet she gravitated to, but needing to be the one who generated ideas. Cari said, 'Dad,

Mum's already got it sorted,' but she could see this was the only way he could handle what was going on, and part of her felt compassionate, as if he were a small boy threatened with being left out. She loved him and knew he loved her and wanted him to approve of Andrew and notice what her mum needed, but still be himself. She wished Robyn would arrive.

Andrew's own family was minimal. How minimal, Cari had not quite realised until now. He was his mother's only child; his parents had separated before he was born. His father had remarried and chosen to have little to do with them. There was a half brother and sister he had met only once, in a meeting so strained he had no wish to repeat it. His mother was a civil servant in London, living alone.

'What does she do, apart from work?' Cari asked.

He shrugged. 'Goes to the theatre with friends. Feeds the cat.'

The theatre-going mum arrived the night before the wedding. She was smart-city-suit dressed, punctual, found things to talk about to everyone. 'And if you hadn't known she was Andrew's mother,' Robyn said, 'you would never have guessed.' He and his mother spoke to each other like interested acquaintances, both intelligent, articulate, detached. Throughout the wedding and reception she seemed to be observing from the outside, a sociological view. There was nothing about her behaviour that anyone could have taken exception to, it was just that her body language made clear that she wasn't really part of this. The next morning she said her thank you's, wished them well, and returned to London.

Cari was outraged. Andrew shrugged. 'What did you expect her to do? I left home six years ago. It's hardly an emotional occasion.'

'Well it should be. I don't mean the wedding. You. It's something important happening to you and she ought to be able to show a *little* more that she notices.'

'I don't want her getting in on what's happening to me,' he said firmly. 'She's had the sense to realise that, finally.'...

'*That's* the problem,' Cari said out loud now, here on the island alone in the night kitchen. Andrew had always been like that, she realised, had always needed space more than he needed closeness. He had wanted her, it had been he who had done the wooing, she who had thought, why not? – but he wanted only so much and only at certain times. And when he switched off, she was left, alone.

Had she not known that? And if she had, why had she thought they could ... ? But she had. It was she had pushed the decision to marry, to make it permanent. Maybe she had thought it would change something? It was only two years ago, she couldn't have *forgotten* how she felt, but the whole thing was such a blur. She remembered drifting around the house the day after, collecting up things, thinking, 'This is definitely leaving home now, I have to decide what to take with me.' And feeling a confusion of emotions, none of which made practical sense. Mainly – bizarrely – anxiety about Robyn, who was about to set off travelling again, no idea where she was going or when she would be back. But so stupid to worry, Robyn was far more able than she to take care of herself.

'Come and sit on my bed while I pack,' Robyn said. 'You can help me decide what to throw out.' She piled things out of the rucksack, excited by the very unknown that made Cari nervous. Cari thought, she has medals for life-saving, she's done hang-gliding, what is there to bother her about setting off in a train across Europe?

'How did it happen that we turned out so different?' she asked.

Robyn looked up in surprise. 'Why shouldn't we? We just are different. What about this jumper? Am I going to need two?'

'Depends. If it's the Himalayas in winter, yes. If it's Rome in summer, no. But wouldn't you think, with the same parents, the same crazy things they put us through?'

'What crazy things?' Robyn asked.

Cari said nothing. Robyn knew perfectly well, she was just deciding to forget. Robyn said, suddenly definite, 'Out it goes. I can always pick up another if I need it.'

'See, that's another way we're different,' Cari said. 'You've decided now and you'll never give that jumper another thought.'

'Why should I?'

'You shouldn't, but I would. Pointlessly. I'd go on worrying about it all the way to Paris. Like you always know when you've fallen in love, and when you've fallen out of it.'

Robyn stopped at that, to look straight at her. 'That's an odd thing to say when you've just got yourself married.'

'It's a backlash. Whenever I think I've decided something the opposite thought comes flooding in.'

'You read too many novels,' Robyn said.

She's right, Cari thought, I'm just layers of all those different perceptions, too many people's point of view. She said, 'It's being back home – I get confused about who I am.' Back home, yet no longer her home. The very shapes of the rooms defined the child in her, shifting up from regions forgotten. Not being taken seriously. Or the opposite, too much responsibility before she was ready for it. She could sense her mum trying, treating her as an adult when she needed a reassuring cuddle, or as a child when she felt herself an adult. How could her mum be expected to know? The child in her answered, 'She *should* know. She's my mum.'

Now Robyn was leaving, the one person who really knew

her. Then she remembered, Of course, I'm going away too, with Andrew. We're married …

A sound from the bedroom. Here, now. Her chest constricted, preparing herself for Andrew to come in and find her. What was she afraid of? Why shouldn't she be sitting here drinking tea, if she couldn't sleep? She listened intently but the noise did not recur. Outside all was still – the storm had blown itself out and she had not even noticed.

She looked down at her hands, still gripping the mug, and felt weighed down by sadness, at all the things never intended, never fully understood.

≈≈

April arrived on St Martin's, as it often did, with a change in the wind. More skittish, little breezes arriving and disappearing, brushing clouds away to flash sunlight then hiding it again. And an accompanying lift in the spirits, coming and going like the sun, but definitely there.

Hugh was out at the back scraping mud off his boots and thinking about the wind when his attention was caught by someone walking up his track. Odd. The track led nowhere except here. A day tripper over from St Mary's, probably, taking the wrong turning by mistake. But the person heading up towards him, complete with backpack, walked like someone who knew where he was going – except that as it got nearer he began to realise it was not a man. Nearer, and now he suddenly recognised her. One of the three he had taken over to St Mary's. Christ, what had she said her name was?

She stopped, a few yards from him, clearly shy that she might be intruding. 'Hi. I'm Cari. You've probably forgotten.'

'I had, actually. The name. Not you.' He had taken them in as a group, not noticed how young this one was. And slim, so little to her. 'Where are the others?'

'Gone back. That was their last day.'

'And you?'

'I live on St Mary's.' She was wriggling her backpack off. 'I've brought your jerseys back. You saved us all from pneumonia!' A momentary embarrassment as now she lifted something out of the rucksack that wasn't a jersey. She held it out to him. 'And a small thank-you present.'

A square tin, not new. He opened it, to the smell of – flapjacks! 'You made these?'

'You said, There should be something decent to give you with your tea. Like flapjacks.'

They both laughed. Suddenly buoyant he said, 'Come in, let's do it properly this time.'

It did not occur to him today to be apologetic about the state of the house, his life, his person. He simply gave himself up to the enjoyment of company. She wanted to see the farm, the water pipes he had laid, the fuel efficient stove he had designed and built. She asked about the rotation of bulbs and potatoes, and listened like she really wanted to know, wasn't just making conversation. Her appreciative eyes gave back to him the pride in having made all this.

'There's a great view from the top of the high field,' he said. 'Would you like to walk up there?'

'Sure.' And as they set off, 'You're an islander?'

He laughed, thinking of how Thomas Penruth would react to that assumption. 'Afraid not. All I can claim is a bit of time here as a boy.'

She stopped. 'You too! I was here when I was eight. How about you?'

'A bit older. Thirteen or so.'

'And then you decided to come back.' She said it with a certain satisfaction, as if it pleased her to find someone behaving so sensibly. 'How long ago?'

He was amused at her persistence, but had to think, working it out. That year on St Mary's, working with Garth on boats while he looked around to see if he could find a way to stay. '1968, it was. Sixteen years ago.' It was longer than he had realised. Made him feel – stuck?

Cari was staring at him. '1968? That's when I was here!'

He laughed with her, thinking, she's half-child still. That simple enthusiasm for small things.

'What made you come back?' she was asking.

He smiled. 'I would have thought you would know.'

'But I'm sure there's a story.'

There's always a story, but he wasn't about to tell his to a stranger, and one so young. Still, he didn't want to shut her down. He said, 'Always wanted to be outside, I suppose. And the sea. I worked on farms a while but I didn't take to being bossed around by farm managers.' They had reached the top. He turned, looked out over the bay. 'See, that's really what I came back for.'

She stood quietly taking it in. 'The first time my dad brought us to St Martin's it was weather like this. It stunned me, the long sands, the sun glinting off them.'

And he too was remembering his first summer, watching children on the beach while he worked on his boat, and thinking, *this* is the place for children to grow up.

Without knowing he was going to, he had started telling her about David. When he came to a halt she said, 'I'm sorry.' He shrugged, run out of words.

'When did you separate?'

'I didn't,' he said, too harshly. 'She did.' Get a hold on it, he told himself. 'It's over a year. Which feels a very long time. And in other ways, so raw it's like yesterday.'

'I'm sorry,' she said again.

'I don't know why I landed this on you.'

'It's good to be known,' she said simply.

He looked at her thoughtfully. 'Yes. And you're clearly older than you look.'

'How old do I look?'

'About eighteen. No, I don't mean that really. Maybe it's just that I feel suddenly a lot older this last year.' He started walking down, heading back to the house. She followed, not saying anything, for which he was grateful. When they got to the house he said, 'They live in Basingstoke now.' He heard the disdain that his voice loaded on that single word, and tried to laugh it off. 'What an exchange for the kid. Losing this, and getting a flat in Basingstoke.'

She left on the two o'clock boat. He hadn't realised she was going so soon and he hadn't done anything about lunch.

'I can take you back later,' he said, but he sensed the awkwardness of almost-strangers creeping back.

'I have to get back.'

He started putting some apples and a hunk of bread into a bag. She protested, 'It's not a long journey, I can eat when I get back.' But he insisted, thrust it in her hands.

She waved as she walked away down the path. It was only then that he realised he had asked her nothing about herself. Not even her second name.

≈≈

Routine, Anna told herself, you have to get back to your own routine, it's the only way to calm the mind. But a routine of what? Of almost nothing happening. Moving around alone, learning the silence again. Walking down to Old Town cafe to buy a newspaper. A few words with Eddie behind the counter – 'Nice and calm today,' or 'Looks like we're blowing up for something.' Maybe it was that she came for, rather than the newspaper, that most minimal of interactions. Walk back home, make a cup of tea, settle down to the paper. Once a week was all she could get herself to do, but she kept to that, trying to remind herself that what happened elsewhere mattered.

Greenham Common: Women protesters evicted from nuclear base. It stirred distant feelings, of her long-ago self taking her first conscious step away from Max's view of the world by joining an anti-nuclear protest. She would never have thought of it if it hadn't been for her friend Elaine, but what Elaine was saying made sense. Anna remembered the bombing of Liverpool in her schooldays, and the gut feeling that said, 'It shouldn't *be* like this.' So there she was, with Jason in a pushchair and Gail a four-year-old with two little plaits, joining a straggling collection of mums and children, grannies and students on the steps of the town hall. Blowing on their gloved hands and singing to keep warm in the coldest March she could remember ...

Shut it down, shut it down. It's got nothing to do with life now.

Out on her bike. But now she saw herself as Gail would see her, going nowhere. Like her life. The High Street with its morning drift of holiday-makers peering in at each of the shops. The Parade where an old lady was letting her dog off its lead for his morning sniff and pee. Past the museum where a hopeful couple in anoraks were reading the notices on the board outside to see what entertainment the island offered – Geoff's Thursday slide show, Birds of the Islands, in the Methodist Hall; the Scillonian Entertainers' summer season. Past the church, where there would be no choir practice tonight even though it was Tuesday, for Neville Hill was a man of regular habits. School was on holiday, and so was he.

It was going to feel a long, silent evening without it. She couldn't paint in the evenings, it never worked. She tried to settle with a book but she ended up just staring out of the window, watching the light fade.

Term started. From the moment Anna came into the church hall for choir she felt an undercurrent, something not being said. They sight-read their way through the new piece, holding in there when the rhythms got out of control, till Neville stopped them, saying mildly, 'Bit of a runaway train there in the sopranos,' and they laughed with relief at being able to catch their breath. 'And tenors, I know you're a bit low in numbers, so you're going to have to pull out the stops on that *forte*.'

It was only then that she noticed, looking at the tenors to see who was missing. Paul Cooper, one of the teachers from the school – and he never missed a practice.

At break-time she asked Vera, Neville's wife. 'Is Paul not well?'

Vera looked at her rather oddly. 'He's gone.'

'Gone?'

'He went back to Devon for the holidays, you know they have a house there. Wrote to Neville, not coming back. The letter got here the Friday before term started, no notice whatsoever.'

'What's happened?'

'No one has the least idea. *Exceptional personal circumstances*, his letter said. They'd better be exceptional, I can tell you. He was teaching the exam classes for history, *and* organising the senior class trip to the mainland. Can you imagine, just walking out on it all. Neville's rushing around frantically trying to sort out replacements.'

Anna glanced over to Neville, who never rushed, and was never frantic. But he did look strained. Maybe that was what she had felt when she walked in. Neville's calm was part of what made Tuesdays feel safe and pleasurable.

Vera moved off to get some coffee. Anna tuned in to the conversations around her ... It's his wife. She never liked the islands. She didn't come back with him after Christmas, did you know? He was having to go back every second weekend. I thought that was because there were builders in the house? A new kitchen doesn't take three months. I reckon he got back at Easter and she gave him an ultimatum. Me or the islands. But then why not say?

'OK, everyone,' Neville was calling out. 'Let's get back. The *Nunc Dimitis*, page three.'

≈≈

Everyone had known about Paul Cooper before term started, it seemed, everyone except Cari. She had come into the staff room and felt an atmosphere like storm warnings, and not had an idea what it was about. 'Where have you *been*?' asked one of the other teachers. In a tunnel of her own, not hearing anything.

A reshuffling of duties. She was the only one on the staff with a history degree, so she would take over Paul's senior classes. Janet Ross, the teacher she was replacing on maternity leave, would come back three days a week and take back some of Cari's English classes. Neville himself would pick up the rest of

Paul's load until the education office in Cornwall could send them a replacement.

'What we're still missing is someone to take over the school trip,' Neville said. Cari thought he was looking her way and tried to avoid his eyes – no way was she going back to the mainland, even for a week.

Neville's eyes passed over her, came to rest on Fran Norton, maths teacher. 'Fran, what about you?'

'Can't say it's my dream assignment. I presume we have a parent lined up?'

'Winifred Downey, she's done about four school trips, she'll run it for you. And given the situation, we'll ask around for one other.'

'Oh, all right, I dare say I'll cope.'

'Good. We'll take other things off you. Primary school liaison, maybe?'

Cari asked, 'What does that involve?'

'Visiting each of the schools on the other islands, any time over the next month. Then we do an open day for them here, so they know what they're coming to.'

'That's me,' she said.

'Sure? On top of exam classes for history?'

'It'll be fine.'

Not just fine, it'll be a relief to have something new demanded of me, no time to think too much.

Back home, telling Andrew. 'It's going to be a big extra push till I've come to terms with the history syllabus.' Feeling relieved to have something new to tell him, that was safe to tell. Then preparing late into the night, and every night that week. Getting behind with everything else and not minding, scrappy meals, clothes lying about in piles.

≈≈

This is distinctly odd, thought Anna, out on her bike, I have begun to worry about someone else's problems. She kept thinking of Neville, running a school, more than enough to handle, and suddenly this thing with Paul Cooper. But why was *she* thinking about it? Almost as if she were back working, a problem in the practice, up to her to work out what to do.

'You must be recovering,' she announced out loud. And instantly felt cautious. Keep clear. Not your problem.

How unlike Paul to suddenly opt out of everything he was involved in. A man of few doubts who enjoyed generating plans and carrying everyone along with them. She had seen him in full action when she had stood in for Bella at the parents' meeting about the trip to the mainland he was planning for Yvonne's class. A nice-looking young man – but then she realised he was not so young, it was the unruly blond hair that had given that impression. And that air of unconscious confidence that she associated with those for whom the prospect of middle age did not yet exist, who had no inkling that you might one day lose your sense of what you were doing with your life. He was explaining his plan to send the older pupils out in twos and threes on different tasks, finding out information from the museum, the council office, the college. 'Teenagers hate being herded around in groups,' he had said – undeniable, but she reacted rather to the proprietorial way he said it, as if he had been the first to discover it. 'At sixteen most of them will be heading for the mainland and will have to make their own way about. We'd be irresponsible not to give them a gradual introduction to what they're going to have to deal with.'

The mainland. The other place where everything was assumed to be more complicated. Just too much noise, that's what it really was, too many messages telling you what you want, what you need, what others around you need, what you must do and know about and have read in the papers in order to be – what? Able to keep your end up in conversation? Know who the others were all talking about? Something more than that. More like keeping your grip on the bar of the roller coaster, lest it hurl you off. Thank God that was all behind her, and for good ...

At which point her wheel hit a stone in the road and she came off her bike – in full view of the police station and two passers by. She lay sprawled on the road half-trapped under her bike and had to face the indignity of having to be extricated by – Oh Lord, it was the young woman she kept passing on the road, now bending over her in concern, helping her onto her feet. It seemed worse, somehow, that it should be her. To be seen like this.

Why should it matter? Why should anything matter?

'Are you OK?'

'I'm fine.' Standing on her own feet again, involuntarily running her hand over a bruised knee. And her damn hip wasn't going to like this.

'Your arm,' said the young woman. 'You've scraped it quite badly.'

'It's nothing. You've been very kind.' Now go away and leave me.

A policeman had come out of the police station.

'That was a bad one.' He was grinning. A young man with pimples. 'How are we doing now?'

'I'm fine,' she said, 'absolutely fine. It's really nothing. So stupid of me.' She felt absurdly put off her stride that she should have landed in a situation where she appeared to need help from these young strangers.

The young woman was examining her bike. 'The wheel's buckled.'

'It's pushable.'

'I could wheel it over to the bike shop for you, if you like.'

'That's very kind of you but there's no need. I can take it myself. I'm absolutely fine.'

'Now you just let me walk with you then,' the policeman insisted. 'In case you feel shaky.'

She was starting to say, 'I'm *not* shaky,' when she realised that actually she was, and that she was grateful. She turned to the young woman. 'You've been very kind.'

'It's nothing.' And she walked on.

Anna started pushing the bike. 'I'll do that,' the young policeman said, and took it from her. She walked alongside, feeling ridiculous. She consoled herself that maybe she was an event in his day.

'There can't be much for a policeman to do around here,' she said.

'The way I see it is, you need the police to be there in case things go wrong. But it's much better if they don't.'

'Do they ever?'

'We have two cells and one we never use, except to store the bicycle and the Christmas lights.'

'And the other?'

'They had a drunk in there overnight once. But that was before I started.'

She was feeling better by the minute. They left the bike at the bike shop and headed back. 'It's really not necessary for you to come,' but by now the protest was half-hearted. By the time they got to her house she knew his name was Ron Bailey, he wasn't married, and he lived with his mother. He had offered all that without asking her anything about herself, which made her even more friendlily inclined. At the gate she thought she was going to send him off, but to her surprise she heard herself say, 'I'm going to have a whisky. Will you join me?'

Ron shifted, embarrassed.

'Just a little one,' she said.

It was almost the end of the day. His resolution wavered. And he came in and sat in her living room, not having any idea that he was the first person outside of her closest family that she had ever let in.

He said as he lifted his glass meditatively, 'I hardly ever do this, you know. It's not being a policeman, it's my mother.'

'She disapproves?'

'Teetotaller. Strict as they come.'

'Well, pop by here when you need a bit of wicked release.'

But when she was finally alone it was not this appeallingly simple young man she was thinking of, but the young woman who had been there when she discovered herself on the ground. Seeing her close up for the first time, her face bent close to hers. Something about that face – nothing you could pinpoint, except those grey-green eyes that missed nothing. A bit unnerving.

So bizarre, Anna thought. We've both been watching each other for months. Our eyes were saying, 'I know you,' but neither of us could acknowledge it.

So bizarre, Cari thought, as she went on her way. Seeing her close up for the first time, but feeling she knew her face already. And then that expression on it, panicking at being caught in a vulnerable position. Why would it matter so? Cari had been on the point of saying, 'I've seen you going around on your bike, I'm glad we've met,' but that look in the older woman's face had silenced her. No way of knowing what was going on in there.

≈≈

It was Wednesday that Anna came off her bike. By Thursday the following people knew about it: Ron Bailey, the policeman, and Cari, of course, because they were there. Len Venables, the bike shop man who fixed the buckled wheel. Steve Tointon who ran the Yachtsman's Friend next to the bike shop, because business was slack and he happened to be standing at the door looking out at the harbour when Anna arrived. Old Mrs Bailey, Ron's mother, for he always tried to find something to tell her each evening, to make up for the fact that she didn't get out much. Vera Hill, wife of the head teacher, because she always popped in on Mrs Bailey on Thursday mornings after the church meeting that the old lady could no longer get to. Neville, because Vera told him when he got home from school on Thursday afternoon and they sat together over a cup of tea.

'It's time someone spoke to her,' Vera said.

'What precisely would you have someone say?' Neville asked. 'It could happen to anyone.'

'It happened to her because her mind's not on where she's going. She needs help and she won't admit it.'

'Then there's not much anyone can say until she does.'

'Bella could.'

'Perhaps Bella already has.'

Bella had tried, but not very successfully. She had heard about Anna's fall not from Anna herself but from her husband Thomas, who heard it from Garth Westerman, the St Mary's boatman who delivered the mail to St Martin's. Thomas had gone down to meet the boat to see if the new clippers he had ordered had arrived.

'Your wife's cousin had a bit of a fall,' Garth said. 'Off that bike of hers. But no damage done.' He felt they ought to know,

Anna Feldman being the odd sort of person she was.

Garth had heard it from Len, the bike shop man, with whom he sometimes had a pint in an evening. Len had sold Anna her bike in the first place and he kept a tactful eye on it, noticing how it was functioning if he saw her cycle past; which by extension led to him feeling protective towards Anna.

'Should be OK now,' he said as he handed it over. 'But if you have any trouble don't mess about with it, bring it back in.'

He told Garth about Anna's fall because he knew Garth was a friend of Hugh Stanford's, and Hugh had taken a friendly interest in Anna's son, though for some reason Len hadn't quite fathomed it seemed that Anna and Hugh now had nothing to do with each other. An awkward bugger, Hugh, liable to fall out with anyone if they so much as looked at him the wrong way.

'What's it all about, d'you know?' he asked Garth.

'No idea,' Garth said. 'Not the sort of thing Hugh ever tells anyone.'

And there the trail stopped. Garth on principle never passed on town gossip to his wife, which irritated her, quite reasonably, for a boatman is in an exceptionally good position to hear it.

'I heard you came off your bike,' Bella said when she came over to St Mary's to do her shopping.

Anna said, 'Honestly, you can't sneeze in this place without everyone discussing it.' But she felt dishonest as she heard herself say it, for she knew in truth they had all been exceptionally tactful. Not probing, letting her be.

'You're OK?' Bella checked, not to be put off.

'My hip's a bit stiffer than usual and I have a beauty of a bruise on my arm. Otherwise fine.'

Bella left it at that. 'I'm worried about Yvonne. She's been looking peaky for months. I suppose it's just the time of year.'

'Hormones,' Anna said. 'They grow in spurts, sometimes too fast for their strength. It'll sort itself out.'

'I hope so. Sometimes I wonder if it isn't something she's worried about, that she's not saying.'

'Is she a worrier? She never strikes me that way.'

'Not exactly a worrier. But she doesn't like it when things change. Like when Sylvie Stanford left and she didn't have her little friend David to play with anymore. She gets very attached to people.'

Like she did to Jason. Bella didn't say it but they both of them heard it.

'Can she stay overnight with you again before the school journey?' Bella asked. 'She loved it last time.'

'Of course.'

'And maybe she'll talk to you. Sometimes it's easier, not to your own mother.'

Again Jason was in the air between them. It seemed impossible this morning to steer clear of him.

≈≈

Saturday morning. Hugh stood at his door, assessing. Soft April weather, warm with a slight breeze. Ideal for sailing, if he could get the essential work out of the way.

Funny, someone walking up his track. Well, what do you know, it was her again, the bringer of the flapjacks. But looking like she was going past his house this time, heading for the hill behind.

He called out, 'Hello there!'

She turned, looked back. He strode towards her. She stood waiting till he was close enough to talk to.

'I assumed it was OK to use your track. I thought I'd walk up over the heath, to see if I can work out where we got lost up there.'

'Of course. Maybe I'll come with you.'

She hesitated. 'I didn't mean to take you away from your work.'

'There's nothing that can't wait an hour.'

But maybe she *wanted* to do it alone? And if he hadn't happened to see her and call out, perhaps she would have gone past and not stopped? But surely? He had no idea, that was the truth. He was hopeless at working out what women were thinking, always had been. They drew him, a force so obvious that it seemed impossible they did not see it themselves, and then they erected these indefinable lines as to how much response was pleasing and how much an oppression.

'Last time I didn't even ask your second name. If you hadn't come I'd have had no way of finding you again.'

She laughed. 'Lawrence. And I teach at the school.'

The not-sure-ness was slipping away. He said, 'Just come in and give me a few moments to get cleaned up.' They moved towards the house, chatting as if the knowing-each-other were already a settled thing.

The heath was yellow with gorse, echoing his pleasure. She talked easily, mostly about the children at the school. At the edge of Bread and Butter Cove they stood looking down into the deep dip that Cari had last seen at the height of the storm. Today it lay silent and secretive, the sun glinting off the piles of black plastic that filled its bottom. Then they climbed down over to Wine Cove, which he thought from her description must be the one she and her friends had started from. He hadn't been there himself for over a year. Sea sandwort marked the band between the high tide mark and the dunes, low cushions of glossy green leaves.

'I know that plant,' she said, 'there's some on the sand in my cove.'

'You have a cove?' He was amused. 'Which one is that?'

'On St Mary's, looking over to here. You can't see it from the land at all, there's just a headland and a cliff falling straight into the sea. You have to know just where the path is or you'd never find it.' She knelt down, fingering the leaves. 'No flowers. I'm sure when I was a child it had flowers. Little, sort of creamy white.'

'They only come in high summer. A few months, and you'll see them.'

'I don't know if I'll still be here then.'

Why? he wanted to ask. But he let it go. Instead he said, 'Tell me about your cove. How did you find it?'

She stretched herself out on the sand, leaning back on her elbows. 'I saw it first from out at sea when my dad took us sailing round the island.' It had been high tide and there was no more than the smallest triangle of sand caught between V-shaped sloping walls of rock. Enchanting in its isolation. Then back on land she and Robyn stumbled on the path. 'We found it by accident really, but you know how things can be when you're a kid, it didn't *feel* an accident, it felt like it was a secret the island was sharing, just with us.'

They had been exploring in the pines up at the north of the island. It felt like a forest, big enough to get lost in. Then they emerged from the trees into the light of a steep headland, and found in a tangle of brambles and bracken a perfectly round gap, the size an animal might have made, yet holding a hint of more. They had come back next day with scissors and a small saw, borrowed without asking from their dad's tools, and set out to find where the hidden path would lead. Arms and legs

116

scratched, clothes torn, but ever more determined, they emerged at a point where the bracken gave up and the land sloped suddenly away beneath them, and they could look down on that magic scrap of sand. By zigzagging they found footholds down to where the boulders became round and easy to clamber over, and finally to the sand, silver and soft on their sunbaked feet. They were captivated by their own cleverness. When they climbed back up they pulled the bracken back over the place where the path started so that no one but them would ever find it ...

She had forgotten about Hugh standing near her. She got up abruptly. 'Let's get back.'

Back at the house he put the kettle on. While he waited for it to boil he took out a pile of accumulated peelings to dump on the compost. She followed him. A compost pile, a place for burning, a pit for burying other rubbish, just like he'd described on the afternoon of the storm. She remembered his vehemence about the black bags. 'Who are the people who'd like to throw you off the island?'

He shrugged. 'A bit of an exaggeration. But the man who built the cottages and dumps the bags is definitely not too keen on me. I wouldn't expect him to be, I'm hassling him, I'm not going to let him get away with it.'

That was like her dad, such definite ideas, other people were bound to react. But even if that meant trouble, at least he was alive. She couldn't deal with people being absent from themselves.

She suddenly remembered Andrew. 'I'd better get back,' she said. 'I've got loads of preparation to do.'

'Come again,' he said as he stood at the door and she ready to be off. She hadn't reply, just waved. He could have walked with her to the quay, but he didn't. No way was he going to give the gossip mongers of St Martin's any spurious fodder.

After she had gone he wandered restlessly about the house, starting a task and leaving it. Going outside to get stuck into some work and then giving up before it was done. Coming back in, staring at the mess in the house, thinking, I really have to do something about sorting this place out. Too much clobber. That tackle, that should go out in the shed for a start.

He began to lift and shift. It had made him restless, someone new blowing in like this. No question of attraction, the girl was much too young. Not his type anyway, didn't go for the gamin, and the last thing he needed was to get involved with any woman again. It was something more basic than that. The companionship. Someone he could be at ease with.

≈≈

A letter from Gail. 'Pictures by the children for the grandmother who paints' – Penny's an abstract splash of colour, Noel's a set of creatures with circular bodies and stick legs and arms heading off in different directions. A curious object in the middle with many pink arms. Gail's handwriting at the bottom – 'The man with the lobster pots.' Anna stuck the paintings on the wall above the sink and felt remarkably like a normal grandmother. Except for that last plea in Gail's letter – 'Please get a phone, Mum, it's so silly not to.'

Anna toyed with a range of replies as she washed her breakfast cereal bowl. 'I need the peace.' No, that wouldn't do, too excluding. 'You can't just get a phone out here, there's a long waiting list.' But there probably wasn't, she hadn't tried to find out. If she said that, Gail would take it as permission and get on the phone and sort it out. How about, 'If I had a phone I'd have to give the number to my friends in Chichester, and then they'd all phone me and want to come and visit.' Gail would say, 'That would be good for you.' But it wouldn't. It definitely wouldn't. Having Gail here was one thing, the others no. She wasn't ready.

Neville Hill's house was near the centre of town, part of a grey stone terrace fronting directly onto the pavement. Anna had been inside once when Vera had hosted a gathering with the choir, but she wasn't on visiting terms. Not with anyone on St Mary's, actually. But here she was, late afternoon, which must be about the time Neville got back from school. He'd be sitting with Vera, having a cup of tea. She would be intruding –

But she had something to say to him that had now been going round in her head for days so the only thing seemed to be to say it. She lent her bike against the wall. Knocked. Felt absurdly junior.

The door opened. Vera – 'Anna, how nice. Come in.'

'I hope I'm not interrupting.'

'Of course not.' Then, calling over her shoulder, 'Neville, come and see, Anna's here.' She ushered her in. 'I was just about to go and get some lamb before the butcher closes. But there's time yet. You'll have some tea?' Vera steered her into the room that Anna thought of as the soft room, more armchairs than you would think could fit, all with big puffy cushions. Chintz and anti-macassars. 'Sit down, my dear. How do you take it?'

'Whatever's in the pot will be lovely.' To Neville, 'I won't stay, I was just wondering if there was any way I could help. With Paul going so suddenly. Maybe with things in the office, to take a little pressure off you?'

Neville looked taken aback, then touched. 'That's very thoughtful of you.'

119

Now she was embarrassed, it sounded so unimportant. To excuse herself almost she said, 'I have all day to do nothing. And St Mary's has been kind to me. It's time I repaid a little.'

'You're very kind. But I think we're coping.'

Vera snorted. 'Except you can't get that stupid education office in Cornwall to send you a supply teacher.'

'They're short,' Neville said mildly, 'and their regulars wouldn't want to come out here. They want the odd days, not a way of life.'

Vera got up to go. Anna shifted in her seat. Vera said, 'Stay, stay, no need to rush.' Then to Neville, as she put on her coat, 'What I want to know is, what are you doing about Paul?'

'What would you like me to do, my dear?'

'Someone needs to hold him to book.'

She left. Neville said, 'Vera is a woman for direct action.' And then, 'So, you're feeling like doing something more, then?'

'It's not that. Quietness suits me. But I do feel singularly selfish sometimes. I attend to nobody's needs but my own.'

'Fine, but not clerical work. Not someone with your talents and training.'

She felt herself clamming up, against a threat.

'Forgive me. Does that feel an intrusion?'

She shook her head. 'Not from you.'

'Anna,' he was speaking gently now, as to someone who needed careful handling. That's me, she thought, that's how they see me – 'Bella has talked to me about you. You shouldn't mind that, I've known her a long time and she's been concerned.'

'What exactly did she say?'

'That you're a high flyer, from a family where no one apart from you has ever gone to university. That you're a doctor, and not just an ordinary one. Training new doctors, presenting papers at medical conferences.'

She pushed it away. 'Bella has *no idea*. She knows nothing about that world.'

'Maybe. But she knows it's not right that you're not letting yourself use all that. Not right for you.'

She felt suddenly very tired. Why am I here, letting him talk at me? I want to get back home.

'Why is it so difficult to think of, Anna?'

'Please, Neville. I've retired.'

'Nonsense. You can't be more than my age.'

'It's not chronological age that matters.' Then, making a real effort – she had intruded herself on him, he had concerned himself with her, she owed him more of an explanation – 'Bella's wrong, all of that is no loss to me. My work was the clearest part of my life, the only bit I knew I was doing well. But after what happened I knew I had to start again differently.' Then, a note of urgent appeal in her voice, '*I can't go back.*'

I can't go back –

But she was going back all the time. Constantly working it over, trying to rerun it, differently. If only she had – if only she and Max had – if she hadn't ...

If she hadn't taken Jason to see her father's island.

But that was ridiculous, what difference would that have made?

If she hadn't gone back to work, if she had been there with Jason after school when he was small and malleable, as long as she had been with Gail ... Yes, that. Maybe he would have stayed longer the way he was as a child, quietly companionable, never saying much but responsive, affectionate. That small smile of complicity when he sensed a joke in the air. Wordlessly coming to show her something he had found, eyes always so sharp – a leaf with an unusual pattern of veins, a stone with beautiful markings.

If Max had been a different kind of father, given more *time* to doing things with the boy, and not thought he could do it all through money, indulgent to a fault with expensive gifts, the big gesture. Or if Max had just stuck to his enthusiasms longer, instead of starting Jason off on a passion for sailing and then leaving it to others to take him out, so that it was always something Jason did without them, that took him away. And because Jason wasn't given to putting things in words, it was no use asking when he came back, 'How was it?' for all he would say was, 'Yeah, good,' and then disappear to his room.

If only she had never brought him here.

The summer of 1975. Hugh had been down at the beach working on his dinghy when he became sure someone was standing behind him, watching. He looked up. A young lad, twelve, maybe, or thirteen. He nodded in acknowledgement of the boy's presence then went on working. The lad would say something when he was ready, best leave it to him.

Eventually he did. 'Can I help?'

Hugh handed him the end of a rope. 'You could hold onto this.'

The boy took it, followed his movements, guessed what he needed next, and was doing it before Hugh asked.

Eventually Hugh asked, 'D'you sail?'

The boy nodded. 'But not enough.' Then, 'My dad has a yacht, back home.'

'Where's that?'

'Chichester harbour. But he's too busy to come out often. And it's too big for me to handle alone.'

They worked on silently, the feeling between them increasingly companionable. After a bit Hugh said, 'I do sailing lessons. You could see if your dad will pay for a few while you're here.'

'I can pay,' the boy said instantly.

So it's like that, is it, Hugh thought. Little rich kid. And wants to do things without reference to his father. Well, he could understand that.

'You'd need your father's permission at least.'

'He'd say yes. He lets me do what I like.'

Hugh looked out at the sea, as calm as he had ever seen it. He felt the boy's intensity. He was probably a bit older than he looked anyway. Short sturdy type, not easy to tell. Hugh said, 'OK, just a quick one.'

Out in the dinghy he watched the boy's hands move and touch with unselfconscious ease, and his eyes judge the wind with the instinct of a natural creature. He had the strangest sensation of watching himself at an earlier age, or even some future one.

They beached. The boy said, 'Thanks,' in a tone that said far more than the word.

'I shouldn't really have done that, you know. If you want to come out again you make sure your father knows and agrees.'

The boy nodded. 'I haven't got the money on me, I'll go fetch it right away.'

'Forget about it for this time.'

'No, really.' The boy was embarrassed.

'It wasn't a lesson, you were a good sailing mate. And maybe I'd better know your name. I'm Hugh.'

'Jason,' said the boy, and was off.

He told Sylvie. Stupid, he should have known how she would react.

'His father's rich enough to have his own yacht and you don't charge him for a lesson?'

123

'This boy's different. I didn't feel money came into it.'

Jason was there again next morning.

'So what does your dad say?'

'It's fine.' And they set out again.

Three days later – Sylvie peeling potatoes for dinner, Hugh oiling tools at the kitchen table, David out playing near the chickens. 'That boy you keep taking out,' Sylvie said. 'Do you know who he is?'

'A holiday kid.'

'He's Bella's nephew.' Sylvie watched with satisfaction the reaction on his face. 'His mother has been wondering where he disappears to each morning.'

Hugh looked at her, assessing. 'I told the boy to get permission. He said he had. D'you expect me to go and accost them personally?'

'You're a fool, Hugh. Something happens to the boy out there, and you're in big trouble. If they pay for lessons it's a different matter altogether. Then it's them taking the risk.'

'Right, at least we're gettting to it now. It's the money, isn't it? That's what's riling you.'

'And why wouldn't it? D'you think we have so much then we can afford to be so casual? D'you think I want to spend my whole life working like a navvy, while you potter about in boats?'

And before he could reply she had got up to check something on the stove, turning her back on him. Over her shoulder she said, 'Go and get David in, it's time for his bath.'

Jason was waiting at the boat. Hugh said, 'Now then, I'm told your mum would quite like to know what you're up to.'

'Who told you that?'

'This island's a small place. You said you'd checked with them.'

'I told my dad. Maybe he didn't tell her.'

'So that's it,' Hugh nodded. 'It's your dad who lets you do what you like, your mum who might say No. So you take care not to ask her.'

Jason grinned. 'She's OK, she just gets worried and I can do without that.'

'Well you go and deal with the worry before we go out again.'

Jason looked as if he were about to protest.

'Go on,' said Hugh firmly. 'Get back there and tell her. You're not going out again until you do.'

An hour later he was back.

'Yes?' asked Hugh.

'Yes,' Jason said.

Jason made no other reference to his family and Hugh let him set the pace. He himself didn't talk to Bella about it, it was a busy time and he didn't happen to go over there. Anyway, the boy had told his mother now, so what more was there to say?

Each day they went out a little further, stayed out a little longer. Past seals sunning themselves on rocks, and cormorants with long necks staring at them. He could not say, looking back, how long it had been – weeks at least, over a long summer. A time without time, where the days took on their own rhythm. Finding time, however busy, for the pleasure of being out on the water, man and boy, sheets of canvas flapping above, lifting and dipping on the back of the sea. The boy's eyes as alert as Hugh's own, following the small changes in colour in the sea that signified a shoal of fish feet below the surface, a current of water running at an unexpected angle.

Then a day when Jason said, 'We leave at nine tomorrow,' in

a voice so filled with adolescent despair that Hugh had to laugh. 'Life will continue,' he said, 'surprising as it may seem.' And because Jason couldn't laugh with him, 'I'll tell you what, we could do a dawn sail. Back in time for breakfast.'

But it wasn't just for Jason. He hadn't done that himself since David was born.

Leaving the house in the four-thirty dark. Down the path, that his feet knew so well they didn't need the torchlight – to find a quiet shadow already moving about the dinghy. They pushed out and set sail, the sea to themselves, and through a still dawn headed out to the Eastern Isles to watch the sun rise over a world of rock and water and sky. To land on a small beach nestling between rocks no human hand had cut for stone, to clamber onto heathland that no one had ever attempted to cultivate. To sit and watch kittiwakes wheel and cry in the air above them, oystercatchers scurry past on the beach, picking at shells. As they sailed back their eyes skimmed the water, watching for signs of the grey mullet that must be there somewhere, invisible under the water – a flip of silver and there they were, heads out above the choppy water, rolling onto their backs.

When they had beached Jason said, 'That was the best.' And then, passionate again, 'I wish I wasn't going.'

Hugh said lightly, 'Maybe you'll be back.'

≈≈

The weekend at last, and Cari got stuck into a quick bout of housewifeliness. Whipping around with the hoover, shoving clothes into the washing machine, a lot of winter things that had been lying about for weeks. Machine on, she settled at the table with her history books. How could she make the stories of remote times and places real to these island children? She had to connect them with what they already knew — with the island's history, maybe? A handful of human beings, cut off from all the rest. Not so unusual, when you came to think of it, only an extreme version of the human condition. We each know only what we experience yet something impels us beyond self, beyond the limits of time, of the land we can see, across seas, to imagine. It was that capacity in them she had to find some way to touch.

Andrew wandered through to get another coffee.

'How's it going?' he asked.

'OK. And you?'

He grunted 'Uh huh,' and went into the kitchen.

She glanced at the time – she'd been going an hour. This is the first Saturday for ages, she thought, that I haven't felt resentful. Maybe this is what it would take for things to work between us, if I always had something I was as absorbed in as he is with his work.

Andrew came back in with his coffee. Said nothing. Went back to his study. Closed the door.

Irritation surfaced again. What about offering me a cup while he's getting his own? And why does he always have to close the door? It's not as if I've got the radio on.

Her concentration was thoroughly broken now.

The washing machine rattled to a stop. She got up, went to the kitchen. Here we both are with work to get through, but it's me who's doing the laundry. She opened the machine door – stop it, that's not what it's really about – lifted out the amorphous wet pile – it's nothing to do with Andrew, first day of my period, that's all, I get irritated by ridiculously small things – dumped it in the plastic basket, carried it outside.

A beautiful day – she couldn't spend it all indoors. As she

lifted clothes and pegged them to the line, her mind slipped back to her last visit to St Martin's, to Hugh saying, 'Come again.' Would she? It would be so easy to do, so natural.

Natural, yes. But too confusing.

She no longer understood herself. She felt off balance, blown about by arbitrary winds, not knowing any more what she wanted or from whom. Karl, who in one intense week had woken her into restlessness was already fading into unreality, but the changes in her continued to rage. Now here was someone else, saying, Come again. Offering friendship, which she realised now she badly needed. A man who understood the islands the way she did, who had recognised that in her so that she felt already they knew each other. If she let the friendship happen there would be stories to hear but nothing essential to explain. Yet the very clarity of that awareness made her afraid.

She lifted up a jersey. Funny, this one didn't look familiar. Definitely not hers, or Andrew's either. Grey, polo neck, frayed at the wrists –

Must be another of Hugh's. She had taken three back, she was sure of it. But maybe one of them had been wearing two? She stood holding it, trying not to feel anything that wasn't practical. Just, 'Well, I'll have to take it back.'

She explained to Andrew at lunch. 'I'll have to take it back. I can get the morning boat tomorrow and come back on the early afternoon one.' Explaining too much, for it seemed too much, third time in two weeks.

He said, 'Sure,' as if it was a matter of no particular concern to him.

Was it? She had no idea.

Hugh wasn't in when Cari arrived. Such a possibility had not occurred to her and she was taken aback at the sharpness of the disappointment. She knocked again, waited, then pushed the door open, feeling like a thief. She put the jersey on the kitchen table and after a bit of a search found a pen and an old envelope on which she wrote, 'Seem to have left this one out last time. Sorry to have missed you.' Then she thought maybe that was a bit much, scrumpled it up, and started looking for another scrap of paper.

At that point Hugh appeared at the kitchen door. She felt like a guilty child, but it was mainly the scrumpled piece of paper she wanted to hide. He just stood there looking, an expression on his face she couldn't read.

She said, defensively, 'You weren't here.'

'What can I say? I wasn't.'

'Your jersey. Another one. I found it. It must have got left out.'

She was sounding ridiculous, like she was covering up something, like she had to convince him she hadn't done it on purpose. But he wasn't noticing, he was looking in the oddest way at the jersey.

He hadn't realised that it hadn't come back with the others. Maybe he hadn't wanted it to. That was the one Sylvie had knitted the year David was born. A time when things still seemed simple; pleasure in the present, a future planned together. They had laughed about the pattern, he remembered, traditional fisherman's knit, untreated wool that kept its natural oil so that sea spray hardly got through it. A good one for sailing. But the pleasure had become tainted by her resentment of the time he spent out in the dinghy, by his trust betrayed. The jersey had been shoved to the back of the deep chest of drawers; pulled out for the storm-drenched strangers, not noticing what he might be unearthing. Now here it was coming back to him, the past refusing to be shut away.

He took it from her. 'Thanks,' he said, and put it to one side.

Then they were stuck again, not knowing what to say. He broke it with, 'It's a beautiful morning, let's get out.'

'Yes,' she said, released. 'On the heath side where we won't meet anyone.' Embarrassment flooded her again. 'I didn't mean—'

'No of course not.'

They moved to the door, almost bumping, each standing back to avoid it. Then through, and with relief into the fresh air, the awkwardness gradually fading as they walked. Out at the back and up, away from all habitation.

'Chapel Down?' he suggested.

She nodded, followed.

They past the stones of the cairn, a mound of rocks cleared from the field by some earlier farmer, perhaps; maybe something more. Perhaps marking a grave, pitiful defence against the sureness of mortality. A little further on, a low stone wall where the birdsfoot trefoil made yellow patterns against the grey of the lichen. Cari perched on it, her hands trailing the rough surface. Hugh came over to straddle it; not too close. He noticed for the first time that her eyes were an unusual grey-green.

He said, 'Do you know, I still know almost nothing about you.'

She laughed, embarrassed again. 'I don't know what to tell you.'

Because I don't have anything to say, I don't know who I am. I've spent all my life so far not thinking about myself because it was too confusing. Reading novels. Watching other people. Making up stories. Escaping back here to the islands.

Now was the time to say, 'I'm married.' But it felt awkward shoving it in like that, as if she were warning him, when there was nothing happening to require a warning.

He said, 'You know when I talked to you about David the other day?'

'Yes?'

'I hadn't done that for a while, with anyone.'

She nodded. 'I can imagine.'

'There's a girl on the island he always used to play with. Maybe you know her. Yvonne Penruth.'

'Sure I know her.'

He seemed to have lost the thread, was looking out over the sea. She thought, He's a strange man. Too much buried in there.

He turned and started again. 'Thomas Penruth was one of my first friends on the island. I'd have said my closest. I've known Yvonne since she was a baby. She's older than David but from the time he could walk she was taking him trailing about with her. She was a great kid.'

'Was?'

'She's not exactly a kid any more.' He got up off the wall, moving to avoid her scrutiny. Those eyes made him feel looked through, but somehow he couldn't stop himself telling her things. 'And I hardly see her anymore. Or Thomas either. There's something odd going on. Thomas just started going distant on me, for no reason I could fathom. Never said anything, just I began to realise he hardly ever came round any more, and if I went there it didn't feel comfortable. So I don't go often either. At first I thought it was this rubbish dumping business — it's Thomas's brother who owns the cottages. I thought, I've know the man for sixteen years, why doesn't he just tell me? But now I don't think it's that, because it isn't just him who's staying away, it's Yvonne too.'

'Staying away?'

'She used to be in and out of our house, like David was in

theirs. Staying over for supper. Coming out in the boat. Now I hardly see her. Of course it's different now David's not here, I wouldn't expect her often, but never is unnatural.'

Cari was picturing Yvonne, her figure full, poised on the brink of adulthood. At times so responsive, but recently – not withdrawn, exactly, but focused on something inner. Waiting the year out till she would be finished with school. She said, gently, 'Girls change a lot at her age. It isn't necessarily anything to do with you.'

'Sure,' he said, but sounded unconvinced.

She said, 'Even while I've known her, she's changed. I see it especially when she's with her friend Kelly – Kelly's still a giggly fifteen-year-old but Yvonne's moved on. She's gone beyond being a kid.'

Hugh said, 'That's just it. That's what Thomas can't deal with.'

'What are you saying?'

'That he must have warned her off me. It suddenly came to me, it was soon after Sylvie left that it happened. As a family man I was safe. As a man alone, I'm a threat.'

The tone was ironic, but Cari wasn't deceived. It was pain speaking. Suddenly it all felt too much. She said, 'Let's go back.' Then, as if to apologise for the abruptness, 'I can't risk missing that boat.'

He thought, She says that every time. There's a man back there, waiting for her.

He was alert now to possibilities, no escaping the fact. No use watching the boats from St Mary's, no chance of Cari coming again until the weekend. But she might phone. But she wouldn't know he had one. He could go over to St Mary's, he might see her. By accident. But he had no idea where she lived. He could get some things he needed from the Yachtsman's Friend; that was near the school, she might walk by at the end of the day.

'Are you crazy?' he said out loud, since saying it silently didn't seem to work. 'Get your mind back on work. As if you don't have enough troubles.'

But his mind wasn't letting him have any peace.

He began to think about the time he had first met Sylvie. He didn't want to, but it kept presenting itself, as if to remind him how flawed his own judgement had been, what madness it was to let himself be led by his emotional needs. How sure he had been at the time, his own conviction driving across her hesitancy. Only to backfire.

The summer of '69 it was, a time when for the young everything seemed possible. Hugh had been on the island a year. Sylvie arrived with a group of friends – long skirt and beads, backpack and guitar – typical hippie she was in those days, full of untested ideals, looking for an easy life over the summer. They camped – and Hugh, seeing her for the first time in that setting, was misled into thinking that the simple life suited her. It only suited her when the weather was good and she had her friends there to sit with in the evening and strum guitars by the fireside. He was fixing up his house, working all the hours of daylight. At first as he watched them he was thinking how much he would dislike to be idle all day; but also that he liked the way they laughed together, and put their arms around each other easily. And that he was on the outside.

He was often at Bella and Thomas's place that summer, giving Thomas a hand in his fields. Thomas had put his knee out of joint and was only able to hobble about. That was how they had got together, he twenty-two and never tired, Thomas fifty and deeply frustrated that his body had let him down. He had farmed all his life and never before needed to ask for help. Hugh understood that and made it clear he saw it as an equal exchange, his physical labour for Thomas's experience, helping him learn what he would need to know about island farming.

Thomas's land was next to the road, the only real road along the spine of the island. Working there Hugh would see Sylvie and her friends going to and from the campsite. They stopped to chat. He invited them over to see his own house, still without its roof, so he too was camping. They ate together sometimes, he with the whole group. And then just he and Sylvie, drawing her little by little into his world. Wanting her. She was buxom and bonny – he could only think of old words for her, words that took him back to childhood, though she was so much a creature of her time. Desire pushing, but more than that. He wanted her to stay. Wanted for the first time to open himself to a woman, in trust.

Then she was off, back to the mainland. 'Stay,' he said. 'You could have this forever.' He had thought she only needed encouragement, to take a small risk and gain a freedom she could never know if she stuck with the life she had drifted into. Waitressing, travelling, back to waitressing – what future was there in it? he demanded. Why settle for something so limited when she could choose to join him, and together make their own? Only years later, after so much had gone wrong, did he begin to realise that she was giving him signs right from the start, that he should not have urged her so persistently to join him.

And why, in the end, did she agree? What did she think she was coming to? Did it just seem too easy, the lover who had it all sorted, a house waiting to be moved into, an Eden to wake to every morning? A year of vacillating, short visits. Not sure. Maybe in a few months. And when she did finally come to stay, it was in the way she had done everything else, by drift. There was no passion in the project for her, no connection with anything she had longed for, or lost, or loved. And not being naturally given to hard work, the island became to her not freedom, but a trap.

He had felt the signs, even before they were there. Knowing she would leave him, before she knew herself, because that was what was bound to happen. Starting to protect himself, withdrawing where he could not be hurt – and maybe his very withdrawal hastened the process. Getting angry, and then anger suddenly deserting him, because what good would it do if she didn't stay of her own free will?

And he? With the years of bitterness between them now it was hard to take himself back to a state where *she* had been what he wanted. Not just a woman but *this* woman. But it had been so, and facing that knowledge of himself, he was afraid.

≈≈

'I'm going for a walk,' Cari said to Andrew, and didn't suggest he come too, nor explain why she was taking a pair of garden clippers. But then he was working and didn't notice.

Out on the road, past a couple of farms and a bulb research centre. Then off into the pines, leaving behind all signs of settlement. It took a while to locate the start of the path after so many years, but that seemed appropriate – their own place, still inviolate. She was surprised now that she not been back before to find it. She had left it, secreted as part of childhood. Now it was being unearthed, connecting to something new. The bracken thinned out. Soon she would be on that last stretch, the sudden drop of the land.

And she remembered now – an almost painfully vivid memory – the time she and Robyn had arrived to find the tide was out, the cove hardly recognisable. The beach that before had nestled safely within the V of the cliffs was gone and in its place was an expanse of sand that stretched out, *way* out, shining from the tide that had washed over it as it departed. They kicked off their flip-flops and ran out onto the sand that was firm and damp-cool beneath their feet, running in joy and freedom till the small waves tickled their toes, out to where the sea really began. It was shallow as far as they could see and the sea bed so smooth that it kept drawing them further, way further, before the water even came up to their knees. She turned to look back – The land was so far away now that they were seeing it as if they had come sailing in from the sea. They could see the whole line of coast, the dark green of ferns and brambles clinging to the cliffs, the little inlets, lots of them, far more than you would know about from walking at the top. Now she wasn't sure which was their cove, they all looked the same. She began to think of stories she had heard of the tide coming in much faster than people realised, and instantly she saw pictures of herself and Robyn running back over those huge stretches of sand, running, running, while all the time it was becoming sea and they never seemed to get any nearer.

Now, adult yet not quite able to dismiss that childhood fear, she reached the edge. She stood poised before beginning the climb down, savouring the dark green of the bushes, the moody blue-green of the sea. Then moved her gaze down to find again the scrap of beach and rocks below –

To see someone else down there before her. A woman moving slowly over the rocks, showing no signs of having heard anyone approach. She lifted her head, just enough for Cari to be sure that it was her. She seemed about to move on; then she paused, her attention caught by something she had seen in the sand.

On bare feet Anna made her way slowly across the wet sand, absorbed in the ritual that she herself did not understand but that drew her continually. The absolving touch of the crunchy-damp grains under her soles, white sand reflecting sunlight, myriad particles of glass. She watched her own footsteps imprint themselves. She bent to touch one, to touch the life in it before the next small wave crept over it, and then retreated, and the print was gone.

Something made her unsteady on her climb back up the cliff that day. Some aura from another being, she presumed. In this place she half expected messages, though she had no expectation that she would be able to interpret them. But she took note of the feeling and placed her feet carefully on the uneven surface. The rocks were shiny-wet from a short burst of rain, the leaves of the small plants that crept over them slightly slimy. Scurvy grass, fleshy-stick leaves of rock samphire. She reached the point where the steep slope began to ease out – and slipped. She lurched out to grab hold of a clump of bracken ahead of her and managed to steady herself, leaning into the slope of the land.

She lay there, panting, waiting for the panic to subside, to be replaced by an awareness of shooting pain in her ankle. Don't move, she told herself, addressing herself as if she were wise and calm. You're safe just lying here. Wait like this for the pain to calm down before trying to move again. But the other voice said, if that had happened just ten feet lower down I would have crashed down to the rocks at the bottom and lain there half smashed up for days, and no one would even have known.

Her immobility in this odd position gave a bizarre quality to what she was experiencing. She began to consider detachedly the picture of herself down there on the rocks. It wouldn't be the dying she would mind, she decided, but the pain. Of course the impact might knock her unconscious, but that couldn't be relied on. She remembered, suddenly, a picture from the life she had left behind. She was standing by the bedside of a frail old woman who had slipped in the bathroom and broken her thigh. By the time Anna got to see her she was lying in agonising pain, her small face white as the sheets that covered her, while men in white coats starched and dulled from endless laundering stood around the bedside and debated the risks of operating.

She definitely did not want to be where that woman had been.

The throbbing had calmed down a little. She edged herself round into a sitting position, carefully wiggling her toes to test them. OK, nothing broken. She shifted into a position marginally more comfortable and sat looking out over the sea while her analytic mind considered yet another angle of the question, her death. Her mother had died at fifty-six, exactly the age she, Anna, was now. Maybe she too had had her span and her life was about to end? Did that thought bother her? Not really. In fact there would be a certain logic to finishing up here, the completion of some private pact. What she did with her life now was no one else's business.

Bella, of course. She had almost forgotten her faithful, unquestioning cousin. Bella would grieve; but then she would get back, as she had to, to the endless round of tasks. But Gail. Yes, she would feel sorry about Gail. Better to live.

She could feel her hip stiffening from sitting too long in one position, from the damp under her on this ledge poised above the sea. Carefully she stood up, testing how much weight she could put on the ankle. Carefully she turned, and started up those last few feet to the top. Then she hobbled back along the path, the fronds of bracken parting to let her through, then closing again behind her, as water does behind a boat.

Out at sea Hugh headed the dinghy across towards the northeast tip of St Mary's, sailing near enough to check out each small arc of sand caught in the curves between cliffs. 'My cove,' Cari had said as she sat on the beach half leaning back, legs stretched out, belly flat, small breasts pointing her T shirt. He had laughed at the childlike quality, but also at the echo she had no idea she had set off. For Jason too had laid possession to it. The lad had been about sixteen then, back on the islands without his family, camping with friends. The others came out in the dinghy a couple of times but were more interested in hanging about on St Mary's in search of girls. So it was Hugh and Jason again, alone out together, which suited them both. Hugh had become aware that Jason's eyes had found something new that interested him. He turned his head to follow the direction. An enticing fragment of sand caught in a V-shape of cliffs rising steep above it. Their eyes met. A slight nod, and they each adjusted their hold on the rope, shifted their bodies' weight, and headed in towards it. Then they both glanced up again, to acknowledge with a smile their pleasure in that instinctively attuned movement.

'What's it called?' Jason asked when they got nearer.

'Don't think it has a name. Not that I've heard. We'll call it Jason's Cove if you like.'

And now Cari's too.

The sun was high overhead by the time Hugh brought the dinghy in and dragged it up onto the beach. The father of the American boy he had taken out was waiting to pay him for the week's lessons. Hugh looked at the wad of notes he was being offered. Even with a generous tip thrown in this was above the odds.

'No really,' he said.

'You take it. It's been great, really great. Done my boy the world of good.'

Still Hugh hesitated. But why say no when the man clearly wouldn't miss the money, and he needed it?

He took it. 'Hope you'll make it back one day.'

'We sure will try to.'

They set off. Hugh counted the notes – sixty pounds. That was twice what he would have charged.

He pocketed it and started pulling down the sails.

Something made him glance up – a sense that he was being watched. A flash of absurd hope – maybe Cari ...

He swivelled round. It was Yvonne, who for months had hardly come near him, now standing about six feet away.

'Hi,' she said, trying to sound as if this were a normal encounter.

'How did you get here? I didn't hear you.'

'I was there.' She pointed to an upturned decaying rowing boat, just below the grass bank. 'On the other side of it. I watched you come in.'

'You devil!' They laughed.

'David didn't come this holiday.'

'No. He had to go to Austria.'

'I was wondering. It seems ages.'

'For me too.'

'He used to write to me sometimes,' she said. 'But he hasn't for a while.'

'Well, you know how kids are. It doesn't mean –'

'I know. I'm not much of a writer myself.'

She was still standing in the same spot, as if the distance had been precisely measured not to overstep the taboo. He turned back to go on pulling down the sails. 'I thought you were working in the shop Saturdays?'

'We close for lunch.'

'Of course.'

She squatted down on the sand now, watching him.

'You must have earned quite a bit. Are you saving for something?'

'A cassette player. We're going to the mainland soon, school trip. I can get one then.'

'I thought you'd just been last term?'

'That was just Penzance. This time it's Plymouth. Mr Cooper said we need the experience of getting around towns on our own. Everyone's been to Penzance, it's no challenge.' Then, voice different, tentative, 'Did you hear, Mr Cooper's left.'

'I did. What's happening to his classes?'

'We've got Mrs Lawrence.'

Mrs Lawrence – Tell me about her, he wanted to say –

Yvonne was doodling in the sand. Avoiding looking at him. 'I can't believe he went and did that.'

'You liked him, didn't you?'

She nodded, inarticulate.

Hugh waited. Then he said, 'Tell me.'

'Just – he never talked to us as if we were kids.'

Then suddenly she looked up, and for some reason he was convinced she was about to ask him for something. He had no idea what but he knew he would have to say No, and he also knew he wasn't going to be able to.

'Hugh, I wanted to ask you –'

He cut in, too quickly, 'Yvonne, just think. Maybe you should ask someone else.' He almost said, Someone your father is on speaking terms with.

'I haven't even said what.'

'It doesn't matter what it is. I don't want you in trouble.'

'I'm in trouble already.'

Say nothing, he told himself, keep out of this, whatever it is. She was looking straight at him, the skin around her nose and

141

cheeks pinched. 'I need money for something, and there's no one else I can ask. I didn't want to ask you.'

He walked over, sat down facing her. He couldn't let her talk over six feet of space, not about something that troubled her so much. He said quietly, 'Tell me what's going on.'

'Please don't ask me.'

'I have to ask you. You're grown up enough to understand that I can't lend you money without knowing what you need it for.'

'It's not a cassette player.'

'I know that.'

She said nothing. He waited. 'Yvonne.'

'It's not drugs either.'

'I know that too.'

'Hugh, I can't, it's not my secret. If it was just me I would tell you. Honest. I just want you to lend me some money and promise not to tell anyone, and everything will be OK. I'll work in the summer and pay it back then.'

'What kind of money?'

She said, hardly audible, 'Fifty pounds?'

He did not move, staring out to sea. Then he put his hand in his pocket and pulled out the wad of notes the boy's father had given him. 'Take it. And now get off this beach before someone sees you.'

≈≈

Cari could not shed the feeling that she was doing something illicit, joining a boatload of holiday-makers on a Monday morning. A low-level sense of guilt had become habitual to her now, and heading for St Martin's triggered it, though all she was doing was carrying out her duty by going to visit the school. She had not even told Andrew that she would doing this today – she had almost said something at breakfast, and then hesitated, and the moment was lost.

She sat near the front of the boat, where the boatman was chatting to the young man who collected tickets. She wasn't listening particularly, but the word 'Hugh' came stabbing towards her, and she strained to catch the rest of what they were saying. Just then they hit a wave caused by a passing boat, and the boat bumped and the spray came over and the passengers shrieked in excitement. The boatman grinned. His mate announced to the rest of them, 'His wife was cross with him this morning so he's taking it out on you.' Everyone laughed. And whatever they might have been saying about Hugh was lost.

The islands had never seemed more beautiful to her, colours cut clear as crystal by the sun, light sparkling on the water. The sort of beauty that is inseparable from a knowledge of loss. She remembered the sea looking like this in her childhood, on days the wind was quiet and you could almost imagine it would let you alone to sail safely on to where you wanted to go. She remembered feeling the callousness in that beauty, that if it suddenly changed mood it would pay no attention, however hard you screamed.

The boat pulled up next to the quay. She was the last out, in no hurry, savouring this day of freedom. She tuned in again to the boatman talking to a couple of locals, handing over mail and loading on parcels to be delivered to St Mary's. 'Tell Hugh that the part for his motor hasn't come yet,' the boatman said.

Up the hill, down the one real road that ran the length of the island. Winding past small grey stone houses with pink and yellow splashes of colour from the gardens. Past the post office, the cafe, then fields and a few farmhouses. That one on the left, ahead – Yvonne Penruth's house, with the path from the beach coming up next to it. That was where she and Karl and Eva had crossed over to the other side of the island, lifetimes ago. Difficult now even to revisit the feelings of the time. A soap bubble that had caught her with its light and colour and then burst, and life had moved on. To – what?

She arrived at the school. It was smaller even than she had imagined, seven children and one teacher in a single room. A luxury in a way, time for so much individual attention, but quite a challenge too, to keep life varied enough. The teacher introduced her, got the children to show her what they were busy with. She spent time with the whole group and a bit more with the two oldest who were coming to St Mary's next year. Then the task was done. She gave the little ones a cuddle, waved to the bigger ones, and she was out again, in the sun. And she didn't have to go back to school.

'Take what's left of the day to catch up,' Neville had said. 'I'll cover your classes.'

She knocked. Hugh opened the door, stared.

'Good God, are you absconding?'

'They sent me over.' Now that she had done it, done what she had known all along she was going to do but not let herself think about, she was suddenly shy. 'To visit the school here.'

He said, instantly, 'I'll walk over with you.'

'I've done it. It took less time than I expected. I just thought – since I had time –'

It started raining. 'Come on in,' he said.

It rained and rained. Hugh said, 'If this weather would only lift I could take you out in the dinghy,' feeling that he ought to offer some way of entertaining her, that his company alone could hardly suffice. But Cari only laughed and said, 'I'm better on

144

land. Anyway, listen to that wind, no way is it going to lift.' So they stayed in the kitchen and talked. This time it was her doing it all. About the children at St Martin's school – she had noticed everything there was to see about them, as far as he could tell, and all in one short visit. About Paul Cooper doing a bunk. About her childhood on St Mary's. He waited for her to come to the man in her life, but she didn't.

It was nearing lunch-time. He was waiting for her to say, 'I'd better get the two o'clock boat,' but she didn't. Maybe she saw him watching for it, for she said, 'Neville's covering my classes.'

'Right, lunch.' He got out bread, cheese, pickles, washed a couple of tomatoes. 'Pretty basic, I'm afraid.' Thinking, there's something bizarre going on here. Feeling alert, waiting for it to show itself.

They started eating. To cover the space he said, 'Neville taught me, you know.'

'He did?'

'The year I was on St Mary's, as a kid.'

'What was he like?'

'The only teacher I ever got on with.'

She laughed. 'I can imagine.'

'He was new himself, maybe he saw I wasn't having an easy time. Found out I liked birds, lent me books about them. I never knew till then you could learn anything useful in a book.'

Her eyes listening, intently. He dried up.

She said, 'It feels like I've known you forever.'

Now it was she who stopped, as if saying even that much were compromising. The silence had become charged. He tried to concentrate on spreading butter on bread. She's lonely, this woman, he felt the message pound through him, she's lonely, that's why she came looking for me. *Don't get involved.* She's got a man back there, keep well clear of this. But the very air

145

between them was beginning to pulse. He felt desire wakening, unfamiliar, painful, like blood throbbing back into hands that have been yellow and stiff from cold. Please, no, he told himself, life's complicated enough as it is. But he was defenceless.

Her voice, small like a child's now, 'I don't know what's happening to me, I feel out of control.'

Afterwards, only after his arms were around her and he was holding her tight, protecting her against he did not know what, only after she had accepted his arms and rested her head against him and wept, and he had rocked her and stroked her hair and carressed her cheek, only then did she tell him – pulling herself away from him to make it possible to talk.

'I need to tell you,' she said, 'I'm married.'

Of course. To someone she liked, she insisted, someone she used to think she loved. Her Andrew had done nothing, she said, nothing had changed between them. But she was protesting too much, trying to find again the loyal wife to set up against the other self that had spiralled out of control, following its own need. And then a long story he didn't want to hear, about the man who had been one of those she got caught in the storm with.

'There are things going around inside me that I never even knew it was possible to feel. I thought maybe when Karl had gone it would be like taking myself outside the field of a magnet, all the iron filings would just quietly rearrange themselves and I'd become normal again. But I see now it wasn't him, he just accidentally triggered it off, it's something in *me*. And the thing doesn't care who calls it up, it just needs out.'

She could not have said it more clearly. He, Hugh, was an accident, the next accident. Of course he had known it, yet he too had not the will to say No to this gift that he had not looked for but had come blowing into his life; to the power of bodies and spirits so suddenly and unexpectedly attuned. They sat at the kitchen table keeping that painful small space between them, and the rain battered at the window, and they both knew they were about to step over a line that once crossed could never be uncrossed, and the fear was all over her face – eyes too alert, body so slim, so vulnerable.

He put out both hands to hold hers and said quietly, 'We could run away from it or we could say, Thank God for the storm that blew you in here.'

He gave her another moment or two, to be sure she would not feel he was pushing her. She made no move to remove her hands. He said, trying to make her smile, 'I have a good solid bed, the best piece of furniture in the house. I made it myself.'

She let him lead her to it. They lay down together, both of them fully clothed. He lay with his arms around her, caressing her back gently through her T-shirt but stopping himself from doing more in case he should trigger off guilt, panic. She lay in his arms like a child, letting him hold her against the fear of her own need. Eventually some balance shifted and she began to touch him and to move. Her movement released all that he had been holding back, and his hands were under her T-shirt and pulling at the zip of her jeans and his. Then she too let herself be taken over by urgency, and they each pulled their own clothes off and threw them aside and were back lying together, and he was touching again the wonder of a woman's body, warm and soft and with that smell of fresh underarm sweat that drove all thought from his mind. He had become one with the wave, and was on her and moving in her, and the loneliness and pain of years dissolved in the moment of coming.

Three

The estuary, winter, early 1950s

They would let themselves quietly out of the door before dawn, Hugh and his dad, their breath like steam. Hugh's hands and toes would lose feeling as the cold got to them. He felt the wind on knees exposed between little-boy shorts and long socks. They made their way past the sleeping terrace of houses, alongside the allotments, then onto the raised path that ran through the flat fields, the only sound their feet crunching the frosted grass. Arrive at the high bank that hid the river from their view. Over it, and scramble down to the boat that waited for them, moored to an alder tree half hidden among rushes on the bank of the estuary.

The sound of the boat was the *siff-siff* of oars parting the water. The colour of the water was black, heaving swells of darkness, small movements of metallic glinting when there was light from the stars. The oars rested in his dad's hands as an even denser mass of dark came closer, and Hugh knew they had reached the island. Gradually he could make out the branches of willows, and he would duck as the boat slipped under. They climbed out, tied the boat, and in the first glimmer of dawn light they picked their way through the tall marsh grass toward the hut.

The hut was their secret, hidden by bushes, not visible until you were almost touching it. It was made of slats of wood, and was just high enough for his dad to stand in. It had no windows, but a thin slant of light from one side made by removing a plank, a narrow opening that ran the length of one wall, just at his dad's eye height. Hugh remembered ever afterwards that sensation of everything being black as the door closed, then the sound of the plank shifting and the long horizontal shaft of light. Then he stood on the low bench that his dad had built specially for him and put his face close to the space. His eyes took in the magic world on the other side – the framing branches of leaves; beyond them the reeds; beyond that, the shifting light on the water.

And the birds.

Then back to the house, where the fire was on, the kettle steaming, his mum stirring porridge.

Those were the times when his dad was back on leave. Looking back Hugh had no idea whether it had been days or weeks, only that it was special, time out of time. His dad worked on ships that sailed across the world. Each time he came back Hugh was half a year older. He would be there, and they would go down to the estuary and the boat, their place, their time. And then he would be gone.

'You can't keep that man away from boats,' Hugh heard his mum say to her friends. 'In the navy in the war, and in the navy he stayed when everyone else came back.'

His mum worked at the canteen. Hugh had to go to his auntie after school, till his mum fetched him. And sometimes in the evenings too, when she went out with her friends. His auntie grumbled but his uncle said, 'She's working hard, bringing in the money, no reason why she shouldn't.' Sometimes instead of going out she brought her girlfriends from the canteen home, and that he liked much better. They put on gramophone records and danced in the living room, bumping into the sofa and the chairs. When they had gone his mum plumped up the cushions on the sofa and said, 'Well that was a laugh.'

Sometimes – how often? Was it only a couple of times but so fixed in his memory that in later years it seemed constantly repeated? – he and his mum set off to the station, and he sat next to the train window as it travelled through fields and low hills, away from the estuary and the sea that were his dad's world. They got off at a small station surrounded by fields and a scattering of houses, and his mum told him the names of everyone who lived in every house. She talked with the women and joked with the men and carried the latest baby around on her hip. Hugh roamed around outside, free, none of the 'Don't go without me' of the streets in town. Sometimes one of his uncles showed him which fields grew potatoes and which ones onions, and let him help look for eggs in the hen house. Then he and his mum had to back on the train because tomorrow was Monday.

Then things changed. His dad came back, and this time for good. He'd had enough, he said, he wanted to be home, so he got work in the boatyard down at the harbour. The house was crowded – his dad was a big man and took up lots of space. His mum seemed to get cross much more often. His dad didn't like it when his mum went out with her friends. His mum said, 'You can't just arrive and start ordering me around when for years you've hardly shown your face.' But there was still the estuary, and sometimes after a Saturday evening of raised voices Hugh would wake when it was still dark to see his dad standing next to his bed, saying quietly, 'Coming with me?' And they would slip out of the door, past the sleeping houses, along the raised path, to the boat. And onto their island as the dawn arrived. To be where everything was still and they were the only people on earth, and they could feel the air shift around them, and smell the sea, and watch the birds.

He was seven when his mum disappeared. No one told him where, or why. His auntie started to come in every day and took over the cooking, and only let him have one teaspoon of golden syrup with his porridge. His dad ate breakfast in silence, went to work and came back, and for months said almost nothing in the evenings either.

Hugh hadn't minded school before but now it seemed to him an overwhelming place, crowded, noisy, closed-in, rough. In class he was expected to sit without moving for hours. In the playground he seemed surrounded by boys bigger and tougher than him. He longed for affection and gentleness but knew it would be dangerous to show it. He had one close friend, a largely wordless companionship formed around collecting snails, but with others he was awkward, and when they wouldn't let him alone he got into fights without knowing how it happened. Being punished made no difference for it wasn't within his control.

At home his mum was never mentioned. He tried to keep hold of her through small rituals that linked him to her. Porridge with golden syrup was the only breakfast he would consider. He splashed his face with cold water every morning. When no one was looking he plumped the cushions on the sofa. He took tea to his dad, making it the way he liked it, the way his mum used to. And at school he began to find his role. Tough as he was with boys his size, he was always gentle with younger children. He picked them up if they fell and grazed their knees. He noticed the ones who were being left out and stood up for them. He felt this as something that connected him to his mum, though how he could not tell.

His dad began to talk again. Not much, that was never his way. But he let Hugh help him when he was doing things in the shed and occasionally he took him down to the boatyard to watch what the men did. Later Hugh took to going there straight from school and finding ways to make himself useful.

There was a sense of possibilities about the harbour, boats always setting off and coming back, the sea stretching out beyond where you could imagine.

He was thirteen when his dad announced that as soon as the school term ended they were going to an island out to sea where a friend of his had fixed up work for him over the summer, repairing a yacht. At first what excited Hugh was the idea of actually setting out in a ship, being one of the people who travelled rather than the watcher from the shore. But from the moment of leaving land another excitement was born, to do with the sea itself. He was on it, part of it almost. It was so vast, so open. He felt his chest expanding, his eyes become sharper. For the first time since his mum had disappeared he stopped feeling tight and closed-up.

His dad's work on the island lasted longer than he had expected, and the summer turned into a whole year. Hugh had taken over managing the household, a minimal functional style that he had worked out for himself but which owed something to his auntie's training. He went to the island school, which he found unnerving at first because it was so small – he had learnt to use the size and anonymity of city schools to his advantage, avoiding attention from those in authority. But he made one real friend, a boy called Garth, a year or two younger than him, who knew all the island birds and showed him places where they nested. Occasionally when they were out together at weekends he would think about how this island contrasted with the one in the estuary that he and his dad had shared as their secret place. This was vast in comparison, but there were moments when it evoked the same sense of wonder. The wind, the water, the silence of the pre-dawn dark. The movement of the rushes, as they watched the birds.

He did eventually find out what had happened to his mum. By then they were back on the mainland and it was his auntie who told him, though why she chose finally to break the silence he never worked out. His mum had gone to Australia, she said; and though the word was never used, he understood that it was with a lover. His auntie would say no more; perhaps she knew no more. And he couldn't bring himself to ask, for even thinking the questions evoked a terrible confusion of loyalties. His auntie was his *dad*'s sister and had always disapproved of the things his mum had enjoyed doing; maybe more so because his uncle had taken her side. He didn't want to hear his auntie's version only.

But there was no getting away from it, she had gone, left them. Had she not at least written? Maybe she had and his dad not told him? Or had she simply cut off from everything about her past life, including her child? Too complicated, too many feelings let loose. He shut down the questions. The next day he got into a fight with one of the teachers, stormed out of school, and that night told his dad he was never going back.

'*Why?*' demanded his dad. But he did not know. Could not tell.

In the years before some inner compass finally brought him back to the island, in those lost years when he felt constantly on the edge of chaos – getting a job, taking offence at his boss, leaving suddenly, starting again somewhere else – two things only remained constant. One was his passion to save enough to buy his own boat. The other was less tangible. He struggled to find within himself traces of the time before his mum had left, when things were still whole. But memory, in wiping out feelings it would have been too painful to hold on to, had closed off so much else he would have liked to reclaim. He was left with isolated fragments. Certain sounds would remind him of the sound his mother's feet had made as she came down the stairs in the morning. A chance encounter – sitting next to a young mother with children in a bus – would unnerve him by reawakening the warm smell of being close to her body. He remembered her taking him on the train to the village where she knew the names of everyone in each house. He remembered her dancing with her friends, and plumping up the cushions after they had gone.

But that was all.

≈≈

St Mary's, late April 1984
Cari and Andrew sat opposite each other at dinner. A monumental silence seemed to have engulfed them and there was nothing she could do to break it. Every attempt at conversation felt artificial, struggling through the fear that she had damaged the intimacy between them beyond repair, trying to hide from the confusion of not knowing whether she wanted it back. She delayed going to bed each night and was grateful when her period came on, to give her an excuse. She was afraid even to start a simple cuddle in case it made him throw back at her what he must be feeling. Then she would swing again, thinking, maybe he isn't feeling anything, maybe he's simply gone down a plughole of his own concentration and hasn't a clue what's been going on for me.

In the staff room, in the shops, in the pubs, Cari overheard people chewing over the scandal of Paul Cooper's disappearance. An astonishing number of people now admitted to never having trusted him. They had always thought there was something not quite right about how matey he was with the older children. Teachers ought to keep a proper distance. The head ought to have made him resign at Christmas when his wife left.

They've forgotten all the good things about him, Cari thought, the hours of extra energy he put into organising outings. Listening to the character assassination was like watching someone else fall off a cliff, while she, Cari, was still hanging on; but only just. What if it someone had seen her up on Chapel Down with Hugh? Maybe more than once? Someone who knew she was married and who thought it their duty to report back to Neville? To say, 'We can't have that kind of woman in charge of our girls.' What if Andrew were suddenly to say, 'I can't take this any more, I'm going back?' And she said, 'I can't come with you, I'm not ready to leave?' *She* would be the one getting it then. Exceptional personal circumstances – she had her own version of those. Something happening she couldn't explain to anyone, even herself.

She thought about phoning Hugh. There was a phone in his kitchen, she had seen it. But what would she say? She couldn't say, 'I'm coming again,' and she couldn't say, 'I'm never coming again.' She couldn't say, 'I have this glow all through me whenever I think about us together. It's so beautiful, I can't stop holding it, even though the rest of me is saying, You're crazy, shut it down.' She couldn't say, 'I'm restless whenever I'm in the house, I have so much to do but I can't concentrate. Yesterday I just had to get out, wanted to come to you, knew I couldn't, went out anyway, didn't know where I was heading' ...

– Arrived at my cove. The tide was half way out, a wind blowing, quite strong. She walked out over the sand till she got to where the water was up to her calves. There was a kind of haze, something shiny out near Great Gannick but she couldn't see exactly. She watched it, fantasising that it was his boat, that he was looking this way, thinking of her. Then she squatted and watched the movement of the waves, imagining through them the rhythm of their naked bodies moving together. Thinking, This is enough for the rest of my life. It doesn't matter what happens now, I've had this.

She couldn't use the phone booth in town, far too exposed. But there was one up on Telegraph Hill. She could detour on her way back from school. But no directory in the phone booth. She could phone directory enquiries. But then she might find herself speaking to someone down in the town, the mother of one of her pupils. Besides, she still had no idea what she would say even if she got his number.

She came out of the phone booth – to see, going in the opposite direction, the woman on the bike. She felt exposed, caught in an illicit act.

≈≈

Hugh was having trouble sleeping. That had never happened to him before. At the worst time after Sylvie had left misery had had the opposite effect. It was the evenings then that were the hardest with the house so bloody empty, so he had taken to going to bed more or less as soon as he had eaten. His body had seemed to know that cutting out was the only way to survive, and sleep had come almost instantly. A heavy, dead sort of sleep, from which he woke tired the next morning, reluctant to face yet another day. Now the opposite was happening, no death-wish but life stirring, afraid to let go in case he missed the crucial moment. So irrational; and so cruel, to be brought back to the awareness of desire only to have to face his impotence.

Three days since Cari had lain with him, and no word from her since. Her silence spoke clear enough – I can't let it happen again. She was right, of course she was, and he had complications enough without adding an injured husband on St Mary's.

But he kept seeing pictures of her, Cari lying next to him, Cari sitting opposite him at the kitchen table, Cari perched on a stone wall on Chapel Down, her dark hair swinging as she walked – at a time when he had thought her physical presence was having no effect on him; but he had it memorised.

Let go, he intoned to himself through the wakeful night. Let go, he told himself as he stared out across the sea of many moods, the waters between the islands, and tried to read in them the spirit of what moved the woman he had no claim to. *Let go.*

He knew that the time had come to do something when he went over his usual limit at the pub on Saturday night. Before he realised it he had started being abusive to some poor sod he had never seen before, one of the self-catering cottage people. He caught hold of himself in time and tried to cover it with a matey arm around the guy's shoulder and stood him a pint. Then he walked out into the night, went round to the tap by the back door, put his head under it and turned it on full.

It was a long time since this had happened and the alarm was sounding in his head. He had been close to breaking the one fundamental rule of survival, never alienate visitors. Private feuds among the residents were one thing, as long as they were kept well out of view. But pleasantness to visitors was the islands' essential commercial asset, the one thing they needed to add to what nature had so liberally provided, to make sure that people kept coming. No one would forgive him if he transgressed that rule.

He spent the next day doing the most physically tiring things he could find, chopping wood, digging a new pit for refuse. It served, but only just. He had lost the capacity to work for himself. Each completed task awaited an admiring eye. He had known he was lonely but until Cari came he had not let himself feel the depths of his need. One small touch of nourishment and now his whole system rebelled, demanding more.

Eventually he took the only action he could think of and telephoned the school.

A woman's voice answered. He held the receiver, paralysed. Then put it down without replying.

This was pathetic, he was sweating with embarrassment like a pimply school boy. How was he going to get past the damn school secretary? He had not the least idea what to say. 'Who shall I say it is?' the secretary would ask – and who *should* he say? He could see the woman looking in puzzlement at the receiver that had gone blank. If he phoned again she would be suspicious, And she was a friend of Sylvie's, to boot. He had seen them wave to each other once in a crowd at a gig race that they had all gone over to watch from St Mary's. 'Who's that?' he had asked, by now distrustful of any signs of a life of her own that didn't include him.

'Laura Edmonds. One of my friends from the choir.'

Bloody choir again. Why had she suddenly needed to go off and do that? She'd never sung in her life that he'd ever heard. 'I did,' Sylvie said, 'at school. And I loved it.' But he knew it was about getting away from him. She denied it and then refused to argue any more – which drove him mad and she knew it. Later she said, 'It's St Martin's I need to get away from. It's getting me down, it's just too small. I need more company.' But it came to the same thing.

'And how are you going to get back?' he demanded. 'I'm certainly not taking the boat out at night to fetch you.'

'I don't need you to, Anna says I can stay overnight with her.'

Overnight now. 'And not see David before he goes to school next day?'

'For one day a week, Hugh! And you do his breakfast anyway.'

Unanswerable. But not the point, he realised – it wasn't David who would feel abandoned. And when had she suddenly come to be such friends with Anna?

'Anna said the choir was a lifesaver in her first months.'

'So you need your life saved,' he shouted, and walked out of the house, to start up his tractor and head for the top field, which needed turning, though not necessarily today. To the end of each furrow, turn, and back again, trying not to think about Anna and Sylvie sitting up late into the night every Tuesday after choir, and Anna listening while Sylvie churned over her resentments, and Anna believing her, never considering that there might be things *he* could say.

'Anna says,' Sylvie would say when she got back on Wednesdays. Anna says. But even without saying anything Anna was dangerous, for the image she held up – a woman who had made a new life for herself by walking out on the man she had got tired of.

Christ, he was working himself up again. *Stop it*, let it go.

Dial again. Ringing tone. Adrenalin pumping. Same voice answering.

'Can I speak to Mrs Lawrence?'

'May I say who is calling?'

'A friend.'

Voice more official, 'Please hold on.'

Heart thumping as he waited.

'Hello?' Cari's voice.

Everything went quiet inside him, lulled by the absurd relief of the sound. 'Cari,' apologetic now that his own needs were minimally met, 'I'm sorry to barge in at the school, I didn't know what else to do.'

'No one has ever phoned me here. I thought maybe it was my

sister, something gone wrong. She's travelling, I never know where.'

'I want to see you again.' He hadn't thought past this minute but now in the urgency a plan emerged, as if long prepared. 'I can come over to your cove this afternoon. Can you get there?'

God, please don't let her say no.

She said, 'You know which it is?'

'I was there just the other day.'

A pause, as she took that in. Then, 'OK. Make it four-thirty.'

≈≈

Getting to Jason's beach followed a ritual, unalterable and therefore comforting. First Anna leaned her bicycle against a tree at the turning in the lane. No lock; no need. She patted its saddle, telling it to stay there and hide her tracks, and then she set off down the lane. Early May, the air gentle, colour in the hedgerows. She paused as she reached the half-concealed entrance to the side path, checking there was no one is sight and then pushed through the tangle of growth. Escapes from the windbreaks, purple bottlebrushes of hedge veronica, small glossy-red trumpets of escallonia.

She emerged into the light, sweeping back from her face the loose strands of hair that had got caught on the bushes as she passed, and stood taking it in, that incredible sweep of space. Green to the edge of the land, the water beyond, the sky doming over it all, white clouds sailing. Earth, water, air; and way below, the cove. Seabirds circled, crying a plaintive *kak, kak, kak,* then a yelping wail, *keeow, keeow.* She began to lower herself carefully over the hump, steadying herself with her hands. And as she did so she heard another sound.

A voice, human this time. Coming from down below.

Anna froze. A scuffle of light wind, taking the voice with it. Then the wind turned again and she heard, as clear as if it were right next to her. 'We're alone,' it said, a man's voice, and she could have sworn she knew it, though distorted by the wind she could not be sure. 'We're alone,' reverberated inside her, this voice that had robbed her of the aloneness of this place.

She turned, moving as quietly as she knew how to head back up the cliff. But as she breasted the next curve in the land she heard another voice, a woman's this time. 'I'm scared.'

Flee. Flee, pursued by some emotion too strong to name. Back along the bracken path, pulse racing. Through the overgrown shrubs. Onto her bike. Off, wind in her hair. She cycled as if in a small invisible capsule of air that moved around her, travelled with her. Her private air, that no one could invade.

She closed the door of her house and stood leaning with her back against the wall, panting slightly. Then slowly she began to move through the small rooms, hanging up her anorak, going to the toilet, then to the kitchen, packing away the dishes from the draining board. Automatic actions, calming in their familiarity. She poured herself a whisky and went to stand sipping it as she stared out of the window at the bay. This is just absurd, she told herself. Stop panicking. Nothing has happened. Nothing has changed.

The whisky glass was empty. Pour another.

We're alone, said the voice from the cove. *Totally alone.*

The voice had got inside her, to a vulnerability she tried to tell herself she had moved past but that was there forever, waiting only to be exposed. Please, she asked – who? The voice? The sea? The cliffs, that listened to no plea? Please, she said aloud to that disturbing image of desire overheard, not quite witnessed, Please, to the voice that she was convinced she knew, though she would not name it, even to herself. *Please leave me alone.*

What was it that had panicked her so? That her privacy had been invaded, yes. That someone else had taken over this one spot on the earth she had assumed to be – not hers, precisely, but *available* to her alone, for she alone understood its significance. A space more spiritual than material, but the essential precondition for that was the absence of any other person. What would she do now that that had changed? Would she go back? She did not know. The instinct for self-constructed rituals began to work away inside her – *find a way not to need it*, her rational mind told herself. Perhaps the cove had served its purpose. Find a way to give back that small, fragile beach to the sea that had created it, wearing down the rocks of the cliff grain by grain, back to the sea from which we came and which receives its own back. Never caring, never noticing, continuing backwards and forwards, in and out, the rhythm of the tides, cancelling feeling.

≈≈

No one could see them. There was nothing but the sand under their legs, the slow-moving clouds above their heads, the protective sides of the cove keeping the world away. He could hear the waves lapping against his boat, pulled up on the sand just yards away.

'Have you brought it far enough in?' Cari asked. Anxious, about every little thing. The boat was right there, near enough for him to pat its side to reassure her.

'The water's yards away. It doesn't get any higher than this.'

His hands were moving over her, bodies tight against each other, 'Hugh, we can't –' Trousers loosened, denying her words. T-shirts lifted, flesh on flesh, desperate to get closer still. 'Hugh –'

He didn't know how to handle her fear. If he pushed past it she might feel that he had forced her.

She pulled away, wriggled her trousers back up, sat up, moving away from him as she did so. They stared at each other. 'I feel a fool,' she said.

He got to his feet, pulled his trousers up, did up the zip and turned away from her, walking to the wall of the cove. He stood there viciously pulling plants out from the crevices of the rock. His back to her he said, 'I'll go mad if I have to go back into that silence.'

'I'll phone you.'

He turned. '*Yes*.' Then, petulant, like a child some adult is trifling with, 'You could have phoned all this last week. You could have talked to me at least, like you're talking now.'

'I wanted to.' She broke off, earnest for him to understand, 'I was trying to let things get back to normal again.'

'Normal meaning saying No to something so good.'

'Normal meaning how other people are, how I used to be. Just getting on with each day as if everything is settled.'

'If you don't phone I'm going to keep phoning the school.'

'Hugh, please! It's not safe. Once was enough to make the secretary curious. Twice and they'd all know.' Then suddenly she started talking as if he were someone else, someone to whom she could confide, who would hear without taking advantage. 'I can't tell you what it's been like. I feel everyone's waiting, to watch me fall. All through my childhood I thought of this as the safest place I knew. Because it was contained, small enough for everyone to know each other and feel connected. Now –'

'Yes. Exactly. You can't bloody get away from them. It's not the people that keep me here, that's for sure.'

'You can't live without other people.'

'There's the land, the sea. The rocks. The birds. You only need one or two people to be close to. You can survive without the rest.'

'Not me, I'm not made like that.' Then, 'When I didn't phone – I was also trying not to stir things up for you.'

He jerked away, a whole-body movement of denial.

'And there's this whole other agenda in your life, Sylvie, David, people on the island being mad at you. I can't cope with being drawn into that. You think I'd be a solution, but I wouldn't. I'd be just another complication.'

He got up, walked to the water's edge and began mechanically picking up stones and throwing them out to sea. After a few minutes the activity developed its own rhythm. He cut out from thinking, just concentrated on each throw.

She was standing behind him now. He felt her hand on his back, touch warm. He didn't turn. Her voice came over his shoulder, quiet now. 'And for me you represent things you don't even know about. Two days ago I caught myself singing The Raggletaggle Gypsies. In the cottage, with Andrew there. I was horrified, like I'd been saying aloud, for him to hear, I want to walk out on all this, everything we've had together, and –'

He turned. 'And what?'

'The gypsy. In the song she runs off with a gypsy. Because he sings so sweet.' She was looking at him, unblinking. 'A man with mud all over his clothes and life bursting out of him, not confined by buildings.'

She stopped. The only sounds were those of the sea behind them. He could not speak. He reached out his hands to touch her again.

'Cari, we're alone, totally alone.'

She said, 'I'm scared.'

167

It took her longer than usual to climb back up from the cove, for she stopped every few steps to watch Hugh's boat disappearing into a shiny speck on the far water. Then she thought she saw a shadow move in the bushes ahead of her. She waited, breath suspended, for it to move again. Nothing.

She climbed on but her fragile equilibrium was shaken. She was afraid if she rushed she would lose concentration and slip. Her body was alive still to his touch, the nearness of his flesh, and just beneath that, to the fear that had made her pull away. 'I don't understand you,' he had said, and there had been nothing she could say, for she didn't understand herself. When you are loving with your entire spirit and touching all over, why does that one act matter so much more than any other?

Out of the overgrown part now and hurrying along the lane. She slowed down as she neared the house of Mrs Tremain, the farmer from whom they rented the cottage. Cari walked softly over the crunchy stones, hoping no one would be about. You can't have so much light in you without it showing, she thought, and she tried to rearrange her face at least.

Mrs Tremain was in the yard. 'Ollie's gone missing again.'

'Missing?'

'He does this sometimes. Working on the passenger boats they get odd days off, never weekends because that's the busy time. Sometimes takes them in Penzance, but he never thinks to tell me. So I've got dinner waiting and no Ollie. I'm beginning to think there's a girl over there.' And then, as if the thought connected, 'You're back late today.'

'There's so much to do since Paul Cooper left,' Cari said, but too quickly.

'Actually I'll be glad if Ollie has another girl. He's been mooning around after Yvonne Penruth for far too long, and everyone can see she's not going to have him.'

No one ever gets the ones they want, Cari thought. We'd all be far better off without desire.

Andrew had the meal ready.

'You're late.'

'I stayed to finish things off at school rather than carry it back.'

She had never done that before, why now? She tried again. 'I wish we had a phone, then I could tell you if that happens.'

Now she was making too much of it, it must be obvious. This was awful, she couldn't go on like this.

Everywhere she went now she had to summon up an effort not to see Hugh's face. When she thought she was managing, her dad kept reappearing instead. She looked out at the harbour, where once in childhood her dad's boat had moored. She walked past The Yachtsman's Friend, family business of young Brad Tointon in her fourth year class. Passing it she was assailed again by the musty smell of coiled rope, could see without even going in the wooden slatted steps that led up to the half-lit upper room, where once she and Robyn had explored the stacks of strange objects piled up in baskets while below her dad discussed the exact requirements of what he was looking for. She liked the straightforwardness of the place, no thought of display. Like her dad himself. Like Hugh.

She couldn't go straight home after school, however much she knew it was important not to be late again. She walked through the town on the pretext of doing a little shopping, past the pub where she and Andrew had sat in their first weeks here, listening to the men tell stories about dangers at sea. It had been her dad's energy she had heard in their voices, unavoidably attractive yet untrustworthy, *his* hands on the ropes, his face

169

staring out to assess the waves. It made her afraid, that pre-occupation with strength, for however powerful they thought themselves the waves were always stronger. But there was something about them that she couldn't stop watching. When Andrew spoke to her she had to flick her attention deliberately to notice him.

'Which one are you fancying?' he had asked, teasing. But there was something beneath the light tone that she had shied away from. When they had made love that night it had been an effort to work up any enthusiasm. His body felt pale, uninteresting, his need too localised, wanting release but no life force behind it that connected to her own. She had felt unnerved, as if she had allowed herself to see something it would have been better not to know.

A morning on Tresco, visiting the school. Just getting off St Mary's for those few hours gave her a kind of distance on herself. All marriages have sticky patches, she told herself in the boat coming back. It's just a matter of effort, *deciding* to make it work.

'I'll cook tonight,' she told Andrew when she got in. 'I bought some prawns for a treat.'

'What's the occasion?'

'Just, I've been so busy lately, I thought it was my turn.'

He said, as they sat down to eat, 'Cari, I've been wanting to talk to you. I've decided I have to go back.'

She stared at him, stunned. So sudden. No discussion, just, 'I've decided.' He was talking now, detail she couldn't follow about his mathematical problems, the need to talk to his supervisor. It was several minutes before she realised, it's just his work he's going for, he's not saying he's leaving me.

'Yes,' she said. And 'Yes, of course I see.' And 'It'll be fine, don't worry about me.' But still she couldn't believe the calm tone, and was too afraid to ask, 'Is it *only* your work?' But the not-asking was like a cloud descending, smothering what small naturalness had been left to them.

Now a misery of hyper-sensitivity, needing to hold on yet unable to take that first move. She remembered, and painfully, the things she had loved about him when they first got together. The shared laughter over little things. His amazement the first time he saw her open a milk bottle, sticking her thumb through the silver top where he had been taught to lift it carefully all the way round. How she had teased him out of his embarrassment when his nose got red on cold winter mornings. Andrew explaining to her how a radio worked, which no science teacher had ever succeeded in doing. Andrew's pleasure in puzzles of all kinds, the more complex the better; and that phenomenal ability to concentrate that she could watch still with awe even though it was the thing that also removed him from her. In the first heady months of being together that intense focus had been turned onto her and she had come to life in its beam, rescued from that state of vagueness that had been her adolescence.

Andrew had been her growing up; now she was leaving him behind. She sat listening to him, watching his gesticulating hands across the table. There was something odd happening to her vision, he seemed to be moving further and further away from her. But it was she who was moving, letting the wave catch her and carry her out, deeper than either of them had ever ventured, while he stood there in the shallows with the water lapping about his ankles, getting smaller every minute and saying, 'I expect it'll be about three weeks.'

Three weeks could mean anything. 'Three weeks for you to sort yourself out, and when I come back I need to know where this is all going.' Or simply, 'Three weeks to work with my supervisor.' Perhaps he would wake once he was away from all this and allow himself to see what he had been closing his eyes to. She could imagine him already in Birmingham, saying, like Paul Cooper's wife, 'There's no way I'm going to stick myself back on that island.' What was there here for him to come back to? She would get a letter, perhaps. 'Dear Cari, This probably won't come as a surprise to you. I'm sorry I didn't find a way to say it before I left.'

Please, she pleaded silently, as on his last night they went through the motions of love-making, like strangers afraid to offend. Please, said her arms, clinging too closely and not feeling any responding tenderness in his, I didn't mean to. I really didn't. Please let me try again.

≈≈

Anna was grateful to have Yvonne coming. She felt in need of distraction, a bed to be made up, flowers in a little vase. Yvonne would be easy company. Brought up to an assumption of closeness because Anna was family, and yet detached; the ideal combination.

They sat together in the kitchen that evening before the school trip, perched companionably on the children's stools, eating carrot cake and chatting. The cake was still warm, a last-minute idea. Anna had got out the baking tins to distract herself from the sight of Yvonne packing and repacking her already packed bags, changing her mind about which face cream to take, trying on clothes and taking them off again. Whose eye did she imagine judging her clothes? Surely not her classmates, whom she saw every day? An unknown young man she might meet in Plymouth? Or perhaps even a known one, someone who had been on the islands on a holiday? Or met when Bella had taken her to visit her gran?

Make something, she decided, and moved to the kitchen. Absurd really, for by the time the cake was ready Yvonne would have gone to bed. But she did it anyway, pleased to be able to still the mind with small decisions of form, of texture. A carrot cake emerged, steaming and luscious. She looked at it with pleasure, at the brown shine on the top, the fat shape. 'Cake,' she called through to Yvonne, 'come and try it,' and said, 'So *there*' to the earlier self that would have told her own children, 'You'll have bad dreams if you eat just before you sleep.' So much unnecessary clutter she had landed them with.

They sat together to munch. Anna asked Yvonne about things at home. Yvonne told her about her new history teacher. 'We used to have her for English, now we have her for history too, *and* she's our form teacher.'

'Is that tolerable?'

'It's great. She's really cool.'

'Define cool.'

This was clearly beyond Yvonne. 'You *know*.'

'I don't, that's why I'm asking.'

'Well, she's — I don't know. She tells great stories, makes it like you are really there. And we can say whatever we're thinking, she doesn't over-react like some of them. You sort of get the feeling she knows you, and it's OK.' A flash of something indefinable crossed her face, evoking feelings far from cool.

After Yvonne had gone to bed Anna sat for a while in the almost- dark of the living room, legs tucked up under her in her armchair, sipping a whisky. Light off, so she could look out at the night and make out the shape of the old harbour wall, the dark space beyond that was the water. It felt wholesome to have the girl sleeping upstairs but maybe it was a good thing it was only one night. She was remembering now Bella's worry about the girl looking peaky. For the first few hours she had seen no trace of it, until that flash of vulnerability, gone almost before it had shown itself. Being her *age* is vulnerable, she told herself; but now the anxiety had got into her too. The islands were so protected. She felt as if she were watching a nineteenth century novel being enacted, Hardy maybe, or George Eliot, the farm girl preparing to set off for the city, heading for disappointment.

'Don't be ridiculous,' she told herself – silently, she had thought, but then she realised it was aloud, a thing which happened too often for comfort these days.

Yvonne ate nothing at breakfast, could hardly wait to go. They got the bus into town. Anna felt the warmth of the girl's leg against hers on the bus seat. There was a scent about her that owed nothing to whatever she had carefully applied this morning, just the freshness of a young, healthy creature. No acne marred the smoothness of her face, no embarrassed slouch to hide the lift of her breasts.

A small crowd on the pier. Yvonne's friends were calling out to each other, getting into excited huddles. Anna saw the looks on the faces of the parents, with difficulty accepting their irrelevance. It doesn't matter at all, she wanted to say. Nothing matters except that they exist and that you are allowed to love them.

Across the sea of heads she watched Neville, central figure in this small community though he too had come to it as an outsider. Admiring as always the light way he wore his role, chatting to those nearest to him, not fussing anyone with instructions. He turned her way and she waved. He lifted his hand in an answering movement, and after a few minutes detached himself from the conversation to get near enough to say, 'I've photocopied the Bach. Come over and get your copy this weekend if you like.'

'I'll do that.'

He moved off. That man has it all, she thought, watching his head bent now to answer a question from a teacher who was tensely trying to keep track, ticking things off on lists. Neville said something that made the teacher laugh, momentarily shedding her tension. Does he *never* feel any of his own, Anna wondered?

The teacher was back fussing. 'Pick up that bag, Kelly, you don't want to leave it behind.' In charge and not liking it. 'You lot over there, can you come here where you can hear me.'

A little to one side she caught sight of the young woman again, the one who had helped her when she came off her bike. She was watching the school party as one watches people one knows, and now it was suddenly obvious to Anna who she must be, the new teacher. And a young man with her this time. Her arm linked through his, her slight body clinging too close. He let her arm rest there but as if it were something he didn't quite know how to free himself from. A briefcase in his other hand, a suitcase at his feet, mind focusing on what he was going to. Her closeness was the afraid-not-to-be-near kind, not the need-to-touch of desire, and just watching it made Anna uncomfortable, so painfully at variance with the way this same young woman walked and stood when she was alone. Stop *clinging*, she wanted to say, it won't get you anywhere He doesn't *want* your arm, just let go and stand free.

She turned away. Someone else's misery, not hers. Why feel it so personally? Was it not enough to feel the things that were hers? Too bloody permeable, she was, no barriers to keep out what she was not called upon to handle.

A sudden flurry in the crowd, movement up at the front.

Parents checked yet again that their young had enough money, their tickets. The youngsters said, 'Of *course* I have, mum,' and detached themselves from the embarrassing concern. Yvonne came flying back, 'Thanks Aunt Anna,' and was off with the rest of them, all pushing forward now.

The young couple seemed stuck, not knowing how to handle the parting. He hugged her – too suddenly, too briefly. Then embarrassed by his own display he bent to pick up his case and walked towards the ship, not looking back.

Last hoot of the departing ship, deep and mournful. The crowd began walking back along the pier to the town, chatting as they went, but the young woman stood looking out to sea, watching the ship as if it were taking a stage of her life off with it and she did not know how to proceed to the future.

Anna waited for her to turn.

Cari turned, saw. They faced each other, neither moving. Cari was aware dimly that the pier was almost deserted now, just a few men moving trolleys and coiling up ropes, but her attention was wholly absorbed in the woman before her, no longer passing by.

'Hello.'

'Hello.'

'You helped me when I came off my bike.'

'I remember.'

'I was so confused, I probably didn't thank you properly.'

'No, no, you did. I hope you were OK.'

'It was fine.' Pause. 'I'm Anna Feldman.'

'I'm Cari Lawrence.'

The voice was entangled with the calls of seabirds wheeling overhead … Something nagging at the back of her mind, not just the bike incident. Where? When?

Anna said, 'What would you say to a cup of tea?'

'I'd love that.'

'The Harbour Restaurant does good cakes. Or we could go to my home.'

'Your home.'

'It's a bit of a walk. Old Town.'

'I know,' Cari said, cautious, as if trespassing.

You know. Of course, why should I be surprised? And in that acknowledgement of how connected they already were, the pieces came together in Anna's mind, and she knew where else she had heard Cari's voice. *I'm scared*, the voice had said, coming up the cliff face above Jason's beach.

They came over the top of the rise that until now had hidden Old Town from view. Below them the bay nestled in the soft morning air. Later than spring, earlier than summer, the light magical. Dark green yews in the churchyard, the morning sun glinting in from the sea, the houses clustered on the far side.

Anna said, 'Each time I look out over that bay I think, I can have this every day!'

'Yes,' Cari said. And then, caution loosening, '*Yes.*'

They reached the gate. Anna opened it. 'Welcome.' Inside she threw her coat over the back of a chair. 'Make yourself at home, I'll get the kettle on.' Thinking, this feels easy, like she's been here before.

Cari followed her into the kitchen. Kettle boiling, warm the teapot. Mugs. Milk. Anna opened the cake tin. 'You're in luck, I did some baking yesterday. The problem once your children have grown up is that your instinct to nourish keeps popping up, and then you have to eat it all yourself.' Plates on the tray. 'With obvious results.'

'You're not fat. Just nice and rounded.'

177

'That's very tactful. But it threatens. Particularly if I get too stuck in my painting and don't get out on my bike enough.' She cut two slices. Then looked at Cari and cut a third. '*You* could do with some fattening up.' She picked up the tray and led the way back to the living room. Settled into chairs, mugs in hands.

'So you're a teacher.'

'Yes. How did you –?'

'I'm Yvonne Penruth's aunt. She says you tell good stories.'

Cari laughed, a little embarrassed.

'What kind of stories?'

'Anything, really. But especially since I took over their history. You have to try to make sense of it for them.' Then, 'Was it your daughter who came at Easter?'

Instantly defensive. 'Yes.'

Cari, apologising, 'I saw the children playing in the sand.'

So stupid to react like that. Why shouldn't she ask? Anna made an effort. 'They loved the beach. They hadn't been before.' Then that seemed to need an explanation – 'Gail needs a little space from me. That's partly why I came here.' Then honesty wouldn't let her leave it at that. 'Actually it's a bit more complicated. But that was part of it.'

'That's amazing.'

'Why?'

'It just is. I can't imagine many mothers doing that.'

Anna shrugged. 'There were special circumstances.'

Cari applied herself to the cake. 'This is really good. Does it work for you, being here?'

Anna thought about the question before replying. 'Me, yes. My daughter's not so sure. My friends are frankly appalled. They're city people and think life stops if you're not rushing around.' I don't know why I'm saying these things, she thought, this girl can't possibly have enough life experience to

178

understand. But she heard her own voice once again voluntarily offering, 'I feel like I dumped all the clobber that was weighing me down and have freed up extraordinary amounts of time.'

Cari's mouth was full of cake. When she had swallowed she said, 'It shows.'

'What does?'

'That feeling, that you're becoming free.'

Anna said, sceptical, 'How?'

'It's what first made me see you. The way you go about on your bike, like it's entirely up to you where you go and how long you stay. And your hair!'

Anna's hand went up automatically to tuck the loose bits back under the pin.

'Don't, I love it like that.'

Anna dropped her hand. 'I calculated once how much I had been paying hairdressers to keep it under control all those years. It was far more each month than I spend on my painting equipment.'

'Does your painting support you?'

Anna laughed. 'Afraid not. I'm living on the back of the past. When my marriage ended we sold a sizeable house and I was left with half the proceeds. If I'm careful, it does for the basics.'

'You sound so – practical. Didn't you mind? Your marriage ending?'

Anna looked at her hand. 'Do you know, you're asking a lot of very personal questions.'

Cari looked stricken. 'I'm so sorry. I didn't mean –'

'But the odd thing is, I don't mind.'

'I – I don't know what to say. I feel really bad now.'

'Why? I've just told you I don't mind. And the answer to your question, it was a relief. I don't understand why I didn't end it years earlier. But twenty-eight years together, you forget who you are separately.'

'Twenty-eight years! I can hardly imagine it. It seems complicated enough after three.'

Yes, Anna thought, it looked like it, the way you hung on to him. Aloud she said, 'Most of the complications happen at the beginning. The rest is just working out what you were afraid to face then.' Outside a cloud shifted and a sudden shaft of light fell in on them. Anna said, 'I don't know what we're doing in here. We ought to get out and walk.'

They headed up to Tolman Point, on the path Anna walked so often alone. For a while it was too narrow for them to be side by side. She watched Cari ahead of her, envying the easy swing of limbs of someone young enough never to have felt a twinge of stiffness in the back. She sensed the girl stepping out into the space created by her husband's temporary departure, that rare experience of having no one else's interests to consult.

They reached the top and sat down on the heath. Cari's fingers trailed lightly over the birdsfoot trefoil that carpeted the spur of land, yellow heads tinged with red. What was she thinking? There was an insecure look that Anna wanted to banish.

She said, 'Yvonne talked about you quite a bit.'

Cari looked up, pulled back from wherever she had been.

'She feels you're very understanding.'

'Understanding?'

'Yes.'

Anna saw in amazement that Cari's eyes were slowly filling. She put out a hand to take the girl's. 'Oh my dear –'

'I'm sorry,' Cari said. 'This is so stupid.'

'Don't be sorry. Cry if you need to.'

'It's just that – I don't know what she means. I haven't done anything to – There hasn't been any call to –'

'You don't need to have done anything. It's who you are.'

'The truth is,' Cari gave a quick wipe at her eyes, 'I'm not feeling very good about myself.'

The story lurched out, a litany of guilt. A brilliant mathematician husband, attention always elsewhere. A man on St Martin's who had rescued them from a storm, a man in an isolated farmhouse, resourceful, alone, full of life-energy. The rest was so obvious that Anna would have wanted to laugh – but for the knowledge of who that man must be. Someone ought to warn this girl, that life-force of his can be dangerous.

But stronger than that was her distress at the girl's self-denigration, her inability to accept what she was feeling. Her words were the kind you hide behind. She did not once say 'desire' and shied even from 'love'. 'Obsessed' was what she said, a word with no dignity. She was tugging helplessly to free herself, hating her own feelings, her panic so pervasive that she had lost any sense of what it mattered to hide.

The outpouring came to an end. Anna said quietly, 'You're afraid.'

'Yes.'

'Of what, exactly?'

Cari stared. It was so obvious. But maybe it wasn't, even to her. Slowly she said, 'Being found out, I suppose. Especially by people at the school.' Then, flipping back into guilt, 'That's awful.'

'Why awful? Of course you don't want to be exposed. It's a very private experience.'

'But Andrew – until I said that, I thought what I was afraid of was damaging *him*.'

'It's that fear that's the really destructive thing.' She heard her tone, more vehement than she intended. Modifying it slightly, 'I

181

saw you together on the pier. It was like watching the person I was in the early years of my marriage and I cannot bear to see any other woman putting herself through that. If you go on feeling your prime responsibility is to appease him, it'll be a struggle to find out what's left of you. And there *certainly* won't be enough for Andrew to love. If that's what you want.'

Cari cried out, as if trying to fend off Anna's force, 'I *don't know*. That's the whole problem. I don't know what I want.'

Anna said, her voice quiet now, 'How can you expect to when you spend every ounce of energy denying yourself?'

Cari stayed for the day. They both understood that too much had happened for them to attempt now to hold the shape of what they were to be to each other within the bounds of a neighbourly cup of tea. Besides, Anna could see the girl was afraid to go back into an empty house, full of reminders of the absent Andrew. The mother in her responded, finding things to distract the girl. Together they got lunch and cleared up. Anna got her doing a little digging in the garden, saying her arthritis was playing up. In fact it wasn't, but the small deception helped Cari feel good that she was helping. It was surprisingly peaceful having her there, someone almost Gail's age but with no history between them. And after the intensity of the morning they both instinctively avoided any topic too personal.

But eventually the need to be alone overtook Anna. Cari saw, was instantly remorseful. 'I've tired you.'

'Not you. But I am tired.'

'I'm going, right now.' Then, momentarily shy, feeling the newness of it all, 'I can't tell you what you've done for me.'

The tone was too grateful, it made Anna nervous. 'It's nothing. People do things for each other, if they're lucky enough to be in the right place at the right time.'

≈≈

Cari woke in the bed in which she had slept alone, the first time for three years. She stretched, catlike, feeling the space around her in the bed. Luxuriating into it. Then letting the pictures from the extraordinary encounter with Anna sift back to her. So much to take in, to absorb. She had thought last night she would never sleep but she had gone out like a light, not even dreamt. And slept – she checked her watch – amazing, eleven hours.

She flung off the covers, went to the bathroom, then to the kitchen. Ate leftovers, everything that was going. Then to make sure she made two slices of toast and layered them thickly with butter and marmalade. She put them on a plate and took them back to bed. She picked up the novel that was lying on the floor beside the bed. The morning drifted away, her mind a beautiful blank. She did not think about Andrew, or Anna, or Hugh, or her own wishes or desire, or anything in the least disturbing. She read and slept and woke and ate, and went back to read again, and the space to herself was like a therapy nature had devised to counteract the effect of too much intensity.

By early afternoon her mind switched on again. She sprang from bed, feeling light and energetic. She opened the door and looked out at the day. Almost the last day of April, and the world was out there, fresh and inviting. The burden of the last confusing weeks seemed to have slipped magically from her, like a boulder that the wind had been wearing away, suddenly loosened that last little bit, going into free fall. She was free, extraordinarily free from anyone needing anything of her.

Sunday, middle of the afternoon. In Hugh's kitchen the phone rang. He stared at it, suspicious. It stopped. Rang again. He grabbed it. 'Hello.' Protecting himself in advance.

Cari's voice. 'Hi. It's me.' Shy, almost. 'I thought about coming over.'

No word from her since he had left her on the beach. No mention now of what had changed. He didn't bother to try and work it out.

'Go down to our place. I'll be there in twenty minutes.'

It had begun to rain while she waited, a soft continuous drizzle. She came wading out to him, carrying her shoes. Wet legs, wet face, her hair in wet strands over her face, making her look about fifteen years old. He reached out to grasp her hand and lift her in. Then he revved the engine and pushed the tiller over and they were off, the front of the boat lifting and bumping against the thrust of the waves, a trail of parting water behind them. The Eastern Islands loomed out ahead.

'A little detour,' he called, across the noise of the engine. 'It's magic in this soft rain.'

'Hugh it's not safe,' she called. 'You can't see the rocks.'

'I know this bit of sea like my own fields.' But he slowed the engine down by way of compromise. Little Gannick approaching, engine now just a low throb. Edging the boat gently through the channel between the islands, surrounded now by circling birds. Kittiwakes calling out in unison, sounding a warning. Absurd, no one could ever reach their nesting sites there on those high rock ledges. He looked back to watch Cari's reaction. Her eyes had relaxed. She's trying to like it, he thought, for the pleasure it will give me. And then a few minutes later, She really *does* like it.

'They're beautiful,' she said quietly. 'What are they?'

'Kittiwakes. Listen.'

Kittiwake, kittiwake, they called.

Engine right off now, and drifting quietly past the sands of an island, visitors in this world that belonged to the birds and the seals. Near the end of the channel a small cross-wind caught them. Switch on again, and off, out into the last bit of open sea.

As they pulled the boat up onto the sand of his beach Cari said, in a throwaway line. 'Andrew's had to go to see his supervisor. In Birmingham,' and then she changed the subject immediately. 'Look Hugh, those birds, are they the same as the ones we just saw out there?'

'You wouldn't find kittiwakes here, far too exposed.' But wanting to say, *How long has he gone for?* and knowing he couldn't ask. She's telling me this afternoon is a gift, time out of time, but no questions asked about tomorrow. OK, if that's how we have to do it.

They climbed the wet grassy bank and onto the path. 'Quick,' she said, 'let's get inside so no one sees us.'

They pulled off their wet things as soon as they got into the house and stood there, naked together. He began rubbing her down with a towel, 'Like I used to do with David,' he laughed. She pulled the towel from him, dropped it to the floor and wrapped her arms around his body. 'This way's even better,' she said. And then to bed, tumbling in together like children, then instantly slowing down, awed by the chance to be here again. Touching gently, hands affirming, eyes confirming, till desire pushed aside the quietness and they were moving together, driving through all the accumulated tension and denial and trying to learn to accept. Then when the intensity was spent, lying so close, so quiet, so safe. Touching again, checking again. You are here, I am here.

Till Cari said, 'Look outside, the rain's stopped!'

Hugh said, 'So it has.' Then, judging her mood, 'What about Tresco? It'll be light for a couple of hours yet.'

She said, 'Why not?' and they were off in the boat again. They landed beyond Lizard Point. The beach was empty, tourists all gone back to base, the place to themselves. She ran in the freedom of that spacious privacy, ran like a child let loose while he was still pulling the boat up the last few feet of sand. He charged off after her, heavier by far but with more stamina. She ran with the easy-limbed fitness of the young till her wind gave up and he caught up with her, and together they dropped down onto the sand, to lie panting.

'You didn't catch me. I slowed down to make it easy for you.'

'What a lie! I had my arm on yours before you stopped.'

Her eyes were laughing back. Quieter now, lying on their sides, watching each other's faces. She said, 'I can't remember when I've had so much fun. Ever.'

Afterwards, remembering that afternoon, it seemed to Hugh that she had been like a creature freed from unnatural restraint. Bonds loosened, finding her limbs, opening out into the space. Cautiously at first, as if she still couldn't quite believe she was safe – safe against the sea, safe with him insisting on steering. Then gradually accepting it and flying with it.

Once she said. 'How long do you think we've got?'

'That's entirely up to you.'

She looked suspicious. 'I'm not crossing the water in the dark.'

'I wasn't thinking of that. But you could stay the night and I could take you back at first light.'

She stared. Hugh saw indecision creeping into her eyes and moved fast. 'In fact,' he said firmly, 'it would be crazy to do anything else.' She continued to stare. 'There's no one waiting for you, Cari.'

She laughed, embarrassed. 'It's so silly, it just *sounds* different.

Cari spent the afternoon with Hugh. Cari spent the night with Hugh.'

'Who's saying it?'

'Anyone who finds out.'

'They're not going to find out.'

'Mrs Tremain might see I haven't come back.'

'*Does* she come and see?'

She laughed, admitting that she was caught. 'We only ever speak if she's outside her house when we're walking past.'

'Well then.'

'But I'd have to get back really early. Before she gets up.'

'With the dawn,' he promised.

He cooked for her when they got back, refusing to let her help. He pulled an old wicker armchair near to the stove, plumped up its cushions – an oddly feminine action in such a large man, she thought, but liked it the more for that – and got busy. She watched him move, filling a large saucepan with water, putting it on the stove to boil. Reaching up to a high cupboard to pull out a packet of pasta. Bending down to an old box under the sink and coming up with an onion, a couple of carrots, an aubergine. From the window ledge, two tomatoes. He started to slice onions, with every sign of satisfaction in the task.

She said, 'Let me help chop vegetables.'

'You're on holiday,' he said. 'You just sit there so I can look at you. And tell me something.'

'What?' She was cautious. Don't break the rules, said her eyes.

'Why are you nervous of the sea?'

Whatever she had expected, it was not that. She answered as if to dismiss the question. 'It's dangerous, that's why.'

'Of course it's dangerous. But I don't take risks.'

187

'It's not you. It's me.' Then, 'I was overexposed in childhood.'

'Meaning?'

'We had to go along with my dad's big plans. You couldn't say, 'I'm afraid' to him. He didn't recognise fear.'

She paused, as if testing his reaction. He said nothing. Vegetables all chopped. Oil in the pan, tipping in vegetables, starting to stir. He looked up. 'Go on.'

'He took us all right across the Atlantic. When I was eight and my sister only four. My sister was too small even to know it was dangerous. I was convinced my parents weren't taking proper care she didn't fall in, so it was up to me.' She stopped again. He looked as if he were concentrating totally on his stirring. 'See,' she said, accusing, 'You can't understand. People who love sailing never can. All you can see is the challenge. And that makes me nervous, because if you feel like that you'll push the limits.'

'You're wrong,' he said, calmly, lifting out a strand of pasta to check if it was ready.

'How?'

'I'm not into testing myself.'

'How can you say that? Your whole life here is testing yourself!'

'You've got me wrong. I'm a peasant, ploughing the same old furrows each year.' He carried the pot over to the sink to drain. 'I've learnt these waters because they're the element that surrounds me and if I couldn't negotiate them, I'd be trapped. But I mean *learnt* them, seriously, and it never stops.' Pot on the table, back to the vegetables at the cooker. 'Noticing each time I go out the quality of wind, and the tide, and what all that does to the water. Testing the pull of the engine against the waves in different weather conditions and in different places. Over at the Eastern Isles this morning, when I switched the engine off, that would have been a crazy thing to do if I hadn't known that channel and known exactly what was going on with the sea and the wind.'

'I could feel it,' she admitted.

'See? I've done stupid things in my life, but not that kind.'

'Like what?'

He shrugged. 'It's people I have trouble with. Or they have trouble with me. Or something.' He lifted the pan of vegetables off the stove and landed it on the table in front of her. 'There you go.'

She helped herself to a large pile of pasta, spilling over the plate. 'I'm hungry,' in answer to his amused eyes. 'It's all that running, and the wind.' Then, 'I *did* like it, Hugh, on the boat.'

He felt more satisfied with her admission than he could find a reason for. 'There's more, any time. Yours for the asking.'

She got down to eating. 'Next weekend, maybe.'

'Why not before? After school.'

But she wouldn't answer. 'This is good,' she said, mouth half full.

The whole night together. The illusion of safety, of infinity of time. He lay with her curled up against him, letting his fingers trail over her skin, and the feelings of the extraordinary day seep through him. Loving and being loved back is all we need to become human, he thought. Why is it so hard for people to find? He was calm in a way he had not known since his first years on the island. She offered him no future, he was not fool enough to think she did. For this chance moment she would open herself to him, to the freedom to explore. She would bathe in the delight of being desired, and by feeling his hands over her would discover herself to be desirable. Then her man would return and the other Cari would surface again, the one who was responsible for looking after, for making sure no one got hurt.

Except me, of course. He could not banish tomorrow as thoroughly as he had persuaded himself he could. Tomorrow, next week, three weeks, it scarcely mattered. It would end. She would agonise about what she had done to him but she would do it anyway because he was not her responsibility and Andrew was. And he would be left again. And nothing to be done about it, except to have what he could have while he could have it, and marvel at the power of present delight to cancel out the sure knowledge of future suffering.

She was so still he wondered if she was asleep. But then she stirred and murmured, 'Don't stop. Your fingers. Keep doing that.'

He started up again. 'You remember the kittiwakes? The birds that were circling around us early this morning?'

'On the cliffs?'

'Them. I was thinking, you have something in common with them.'

'Me?' She sounded more awake.

'D'you want to hear?'

'Of course.'

'They take extreme precautions to be safe, nesting on ledges no one could scale. But once the chicks hatch out, if they moved around they would drop into the sea. So nature programmes them not to stir until the day they're ready to fly.'

But he had broken the rules. She went still in his arms, voice panicky, 'Please, Hugh. I don't want to think about it.'

In the early hours he was shaken out of deep sleep. He could not say what, other than a sense that all was not well. Already he was tuned in to the changes in her, unable to sleep when she was wakeful. He pulled her body closer into the curve of his, wrapping his arms around her.

The voice of an anxious child. 'I didn't mean to wake you.'

'Something's bothering you.'

'It's so silly.'

'Tell me.'

'It's just — I woke and remembered Andrew, and felt sad for him.'

He did not move, protecting himself against the intrusion. Old feelings of abandonment stirred. Fear beginning to grip — not again. Please. She can't come this close and then leave.

It was a while before he could speak. Eventually he said, trying to sound detached, 'Andrew doesn't know.'

'I don't know what he knows. He must know something's changed in me. And when he comes back —'

Silence. What to say?

'Hugh, I talked to someone.'

He raised himself up on an elbow, to stare down at her in amazement. 'About us?'

'I didn't mean to. It just happened. But I didn't say who.' Then, 'And it's only because I talked to her that I'm here now.'

'Who?'

'A woman I've only just met. It was like, like there's something bothering you and you tell a complete stranger on a train, and you can do it because they don't connect with anyone you know.'

'Everyone's connected here. Go on, who is it?'

'She's called Anna Feldman.'

He stared, as if unable to take it in. Then he dropped back, lying now a little apart from her. 'Christ,' he said.

'Hugh, what is it?'

He was silent a moment, trying to make his voice sound reasonable before he said, 'She's the last person I would want to know anything about me.'

'I'm sure she wouldn't −'

He cut her off. 'You don't know her. She's an unhappy woman. She doesn't know what she's doing.'

'Hugh, she's −'

'I know what she is.' Then, wanting to banish whatever divided them, 'Let's forget it. But just don't tell her anything more.'

Hardly any sleep after that, too few hours before they had to be up. Just lying holding each other, and one final, wordless lovemaking. Then up, pulling on clothes in the half dark. Down through the mist along the path. Into the boat. Out onto the sea. All in silence, moving in unison.

There was a low mist over the cliffs as they came in to the small beach. Hugh turned off the engine and jumped out, to drag the boat up and give her a hand out onto the wet sand. Silence lapped around them. She stood still, absorbed. He watched, not wanting to disturb it. Eventually she turned to him. Whispering. 'It feels like we're visitors on the planet.'

'Come in my dinghy next time, It'll be quiet all the way over.'

A soft, just audible laugh, a shake of the head. His eyes held on to her laughing face. 'I'm mad to have let myself start loving you.'

She put her hand to his lips, 'Shhhhh.' Don't talk about the dragon and it might go away. She gave him a last hug and headed up the path. He watched her go, till she was lost in the bushes that clung to the steep sides of the cove.

≈≈

School was out and the bus had just gone past. Sounds of children's voices lifted up to where Anna worked in her garden, feeling the soft warmth of a May breeze on the back of her neck.

While her hands worked her thoughts drifted. Yvonne and her friends, in Plymouth now, feeling grown-up; Cari, their extraordinary enounter. Young enough to be her daughter, walking into her life as if she had been waiting for months to be there.

Anna straightened up, looked down to the bay – and saw Cari coming up towards her.

'The light's amazing today,' said Cari as she reached the gate, plunging straight in as if this were simply a continuation of a conversation. 'I thought I'd walk back this way.'

'And walking's given you an appetite, I expect,' said Anna.

'Well actually,' said Cari.

'Come on in,' smiled Anna. 'I needed a break anyway.'

'Oh good,' said Cari, and they both laughed.

The ease of old friends, when they were still so new to each other. The openness, and the things which could not be said.

Cari said, 'You were so helpful to me on Saturday, and I made you tired. I'm not staying long this time.' The voice of a child, promising to be good.

Anna smiled. 'The tiredness was temporary. Stay a while with pleasure.'

'Actually,' Cari said, 'there was something I wanted to ask you.' Not one thing, so many things. Why you so immediately told me to do what I wanted to do, not what I thought I ought to do. What Hugh knows about you, that I don't. What you know about him. Why he doesn't trust you, when it's so obvious anyone should. And none of these questions can I ask.

Anna said, cautiously, 'Go on, ask.'

'I wondered if I could I see your paintings?'

No one aside from her family had ever made it into the upstairs room. Now Cari was sitting in the window seat with apparently no consciousness that she had come in further than was normal, and was carefully lifting one painting after another and holding them to the light. She said little but her whole body spoke her deep interest, and Anna found it oddly moving to have her there.

Cari was pausing longer than usual over one painting. It was the one of the pier with the passenger steamer arriving; not quite finished. Anna watched, wondering what precisely she saw in it that was keeping her looking so long.

Eventually Cari looked up. 'There's something unusual about this one,' she said.

'Can you say what?'

'It's like – I don't know, there's a feeling of being *in* it. One way, it's like you're standing on the pier looking at the ferry. But the *feeling* is the other way round, like you're one of these people, looking out.'

Anna said, slowly, 'That's exactly what it was.'

'That's *you*, arriving?'

Anna nodded.

Cari looked at the painting again, and then back at Anna. 'And there were four of you?'

Anna nodded again, minimally. Her brain felt vague, as if she were losing focus. Cari's voice was coming from further away. Everything seemed to be slowing down.

Cari said, 'An odd thing happened the first time I saw you down at the pier. The day your daughter arrived. I was there too.' She paused, as if for permission to go on.

Anna heard her own voice say, 'Tell me the odd thing.'

'It was nothing really. Just – at the pier, I saw you waiting for someone to arrive. You know how it is when you keep seeing people you don't know, you find yourself filling in the gaps.'

Stop her now, thought Anna, the girl sees too much. But she

seemed unable to take protective action.

'I don't know why,' Cari said, 'but I was surprised when I saw it was your daughter who arrived. I had imagined you were waiting for a son.'

Jason. She had been waiting for Jason. Of course she had; why wouldn't she? She had been watching the waves as she waited for the boat to come in, and then seeing Jason once again on the deck as he had been that summer they had all arrived to stay on St Martin's, a boy of thirteen up at the prow, eyes intently looking out at the yachts in the harbour, the gently heaving sea, longing to get out onto it.

She looked up. Cari was framed by the light of the window, not moving. I can change the subject, Anna thought, and she'll have the sense never to bring it up again. But she made herself say, 'The story I was telling you, about why I came here. It was true but it wasn't the whole truth. I did have a son. He died. Here.'

Anna did not know how long they had been there. An infinity of experience to be reabsorbed, yet again, yet again, and the minutes and hours were never long enough to do it. Eventually she came out of the space into which she had disappeared. Cari was still sitting exactly where she had been however long ago it was, the painting in her hands.

Cari saw that Anna was back. Quietly she said, 'I'm sorry.'

Anna nodded, not pushing her away but making it clear she was not going to talk more. Then her eye, searching for something to move them on, caught the light through the window. Darkening.

'The rain's coming,' she said. 'I think you should go.'

Died. Drowned, I should have said.

Why is the word so hard to use?

A freak storm, the islanders said. It blew up out of nowhere, as storms do in March. Just when you think the weather is at its gentlest the black clouds build up over the Atlantic, and before you've had time to turn a yacht around and head back to land they have come rolling in, and the waves that break on the rocks of Hell Bay have built up to a frenzy, and the rain is lashing at your sails, and the sea is tossing your yacht wildly about, and world goes dark so you can't see what you are doing.

Three young men, university students on their holidays, out beyond Round Island, fighting to get back. The lifeboatmen pulling on storm gear, the boat sliding down the ramp out into the wildly tossing sea. Their wives and families waiting at home, knowing that they too could go down in it, as the lifeboatmen of Penlee had done just months before. People watching at windows, listening to the howling wind.

They were out for hours but they could not locate the yacht, and eventually they came back. And everyone waited still at their windows for the storm to blow itself out. Waiting for something they knew was impossible. The next day a few shattered remains of the yacht drifted onto the rocks at the north end of St Martin's. But there were no bodies ever found.

That was the story, that's what they told her.

She was not at home when Bella called. No one was home. The phone rang and rang into an empty house. Jason was dead and there was no one there to receive the news. It was eight in the evening but Max was still in London, working late. She was out having a meal with a friend – a friend she hadn't spent time with for two years, who had suddenly made a reappearance. 'It's ridiculous, never seeing each other,' he had said. 'Can't we just have a meal together?' And she had thought, Max's not here, and even when he is he hardly notices if I am. So she had left a note on the table and gone.

And come back at ten, to find Max there, standing in the middle of the living room, looking lost.

'Bella phoned,' he said, and then broke down.

I had a son, and he died. Drowned. Here. Two years, one month and ten days ago.

That's why I am here.

But it doesn't make sense, to anyone else. Does it still to me? What is it I hoped still to find, or rediscover, or come to terms with, or understand?

They talk about me, the islanders, I know they do. They pity me. Her son was drowned here, poor woman, they say. It's like that sometimes, grief affects people's minds. My friends back in Chichester who have never seen the islands, who if they had heard of them thought of them as a place for a holiday maybe, but unconnected to real life – they begged me not to come back. Elaine, sitting on my bed watching me pack, in the too-big house that was my and Max's creation, Gail and Jason's childhood home, and that now meant nothing to me, nothing at all except a burden to be shed, Elaine saying, 'Anna, I can't bear what you're doing to yourself.'

To myself? Does she understand nothing? Even Elaine, who I thought knew me so well? If even *she* does not understand, how will I begin to explain? That nothing I am doing is my choice. That it's happening to me, like Jason's yacht being smashed happened. We don't *choose* these things, there's a cycle in everything, we get carried by the tides, the moon, birth, death, by where we happen to land in between.

'I don't have a choice, I am a mother,' she had said to Elaine.

Elaine had said, 'You've done everything you could as a mother. What more will you do by going?'

197

There was no answer to that, so she just went on putting clothes into the suitcase.

'And that's not all you are, Anna, it never was, it never could be. You can't find the other parts of yourself now, but they're there, and you do yourself terrible damage if you deny them.'

Other parts? Yes, she supposed Elaine was right. We are so many things. Child, girl, woman. Lover, wife. Scientist. Healer. Friend. Now even grandmother. Yes, they're all there, jostling for space, but it is the mother that speaks in the end. That's why we were made, that's what nature requires of us. The men who take up so much of our energy, husbands, lovers, they are simply the vehicle to enable us to fulfill that function. The women who are our companions, with whom we talk and laugh and cry, whose arms are around us when our men abandon us, they too are in the last resort an extra. When death takes over and leaves us naked, exposed, raw to pain, when all the props we have surrounded ourselves with, insuring what can't be insured, when our friends stand by with misery in their faces but are helpless to help, *this* is what is left – I am a mother. Of a boy whose life was so short, so painfully short. Who lived so intensely, who moved by instinct and had no fear, who saw so much, and said so little. I am that boy's mother still, and my mothering is unfinished. As his life was unfinished. I have no choice but to be where he was, to try to touch that life with my spirit, though it is gone forever beyond my reach.

Four

Liverpool, 1934

Anna MacCaul, six years old at the time her grandma comes to live with them, shares an upstairs room with two sisters of eleven and thirteen. Her parents are in the other room. Her grandma, says her mother, will have to sleep downstairs. Her father puts up a lean-to off the kitchen, just big enough for a bed.

She has come, Anna's father explains, because the government has made everyone leave her island. 'Why?' asks Anna. Because there are too few people on it. It's too hard for them to get food. She has nowhere to go, and Anna's father is her only child. So she will live with them.

Her grandma is installed. By day she sits in the corner next to the fire, old and bent in a shawl she has knitted herself and will never let anyone take from her shoulders. She never goes out. Anna's sisters take little interest in her – they are embarrassed by her strangeness. She can't speak English and she dribbles. When instructed, they do practical things for her. 'Give grandma her tea,' says their mother. 'Grandma's coughing, go and do her medicine for her.' Apart from that they ignore her.

Anna likes to listen when her father and grandma talk, in their private language. She likes its strong sounds and practises them sometimes, making up pretend conversations with herself by stringing together random words. Her sisters find it an irritating habit. 'Tell her to stop,' they ask their mother. Their mother says, 'Leave her, where's the harm?'

Anna asks, 'Why doesn't grandma go anywhere?'

'She's too old to learn new ways,' says Anna's mother. 'She's afraid of big buildings and crowded streets.'

Anna's father says, 'On the island it was different. There were no shops. She made everything we needed.'

'Out of what?' asks Anna.

Her father laughs, and turns to share the joke with grandma. She replies, talking fast, hands moving. Anna's father listens, smiles, nodding, then tells Anna what she's been saying. 'She says the birds gave us everything we needed. Salted meat for the winter. Oil for the lamps. Feathers for the bed. Ointment for wounds.' Her grandma touches Anna's hair, that never will stay in place, and talks away. Her father says, 'She says you have the hair of island children, strong and full of life.'

Even when her father isn't there her grandma still talks to her, telling her long stories as if she is sure Anna understands. And maybe she does, from hearing the same stories so many times, in almost exactly the same words. She watches the hairs on her grandma's chin move, and lets the sounds of the words roll over her and into her, and sees pictures. She sees a little boy, growing up on the island, watching his mother take from the birds salted meat for the winter, oil for the lamps, feathers for the bed, ointments for wounds.

Anna's father is strong – strong arms, big hands. At work he climbs scaffolding, heaves heavy things half balanced against the sky. He appears not to notice danger or constant exposure to bad weather. Now Anna begins to imagine him as a child, climbing the cliffs like he climbs scaffolding.

The pictures stayed with her, a mythical place off the edge of the map. But as she grew older and began to find stories also in books, she filled out the picture, located the island in space and time. She saw it on a map, far to the west of the Hebrides, so remote that hardly anyone from the mainland ventured to visit. She saw on it the things her grandma had described. A scattering of stone houses straggling up from the harbour. The sky dark, the brooding threat of wind and weather. The storms, when for days the people would be shut inside. Then the sun of a late spring lighting on the cliffs, the edges of the island.

Cliffs shaped her father's child-world, and the sounds of seabirds crying, *keeow, keeow* – voices of tens of thousands of wheeling white forms that nested in the cliff face. The birds left the island each year to go somewhere far across the sea. Each year they returned, the gannet in February, the puffins in March. The fulmar stayed almost all the year, they were the birds on whom the life of the island depended. The coming and going of the birds was an affirmation that life existed beyond this fragment of rock battered by Atlantic storms on which the dwindling collection of families struggled to survive.

The sea defined their isolation, as the birds affirmed their connectedness. Once or twice a year a ship would emerge from the sea, would stay for a day or two and then return, loaded with fulmar oil and rolls of tweed that the women had woven from the dark wool of island sheep. Some years the ship would bring people who were not sailors and who had come for no reason except to look. They stared at the islanders, peered at their houses. They admired the thickness of the girls' hair and the agility of the boys. They hovered on the tops of the cliffs and gasped at the daring of the fowlers. Before the ship returned they gathered near the harbour and bought whatever the islanders put in front of them – charms against bad weather, old kitchen tools, knitted shawls. And they left behind them diseases to which the islanders had no immunity, and that claimed the children first.

The boy was the only one of five children to survive. Like every other boy, he learnt to be a fowler. He learnt it from his father, who several times each year risked his life at the end of a rope to raid the nests of the fulmar and bring in the catch of young birds that would keep life going through the months ahead – till finally the rope that should have held him frayed, and he dropped like a stone from the cliff, thousands of feet to the rocks below and the swirling sea. The boy took his place, but he knew he could not stay. He did not want to leave his mother, who was now all the family he had, nor the island, which was all the land he had ever known. But the island was no longer a place for young people. In the end he left on a ship that his mother knew would never bring him back.

With the going of the young men came the slow end for all the others. Till the last remaining islanders rolled up their belongings in blankets, and climbed onto the ship that had been sent to take the away. And saw for the last time the cliffs, abandoned to the birds.

In the corner next to the fire Anna's grandma shrank further into her shawl each year, dribbling, having her tea and medicines brought to her, never going anywhere. Until one day they came back from school to find that she had died, there in her chair. They buried her. Anna's oldest sister moved into the annex. The house felt a little less crowded. The days continued. But Anna was thoughtful for some time after. It was strange seeing her grandma's chair empty. Where had she gone? What was left of her life? Only the stories, it seemed.

For years Anna forgot about them. School became her world, separating her forever from the paths of her sisters and cousins. She entered other lives in her imagination now, the ones that came to her through books, and they took her away from the world of her childhood as fundamentally as the ship had taken her father away from his.

It was only when she herself had children that she began again to think sometimes about her grandma, for the experience of birth and death brings us closer than at any other time to the cycles of life we are part of. By then she was living again in a sea port, far from the one she had grown up in, and sometimes when beyond the sounds of the city she heard the cry of the seagulls, she saw in her mind's eye tens of thousands of wheeling white forms, the birds that nested in the cliff face. She felt the heritage of that cold northern island particularly in her second child, a boy, sturdy and agile as she imagined the island boys to be, exceptionally co-ordinated, and with sharp eyes that would have served him well as a fowler.

But she did not tell her children the stories they were heir to. Perhaps that was because she felt still traces of the fear the stories had evoked when she had been young and impressionable – the violence of the elements, the pull of fate. The men who fell to their deaths from the cliffs, the women who lost their sons to the sea.

≈≈

Plymouth, May 1984
Afterwards, when so many questions were asked, it became important to track exactly what had happened when the school group settled in at the hotel in Plymouth overlooking the sea.

The hotel was a family-run affair, two Victorian houses joined together by knocking down walls. It was full of corridors that ended abruptly and landings on odd levels. The landlady, who they later heard from the staff was a stickler for detail, happened to be away visiting her married daughter that week so it was the landlord who received them. He was clearly one for an easy life.

'You're the only guests,' he told them, 'I've left it to you to decide who goes in which room. We'll do the meals, you do the rest. If you want anything, there's always one of the staff around.' And then he left them to it, spending most of the rest of the week watching television.

The staff were equally keen not to miss the rare chance of taking things a bit easy. They did what they were paid to do and then left, earlier than the landlord had said they would. Fran Norton, the only teacher with the group, and the two mothers who were helping, took a poor view of all this, but there wasn't much they could do. At least the place was clean and the meals arrived on time.

The school party expanded into the unexpected lack of officious control and buzzed around excitedly, testing out the potentialities of each room. Each was a different size and shape, and of course each with a different angle to the view. Within half an hour of arrival it had become established, in that indefinable process by which groups create their own identity, that the most desirable rooms were those which looked out over the sea, not because it was a particularly aesthetic view – it was mostly the cranes and ships of a busy harbour – but out beyond there was a strange rock formation. The stone had been worn down by the disinterested action of sea and wind, but to a collection of fifteen- and sixteen-year-old minds the resulting shapes were as suggestive of sexual activity as if they had been deliberately sculpted.

The three women in charge of the group were ignorant of the power of these rocks and therefore at a disadvantage in understanding the passion which accompanied room allocation. 'Sort yourselves out,' Fran said, waiting impatiently to finalise her list. She didn't like the split into two buildings, for even though internal walls had been knocked down to link corridors, there were still two front doors to watch. The best she could do was put herself in one building and the two mothers, Norah Tointon and Winifred Downey, in the other.

On the first morning they all met up in the breakfast room, and from the excited conversations across tables Fran discovered that they were negotiating swapping rooms for the second night. 'What's all this?' she demanded. The defence was instant and united. The rooms were so different, they said, it wouldn't be fair for one person to be stuck all week with the one whose only view was the dustbins and a shed.

Fran said, 'That's ridiculous. You decide on your rooms and you stick to them.'

Winifred, the mother who had accompanied four school journeys before, said, 'Does it really matter, Fran? I can't see any harm.'

Norah, mother of Brad and in Fran's opinion over-indulgent, said – to the youngsters, mind, not even checking it out with Fran first, 'As long as there's no socialising in bedrooms. You use the lounge when you want to get together.'

Fran backed down. With the mothers unbothered it seemed hardly appropriate for her to insist, but giving in started a roller coaster that took things out of her control. The room swapping became a source of animated negotiation, far more interesting to the young than the sights they were expected to focus on in the city outside. The rooms with revealing views all had two beds, the others either three or one, so every room swap involved the occupants of at least two other rooms simultaneously. Yvonne was the only one who positively wanted a single room and didn't mind about the view. Her friend Kelly was disappointed, briefly, that she didn't want to share, but was getting used to the fact that Yvonne was like that these days. Kelly was going for the highest stakes – one of the rooms with The View also had a four-poster bed – and she found another friend to partner her. At breakfast Fran overheard them say,

'We'll throw in fifty pence.'

'This is becoming a gamblers' den,' Fran said. 'You're each only allowed one more change, and I don't want any money involved.'

They protested loudly, united at the arbitrariness of the edict. It was good humoured but it was also serious. Here they were for their big mainland experience, supposedly being given space to make their own decisions, and Miss Norton was treating them like children. Beneath the words Fran felt their unspoken judgement – if Mr Cooper had still been here he would certainly have let them. She was an inadequate substitute.

This time she stood firm. Later she told Neville Hill, the head teacher, that she knew she should have forbidden the swapping altogether but she was undermined by the attitude of the mothers. Norah clearly thought it was all quite amusing. Winifred said, 'They'll be all right, my dear. It's just a game,' making Fran feel what she was, inexperienced at all this. The landlord had totally opted out so she couldn't even invoke the rules of the house. Fran considered phoning Neville and telling him he had better come and sort them out himself, but she didn't want to admit that she wasn't coping.

For the first day they split into groups, each with an adult, and practised negotiating buses and using the map to find their way around. On the second day they divided into threes and set off along the same routes to collect information to fill in on their sheets, returning to base at the end of each stint. Each time Fran ticked them off on the list.

'We're not about to get lost,' they said.

'It's my job to be careful,' she said.

'Miss Norton,' Kelly said, 'there's this place called Paradise Cafe that stays open in the evenings, and it's really near.'

Fran could see it coming.

'Can we go after dinner?'

'You're pushing me.'

'Oh go on, Miss Norton, it's only round the corner.'

'OK, but the rules are, groups of three at least, and there has to be one of our own boys in each group.' The girls groaned. 'That's enough,' she said. 'And I want you all back in by nine.'

'*Nine?*' – as if she had announced that they were to have a bed-time story. 'We stay out till *eleven thirty* at the Sunset.'

'That's on St Mary's.'

'Mr Cooper said the *whole point* was –'

'I am tired of hearing what Mr Cooper said.' Fran got louder as she felt her authority dwindling. 'It's nine or you don't go at all.' She walked out of the dining room, trying to ignore the indignant noises that followed her.

Five of them went. They duly came back at nine, all together.

'How was it?' asked Winifred.

'Cool. Only it was just getting going.'

It was on the third day, Tuesday afternoon, that the first accident struck. Tracy Austin fell while running for a bus and lay sprawled on the pavement, blood on her face. Her companions acted with great presence of mind, got a taxi, took her to the hospital and from there phoned the hotel. Fran was out with one of the groups. Winifred Downey took the call, dropped everything and went to the hospital. The other girls arrived back about the same time Fran and her group did, with the message that Tracy seemed fine but she had to wait for an X-ray just to be sure she hadn't cracked her jaw, and they might keep her in overnight. Mrs Downey had said that in that case she would stay. The hospital said she could use a bed in the nurses' room.

Fran phoned Tracy's parents, promised to keep them informed. The girls who had just come in went up to shower.

Some of those who had gathered in a huddle to listen moved off, but one group hovered, hoping Miss Norton wasn't going to decide that Tracy being in the hospital was a reason why they shouldn't go to Paradise Cafe; but not quite wanting to ask.

Fran was tired, overstretched, wishing the week was over. She said, 'What are you all hanging about for?' and then saw the Paradise Cafe in their faces and felt suddenly at the end of her tether. And it was at this point that she saw sparks of light flashing and began to lose focus, and realised to her horror that she had a migraine coming on. Too late to prevent it, and when it hit it would last at least twenty-four hours, during which time she would be completely out of action.

Gathering her fast-diminishing ability to put words together she said to Norah Tointon, 'There's nothing I can do, it just blinds me. You'll have to phone Neville. Tell him.'

'My dear, you go to bed and rest,' said Norah.

'*Phone Neville,*' Fran insisted, losing her grip more every second. 'The law says there have to be two adults in charge.' She started up the stairs, turned, her last clear thought as her vision blurred and blind pain began to hit, 'I haven't checked the list yet. You'll have to do it.' She fumbled in her case, managed to pull it out, handed it over, 'Here,' and then knew she could not say another word without her migraine flipping out of control. She took herself off to bed and a darkened room.

The group watched her go, at a loss with all that adult intensity still in the air. For a few moments no one spoke. Then Brad asked, 'What's the law got to do with it?'

'It's in case you do something stupid,' said Kelly. 'Like fall off a cliff. Then they'll blame the school if there was only one of them.'

'*Are* you going to phone Mr Hill?' Brad asked.

'No dear,' his mother said calmly. 'I don't think there's any point in bothering him. She'll be fine in the morning.'

She didn't check the list just then, because half of them had gone off to shower. More sensible to do it at dinner.

The group who had been waiting now finally got their question in. Could they get hamburgers in the Paradise Cafe instead of the hotel dinner?

'I can't see why not,' said Norah. It wouldn't help anyone to have them mooning about. 'Just make me a list of who's going, so the staff know how many to cook for.'

They got paper and pen out instantly, and wrote the list.

≈≈

Wednesday, just after ten. A knock at Anna's door, a rare enough occurence for her to pause before she answered.

Vera Hill standing there. 'Well, how lovely,' Anna said. 'Come in.'

'I won't stop. Neville's just phoned from the school, wanted me to get a message to you. Could you come over for a few minutes.'

'Well, I – of course.' My mind's working slowly, she thought. This doesn't make sense. 'So he's found something for me to do after all.' But it couldn't be, that wouldn't be important enough to send Vera out to find her. Now Anna noticed Vera's face properly. There's something wrong with her, she thought. She looks like a bomb's about to go off.

'Are you all right?' she asked.

'I'm fine,' Vera said.

'I'll just get my coat,' Anna said.

'He's expecting you,' said the school secretary. 'Won't be a minute. Have a chair.'

211

Neville's door opened. 'So sorry to keep you waiting.' Ushering her in, manner courteous as ever, face giving away nothing. He closed the door behind them, pulled up a chair for her.

'Neville, what's going on?'

'It's about Yvonne.'

She stared. 'Yvonne?'

'She stayed with you the night before they left?'

'Yes.' He knew she had. He'd seen her at the pier.

'Did you get the impression,' Neville asked, 'that she had anything on her mind?'

Tuesday evening, the hotel in Plymouth

There were two fewer than expected at dinner. Norah checked the list. Kelly and Yvonne were missing.

'I saw them with the others,' Brad said.

Norah said, 'That's most inconsiderate to the kitchen staff,' but she didn't worry any further.

She was watching television in the lounge when the group came back. 'They were talking rather loudly,' she told the police later, 'and I was bothered about them disturbing Fran so I just went out to *sssh* them, and said, Get upstairs quietly now.' But she did check that all those on the list had got back, and that Kelly was among them. She scolded her for not having put her name on the out-for-dinner list. Kelly had some excuse about a last-minute decision, very sorry she'd forgotten to write her name. Norah didn't actually *see* Yvonne, but because Brad had said they were together, she just assumed ... Half of them were up the stairs already while she was talking to Kelly, and it was so confusing with there being two houses, and all the rooms changing. She had lost track of who was sleeping in which house, so she supposed Yvonne must be in the other one. She didn't know how it could have happened, she realised she *should* have made sure she saw each of them herself, but she was so used to assuming that Kelly and Yvonne went everywhere together. And to tell the truth, she just couldn't remember exactly. So much going on, what with Tracy's accident and Fran's migraine and all the comings and goings.

In the third year classroom the history lesson had just got started. Mrs Edmonds from the office appeared at the door and said Mr Hill would like a quick word. Mrs Lawrence went out. The third years took advantage of the gap to swivel round in their seats and talk. Mrs Edmonds came back in. 'I'm supposed to keep you occupied. You'd better tell me what you're doing.'

'The Tudors. We're revising for a test.'

'The Tudors. Why is it always the Tudors?' They stared, amazed. 'Well, get to it then,' she said, 'get on with your revision.' And she settled herself at the desk at the front with her knitting.

There was someone else in Neville's office. Cari heard low voices before she knocked, came in, and saw that it was Anna.

'I gather you two know each other,' Neville said.

Cari stood still, taking in Anna's drawn face.

'Cari, we're hoping you can help us. I understand from Anna that Yvonne thinks highly of you.'

Cari stared from one to the other. 'Well, I —'

'We were just wondering if she said anything to you before they left.'

'Anything about what?'

Neville watched her face, and sighed. 'Apparently not. I'm sorry to sound cryptic. This is all rather sudden, for all of us. The fact is, something out of order appears to have been happening with our people in Plymouth.'

Wednesday morning, Plymouth
Yvonne had not come down to breakfast.

Norah Tointon asked, 'Who's she sharing with?'

'She's not sharing, she's in the attic room.'

'Maybe she's got her morning sneezes,' Kelly said. 'She won't come to breakfast if she has.'

'It happened when we were in Penzance, remember?'

'Yea, she spent one whole day in her room.'

Norah sent Kelly up to check that Yvonne was OK. Kelly came back saying, 'She's not answering and she's locked the door. Maybe she went back to sleep.'

Norah said, 'Leave her and get yourselves off. I'll sort out some breakfast for her later.' Then, as Kelly was going, 'She was OK yesterday, wasn't she?'

'She was fine.'

'And in the evening?'

'I didn't see her after I got back. I was with the Paradise Cafe lot.'

But she was too. Surely she was too?

By the time they got into her room and found it empty, it was just over sixteen hours since she had been seen.

Neville issued instructions, quiet, precise. 'Anna, there's a boatman waiting to take you over to St Martin's. Garth Westerman. You'll find him at the ticket kiosk on the pier. You can stay a while with Bella, I imagine?'

'Of course.'

'Garth's coming off the tourist boat run for as long as we need him. His first priority is to get you to and from Bella's. I'll be flying out on the next helicopter and I'll be in Plymouth

214

within a couple of hours. Here's the hotel number. Phone me at lunch time, I'll give you whatever news I can. Cari, I'll be calling the staff together at break-time, before I go. Until then I would be grateful if you don't say anything to anyone.'

Garth handed Anna down into the boat, saying, 'Careful, it's slippery,' and then took the tiller and said nothing more all the way across. She was grateful for his discretion. She sat at the back watching the white line of foam the boat churned up through the water behind them.

The boat pulled up beside St Martin's quay. 'Don't wait,' she said. 'I'm unlikely to be coming back today.'

'That's fine. Just phone when you need me.'

Bella was in the house, no sign of Thomas. Bella had begun to say, 'Well, what a nice surpr –' Then she stopped.

Anna said, 'Bella, my dear,' and could speak no further.

Bella's face had got stuck in the last expression it had naturally assumed. Anna took her arm, pulled out a kitchen chair for her, pushed her gently down onto it. She sat with her hand on Bella's arm, searching for words. Hearing her own voice saying, *Bella my dear* … remembering, that was what Bella said to me when it was Jason, in just that tone. *Anna, my dear.* A tone that comes through us from the suffering and having-to-survive of mothers. *Bella, my dear.*

≈≈

The afternoon classes were a pretence on both sides. The pupils knew something was going on. The staff knew they knew. The fact that nothing was being said told the pupils it was serious. Cari marvelled that none of them asked. It's the island that

215

teaches them, she thought. They're like people out at sea, so interdependent that they know without being told that satisfying their individual curiosity is less important than keeping the whole group afloat.

As soon as the last class was over she escaped from the school without talking to any of the other teachers. She needed out, to be alone, to think – to shift the inarticulate feelings that churned inside her. She remembered she was out of Tampax and set off down the High Street towards the chemist. There was a stream of holiday-makers trailing back from the pier. She remembered walking here with Andrew in January, anoraks against the wind, how she had watched the faces and guessed at the lives behind them. Now hers was one of the faces the tourists looked at, knowing from the way she walked that she lived here. Almost five months of her seven gone. But this is *my* place, she thought, this is where I belong. A crisis simply underlines it. Just five days ago she had walked back from the pier with Anna, the day she had seen Andrew off, a short journey taken together that had changed her so that she could never go back to what she had been before. How would she explain to Andrew, who knew nothing of Hugh's existence, or Anna's? 'I know we said it was temporary, and I'm really grateful to you for making it possible, but I'm not going to be able to walk away in two months' time. We're going to need to find a way to –'

To stay? To keep coming back? We? I?

Oh God, what a mess.

Maybe Yvonne has just run away, from something that had got too complicated to sort out.

She stopped in the square, that wasn't a square at all but a widening out of the road, wide enough for the buses and taxis to wait, and behind that a small park, with a red phone booth on either side of the gate. She found a coin and dialled.

Hugh answered.

'It's me,' she said, 'Something's happened. I need to talk. Can you come over?'

She was waiting what seemed a long time before he arrived. She had begun to worry. She had not said where, it had seemed obvious. Then finally his boat appeared.

'Couldn't get the engine to start. Bloody sod's law.'

'Hugh, Yvonne's disappeared.'

His face flushed, then lost colour, a succession of emotions passing almost visibly through him. Cari felt moved, seeing the size of his concern. She took his hand and pulled him down to sit next to her on the sand.

He said, 'She came to look for me, not long ago. She said she was in some kind of trouble, but wouldn't say what.'

They looked at each other without speaking.

'You think you know?' Cari asked.

'What would you guess?'

No need even to say. 'But it won't be one of the boys.'

'How can you know?' he asked.

'I just can't believe it is. They're fascinated, but they're out of their depth. They'll touch the other girls in a testing way, flicking someone's hair or grabbing a pen out of their hands to try and get a reaction. With Yvonne they kind of hover, leaving a space around her. Like they sense she knows things they haven't yet experienced.'

'That day she came to see me,' Hugh said. 'She asked me for money.'

'What for?'

'She wouldn't say.'

'You gave it to her?'

217

'Yes.'

'How much?'

'A lot.'

'*Hugh.*'

'I know. I shouldn't have.'

She stared at him. 'I have a feeling there's something else you know that you aren't telling.'

He held her eyes with his own, challenging them. Either you trust me, his eyes said, or — . Sudden flaring anger, as if she had trip-switched some emotion too basic for him to control.

'Hugh, you need to tell Bella and Thomas. Or Neville, as soon as he gets back.'

'Tell them what?' His tone was hard, instinctive resistance.

'What you've just told me. And that you know nothing beyond that.'

'What use is that to them? It won't help them find her.'

'Hugh, have you no sense of what we might be getting into?'

'I'm not about to start apologising for not having done anything.'

They glared at each other, too worked up to speak. Then suddenly he got up, strode down to the boat, pushed it out to the water and jumped in. The noise of the engine blotted out all other sound.

She watched it get smaller and smaller till she couldn't see it any more. Then she climbed back up, her feet almost missing the foothold a couple of times. Along the cliff top, through the overgrown bushes. The path to the cottage.

When she got in she dropped onto her bed and lay on her stomach in a state of non-feeling. Eventually she realised that one foot had been dangling over the edge and had gone numb. She shifted, curling up into a foetal position, hugging her knees against her chest. She lay for a long time without moving, holding herself against the longing to be lying with Hugh again, against the fear of facing up to what she was doing to Andrew by wanting that. She wanted to disappear, hide, bury her head in her knees, make herself into the smallest of bundles, a foetus, invulnerable ... Words began to form. The only safe place is the womb, they said, and repeated it again and again, a mantra of escape. The only safe place is the womb.

≈≈

Neville was back next morning, issuing instructions in all directions. At the first break the staff were summoned to the staff room. 'I'm afraid there is no news of any substance,' he announced. 'I have cancelled the rest of the school trip. They are on their way back to Penzance and should be here on the afternoon boat. Immediately after we are finished here there will an assembly. I'll tell them what it's possible to tell. At four this afternoon there will be a meeting for all parents we can summon at short notice. There will be another this evening for those who couldn't get to the afternoon meeting.' Arrangements were being made for boats to bring parents from the other islands. The role of the staff was to keep everything as normal as possible, to discourage unhelpful speculation, and to keep the children's minds off the crisis by engaging them in calm, positive activities.

Great, thought Cari. Calm, positive activities. I can't think of a single one.

They all trooped into the hall. To a subdued gathering Neville told the story, such as it was, moving almost immediately to the 'what you can do' phase. 'No one knows where Yvonne is at this moment. But there is one vital thing we all have to do to help her get back as soon as possible, and that is *not to talk about it.*'

There would be no media alert. With the agreement of Yvonne's parents, they had decided it would not be helpful. Yvonne was not a child, she was sixteen and would be leaving school within a few months. Whatever had happened to her, publicity would make it harder for her to come back. But to keep something like this quiet was one of the hardest things in the world. The whole island community would need to share that responsibility, to keep their concern about her as something known only to those who lived here. It would take only one word from a returning holiday-maker and the press would be over in droves. 'We are a close community and we need that closeness now. I cannot stress how much we are relying on each of you.'

A long silence.

'Now get back to your form-rooms and take a breather while I meet with the staff. We start classes again in ten minutes.'

When only the staff were left Neville said, 'There's a little more you need to know. We are now in no doubt that Yvonne planned to disappear, and had been planning something since well before they left. I don't know if that's better or worse, but that's what it is.'

She had consistently chosen a room on her own, only once sharing with her friend Kelly. On the first day that they worked in threes she had left her group, saying she needed to make a phone call. 'You go on, I'll catch you up.' They had said, 'We have to stay together.' She had said, 'Please, it's really important, and please don't tell anyone.' *Really important* could only mean a boyfriend. For such a situation they understood the importance of secrecy but knew they were breaking the rules. They didn't know what to do and compromised by hanging about, just within sight of the phone booth. She came out – not looking as if the phone call had gone well – and they all went off together again.

On Tuesday she chose to be part of a different group, where the same thing happened. They had all come back to the hotel together that afternoon and joined the crowd gathering to hear about Tracy Austin's accident. That was when she must have slipped away. But to act so quickly, she must have been waiting for the chance. She had now been out of contact for two nights.

The police had pushed as hard as they could to find clues about the possible boyfriend, but with no success. None of her friends seemed to know anything. Yvonne's mother could not think of anyone. The only piece of information they got was from her friend Kelly. On the one occasion she and Yvonne had shared a room, Kelly had woken first and was going to have a shower. She thought she would try out the new hair conditioner Yvonne had bought. She didn't bother to ask because they always shared things. But as she got it out of Yvonne's toilet bag she saw a sealed envelope at the bottom. Plump, like it was stuffed with a long letter. When Yvonne woke Kelly said, just chatting really, not thinking about what she was saying, 'That envelope looks like it's got a stash of ten pound notes in it.' Yvonne jumped off the bed, grabbed the toilet bag away from her and said, 'What are you *doing?*' as if Kelly was trying to steal something. When she calmed down she said someone had given the money to her, and it was for some secret she couldn't tell Kelly yet but would soon. She swore Kelly to secrecy.

Kelly had wept as she told the police, sure Yvonne would never forgive her for telling.

End of the day, the longest school day Cari could remember. The corridors emptied in record time. Out onto the road, looking out over the harbour. Where to go? Her home was empty, no pull to go back into it. Anna was on St Martin's. Hugh had walked away from her, and a barrier of hurt and confusion kept her from making the first move to see him again.

Have you no sense of what we might be getting into?

And what sense had *she* had? She would have to somehow try to forget that anything had ever happened with Hugh. Find a way to keep the lid on the chaos inside her, for the last few months till term ended. Then she and Andrew would go, and that would be the end of it, the whole saga.

She headed for open land.

Birdsfoot trefoil, bell heather, sea pink, the spirit of the heath in May ... She lost all sense of time, walking alone through the carpeting colours in the long hours of evening light. She had not eaten, and did not know it. She clambered over rocks, pushed through bracken and gorse, up onto the high headland. Birdsfoot trefoil, bell heather, sea pink. She bent to touch each plant as she said its name, to state her belonging and her knowledge that she could not belong. With her fingers she recited their qualities. Birdsfoot trefoil, small pea flowers, yellow tinged with red. Bell heather, purple bells on upright stalks. Sea pink, light clusters on slender stems that rose out of springy tufts. Then she lifted her head to register again the distance between here and everything else. The land falling away suddenly, the sea beyond, going on forever.

≈≈

Anna woke in the early hours to the sound of Bella moving around in the next room. After a while she decided she had better get up to be with her. They sat together in the still-dark night, not saying anything because there was nothing to say. Eventually Bella said, 'I'll try again now,' and went off to her room, where Thomas snored. Thank God he sleeps, thought Anna, though she was afraid to think of what he dreamt.

Anna moved quietly to the window and looked out. The first strands of morning light. She held her watch to catch the light from the window. Four-thirty. No point going back to bed. She got dressed, pulling on a sweater against the morning wind that was sure to be up, and let herself out. Down past Thomas's fields, now with the summer crop of potatoes coming up, through a little wooden gate, onto a path over the dunes. To the sands where she had lain two summers ago and wondered if she would ever find a way through the pain of Jason's death.

At breakfast she said to Bella, 'I think I should get back for a couple of hours this morning.'

'Of course. You must have things to do.'

'It's just that I left in a hurry. There are things to clear up. It's silly but I'd feel better if I did that, and collected a couple of things.'

'Of course. You do that.'

On St Mary's Anna opened the door to her house, stepped in as if she were entering a stranger's place, and took stock. Breakfast dishes unwashed on the sink. Upstairs, paints dry on the palette. A house suddenly abandoned, like those in Pompei, caught in a frozen moment when the volcano erupted.

She wandered around aimlessly, as if she expected to see things that might be clues to Yvonne's disappearance. Then remembered that she was here to collect things, found a small bag, put in it her toothbrush, a change of underclothes. Picked up things that were lying around, put them back where she had lifted them from. A letter from Gail. The photos she had enclosed. Wandered back into the kitchen, to stand looking at the stools, remembering Yvonne sitting opposite her, eating warm carrot cake, talking about Cari. Just five days ago. Before. After.

Neville pulled up a chair for her in his office. 'Well Anna, strange times. How are Bella and Thomas doing?'

'As you might expect. Hoping for news.'

He shook his head. 'I'm afraid not. A trail of sorts, but we're always one step behind her. One from the hospital.'

'The hospital!'

'No no, nothing like that. But Accident and Emergency had a record of a girl of eighteen turning up in the early hours of Wednesday morning, saying she had a severe pain in her side. Nothing wrong with her, that they could find. She'd given an address no one had heard of. Came to the conclusion she was out on the streets, wanted to get in from the cold. It happens. They let her stay until first light, then sent her off.'

'Eighteen, they said?'

'*She* said. She could pass.'

Yes, she could. And thank God for hospitals.

'Another one this morning – the police have just phoned. A young girl who fits the description was seen on a branch-line station north of Plymouth, late last night.'

The stationmaster noticed her because she was waiting on the far platform after the last train in that direction had gone. He walked over the bridge to tell her, and noticed that she was in a slightly distracted state. Not like someone who regularly sleeps rough, he said, but like a girl who'd been out on the tiles the night before. He told her about the trains and she said she was heading back to Plymouth anyway, she'd just got confused about the platforms. She walked back with him and got on the train when it came. He didn't ask to see her ticket because she reminded him of his daughter, and he thought the best thing for her was to get back home with as little fuss as possible.

'So by last night she was back in Plymouth, sleeping God

knows where. And still no clue what she's up to. The police don't think the boyfriend story amounts to much. They think the only thing that makes sense is that she's trying to get away, to a more exciting life. And for that she'll need money. And to them that means only two things, drugs or sex.'

'They're crazy.'

'I've told them that. They're dealing with messed-up city youngsters all week, they can't focus on what would be different about a girl who's hardly left the islands.' He drew his hand across his brow, an uncharacteristic admission of tension. 'They think I'm naive.'

'You're not,' Anna said, with a firmness that surprised them both. 'You just know her, they don't.'

The thought surfaced, unasked, unwelcome – someone who knows her should be there.

Another silent boat trip with Garth. As the boat pulled in at St Martin's she said, 'There's a possibility I'll need you again today, but I don't know how soon. Maybe an hour, maybe only this afternoon.'

'Just phone my wife, she'll get me the message.'

Bella was alone. 'Thomas is having a rest,' she said. Thomas, resting.

Anna repeated word for word what Neville had told her. The woman was hungry, any scrap better than nothing. Then finally there was nothing more to say.

Anna reached into her bag. 'Look what I found.' She handed Bella a photograph.

Bella held it, trying to focus. Two women and two girls in their late teens in front of a small terraced house, with the rubble of bombed-out buildings in the background. The girls were fresh faced, in dresses with flared skirts, and laughing about something together. The women were middle-aged, thin-faced, with a hard-work look about them. Flat shoes and thick stockings. Staring solemnly at the camera as if unused to being photographed. And so alike they could only be sisters.

A wan smile crossed Bella's face. 'It's another life, isn't it?'

Anna nodded. 'It was the summer I was about to go to university.' 1947. A goodbye photograph. Her sisters had gone off already while she was at school, to the WAFS, and not come back when war ended. Bella's closest brother had died at Arnhem. The other had stayed in the navy. Of all the cousins, just the two of them left, and Anna about to go.

Bella said, 'I wanted to give you something for going away, and all I could think of was a notebook.'

'I remember, it was pink, with hearts on it. I used it as a diary.'

Bella turned over the photo as if the reverse might reveal other lost lives. 'I thought you left everything like this behind.'

'I did. But Gail couldn't bear it. When we sold the house she took over all the things she felt sentimental about. She sent me this, after she was here at Easter.'

Bella was staring at the photo again. 'Your mum. When was it she died?'

'1957. Ten years after that photo.'

'You were always good at dates.'

The old admiration in the tone. I wish she wouldn't keep *doing* that – Anna reined in her irritation. She said, 'I remember dates by other things that happened at the same time. That's the year I got married, and started in Chichester hospital.'

I remember ... I remember that it took Mum dying so suddenly to face me with what I had done to her, hardly ever going back, hardly ever writing. Never quite meaning it to be that way, just always studying, working, never finding time.

Being with Max, not wanting to go without him but knowing he would be uncomfortable if I took him.

Bella had moved to the window and was staring out, over the fields to the sea. Eventually she said, her back still to Anna, 'While you were gone Hugh came.'

Anna waited, stilled by surprise.

'Thomas was out, you were on St Mary's. I think he must have known –' She hesitated. 'I know you don't like to talk about him.'

'Forget it. Just tell me what happened.'

Bella turned. 'I was standing here thinking about who Yvonne knows on the mainland that she might have gone to. Then it came to me, so obvious – David and Sylvie. She knows their address, she writes to David sometimes. But I don't have it, I'd need to ask Hugh. And as I was thinking that, there he was at the door.'

A shadow at the door now. Thomas. He said, 'Bella, come in here a moment.'

Bella got up to follow him to the living room. Anna walked out of the kitchen, to where she didn't have to hear. She stared vacantly across the fields until Thomas walked out again and past her.

Back into the kitchen. Bella stood at the sink, hands in the washing-up bowl but not moving. Anna put her arm around her shoulder. 'I need a cup of tea. What about you?'

Bella nodded. Anna busied herself with the kettle. Bella ran the tap faster, squeezed washing-up liquid into the bowl, far too much. She stared at the foam, bemused. 'You maybe know, things have not been quite right between Thomas and me.'

Anna poured the tea. 'No, I didn't know.'

'I was upset with him because of something he said to Yvonne, that disturbed her, and it wasn't necessary. But I lost his trust by criticising him.'

227

'Bella, leave the dishes. Come and sit and have your tea.'

Bella stood looking down at her hands. Then she lifted them out, pulled off the washing-up gloves, dried her hands carefully on a hand towel. She came to sit. Anna said quietly, 'You'd better tell me more now we've started.'

'It's this thing he has about Hugh. It was last autumn, David had already gone back. Thomas saw them out sailing together, Hugh and Yvonne, just the two of them. It was so odd, just the week before they'd all been out together, but it sort of flipped something inside him, seeing them like that alone together and she grown so. She meant nothing by it and neither did Hugh but Thomas getting so upset made it *seem* like – Like he was turning something that used to be simple into something frightening to her.'

She was rocking now, holding herself. Blaming herself for not having stopped what was not within her power to stop.

'Bella, my dear.'

'The last two years have been too much for her, I know that's what's behind what's happening now. She's lost too many people she was close to, Jason, David, and then Hugh. She looks so bonny and confident to other people, but inside she's confused, she's lost herself.'

Bella, Bella.

'I just don't understand – Hugh used to come to Thomas about farming. Thomas taught him things you only know if you've grown up here. He said Hugh wasn't afraid of hard work – I've never heard him say that about any other mainland man.'

Rocking, rocking.

'The thing is, Hugh always had a way with him, with the children.'

'I know. I saw.'

'From when Yvonne was little Hugh had her trust in a way

Thomas didn't, and it was hard for him, I know it was. And after he spoke to her like that – she closed right up, stopped telling us things.' She looked up, her faced strained. 'I'm so afraid for her.'

I'm afraid too, Anna thought, though it would not help to say it.

Bella had stopped rocking. In a quite different voice she said, 'And the thing that really frightens me – whatever trouble Yvonne got herself into in the first place, it's fear of us being angry that's stopping her from coming home.'

That thought again, more insistent now – someone needs to go and find her, to fetch her back.

Anna heard it as if it had been spoken, and she tried to fight it off. What would be the point? Where would I go? What could I do?

Just *go*.

Someone else, please.

But Bella is in no state, Thomas would be a disaster.

No way of avoiding what had to be done.

≈≈

Anna didn't ask how Neville fixed it but there was a seat booked for her on the helicopter that left an hour and a half after she phoned him. Mid-May, high tourist season, fully booked for weeks ahead – had they thrown some luckless holiday-maker off to make room? And if so, what story did they concoct?

She climbed in, took her seat, turned her head to the window. Fortunately the roar of the engine made conversation with her neighbour impossible. She stared down to watch the islands slowly diminishing beneath her, till they were over open sea and there was nothing more to watch.

She was leaving the islands, the first time for almost two years. It felt strange, but not as threatening as she had assumed it might. Maybe because she was not going back through any process of her own, simply doing what she had to for someone else. And perhaps almost a relief, to have some compelling reason for action.

All she saw of Penzance was the harbour and the walk from there to the station. In the train heading for Plymouth she watched the view pass, like a film of a country she had once inhabited. Green fields, collections of houses, more fields. Land going on and on. Emerging from Plymouth station into a road honking with traffic was the first real jolt. She stood for a few moments gathering her wits, trying to remember what you do in places as loud and in-your-face as this. Then she felt in her pocket for the address of the hotel Neville had fixed for her, asked someone the way, and started walking. By the time she had negotiated two sets of traffic lights it was all coming back to her. I can do this. It's what I used to do all the time.

She checked in and made for the police station. Now she was confronted by a different kind of unreality. She felt absurd presenting herself here. What could she suggest or do that they wouldn't already have thought of? She had to wait a while before anyone could see her, and then it was a rather officious young officer. He talked about Yvonne as if she was simply a case, which of course to him she was. Then suddenly he switched to questioning Anna and she felt even more disempowered, slotted into a role, potential witness. When it became evident that she had nothing to add to what they already knew he didn't exactly say, 'Why have you come?' but his body language did. She didn't like him, but she couldn't say she disagreed with his judgement.

She walked out, back to the street. Again the onslaught, noise, rush, far too many people, cars zooming by, people passing her, walking too fast, not seeing her. Walking round her as she stood there, a temporary obstacle in their way. What to do? She couldn't come all this way and then go back to the hotel and sit there, useless. But she couldn't think of anything else, so that was what she did.

From her hotel room she phoned Sylvie – 'My God Anna, I can't believe it's you, where are you?' Anna responded vaguely – 'Just come over to the mainland to do a few chores.' It would not occur to Sylvie that this was out of character. Anna asked about David, about Sylvie's new job. When the flow ended she said, 'Do you hear from anyone else on the islands?' Just Bella, Sylvie said, a card sometimes. Anna prompted, 'Yvonne and David used to write, didn't they?' But not for a while, Sylvie said.

A blank. Sylvie launched into a resentful story about Hugh and money. Anna held the telephone away from her ear to lessen the force. She felt as she had done on those evenings when Sylvie had stayed overnight after choir and over filled the space in her small living room – the same mixture of compassion and irritation. I don't want to know, she thought, and was surprised at the strength of the feeling. When she put the phone down she was relieved to be once again alone.

She ought to phone Bella. But what to say? She did it, managing to sound as if she might still achieve something. Phone down again. Silence.

She stared around her. There's something about hotel bedrooms, they close you in. The anonymous decor, the bland framed prints on the wall – did anyone ever really paint the originals? They were so lifeless she could hardly imagine it. The curtains were drawn, floor length, a dull brown, formal pleats. For heavens sake why couldn't they let drapery drape? In irritation she pulled on the cord to open them, to find herself looking out onto the back of some other tall blank building. She drew them closed again.

Perhaps she should phone Gail. But why from here when she didn't do it from St Mary's? And how would she explain her presence here? More than any concern to keep Yvonne's story quiet she did not want to give away the information that she had left the island, however temporarily. Gail would seize on it, find in it the sign she had been waiting for, that Anna was getting over the need to put thirty miles of sea between herself and everything about her old life. Gail would say, 'I'm so glad, Mom,' and press her to come further.

Not a personal thing in this room yet she felt the presence of ghosts. The people she had cut off from, whose lives continued without her – Stop it Anna, stop thinking. You're tired, that's all.

She wasn't just tired she was exhausted. She had travelled eons – incredible that this morning she had woken on St Martin's. And it was late and she'd not eaten. She phoned room service. 'I'm afraid we only have light snacks left, madam, the kitchen closes at nine.' She ordered the most substantial thing the light snack menu offered.

Funny how you slip back into things. Being in a hotel alone, picking up the phone to order food. She could almost be starting to look at the conference papers, checking out the list of participants.

Checking Daniel's name was there … Memory pictures taking over now, not to be closed down …

A conference in Southampton at which she was giving a paper. It wasn't the first but there was still a sense of escape about going away on her own, for three days having the luxury of concentrating entirely on work. The hotel was over-the-top, too much crome and glass, everything starched.

'And so much rich food, for a conference about health!' said the man next to her as they served themselves from the buffet – said with light irony, a laugh just poised. She turned, caught by something in the voice and then by the way he stood there, so certain in himself, amusement in his eyes. They began talking, a sense of lightness flipping between them. How is it that people recognise each other so quickly, complete strangers as they were? 'Daniel Gretton,' announced the conference name-label on his shirt, 'Research Fellow in Biochemistry'. How was it possible that within hours they felt as if they had known each other forever, must have lost each other in some other life and were now simply recovering the intimacy that had once been normal? In the space of those three days, each removed from their own lives, they created a way of being that was special to them, that involved no one else. The ease, the lightness – she had always known that possibility must exist, somewhere beneath the tensions that life seemed to generate. Just to be, to breathe, to fly.

And then back to the life that before had seemed normal because the only one she had. To try to remember that this was the real one. Return to being Anna, wife, mother, doctor, friend. Responsible for others. Overcommitted. Time apportioned, never doing a spontaneous thing. Yet in her most private self to hold on to what had happened between her and Daniel. Something she would never regret, but would never be able to talk about.

Shut the door on that anonymous hotel where something extraordinary happened once between two people who were lucky to recognise each other.

Daniel did not see it that way. But then he had no wife, no children. A professional life, yes – he understood that all right, and that was part of the excitement. That they connected about things that mattered to them, that she could talk and argue and be listened to, instead of having to downplay what she did in her time away from home, because it got in the way of what her family needed from her. For Daniel work happened so differently. He seemed to live a charmed existence, able to organise his own time, come and go whenever he chose. He would arrive at her practice in Chichester, openly – he needed to discuss his research, he said. 'When will you be free? A meal tonight?' Phoning home with an excuse – 'For God's sake,' Daniel said, 'what's wrong with the truth? I'm a colleague you met at a conference.' But she couldn't sort out which bits of the truth were acceptable and which threatened all known existence. She knew only that with Daniel there beside her she could find no way to say No to joy. And when she said, 'I don't want you doing this again,' he answered by taking her hand across the table and saying, 'You do.'

And he was right.

Two years of Daniel arriving without notice, refusing to be discreet. Daniel setting up meetings for her to attend away from Chichester, and she went. More conferences, more anonymous hotels. Daniel phoning, Daniel writing. She gave so little in return, never took a move to make the next meeting happen, never put a word to paper. She was anxious all the time at the thought of being discovered – but why? Max had opted out of a real partnership years ago without ever finding it necessary to say so, but she couldn't bring herself to do the same. For herself she was still trying to hold on to what they had once had together.

The summer of 1980 – Jason finished school and Max bought him his own yacht. It had been a deal – You do well in your A levels and you get a yacht. Controlling through bribery – had the man no judgement? But it turned out Max and Jason understood each other, better, it seemed, than she understood either. Jason's school results had for years been abysmal; his intelligence was never in question but he couldn't be bothered. Now he switched into high gear and did it. And exultant, prepared to sail off with a couple of friends for the summer. 'Where will you sail?' she asked. 'Oh, wherever the winds take us,' he laughed and he might just as well have said, 'It's none of your business, Mum.' When he came back he would be gone to university. He had left home. The house was empty.

This, she realised, this was what she had been waiting for, this being faced with her irrelevance. It was this departure that made her recognise finally that there was no point in staying. Max didn't need her, his neglect made that clear. A wife? Well, of course he would want to keep that, might fight even, there were a lot of practical comforts associated. Who else would keep his home the way he liked it? But that she was ready to ditch. It was Jason who had held her, Jason the child who had become separate too young. She had been waiting in case he might still need her; or until he was adult and it was clear he didn't. It was time she moved on –

But Daniel wasn't there to say Yes to anymore. The years of keeping him in a separate compartment, of loading him with all her mess and never allowing space for what he knew, she knew, they could be when they were free together, all that had finally been too much for him and he had given up waiting. And found someone else.

She sat now cross legged on her hotel bed in this room that was like all the others but totally unlike because Daniel was not there. She sat very still and felt she was in his presence and finally able to think about him calmly. I was wrong, Daniel, and you were right. I was afraid, that was all. You understood

235

and you tried to help me past it and I wouldn't let you. That's the way it happened, there's nothing to do now but accept it. For me to accept myself as I was, made by all that had gone before. And myself as I am now, understanding that, trying to move on.

Gradually she became aware of another presence in the room. She felt Cari sitting opposite her in the armchair as she had sat in the window seat of her upstairs room just five days ago, holding a painting to the light. Anna stared at the chair and knew it was empty. I could be mad, she thought, but calmly, as if it didn't much matter. She knew perfectly well Cari was not there but she felt her presence all the same and it seemed natural to do so. The girl had no idea what she had stirred back into life, just by presenting herself, so painful a mirror of Anna's own younger self. Cari crying, 'I don't know what I want, that's the whole problem.' And Anna saying, 'How can you expect to when you spend every ounce of energy denying yourself?' – urgent to save this girl from having to live through it all before she found out.

'You wanted to know what brought me back to the islands,' Anna said now, to the presence of Cari, quietly listening. 'I couldn't find a way to explain. You think you're doing one thing and something else is really happening and you don't discover what it all means until it's happened. You see, there were things I had to work out, not just about Jason or Max or Daniel or anyone else, but about my own relationship to life.'

Cari nodded, as if it were all quite comprehensible.

≈≈

Saturday morning, breakfast in the formal dining room, and she the only single woman among the men on business, the elderly

236

couples, the young families. Her woman-alone state that on the island she had got so used to she could imagine no other, marked her here, making her a social misfit. I have to get out of this, she thought, I have to head home. And then realised, of course, that's what Yvonne would be feeling. What she would be doing. She paid her bill and headed for the station. Train back to Penzance. This time she didn't bother with the police – if they knew anything, the Plymouth police would have heard – she went straight down to the port. *The Scillonian* was due to sail in three-quarters of an hour. She summoned her professional self, so long packed away, and insisted on being taken to see the port officer.

They found Yvonne locked into the ladies' toilet on the steamer, minutes before it was due to set off for the islands.

It was the ship's purser who found her, and he would have done so without Anna being there. It was just a bizarre coincidence that she and the port officer happened to arrive as it was all happening. The purser had become suspicious because young Ollie Tremain, who was on ticket duty, kept flicking glances over the heads of the milling passengers, then quickly back again. Fifteen minutes of cross-questioning in the captain's office and Ollie confessed – he had allowed on a friend with an expired ticket. Just then the officer on duty on the lower deck sent a message to say that a door in the ladies' toilet appeared to have jammed shut and could they send someone to look at the lock.

Yvonne had barricaded herself in, to wait for the ship's hoot that never came. Must have heard instead the voices of women waiting their turn outside the door, then unseen hands testing it. A message over the tannoy, regretting the delay of departure. Then a voice on the other side of the door, the tones of

237

officialdom saying, 'Yvonne are you in there?' And when she sat frozen and made no sound, 'Yvonne, we know you're in there, please come out.' Men's voices now, and heavy hands hammering on the door. The sound of a saw relentlessly working around the lock till its tip thrust in at her. Sitting paralysed waiting for the door to break loose – and then being exposed, to an army of angry people, being treated like a criminal when all she was trying to do was hide from the mess that her life had become.

And Anna, waiting with them all on the outside, saw in the girl's desperate eyes the unspoken scream, *Get out of my life*.

But no sound. Yvonne had gone silent. Blank defiant silence, to salvage some remnants of privacy.

In the office of the Port Authority Yvonne refused to speak at all, but Ollie developed verbal diarrhoea in his panic. He didn't want to do it, he kept saying, but he didn't know how to say no. She was his friend, she was from the island, she had been waiting on the road outside the place where he had a room when he got back from work yesterday, looking awful, needing somewhere to sleep for the night. They had to smuggle her in late at night without his landlady seeing, and out again before it was light. She had slept on his bed and he on the floor. But not slept much. She kept saying, 'I've got a return ticket, Ollie, it's paid for, it can't be cheating.' She couldn't buy a new one, she had run out of money, and Ollie had none to lend her.

But he knew the rules. His job was gone when they caught him.

In the helicopter coming back Yvonne was spectacularly ill. Anna saw it coming and passed her one paper bag after another. The embarrassment became an agony for Yvonne. She turned her head away, unable to receive Anna's concern.

They landed. Stepped out onto the headland, colour at their feet, birdsfoot trefoil, bell heather, sea pink. Yvonne stood taking it in as if she had never expected to see it again. Then she turned to Anna and spoke, her first words.

'Not St Martin's. Your place.'

≈≈

Hugh was the last person on St Martin's to hear that Yvonne had been found. For days he had stayed away from people, working at his fields to catch up the hours lost with all that was going on, but it suited him to have the excuse. He had a sailing lesson booked that he couldn't get out of, but it was an effort to summon the words to instruct. Each time he went out it seemed that the island was unnaturally quiet. Ominous, even. It was like an effect of nature yet his eyes and ears told him it was nothing to do with the sky and the sea, harbingers of storms. Some human-induced violence, threatening.

He tried to eat but felt no interest in food. He went to lie down but his body could not rest, almost painful with tension. Eventually exhaustion took over but his sleep was horribly disturbed. Dreams – hardly dreams, more an irrational semi-waking twisting around of the reality that was too entangled to cope with by day. Yvonne lost, adrift, her face looking up at him as he pulled his boat in to the beach, Yvonne caught in a mess she had not been able to trust him enough to share. Cari saying, 'Have you no sense of what we might be getting into?' Himself tense, angry, turning his back on her – *Why? Why?* He was afraid of giving way to intimacy again in case it all went wrong once again, but the thing was already done, and he had made it go wrong himself.

By Monday morning he decided he must make himself speak to someone, even if only to say Hello. He could at least walk down to the post office stores, he thought, though he didn't really need anything. As he got near he saw there was someone else in there. Profile of a woman leaning over the counter to talk, quiet talk. Hilda Penruth, Thomas's sister-in-law. The talk stopped.

'Well, I'll be going,' Hilda said and walked out past Hugh. Not even hello.

The woman who kept the shop turned to sort things on the shelves. Back to him. A woman he chatted to at least twice a week.

He said, 'I've run out of flour.'

'Plain or wholemeal?'

'Wholemeal.'

She lifted a packet of the shelf, turned and gave it to him. He handed over the money, took his change and left.

Since the adults did not appear to be speaking to him it was scarcely surprising that it was from a child that he heard the news. He had been going past the one-room primary school at a time when the children were playing outside. They ran up to him.

'When's David coming?' asked the biggest of the boys.

'In the summer,' Hugh said. 'That's a new ball you've got?'

'Yep.' The child kicked it to demonstrate.

His sister said, 'It's good Yvonne's back, isn't it?'

The teacher appeared at the door of the school. She gave Hugh a small nod of hello and then called to the children, 'Come on, time to get back in.'

Have you heard? said the voices on St Mary's. Yvonne Penruth's been found but she won't go back to St Martin's. Yes, truly, she's

240

staying with Bella's cousin. What do you think is going on?

In the shops, when there was a lull between customers. Across a neighbour's wall, when the bed-and-breakfast guests had taken themselves off to get boats for other islands, and there was a moment to exchange a few quiet words, no one listening. Down at the pier, when the boatmen returned from the morning run, in the lull before they needed to set out again.

I don't know what to think, they said, but they say it's got something to do with Hugh Stanford. Hugh? So they say. Don't know if it's true. They say Yvonne's refusing to talk about what happened. Looks like she was running away, from something, no one knows what. And now she won't go back to St Martin's. There's got to be a reason. Hugh Stanford? Can't believe it. Well, I don't know what to think. He's an odd sort of person, you have to admit, no idea what's going on there. Look at that business with Thomas Penruth. One minute they're buddies, the next they're not talking. *Something* must have happened.

Garth Westerman came up to join the group, and the talk changed direction.

Garth's wife Rose said, when he got home for tea, 'Do you know what people are saying about Hugh?'

'They don't say it when I'm there.'

'I just thought you should know.'

'This tea's stewed. What have you done to it?'

'You're late, that's what. You know, I always thought there was something odd about Sylvie just up and leaving Hugh. It wasn't like she was new on the islands, been here thirteen years, more. There must have been a reason, more than what she said.'

Garth said, 'That's wild talk, and I don't want to hear it.'

His voice was calm but with that warning ring in it, and Rose knew she'd get nothing from him.

He won't hear a word against Hugh, Rose told her neighbour when Garth had gone back to work. Known him from school days. Hugh was a bit older, kept an eye on him, he says, even though he was the outsider. Garth's always been a quiet one, his mother says he was shy as kid, maybe he liked having an older boy pay attention to him. But it was the other way round when Hugh came back, it was Garth helped him get started. What do I think? I really don't know what to think. I can't say I *know* Hugh, him being on St Martin's and he's not given to coming over to St Mary's unless he has to. And when he does, it's Garth who sees him, doesn't bring him home much. Not much of a sociable type, bit of a loner. Mind you, we get our share of those, he isn't the only one for sure. But it *is* odd, what people say about him being so friendly with Bella and Thomas, and then them all going off each other. And Yvonne disappearing, and now refusing to go back. You can't blame people for wondering.

In the staffroom Cari tried to pretend she wasn't listening.

It can't be true, he's old enough to be her father, he's known her since she was born.

That's the whole point, she's been in and out of that house as if it's her own, and no one else there to see.

People say he's been keeping away from everyone since she disappeared. There's got to be a reason.

Cari's cheeks were burning and she couldn't believe no one was noticing.

In assembly Neville read the school a lecture about the pernicious effect of rumour. The words were abstract but everyone knew what he meant.

≈≈

Bella and Thomas had arrived at Anna's within an hour of their return. Too soon, as it turned out. Yvonne held on to Bella like someone threatened with being dragged away but could neither cry nor say anything about what had happened, except that it had been awful and she never wanted to go back to the mainland again. Thomas stood helplessly to one side, not knowing what to say, how to be. Anna was relieved when Bella took him off.

Bella came again next day, on her own this time. By now Yvonne's face was sullen, announcing in advance there was no point asking her anything. Anna and Bella did things together around the house while Yvonne lay on the sofa like someone who was ill, which in one sense of course she was. Once she roused herself to come and sit with them and watched vaguely as Bella looked through Anna's canvasses. Anna made an excuse to leave them alone together, but within a few minutes Yvonne had followed her down. 'Don't leave me alone with anyone,' her face said.

Anna had no choice about the role she had been allocated. She accepted it, and managed it with as good a grace as she could. Her mind told her to be glad she could be there for Yvonne, a trusted transitional space. She held her when the sickness threatened again. At mealtimes she prepared small helpings of food, carefully arranged, but didn't press her to eat. But once the initial surge of relief and compassion had faded, she began to feel invaded, her time and space overrun, things demanded of her emotionally which she could only with difficulty give.

She tried to tempt Yvonne out on small excursions; down to the cafe to buy bread, even out into the small garden at the back. But that was overlooked by the neighbours, a place far too public. Yvonne would not move from the house. Anna went up onto the headland behind and brought back for her some fragments of the life that was out there, placed in a small vase on the table next to her bed; birdsfoot trefoil, bell heather, sea pink. Yvonne noticed, touched them slowly but sadly, as if she recognised their connectedness but could no longer claim it.

Once only in every twenty-four hours did something of what was going on inside the girl express itself, in a terrified mewing in the small hours of the night, a nightmare of undigested experience. The sound woke Anna and she found it harder than any cry to listen to. She lay waiting for it to go away. When it didn't she got up and went to sit on the edge of Yvonne's bed, stroking her hair and making comforting noises that eventually seemed to calm her, but through it all the girl never woke. One night Anna felt she could bear the sound no longer and thought perhaps if she woke Yvonne it might chase the dream away quicker. But there was too much she didn't know, it seemed foolhardy to intervene.

As they were coming out of assembly Neville stopped next to Cari. 'I wonder if I can have a quick word with you.' She walked with him to his office, thinking, 'This isn't school stuff,' and felt her cheeks becoming hot.

He shut his office door and motioned to her to sit down. 'About Yvonne.'

Cari waited, heart pumping. Someone's seen me with Hugh. He's going to ask if I know anything.

'We need to find some way to help her move on. Anna seems to think you might –'

'Me?'

'It seems Yvonne thinks you understand her.'

The pumping gradually calmed down. Yvonne was stuck, and yes, she understood about being stuck. And afraid, so afraid of all the questions everyone might ask.

Mid-afternoon. Anna opened the door.

'Hi,' Cari said. An odd shyness between them, this first meeting since they had sat together in Neville's office.

'You've come to see Yvonne. I'm glad.'

'And you.'

Anna gave her a hug. 'It feels a long time. Too much happening.'

The hug felt wonderful. Cari longed to be able to tell Anna, to pour out all the 'too much happening' that Anna did not know about, and had in one sense unwittingly set in train. But even if she had felt free to do so, now was clearly not the time.

Yvonne looked up, startled.

'Mr Hill suggested I come after school for a few days, and take you through a bit of what we've been doing. So it won't be too difficult to catch up.'

Yvonne was confused, unable to sort out how to react. A teacher, coming here, calmly getting started on a lesson with her. Then the habit of doing what was set out for her took over, sidestepping the obstinate refusal to co-operate. Anna caught Cari's eye before she left them to it, and passed her a wordless message, Hats off to you, my girl.

Anna went upstairs, pottered about in a desultory manner, unable to concentrate. Then back down to say, 'I think I'll just pop down to the shops while you're busy,' and got on her bike for the first time in almost a week but it felt like months. Wind in her hair again, space around her, no one needing her. Exquisite release.

She was back before Cari had finished her session. She went straight upstairs but could not have stopped herself from hearing even if she had wanted, for she had long since removed the door on the painting room to let in more light and Cari hadn't closed the living room door downstairs. Sounds of packing up now. Yvonne's voice, 'Thank you Mrs Lawrence' — tentative, trying out its normal register again after all the days of denial. Cari's voice, 'It's no problem.' And then, 'Be easy on yourself. It'll take time for things to calm down inside you. You've had a lot to deal with.' Then another sound, a dreadful low animal noise. Yvonne, crying. It went on and on, till Anna had to walk out of the house where she couldn't hear it.

≈≈

There being no future that he could count on, Hugh had begun to count the days, backwards. Four days since the adults on St Martin's had stopped speaking to him. Seven days since he had seen Cari, and he had fouled things up, parting in anger on the beach. Sixteen days since they had first lain together. Thirty-eight days since she had first come to see him, carrying sweaters and flapjacks. Thirty-eight days.

Sometimes he did it the other way round. Thirty-eight, sixteen, eight, seven. Four days of silence, with no prospect of it ending.

He knew now what the silence was about, the eyes averted, the conversations suddenly stopping when he appeared. He knew because Garth had come over to see him, deliberately sticking his neck out to break the silence. They had talked in his kitchen in a way they had never talked before, Hugh's extreme need breaking through the habit of years of inarticulate companionship. When it was time for Garth to go he had insisted that Hugh walk back with him to the boat, so that people would see them together, see someone behaving normally with him.

But still the silence.

In the long hours of isolation a strange thing began to happen. His mind began to shift backwards, slipping between one time and another. People he had not thought about for years washed back into focus for a few seconds and then were carried out again, to be replaced by others. His father appeared briefly, trying to persuade him not to leave school before he had done his exams. He shrugged off his father's disappointment, a thing so long past, and then was disturbed by the picture of himself at some future time being disappointed with David at what he might choose to do with his life. *No,* he said out loud, to the low curve of land, the sweep of sky, we have to break the cycle.

The feeling shifted. Now it wasn't the thought of David's future that worried him but Yvonne's. She needed help and guidance, and he was shut out from the circle of those who could reach her. 'Why didn't you *tell* me what the trouble was?' he asked the wind that carried his words away. And the wind carried back her answer, 'I didn't know what else to do, Hugh. And you couldn't have helped anyway.'

Then Cari's face as he had last seen it, strained, her eyes pleading, *Have you no sense of what we might be getting into?* His anger flaring, not at her but at the rest of them – but only once he had turned and walked away from her did he calm down enough to realise that she received his anger as a rejection of her. Now he did not know how to go back. What was the point, anyway? It had been a crazy fantasy to think that things could ever be that simple. Nothing she had ever said suggested that she was ready to leave Andrew, and he was in no position to urge. There were times when he did not even know if he wanted to. To have her and then to lose her again, would be more than he could cope with. Better get used to the loss now.

But the sadness would not leave him, at the mess they had all made of things. He felt there was something trying to get through to him, some better way of understanding things, some more profound truth than daily life allowed. Then it slipped away again before he could see its shape.

≈≈

Anna opened the door to Neville. Twelve-thirty exactly. Even in a time when everything was awry the man's habitual nature was establishing a pattern.

They sat together, the three of them. Neville passed on scraps of news about the school, trying to tempt Yvonne back to normality. Once he succeeded in raising a small smile, but it didn't last long.

She left them to it, but from the kitchen where she was getting tea she heard him saying, 'I don't want you to feel pressed about coming back to school.'

Now Neville, that is *not* helpful, Anna told the kettle.

'It's really up to you,' Neville was saying. 'You're sixteen, no one can make you stay on.'

'My dad can.'

'I've spoken to your dad. He agrees, it's up to you.'

A silence. Stunned, Anna presumed. She came in with her tray. Neville continued, still that rational voice, as if this were nothing more than a careers counselling session. 'The only thing I would say is that it would be a pity not to do your exams since you've gone so far already. Exams aren't the be all and end all but if you get that piece of paper it does give you some options, about your own life.'

Yvonne looked as if she were about to cry. But she didn't.

They drank their tea, talking of other things. Neville got up to leave, saying, 'Excellent cake, Anna.'

Anna went out to see him off while Yvonne stayed inside. They stood talking at the gate; this too becoming a daily ritual.

'I'm grateful, Anna.'

'Why should you be grateful? She's my niece.'

'It's not as simple as that. As you know.' Then, 'If you can bear it, I think we need to give her a couple more days. I've got the mainland police on my back, it's officially still their case. They've agreed to leave it to the police here on St Mary's but they think I'm being unnecessarily soft not letting them go straight in and start questioning her all over again.'

'And aren't you?'

He raised his eyebrows. 'You've seen what the first round did to her.'

'You can't protect her from what she has landed herself in. Not to mention the people she is damaging by shutting herself up like this.' It was pushing out now, demanding expression. 'She exercised the freedom to act as if she were an adult. She has to be faced with an adult responsibility for the effects of her actions.'

Neville said, voice even, 'Would you like to suggest a way?'

There was no answer to that. For the girl sat there in her living room and if anyone came near to asking her about the days between her disappearance and her being found, her eyes glazed over.

Trauma, Neville called it. Privately Anna was beginning to give it another name. Obstinacy. Immovable as rock.

The school secretary put her head around the door of the staff room, looking for Cari. 'Your husband phoned. Can you call this number. It sounded rather urgent.'

Cari stared at the slip of paper, slow to take it in.

'Use my office. You can be quite private there, I'll be in the photocopy room.'

249

Urgent. Andrew needed to speak to her, urgently. Guilt flared, expecting accusations –

But Andrew sounded normal. Not just normal, back to how they had been before, as if there were no issue between them. He was full of energy about his work, wanted to tell her things. Luckily he didn't seem to need much response so she just listened, trying to get used to the change. Trying to connect with a reality so removed it felt like another planet.

'It's going to take longer than I expected,' Andrew said. 'That's really why I phoned.'

'That's OK. Just whenever you're ready.'

'How are things your end?'

Where to begin?

'A lot seems to have happened since you left.' She couldn't possibly tell him on the phone, none of it. 'When do you think you'll be coming back, Andrew?' She was surprised at the tone in her voice, sounding as if she really wanted him back. Maybe she did? She didn't know anymore, didn't know anything. While he stayed away too many things could happen. If he came back quickly it would stop things getting even more out of control.

Andrew was saying, 'It wouldn't make sense to come away before I've got this sorted, I'd just have to come back again, and it all costs. When's your half term?'

'In two and a half weeks.'

'Why don't you come here then?'

She could not think of an answer. The idea seemed shocking, even physically impossible, like asking her to swim across that sea.

'Come on, Cari, I came with you to your island.'

Did that mean, I did my bit and now I'm staying here, in my place? If that's what he felt why didn't he say it, straight out? But there was so much she wasn't saying straight out, either.

'I don't know how to explain,' she said. 'There are things going on here. Someone who's in trouble, I don't feel I can leave.'

'I'm not saying now, I'm saying in two and a half weeks.'

'Andrew, it's not just that. There are a couple of people who've become important to me. Let's wait till you can come back.'

'New people? Since I left?'

'I sort of knew them before but we've become close, quite suddenly.'

Silence. Then, in a voice that gave away nothing, 'OK,' he said. 'I'll try and get back for half-term.' And then he talked about other things.

Hugh had been out on Chapel Down in the late afternoon on Friday and arrived home to see – unbelievable, but true, Cari sitting on his step! He stopped on the brow of the hill looking down at her, wanting the moment to last. She was looking down his track, staring as if to memorise it.

His body moved forward of its own accord, long loping strides, turning into a run. She heard, turned, jumped to her feet. He stopped, panting slightly, in front of her.

'How did you get here?'

'I got a boatman to bring me over.'

What's happened to her? Hugh thought, she's losing all caution. Then he realised they were standing like awkward strangers. He pulled her towards him, holding her so tightly she had to break out of his arms after a couple of minutes, laughing for breath. Immediately he was contrite – 'I'm a clumsy peasant,' he laughed, and she put up her hand to his face and touched it, so lovingly that his pulse slowed down to almost nothing.

She's come back, he sang inside himself, and could hardly speak for the press of feeling.

She said, shyly almost, 'It's a beautiful evening.'

'You'll stay?'

She nodded. 'The weekend. But we'll have to stay out of other people's way.' She wanted to say, 'I heard what was happening to you here. I couldn't bear for you to be so alone. I had to come.' But she was afraid it would sound like pity and she knew he would hate that. She said instead, 'The boatman wouldn't let me pay him. I think he knew where I was coming.'

'What did he look like?'

'Big shoulders, sort of wispy red hair.'

He started laughing, 'This is bizarre.'

'You know him?'

'He's a friend. You can ask him again, anytime you need to. He'll keep it to himself.'

'I was waiting ages. Where were you?'

'Chapel Down.'

'What for?'

'I just felt like walking.' Where *we* walked, he almost said. But there were too many things pushing to express themselves, and he was unsure which it would be wise to say.

While he cooked she talked, an outpouring of all that had been happening on St Mary's. So easy for her, this complete openness. He soaked it up, quenching the thirst of more days of isolation than he would let himself count. At first he did not want to tell her what was happening to him, afraid to let her see the depth of the pit he had somehow dug for himself here in case it turned her from him. But it came out anyway. There was no way to build defences against her, and once he had started opening he knew that he would never want to hide again.

252

In mid-flow he stopped, looking at her, trying to take in that this was real. 'I don't know how it's happened so quickly. You. Us.'

She nodded but her eyes shifted, afraid.

'When I saw you sitting on my doorstep –'

'Sssh.' She put her finger up against his lips. Please, no statement of love, it makes me afraid.

But we're making statements all the time, he wanted to say. With every thought, every movement of our bodies.

By Sunday night he risked saying, 'Tomorrow – after school – I can fetch you. Take you back in the mornings. Early.'

She thought for only the briefest moment before she said, 'You're right. Nothing else makes sense.'

He took her back at dawn. He said as she stepped out onto the wet sand of the cove, 'I'll be here this evening. You name the time.'

'Six.' She touched his face once more, and turned to climb up the path.

≈≈

Wake to the early morning sun coming in through Hugh's curtainless window, the sound of the seabirds, then drift back to sleep in his arms. Another hour, another ten minutes, time moving on, unstoppable. Walk down the track, the dew shining on each leaf of the windbreaks. Up over the grassy dune, to the sea stretching ahead, the eastern sun lighting a path of silver to the islands where only birds live. Spray on her face as they crossed that water between the islands that once had been land you could walk across, his island joined to hers. Watch Hugh's hand on the tiller, his eyes taking in the sweep of creation around them.

Step out onto the scrap of high-tide beach that had become her place in a way more significant than her childhood imagination could ever have conceived. Climb the cliff path and at the top turn before pushing through the bracken, to watch his boat gettting smaller as it headed back to St Martin's, to start another day's work.

Another day. Another day to walk the path to school, another day to feel her spirits lift to the extraordinary beauty that was around her, lift against all rationality, all knowledge of the things that were bound to go wrong.

For all those days that had no number Cari felt as if she and those closest to her were on a yacht moving across an endless sea, life suspended while they kept each other going. Anyone who was not part of what was happening here was somewhere beyond the horizon, a place that once had seemed normal but now had lost reality, a land they would eventually arrive at when the crisis was over, where children woke up in the same house every day and knew what they would see.

The suspended moment had become the only intelligible time. *Now* had its own pattern, its own demands. The need to keep the children she taught challenged, their absorption a protection against the message of Yvonne's empty desk, that the life that awaited them after school might not be simple. To be with Yvonne, helping give shape to her days, a space to recover. With Anna, sharing the task. With Hugh, keeping his faith in human kindness alive when he could speak to no one else.

That he needed her she could not now doubt. She was moved by the strength of the man and his vulnerability, which he took no pains to hide. But she did not dare let herself think about what it implied or what she herself wanted. Desire she allowed herself and the simple love of the present that expressed itself in touch, in caress. In laughter and a shared response to the light, the air, the land, the sea. These were the things that had brought them together across the experience of lives of such different lengths, lived so differently. Each night that she slept in his arms the sense of comfort was stronger. Beyond that – ? Sssh.

A fragment of shared existence given to them while the crisis lasted, while Andrew was still away. Before time caught up with her.

Once she woke in the dead dark of night from a dream in which she and Hugh were standing on his beach next to his dinghy. 'I *might* come out with you,' she had said, 'just for a very short sail. But if I did you'd keep pushing me to do it again.'

He said, 'I'm not your father, Cari.'

'No, but you're you,' she said, and then felt a rush of affection for all the impossible things that made up You.

The dream moved and now they were out in the dinghy on the open water. She looked up at the sails and realised she had forgotten how beautiful was the curve of canvas filled with wind, how satisfying the tug in her hands of the rope that held it there. She woke, to find Hugh stirring with her, carressing her in his half-sleep.

She said, 'I dreamt I'd let you take me out in the dinghy.'

He grunted, encircling her a little tighter, but he was two-thirds asleep and hadn't really heard.

Look, said her dad, come and see through the binoculars. A small dark speck, bobbing up and down in the sea. Land ahead. The suspended moment coming to an end.

Hugh's first awareness each day was of Cari turning and

snuggling up against him. The childlike quality in her was strongest in her early morning stirring and she would start telling him things that in his half-consciousness state he was in no position to take in. Later when they were both awake they laughed about it, but even two-thirds asleep his spirit was moved that he should be the recipient of that trust. By the time he woke for the second time the child was gone and a woman's warm naked body moved up against his, her hands stroking his back, his belly, tempting him into life.

Up to the day. So short a time life allowed them – by six-thirty each morning they were in the boat again heading for St Mary's. She had found a back route to the cottage, she said, that didn't pass Mrs Tremain's house but she needed to get inside by soon after seven to be opening her front door and waving hello as Mrs Tremain started moving about her yard. As if that hawk-eyed woman was deceived.

The journey back across the water, then to the tasks of the day, but transformed. The hours alone were no problem now for he moved through the day in the knowledge that she would be back at the end of it. The awareness of her lapped against the rhythm of his daily work, the tilt of her head as she listened, her alertness to the small miracles of nature that surrounded them everywhere and that most people never saw. A picture of her touching a tufted mat of sea pink, commonest of headland plants, with the complete concentration of a child. She had looked up, seen him watching her and said, 'Such gallant flowers.' Waving on slim stems, no resistance to the wind.

Another picture, constantly recurring – Cari lying next to him as he drifted awake, light coming through the window, just enough to see her sleeping face. It was the kind of sleep he had lost the knack of, and beautiful to observe. Her face was smooth with youth, no sign of all she was dealing with by day. 'She has broken through my disbelief,' he thought. In what? In himself, maybe, in his capacity to love and to be loved in a way that could be relied on. But then that very awareness made him vulnerable. He said out loud, practising, 'She'll have to go back as soon as Andrew comes back.' But he couldn't make himself believe it.

He thought back to the person he had been at her age, how much he had thought he knew about the world and how little he had understood, and he marvelled at the wisdom that seemed to be hers instinctively. It could hardly have come from life experience for she had had almost none. Home, school, university, a partnership with Andrew he could not understand but which seemed to him to give no scope for the depth of which she was capable. Yet here she was moving into the lives of people she had known a matter of weeks or at most months, and changing them, simply by the way she had of taking in the whole person, understanding without things needing to be explained.

Stay a little longer, he said every morning as they lay warm and flesh blending into each other. I can't, she said.

≈≈

It had been a day of short bursts of rain, then the sun again, sparkling. They tried to settle to history but the sun kept glinting in at the window. Cari said, 'I can't concentrate. Let's get out.'

Yvonne said, 'We might see people I know.'

'There's not many people about. And we can detour if we see anyone.'

They emerged into the light. Yvonne looked about her like someone coming out of a hole, which of course she was. Old Mrs Strawcross was out in front of her house next door. Yvonne tensed up. Cari said, 'She's so deaf she probably hasn't heard you were gone.' They stopped to say hello. Mrs Strawcross said,

'Well Yvonne, you certainly have grown.' Yvonne was actually smiling.

Cari said, 'Look, there's hardly anyone down on the beach, and they'll only be holiday-makers,' and walked her on before she could say no. Across the beach, not stopping, and then up into the churchyard beyond. Safely sheltered by the trees, climbing up the steps between the gravestones to the top, to sit looking out over the bay. No one near them. 'Have you ever looked at the headstones?' Cari asked. 'They're more interesting than you might think. People who lived right here where we are, and just these scraps we have left to imagine their lives from.'

'I know that huge one, that's Augustus Smith. We did a project on him in primary school.'

'Forget about him, let's find out about the others.'

They wandered around, Yvonne tracing her finger over the names and dates. 1875, a young woman lost at sea with the sinking of the *Schiller*. Over three hundred people drowned, only a few bodies washed up. Maybe gravestones weren't such a good idea today.

'Let's get up onto Peninnis. I'd like to see what flowers are out.'

Yvonne followed but said, 'It'll be the same as at the back of Aunt Anna's.'

'Not on your life. There's something different on every headland.'

Rhythm in the legs, the walk itself a therapy. And small heads of colour at foot level. Cari squatted to get a closer look. 'Try and count the number of different flowers you can see from here, without moving.' Yvonne sat near her and began but gave up at fifteen. 'Do you know this one?' Cari asked. Tiny white stars bedded on a mat of succulent leaves. Yvonne was only vaguely focusing. 'It's stonecrop, isn't it? We've got some like that on our wall.'

'Each head is such a shy thing, but a whole clump of them together and they're brave.'

Yvonne laughed. 'You're just like Hugh, he notices everything.' Then, 'He's my friend's dad. On St Martin's.'

Cari kept her eyes down on the flower. Yvonne had said the words 'St Martin's' like someone afraid to admit the depth of her longing. Cari did not trust what her own face might be showing.

Yvonne said, 'It's funny, being up here like this.'

'What way, funny?'

'It feels more like – I mean, it's funny you being a teacher and us both being at Aunt Anna's. It's more like – I don't know. A cousin or something.'

'That suits me. I haven't got any cousins and I'd quite like one.'

'What have you got?'

'A younger sister. We were here when we were little. And we used to count the flowers!'

Yvonne laughed. The laugh hesitated, became shy. 'You know that gravestone?'

'Mm?'

'She was young, wasn't she?'

'Yes.'

'Do you know about my cousin Jason?'

'A bit.'

'You know he drowned?'

'Yes.'

Silence. Then, 'When I was on the mainland, I don't know why, I started thinking about him again. There was one awful night, the worst. I was in this doorway of a bank or something, trying to keep out of the rain and I began thinking about Jason's funeral. It wasn't a proper funeral, there wasn't even a body. It was so confusing, thinking about Jason not being any more. And then it began to feel like *I* was gone. Because no one at home knew where I was, and I was scared to come back so it was like I was lost forever. Sort of like Jason, but another way.'

'And now?'

Yvonne said nothing.

'You're back but you're still scared?'

A minimal nod.

'Being scared doesn't go away. You just have to get used to living with it.'

Yvonne stared. Then she said, abruptly, 'There's something I've never told anyone. After Jason died I had these dreams. About him, that he was there. He was special to me in a funny kind of way because he was our family but I was the only one who got to know him. He didn't use to come to our house but he was at Hugh's a lot and I was too. He was really funny sometimes, he used to make me and David laugh. And I –' She hesitated. 'This is going to sound really stupid.'

'Go on.'

'I got this feeling every time I had one of those dreams that something was going to happen to me that day, different from other days. Nice different. And it did. Every time. I used to think, it's Jason's way of still being there somewhere.'

'That doesn't sound at all stupid.'

'It would to other people.'

'That doesn't matter. You know it's not.' Cari sat up and took her hands, looking straight at her, urgent now to break through after so many days of restraint. 'What you feel about Jason, it can be the same sometimes for people who're still living, people we love but there's some reason we can't be with them. Maybe

260

you can't change that but you can still keep the strong things they mean to you, inside yourself, where no one else needs to know.'

Yvonne's eyes were fixed on hers, holding on, holding on. Then gradually they began to fill with tears and her shoulders began to tremble, and then to shake convulsively. Cari pulled her towards her, arms around her, holding her as Yvonne cried, for both of them.

≈≈

Each morning Cari reported to Neville. That is to say, she reported that there was nothing to report. Yvonne's lessons were proceeding well enough and for that hour each day Cari succeeded in distracting her. But Yvonne said nothing that gave any clue as to why she had run away and nothing of any significance about what had happened while she was gone.

'And you don't ask,' Neville said.

'No.' Then, a plea in her voice, 'I can't, Neville.'

Neville shook his head. After a pause he said, 'I've just had a reporter on the phone from Penzance. That's all we need now. I got rid of him but he'll go and do some nosing around of his own and be back.' Then, 'You don't have any theories, by any chance?'

Cari hesitated. 'I know what people are saying.'

Neville looked up sharply.

Cari said, 'I also know it's not true.'

'I think you'd better be a little more specific.'

'You know. You read us that lecture about rumour. A man on St. Martin's.' Heart pumping, 'Hugh Stanford.'

Neville was looking at her intently, eyes missing nothing. 'And what makes you so sure it's not true?'

261

'Yvonne speaks about him but in passing. Just about being at his house, that he's the father of her friend. It's absolutely not the way you'd talk if you had anything to hide.'

Neville's intensity relaxed. 'Well, thank goodness we've got that out of the way.' He shifted in his chair. 'I've known Hugh since he was thirteen. A difficult boy, guaranteed to create problems for himself. But I'd trust him with a child sooner than anyone I know.'

Cari felt choked up. And trembling, as if she had run a very long way and was suddenly being allowed to rest. She could feel tears starting, and brushed them away hurriedly with the back of her hand.

He passed her a handkerchief. When she was a little more composed he said, 'I'm sure I don't have to tell you, that's one of the reasons why we need to get to the bottom of this.'

Is he telling me he knows why it matters to me? He can't know – But can he? There's not much he misses –

Oh God, I want to get out of here.

'You haven't answered my question. I asked if you had any theories.'

She was silent.

'So you *do*.'

Choosing her words carefully, 'I don't know if 'theory' is the right word. It's just that I have a dreadful habit of imagining what goes on in people's lives. Not just for this. I do it all the time.'

'And?'

She hesitated then shook her head. 'It's not fair, please don't ask me. I can't do to someone else what they've been doing to Hugh.'

Neville sighed. He stood up and in a voice less personal, brisker, said, 'The police need to question her. She doesn't want either of her parents present, or Anna, or me.'

Of course she doesn't, Cari thought. She wants to be left alone.

'She wants you to be there.'

Oh God.

'She feels apparently that you understand her and we of the older generation do not.' Only the slightest irony in his voice.

Cari said defensively, 'If you're thinking she has confided in me, she hasn't.'

'And if she did?'

'What do you mean?'

'I don't know whether you've considered it but she might decide to confide and ask you to promise not to tell.'

Cari felt close to tears again. She tried to speak calmly. 'I want this sorted out as much as anyone.'

'Forgive me, I didn't mean to imply a lack of trust.'

'It's not that. It's just —'

Just what? She had become confused, no longer able to sort out what was her story and what was Yvonne's. She wanted to cry out, *Leave her alone*, for God's sake, something overwhelming has happened to her and no one will leave her alone. Everyone's pushing to make her most private experiences public, to know the details before she can even understand them herself.

Cari looked up. Neville's eyes were on her, the eyes of sensible decisions, co-opting her onto the side of the people for whom life was still an ordered affair. She felt defeated.

'If you want me to be there in the questioning, I will.'

'I would be grateful. This afternoon at two. I'll take your class.'

The policeman was the one who had helped Anna when she fell off her bike. 'Ron Bailey,' Anna introduced. He'd brought with him a woman special constable, whom Yvonne knew because she had come to the school to talk to them about careers in the police. Ron had been at school with a nephew of Thomas's. It was a bit like having family friends over.

Gradually, almost embarrassedly, Ron brought the subject round to what they were there for. Yvonne answered all questions the same way - No. Is there anything you want to tell us about why you went off on your own? No. About where you went? No. About what happened to you? No. About how you got the money? No.

'Yvonne, I don't know if you understand this but if you can't say any more than that the police in Penzance are going to keep thinking it was stolen.'

'It wasn't stolen, by me or by anyone.'

'So where did it come from?' Silence. 'We know you'd been saving from what you earned on Saturdays but it was more than that. If you want people to believe you, we are going to need to know how you got the rest.'

Cari felt her own heart pumping almost audibly and marvelled at Yvonne, whose face still showed nothing she was feeling. When finally she started speaking it was a set speech, clearly prepared.

'I knew I was going to need money for something personal, so I asked someone who's known me a long time and they kindly gave it to me and didn't ask any questions. I told them I would pay it back from working and I will. And it's no good you or anyone guessing who the person was because there are lots of people who've known me since I was so high and it could have been any of them.'

Ron shook his head. 'You're not making this easy.' Silence. 'OK. Leave that.' His voice became more formal, as if reading from a script. 'I have to ask you now whether anything happened either before or during your days away where you felt you had been injured by another party. And if so whether you wish to bring any charges.'

Yvonne must have been waiting for this too but if she had a prepared answer it abandoned her. 'No,' she said, 'No, No, NO! I told them no a thousand times and no one bloody listens. I wish you would all go away and leave me alone.'

'Which leaves us,' said Anna as she and Cari stood at the gate, 'precisely nowhere.'

'Yes.'

'I'm stumped.'

Cari should have been heading back to the school but she made no move. Anna said tentatively, 'When's Andrew due back?'

'He postponed. I forgot to tell you.' Anna waited for more. 'He's not quite sure, but probably at half-term.'

End of communication. Clear instruction, Anna – change the subject.

'I tried to suggest to Yvonne it was time she went home.'

Cari nodded. 'You must be needing some quiet time to paint.'

Anna thought, someone knowing me, my patterns. So absurdly comforting. She risked, 'Cari, I hope you're OK, in yourself.'

'I'm fine.'

But still Cari didn't move to go. She stood at the gate, fingers fiddling with the succulent leaves of the scarlet mesembryanthemum that tumbled over the wall, but her eyes not seeing them.

Cari did not know when it was that she had first become aware of the change in her that could not be reversed. She was doing an emergency load of washing when the first warning made its way through to her consciousness, uncertain as a light at sea. Being away every night had caught up with her and she was completely out of clean clothes. There she stood in the kitchen of the cottage that in a time so long, or so recently, past had been the place of her shared life with Andrew, and that would again be so when the days and hours had finally counted themselves off. As she piled in the knickers the thought walked across her brain that it was a while since she had had to wash blood stains out of them. She stopped, caught there with knickers in her hands, her mind suddenly racing.

At first the thought was so threatening that though she had heard it she could not acknowledge it. She finished the washing, closed up the cottage and set off to walk to the cove, all as if nothing had happened. She said nothing to Hugh. They made love that night as they always did and for Cari if anything with more abandon, as if to defy fate. If there was a part of her brain that said, 'Hold on,' she did not let herself hear it.

The next day the thought intruded again in the middle of a lesson as the children shuffled chairs around to get into groups. This time her mind produced not the question but the answer.

Frantic calculations. But time had lost focus; it was hard to remember the simplest relationships of one thing to another. Of how many days had gone since Andrew had left or since she had spoken to him on the phone. Since Yvonne had disappeared and been found. Since she had first taken the boat alone to St Martin's, to walk with Hugh on Chapel Down and then to lie with him, and in doing so to change the shape of her life.

It can't be, it's not possible. I'm just late.

She shut herself in the staff toilet at lunchtime and made herself count, properly. The sum worked out not too badly. She emerged and went back into the staffroom. A week late, well ten days – for many women that wouldn't mean anything at all. They were often late when stressful things were happening.

'But *you've* never been,' said a voice – Robyn's. Robyn who knew her as no one else did. 'They could set the moon by your periods,' she had said once.

Now that the awareness had lodged it could not be shifted. She woke next morning unusually early, waiting to feel that pull in her lower abdomen, that familiar sticky wetness between the thighs that would announce the start. Please, she pleaded with fate, please. Almost she persuaded herself the wetness was there. She climbed quietly out of bed not to wake Hugh and went through to the bathroom, hope beating against her ribs. It turned out to be that other moistness, from the night's love-making.

≈≈

Though Neville had summoned Cari he did not seem to know how to proceed. 'Sit down,' he began, but then got up himself to check that the door was closed. He returned to his chair behind his desk and started doodling on a telephone message notepad. Cari thought, I've never seen him do that before. Something new and troubling has happened. Perhaps Mrs Tremain had seen her come in and felt it her moral duty to inform?

'I've been trying to decide if I should tell you.' Eyes still on his doodling. 'I have a theory too.' Cari sat very still. He said, 'If I say mine first perhaps you can tell me if you've got the same one.' She nodded. 'I have been thinking,' he cleared his throat, 'that when you have one mystery, it's a mystery. When you have two you may have a clue.' The pen stopped. He looked up. 'I have never had a satisfactory explanation for Paul Cooper's departure.'

Eyes meeting. No need to confirm.

'Tell me what makes you think it,' he asked.

'The timing, more than anything. Paul left at Easter. It was just before then that I began to notice changes in Yvonne, the kind you feel in yourself when –' She stopped, tripped up by her own words. She felt blood rushing to her face, immediate give-away. Neville waited for her to regain composure but made no other sign that he had noticed. 'Anything more?' he asked.

'I heard Paul has a house in Plymouth?'

'Some way beyond. Along a branch railway line.'

'The one Yvonne was found on by the station master?'

'The very one. But she was well beyond his stop.'

But if she had got off at that stop and not found what she was looking for and been distressed, she could easily have got on a train going back in the wrong direction … Neville got up, went to a filing cabinet and pulled out a folder of papers. He paged through them till he came to the one he was looking for and handed it to Cari.

School journey. Penzance, February 20th to 24th. Health record. Brad Tointon, caught thumb in door. Swelling, nail blue, otherwise OK. Didn't think it necessary to consult doctor. Val Strawcross, complained of headaches, given two paracetamol. Yvonne Penruth, morning sneezing attacks, not sure if flu coming on. Advised to spend day in bed. 'Which means,' Neville said, watching her as she looked up from reading, 'that one of the adults in charge would have had to stay behind that day.'

Cari looked up, afraid now – for Yvonne, for Paul, for them all. 'Neville, Yvonne is so definite she doesn't want anyone blamed.'

'That's as maybe. If we're right, the matter extends well

beyond Yvonne's wishes now.' He paused. 'The accusation we both appear to be contemplating is so devastating for a teacher in charge of young people that I don't feel justified in even hinting at it to anyone other than you until we get some clue from Yvonne herself.'

I want to get out of this office, Cari thought, away from those eyes that keep looking at me, saying, It's up to you.

'And you appear to be the only person who has the slightest chance of finding out what's going on in Yvonne's mind.'

The wind rising, and she wanted to go down below and close off her ears. Don't make me responsible, screamed the child in her, I want someone to look after *me*.

'I need hardly tell you,' Neville said in that quiet, lethal voice of the adult who refuses to hear the child scream, 'that the costs of not knowing rise daily.'

Summon the wind, but don't listen as it comes.

She set out after school in the opposite direction from Anna's house. She could not go today. She knew Yvonne would be disappointed and she was sorry but there was nothing she could do about that.

She was running away, hiding from them all. From Hugh, whom she could not possibly tell what she thought was happening in her own body, but not telling made it more difficult each day to be natural with him. From Anna, whom she could not look openly in the face because Anna would see at once that something was wrong. Now from Yvonne, for whom Cari was the buffer against the world that pushed constantly to know Who? What? Why? When? Yvonne whose trust she was about to betray — *had* to betray, as the only way to rescue Hugh.

But her own state seemed daily less rescuable. *When? Who?*

Instinctively she chose the least frequented route to the north of the island, a difficult route along the western edge, no real path near the sea but a process of clambering over slippery rocks and then stretches of pushing through bracken. Eventually she came out at the stone foundations of the ancient village that she and Robyn had clambered around as children, making up stories about long-ago lives. The only other people there were a family of holiday-makers, a father explaining the history to children who only wanted to climb and run. She sat on a grassy sward a little distance from them, watching the unconscious ease with which the children moved, losing her present troubled self to become again a child exploring a small, safe land with edges so you knew exactly where you were. And then lifting her eyes to look out at the untrustworthy sea that in a few hours' time she would once again have to cross and expose herself to vulnerability.

Eventually she got up and set off for the cove; to be there, waiting for Hugh at the expected time and not tell him that anything different had happened today.

The first time Cari did not arrive to teach Yvonne nor send any message to say why, Yvonne watched at the window until an hour after her usual time. For some reason this irritated Anna. 'I expect she just has a lot to do,' she said. 'You can't expect her always to be available.' So easy to be rational on someone else's behalf. But she too was watching.

The next day it happened again. Now what do I do? Anna thought. Am I supposed to tell Neville she's bunking? What if something is really wrong and the girl needs help?

She went upstairs to distract herself by finding something practical to do – couldn't settle – came down again – saw a note on the floor at the door, pushed through the letter box.

Dear Anna, I'm very sorry I didn't make it yesterday and I won't be able to today either. I'm just a bit overwhelmed. I think maybe I'm getting flu or something. Please tell Yvonne I'm sorry to be missing the lesson. I think I just need a couple of days off. But I'll definitely be there tomorrow. Unless I do get flu! But I'm sure I won't. Love, Cari

But why write? Why not just knock and say it?

Meal eaten, dishes washed up. A long May evening outside, the light magical. Anna said to Yvonne, 'I'm going over to Cari's to see how she is.' Yvonne looked as if she might say, I'll come too. Before she could speak Anna said, 'I'm going on my bike. My body's got so stiff, I need the exercise. I'll be about an hour.'

The cottage was easy enough to find from what Cari had told her, past the Tremain farmhouse and a track down the side of their yard. She knocked a couple of times. No answer. She peered in at one of the windows. A living room, but with a remarkably unlived-in look about it. She went round to the side to find the bedroom window. An earlier Anna would have been appalled at her own noseyness but she had got beyond all that. The curtain was half-closed but she could see past it to a bed neatly smoothed down, not a thing out of place.

She got back on her bike, trying to pedal away the hurt of having been lied to, the message of those over-tidy rooms. How stupid of her not to have realised.

Now the picture of the house where Cari was spending her nights presented itself to her, unasked. A house Jason had treated almost as his own, summer after summer, but that she had never been into. The house that Sylvie had kept thrusting before her unwilling imagination. *I don't want to hear*, Anna had wanted to cry but Sylvie was in that state of need that Yvonne now inhabited where the pressure of her own turbulent emotions made it impossible to take in what anyone else could or could not handle.

I came here to be left alone, Anna wanted to say to them all. But other people's crises kept finding her out and facing her with the unresolved parts of her own.

She came back in. Yvonne asked, 'How is she?'

Anna said, 'She didn't answer the door. She probably needed an early night.'

I could be wrong, she told herself as she lay waiting for sleep that didn't come. Cari has other friends, she might have gone to someone else to be looked after. She has never once used Hugh's name. I have no evidence that they even know each other.

Don't be absurd. It's obvious. And Cari as good as told me.

But she didn't, I just happened to trip-switch that first guilt and after that, nothing. And she seemed so much calmer I just assumed –

Well of course she would be calmer, wouldn't she?

≈≈

Hugh watched Cari's face as they ate. He felt buffeted by the air of hostility that seemed to have blown out of nowhere. She seemed to be looking for some reason to launch out at him. Maybe it was something about Yvonne? But today even that was a no-go area. All he had said was, 'Do you think she *is* pregnant?' – a stupid question, true, for how would Cari know? But he had an idea that perhaps there was something that women could sense, and certainly a woman like Cari. But she snapped at him, 'She doesn't need *you* trying to probe as well' – the tone so sharp that he felt assaulted, and quite unfairly.

With difficulty he pulled himself back from the edge of anger. 'I had a letter today.' He passed it to her. 'Take a look.'

To make up for Easter, David could come for four weeks this summer instead of three. If that suits you ... She seemed to take a long time reading it. Eventually she looked up but said nothing. Hugh said, *'If that suits me.* How does the woman manage it? She can't make any arrangement without getting at me. She bloody knows I'd have him here the whole time if I could. There isn't a time that doesn't suit me.'

Cari pushed back the letter. 'I don't want to know, it's not my issue.'

He had had enough. 'Cari, look at me.' She looked. 'I want to know what's going on.'

'Just that you make me tired the way you have to *fight* the whole time. How long is it since Sylvie left and you still can't see her handwriting without going into overdrive. No wonder she left. You'd wear anyone down.'

'Cari —'

'And David, what do you think it does to him that you keep that level of hostility fuelled?'

'Do you think I'd say these things in front of him?'

'You don't need to. They come out of your pores. He'd be a fool if he didn't know.'

He was suprised into silence. Of course she was right. But so easy for her to say. She was watching him, assessing. 'When David comes, what happens? I mean, where do you collect him?'

'Penzance.'

'Sylvie brings him to Penzance and hands him over?'

'Yes.'

'Where? On the pier where people queue to board?'

'She doesn't get that far. At the station. We have a cup of foul tea in the railway cafe and she tells me all the things I have to not forget to do, and then she gets the train back and we go.'

'And David?'

273

'What do you mean?'

'I mean what is he doing while the two of you are sitting there?'

'He tries to pretend he doesn't belong to either of us. Wanders out to stare at the train. As soon as she goes, we start.'

'And going back, same thing in reverse?'

'Yes.'

'So Sylvie does the journey both ways?'

'What do you mean she does the journey? I do it too, on the boat. Which is a lot more expensive.'

'She does the train. Which probably takes longer.'

'What the hell are you getting at?'

She didn't answer, as if doing so would have taken more effort than she could summon. Then the inquisition started again. 'Have you ever been there?'

'Where?'

'To see David. Where he lives.'

He was losing patience. 'Are you crazy?'

'Don't you think he'd like it? To know that you know something about that other life of his and can visualise it if he wants to tell you things?'

He knew he was about to shout again and this time he was too late to stop it. '*I thought you said it was none of your business?*'

As soon as the words were out he wanted them back. I want everything to be your business, he wanted to say. But he was beyond help now, aware only of the sensation of wind whipping up, too fast for thought. Her face that only that morning had lain soft and loving next to his now lashed at him across the expanding distance of the night's anger. She was pushing him to do impossible things, unpicking his life, one corner after another.

'Someone has got to get Yvonne to talk,' she said. 'And

274

you're the only one with any chance.'

'Me? When I can't even get to see her?'

'You could. I could fix it with Anna.'

'No way. Not in that house.'

'You'll do *nothing* to help yourself!'

He heard in her voice a tone too familiar, one that he had heard so many times from Sylvie, *It's you that's the problem. You have to change.*

'I am who I am,' he said, holding fast to the ropes as the wind tugged senselessly. But he wanted to cry out against the hurt they seemed to be inflicting on themselves.

They slept with their backs to each other, empty space in the sheets between them. Got up separately. Breakfast without speaking. Out onto the track, a routine they could follow without discussion. Rain blanked out all view. They walked with faces down away from the rain.

In the boat Hugh sat at the helm with his back to her. *I'm sorry,* she pleaded silently to that rigid back. *I didn't mean to.* It's just that there's too much happening, I can't handle it. And I don't even know how to tell you. His back did not hear. When she climbed out onto the beach their eyes met and she thought he too was asking for a way out. Then his face closed off again, that familiar set of the jaw, the distant look in his eyes, refusal to engage. It would be as easy to hate this man as it is to love him, she thought, and the feeling could flip in an instant. He revved the engine to block out all chance of speech, and was gone.

≈≈

Cari hardly knew how she got through her classes that day. She wanted only to get back to him, to plead for things to be loving between them again. She felt driven by a primitive female need for reassurance, heightened out of all proportion by her fear of what might lie ahead for her. The force of that craving frightened her. For once she was grateful for the sea that divided them, that made it impossible for her to find some excuse to rush back.

Get out, Hugh told himself, go for a long walk. Something was going on and Cari wasn't telling him what it was. Her moods veered unpredictably, sometimes open and loving, needing physical closeness, then suddenly fighting at the least excuse, then pushing that aside to revert to the practical 'I-only-want-to-think-about-the-present' state. She could go on like this till Andrew comes back and then disappear without a word. The threat of abandonment began to creep under his skin and the questions churned over in his mind. He could not free himself from the suspicion that her ambivalence had something to do with the hours she spent every day in Anna's house.

He had walked without realising it to the northwestern tip of the island, a long low promontory looking out to Round Island lighthouse. A long time since he had been to this spot. He had not been aware of avoiding it but it must have been so. He settled himself now on a rock almost as far out as it was possible to be, letting the place and the presence be with him. On those distant rocks, just visible on a good day, two years ago a yacht had been dashed to pieces by a freak storm, a yacht that he might have been on. *Come with us, Hugh*, they had said, and he had wanted to go but Sylvie had not been well so he had stayed to take David off her hands ...

Jason; Anna. What half-truths was Anna telling Cari? And was that why she kept shutting him out so unpredictably?

Today, Anna told herself firmly, we are *not* waiting about wondering if Cari is coming. To Yvonne she said, 'You just get on with the work yourself, I'm sure Cari's given you plenty to be going on with.' To herself she said, I've got to get normal life going again, regardless. And she got out her tools to fix her *Paintings for Sale* notice that had got dislodged in a high wind.

The problem is, she said to herself as she hammered in the first nail, I fooled myself that I had her confidence, and now look at me. And I mind, and it's ridiculous to do so. *I'll definitely be there tomorrow*, her letter had said, but it was tomorrow now, end of school time and the road was empty. *Unless I get flu.* The hammer slipped, landed on her thumb. Damn. She sucked it to contain the pain. *But I'm sure I won't.* So Cari was still flapping indecisively, she thought, working herself up to feel cross so she wouldn't feel the other things. Cari's voice crying, *I don't know what I want —*

But it seemed now she did.

And wasn't that precisely what I told her to do, to stop suppressing herself, to listen to who she is?

Anna bent to pick up another nail, straightened up – and saw Cari coming up the road.

She was holding a single tall grass. She came to a halt a few feet away, the low wall separating them. Like a child she stretched out her hand, offering the grass. 'I came across the nature trail. I wanted to bring you a bit of it because you've been so stuck inside.'

A peace offering. Anna took it, touched despite her schooling of herself. 'Such extraordinary grace it has, from bending with the wind.'

Cari made no move to go inside. She seemed to want to say

something. Anna turned her attention back to her hammer and nails, not sure if she wanted this communication after all.

'Anna, I want to ask you a favour.'

'Ask.'

'One day this week, could you –' It seemed difficult, whatever it was. 'I think Hugh would like to come and see Yvonne.' His name fell with a clatter between them. Anna looked out over the bay, avoiding those eyes that asked for an acceptance she was not ready to give. Cari said, 'I guess you've always known but I couldn't find a way to talk about it.'

Anna realised she was breathing too deeply and tried to focus, to calm it. Cari could do whatever she chose with her own life but it was another thing to expect her to have the man come right into her home. Yet impossible to say no for there was no escaping the logic. Hugh was the one person to whom Yvonne might speak openly. If they didn't set up a meeting before she sent Yvonne back to St Martin's, there wouldn't be any way.

Eventually she said, in a voice that sounded considerably calmer than she felt, 'I'm sure Yvonne will be pleased to see him.'

Cari hesitated. 'The thing is, I wondered if you could arrange to be out?'

It was a minute or two before Anna felt like answering. Then, coldly, 'He doesn't want to meet me, is that it? Well I'm not sure I want anyone in my house on those terms.'

'I hate to ask. But there doesn't seem to be another way.'

There it was, slapped down before her. Hugh had Cari's primary attachment, as once he had had Jason's. She, Anna, had once again to face the knowledge of her irrelevance. I thought I'd got *past* all this, she thought, despairing of her untamable emotions. Envy flailed in all directions, hardly caring where it alighted. On Hugh, for having Cari. On Cari, for having Hugh. On all lovers who had each other, all mothers who still had their sons.

She bent down to gather up her bits and pieces to take back inside. Steady, steady. It doesn't matter. Nothing matters. Just take it steady, do what has to be done. You want this to end as much as anyone ... Then pride surfaced, flipping her into anger. She straightened up and said, 'Why is it always *women* who have to make things easy for men? The way we walk around these male egos –'

Cari stood before her, looking forlorn.

'Oh go on then, do it,' Anna said. 'Tell him I'll go and see Bella tomorrow morning.'

Cari said little in the boat coming over and nothing as they walked up the track. When they got in she said, 'I'll cook tonight,' and busied herself at the cooker. After a while she said, 'This is going to be a bizarre meal. My mind's not on it.'

Hugh said, 'You're tired. Let me do it.'

She shook her head. 'It's time I had a turn. You've got more reason to be tired.'

'Only body tired.' Then, back still to him, she said in a voice conveying no particular emotion, 'I spoke to Anna. She'll be out tomorrow morning. It'll be just Yvonne. You can go then.'

He came up and stood behind her, not knowing what to say. Instead he put his arms around her from behind. She stiffened, as if she didn't want to accept them, then wriggled round and turned to face him. 'You're an impossible man. You know that, don't you?'

He said, trying to keep it light, 'I have been told before.' But she was not mollified and he could feel his own defences rising. 'It may not be obvious to you but I'm trying. I'm just not used to anyone else telling me what I ought to do.' He dropped his arms.

'I had to hurt Anna and I hated doing it. I just don't understand why you can't –'

'Skip it,' he said, obstinacy taking over now, involuntarily. 'I've said I'll go. Leave it at that.'

She shrugged and turned back to her stirring. He moved away and started getting out plates to put on the table.

'If it makes any difference,' he said after a couple of minutes, 'I am sorry I create problems for you.'

She turned and said fiercely, 'You create problems for *yourself*.' He stood still, receiving her fierceness, registering the love in it. He felt at a loss, humbled by her acceptance of him.

They sat down to eat. She said, 'You've never told me why Sylvie left.'

'Cari, let's eat in peace. You don't want that now.'

'I do.'

He said, between mouthfuls, 'Because bulb-farming doesn't pay for trips to the mainland.'

'Oh come, Hugh. You can do better than that.'

'It's true. She didn't like being stuck here all the time. She was OK for the first few years when David was little but then she started throwing back at me that I had pressed her to come.'

'It wasn't just the place, surely.'

He hated this. It was over, why couldn't she leave it?

'Hugh, I need to know.'

'OK, it wasn't just the place. She's the kind of woman who has to be the centre of attention. And jealous. She resented anything that gave me pleasure because it wasn't centred on her.'

'That's a harsh thing to say.'

His voice rose. 'You're asking me how it felt. I'm telling you.'

'I'm also asking you how it felt to Sylvie.'

'Ask your friend Anna,' he shouted, 'she knows better than I do.'

They stared at each other, both shocked by the pent-up aggression.

'*Anna* knows?' Cari said.

'She encouraged Sylvie to leave.'

'She did *what*?'

'I just said it. Do you want it again?'

'Why?'

'Why are you asking *me*?'

'Why would she *do* something like that?'

'How would I know? Maybe because she'd made a mess of her own marriage. And then needed someone else to do the same, to make her feel justified.'

'You're crazy. She's not like that.'

'I happen to know a little more about her than you do.'

Cari put down her fork, pushed away her plate. 'I can't believe how messy this is.'

Hugh said nothing, waiting for his anger to subside.

'All I did was ask you to help me understand the story from Sylvie's side.'

He made an effort to speak calmly. 'Sylvie's story is that I'm an obstinate bastard who can't see anyone else's point of view.' He helped himself to another potato. 'But since I can tell you that, it can't be entirely true.'

Cari said, sadly, 'It's so *heavy*, what happens to people.'

He was silenced by her tone. Him and Sylvie, her and Andrew. Him and Jason and Anna. Even them, Hugh and Cari. There was nothing he could say. Every movement forward of his life seemed defeated by a relentless backwash of loss and misunderstanding. He had to find a way to pull himself clear of the pattern. Tentatively he put out a hand across the table. Cari took it and held it quietly. Her face looked peaky with tiredness. The thought flashed that something might be wrong with her physically, and the urge to keep her safe pushed all the other feelings into the background. He got up to come round to her side of the table and lifted her up to stand against him. She buried her face against him as he held her.

Her voice came up from his chest. 'All these last awful days, I keep looking at you and thinking –'

'Thinking what?'

'That I'd go crazy if I was living with you and had to fight you all the time to try to get you to do such *simple, obvious* things.'

He let go his hold so he could see her face. 'What are you saying, Cari?'

She was staring like a bird that has let danger come too close and now cannot find the instinct to lift off and fly away. She said, 'There's only a week to half-term and Andrew coming back. And we still haven't begun to work out what we're going to do about it.'

He was stilled, by hope, by fear. She said, 'I think I need a little time on my own.' Hope faded, fear rushed in to fill the space. 'Hugh, I said a *little* time.'

'How long is a little?'

'The weekend. Maybe more.'

'What for?'

'I don't know. To get my head clear, I suppose.'

He said nothing. What was there to say?

'Hugh, are you still there?'

'It's not me that might go.'

'Hugh, please. You're not making it easy.'

'Why would I want to?'

He realised he had removed himself a foot or more away

282

from her now, learning already to protect himself.

She said, 'I can't think when I'm here. I'm getting like you, blocking out things instead of dealing with them.'

'Go then.' But his body said the opposite and he was holding her again, holding her against a future he could not keep at bay. One hand moved briefly down to her thigh and his hand rested lightly there, in love, in the need to protect and to be protected, in desire, all of them hopelessly mingled. And in that touch a fragmentary memory surfaced. He was a boy and he stood in a kitchen and a woman was standing at the stove, stirring. She put down the ladle and pulled him over, to hug him against her. He had just come in from the early morning on an island with birds and the freshness of it mingled with the fuggy warmth of the kitchen and the smell of porridge cooking. He rested safe and loved into the curve and firmness of his mother's body. Then she was gone, and he learnt to be alone.

Five

St Martin's, summer 1981

The first Hugh knew of it Jason was walking in at the door, excitement lighting his face, *Come and see — I've got my own yacht.* Nineteen, just about to go to university, buoyant with possibilities.

He turned up at Hugh's house almost every other day, sometimes with his friends, sometimes alone; would walk in as if it were his own. David, at nine, thought him a magical creature. Yvonne, at thirteen, was excited to have so grown-up a cousin. Jason played silly games with them and made them laugh — enough attention to fuel the adoration, but basically it was Hugh whose company he wanted. And he was oblivious of Sylvie's resentment, creating a cloud in the background.

'He just arrives and expects you to drop things,' she grumbled. 'He needs to be told you have other things to do.'

But she was the only one who didn't want him there.

'Can you imagine,' she said, 'a father buying a boy that age his own yacht?'

Hugh said mildly, 'He has a passion, his father has money. There are worse ways of spending it.' But perhaps she was right, it might have been better for Jason to have had to work for it himself. By his age Hugh had been out earning his living; as far as he knew Jason had never even had a holiday job.

'There's something about that boy I can't deal with,' Sylvie said. 'He's secretive. He's been here weeks and only once bothered to go and say hello to Bella.'

'He's at an age to shed families,' Hugh said. 'I didn't pay any attention to mine at that age. Did you?'

'Well all I can say is, Bella minds. Yvonne does nothing but talk about him, and Bella and Thomas never see him. What would it cost him? You should speak to him, you're the only one he listens to.'

'It's nothing to do with me how he handles his relationship with his aunt.'

They both knew they were not talking about what really bothered Sylvie. Jason's company brought him pleasure, and he couldn't hide it. Nor could he explain it so she would have understood. She saw only Jason-on-land, a self-absorbed adolescent. On a boat he shed the awkwardness like an uncomfortable set of clothing and the man within him emerged, simply and without any obvious transition. Hugh watched the unconscious skill of his handling of the boat, the effortless co-ordination of thought and body, the economy of movement to achieve the intended effect. The eyes, awake to every change in the water and wind, following the line of distant land, lifting with the airborne power of birds. They understood each other's intentions, quickly, wordlessly. They were together.

Anna turned up on the island, staying with Bella.

Hugh was appalled. 'What does the woman think she's doing, following him? He's virtually a grown man for God's sake.'

'It's no small thing, sailing over from the mainland. She was worried.'

'Then she can't know much about him. He's as able to handle that as I would be.'

'Imagine if it had been David.'

'David at nineteen? You think I'd follow him?'

Sylvie turned away, got busy. 'She needed a break anyway. Bella thinks her husband's having an affair.'

Hugh looked disgusted. 'Is there anything about this woman's life you don't know?'

For days there was an uneasy sense of an incident about to

happen. Jason appeared not to know that his mother had arrived. She must know from Bella where to find him but she didn't come. Though Hugh tried to detach, something about the whole situation got under his skin. If she wanted to speak to Jason let her do it, get it over and go. There was something he couldn't stand about the thought of a mother holding on to her son.

He was the only person to observe the encounter when it finally happened. He and Jason had been out alone, the first time for a week that Hugh had been able to make time. They had sailed out the other side of Tresco, round the top and back again to his beach. Hugh had thought the weather was looking fickle. Nothing more than a brisk east wind, enough to present a nice challenge, but something about the clouds suggested a westerly on its way. As he was leaving the house he grabbed a couple of spare jerseys in case. He was glad he had for on the last stretch back they needed them. Watching Jason at the tiller in his old grey fisherman's knit that Sylvie had made him years ago, Hugh thought, I'd better get that off him before we get back to the house, Sylvie won't like seeing him in it.

They had come off the boat and were about to head home when he saw Anna. In fairness he had to admit that she didn't look as if she was looking out for anyone, just walking along the track beyond the grass dunes. But it made no difference what she intended.

Jason looked up. Anna saw him. They stared at each other.

Hugh was caught by surprise at his own reaction – he felt a sudden compassion for the woman, trapped by her own unwisdom in coming here. He tried to ease things with a wave, calling out, 'Well, hello.' And since that didn't seem to be enough, 'Wind's pretty brisk out there.' Then he remembered something he had left on the boat and turned back. Over his shoulder he heard Jason walking towards Anna, heard him leap up the grassy bank to stand next to her. He heard voices but thank God the wind was blowing them in the other direction so he was not compelled to hear what passed between them. He went on finding things to do until the woman left.

Jason came back. Without speaking he took from Hugh half the pile of things he had stacked to carry back, and they set off again. Hugh tried to talk about other things but Jason hardly seemed to hear. As they got near the house Jason said, 'She says she's going back tomorrow.' Hugh put an arm briefly around his shoulder. In solidarity, but also hoping to jolly him gently past the tension. Jason shrugged the arm off. Hugh smiled. OK mate, I get it. I too am one of the older generation. Then that flipped him into thinking of Anna, of that stricken look on her face when she realised that Jason had seen her. It seemed to Hugh that the woman understood, what perhaps she had known all along but been unable to act upon, that by her very concern she had pushed the boy away. And this time, beyond where he would ever let her in again.

Sylvie's right, he thought, I ought to help this guy grow up a little. He said to Jason, 'I guess it's difficult for your mother too.'

Jason said nothing. His face was unreadable.

She had come back, nine months later, but her son was gone. No body to bury, no face to see for the last time, to shift the image of all that had gone wrong between them, that there would never now be time to change. Nothing that could be done but stand on this promontory with the people of the island, while the priest's black robe blew in the wind and the sea crashed against the rocks beyond Round Island, and the voices of the small group of suffering humanity sang hymns to the God who had never been able to control the elements. And when it was finally over and one by one the islanders came up to the families of the three young men to offer their awkward words of condolence, Anna had accepted them from everyone else, but when it was Hugh's turn she had turned her head and could not look at him.

He had tried to say something, but she had turned away. A fierce, unspoken accusation. It was you, said her turned-away head. But for you this would never have happened.

For months after Jason's death Hugh kept seeing again that moment when Anna and Jason had faced each other on the beach, and he felt there was something about that incident that he had not understood, not let himself know. He waited, for it to make itself known. He relived that moment of looking up, and seeing Anna staring at them – transfixed, like someone who had been watching for a while before they were aware of her. Of course she would have seen Jason being the self he was with Hugh, calm, no trace of tension, his spirit light from the exhilaration of wind and sea. The ease between them like a language of the body, of the mind. They chatted as they sorted out things on the boat. Jason laughed at something Hugh said. Then he saw his mother, and the ease and lightness was cut out.

It was that she could not forgive.

≈≈

Hugh was up before first light, to a world of drifting sea-fog. He had suspected it might happen for the night had been cloudless. He left Cari sleeping and stood at the door to watch the white drifts swirl and lift to reveal bits of the island at dawn, and hide them again.

When Cari woke she looked at the white world outside in alarm. 'Will we make it across?'

'Not at our usual time. But it'll lift once the sun gets going.'

'Christ. Something like this was bound to happen.'

'Don't panic. We always go far too early. You can miss your ritual Good Morning to Mrs Tremain and go straight to the school.'

She said nothing, still staring out of the window.

'Let's eat,' he said. 'It might have lifted by the time we're ready.'

It had, but not enough. He watched as two sets of fear competed in her face. Each threatened exposure, one to the untrustworthy sea, the other to the unkind judgements of people she thought her friends.

She waited until the last possible moment and then capitulated. 'Let's go,' she said.

They made the journey across without incident. In her anxiety not to be late she was poised to get out before he had even beached the boat. He brought the boat right in to the triangle of beach, the cliffs above it magically draped in wisps of white. He said, leaving her no chance to argue, 'It'll be treacherous on the path up. I'm coming with you.'

She went up ahead of him, and he watched in love as her feet found each foothold with the sureness of habit, the lightness of youth, but too fast. At the top he took hold of her hand to calm her before she set off along the bracken track. They stood looking out over the panorama of mist that laced the sea and the Eastern Islands. Then he turned to give her one last hug.

'Go carefully,' he said.

By ten-thirty the mist had disappeared completely, to leave a day of spectacular clarity. Hugh paused in his work to sit outside the kitchen door in the sun and absorb the gift of air and sky, trying to return to a state when this had been enough. The St Mary's boat came chugging round the edge of the quay, to deposit the day's quota of holiday-makers. Anna would be among them, going to see Bella. Time to get himself over, to see Yvonne.

He began to pull off his muddy wellingtons. He had no idea what he would say to the girl. He was weighed down by loss, and couldn't think. He turned his mind instead to the problem of how to get to the house unnoticed. He would make for the last inlet before Old Town, he decided. Being low tide he would be able to pull up a long way out from where anyone from the farms that overlooked the bay were likely to notice. Then he could walk round to Anna's the back way, over the headland, where the only people he was likely to encounter would be holiday-makers. That left only the houses of her immediate neighbours. If one of them saw him going in the scandalmongers would have a field-day of it, particularly if they had previously seen Anna going out. But they had damned him anyway, so it hardly seemed to matter.

He knew which her house was, without having any idea how he knew. It was just *there* in his head, from the intensity of his rejection. Tuesday nights, trying not to think about Sylvie there. *Anna says*. He didn't knock. There seemed no point, he could see Yvonne through the front window, and he knew she would be alone.

He was inside before she saw him. She jumped from the sofa, ran towards him. He had not had the least idea what to expect – holding her in his eyes all these weeks and never knowing when he would see her again – and now to find her so obviously glad to see him. She seemed to feel an almost childlike relief, as if he symbolised some zone of safety she had thought she had lost. For a while he almost forgot that he had come with a specific purpose, for they slipped into talking the way they always had. She wanted to know about David, as if he were the one who had gone missing. And then they started on 'do you remember?' Do you remember the time you and David had gone off together and you came back crying, thinking you'd lost him? Yes, yes, and he was hiding in the chicken-house the whole time. He could hide for *ages*, you'd think he'd have got bored waiting to be found.

'And that time he fell in?' she said, 'When we were out in the dinghy and he leant back too far? And you just *laughed* at him, splashing about, and I was so mad at you.'

'He could swim, you know,' Hugh said mildly, 'and the sea was about as dangerous as a paddling pool that day.' He was smiling as he remembered, her flailing arm, her yelling, 'Go get him, go get him,' while he ignored her and brought the yacht around and waited for David to catch up with them, and stretched out an arm to help haul him up over the side … The luxury to be talking normally. So many days since he had said anything more than 'Hello' to anyone other than Cari, and now here he was, able to be himself, not watching what he said, not tensely expecting rejection.

Then a look on her face reminded him what he was here for. He launched right in, conscious now of time slipping by. 'Yvonne, you've had us all worried sick. What have you been up to?' She glared at him, all childlike confiding gone. 'You ran away, didn't you? That was what you needed the money for?'

'Hugh, I'm sorry about the money. I –'

'Forget the money. I just need to know nothing bad happened to you while you were gone.'

'They think I'm pregnant, don't they?'

'The idea has occurred to them.'

'I'm not.'

'I'm glad. You want to choose your time before you do that. And choose the person carefully.'

She shot him a look – don't push me, I'm not telling.

'OK, I'm not trying to force you to say anything, you know I can't. But I do want to know, why are you still here, not at home?'

'You told me once *you* left home at sixteen.'

'That was completely different.'

'Why?'

'Number one, I wasn't behaving like a child, asking someone else to look after me. And number two, I knew what I wanted to do'

Curiosity distracted her. 'What did you want to do?'

'Work like hell, save money, buy my own boat.'

'So did you?'

He laughed. 'It took a while longer than I'd imagined.'

Then she plagued him for stories – Why did he want to get away from home? How did he know where to go? How did he get his first job? Why didn't he stay? Had he ever had a time when he didn't know what he was doing next, had almost run out of money, had nowhere to sleep?

'Sheltering in doorways on cold nights? Yep, I've done that.' Pause. 'You too?' She nodded. 'No fun, huh?'

'It's horrible.'

'And probably worse for a girl.'

'There was this *awful* man, he stank, and he wanted to sit right close to me. Said it would keep us both warm.' She shivered, remembering. A couple of years ago, he'd have put his arm around her, given her a hug, said, 'Don't worry, it's over.' Now his arms hung useless by his sides, self-consciousness taking over again. Looking for a way to distract her he started telling her stories again. 'The time I did it, I'd had an argument with the guy I was sharing a flat with. I walked out, the big gesture, *no way* was I going back. Down the stairs – we were on the top floor – and as I got out and slammed the door behind me – no keys, of course – I realised it was snowing. Too busy being angry to even think of a coat, and it was *cold* that winter, seriously cold.'

'What did you do?'

'Found a pipe by the side of a road, climbed into it.'

'A *pipe?*'

'A big one.' He made an O with his arms to demonstrate. 'For drainage. My back felt like a bent nail the next morning but it was wonderfully sheltered.'

She was laughing, almost hysterical. Release. Gasping she said, 'You know what I did?'

'Go on, you tell.'

'This man – when he kept on at me, I got up and walked away. *Really* fast and trying not to look like I was running. You know?'

He grinned. 'I know. Done that too.'

'I was too scared to look back in case he was coming after me. There was this dark lane, I slipped down it, just to get away where he couldn't see me. And then it turned into a sort of alley between the backyards of two rows of houses, with all little sheds, one at the bottom of each yard. And *nobody* around, everyone asleep. So I just started testing the doors of the sheds till I found one that would open, and I curled up in there, with all the tools and garden pots and junk.'

'And slept?'

'Sort of. But I was so scared of being found, I was out before it was really light.'

She was telling it now with bravado – I had an adventure. Time to bring her back. In a different tone he said, 'It's better knowing where you're going to sleep. And you've got something I never had.'

Defences up again. 'What's that?'

'A mother. Who'll take you back, no questions asked.' Silence.

'You need to get on with your life, Yvonne. Doesn't matter what it is, you'll work that out when you're ready. But move.'

≈≈

Anna felt distinctly odd coming back into her house, expecting to sense the man's departed presence. Mud from boots on the doormat, perhaps, or the smell of old sweaters, a male aura in this house that had never witnessed anything more sexually disturbing than Neville with his headteacher calm or Ron the policeman with his once-a-month small whisky. But there was nothing.

'How did you get on today?' Anna asked.

'OK,' Yvonne said.

No mention of a visitor. Anna felt a flare of anger. She can use me as a retreat when it suits her but she won't trust me even to say, Hugh came.

You'd think, she said to herself as she started making supper, you'd think a girl who hasn't seen her parents for days might ask how they are, or what's happening on St Martin's. But no.

Yvonne's eyes kept following her as she moved about the kitchen. Anna tried to ignore them. Irritation said, if she wants to know, why doesn't she ask? Compassion said, because she can't find a way. Anna said, I'm not listening to compassion, I'm tired of this.

Yvonne got up and went through to the living room. She slouched on the sofa, staring out of the window. Anna watched her through the doorway. Backs are so eloquent, she thought, teenage defensiveness in every muscle. She said to the back, 'Your mother's worried about something. I promised I'd ask you about it.'

Without turning Yvonne said, 'If she thinks I'm pregnant you

297

can tell her not to worry. That wasn't what the money was for.'

'I'm not going to tell her. It's time you started telling her things yourself.' No answer. Anna said, 'I gather Hugh came.'

Yvonne whipped around. 'How did you know?' And then, when Anna didn't reply, 'He was looking around like he'd never been here.'

'He hasn't.'

'He doesn't talk to you, does he?'

'We never see each other.'

'So how did you fix it?'

'I didn't.' Anna paused. 'It was Cari.'

Yvonne stared, full concentration now. Anna said, looking her straight back in the eye, 'And you're the only other person who knows that. So look after that knowledge, privately.'

Yvonne nodded, eyes never leaving Anna's face. Good, thought Anna, for once she's managed to focus on someone other than herself. 'I just wondered,' Anna said, 'whether Hugh had told you. About what's going on on St Martin's.'

Yvonne looked nervous. 'What do you mean?'

'He's having a hard time, your mother says.'

Yvonne stared. Then she said slowly, 'It's my dad, isn't it?'

'Not him directly. But what people think he thinks.'

Yvonne got up, but didn't know where to put herself and slumped down on the sofa again, staring moodily out of the window. Eventually she spun round and burst out, 'I feel like I'm in a deep hole here, shut away from everything.'

'You're choosing that,' Anna said. 'You can choose any time to come out.' Yvonne's eyes flashed denial, then misery. Anna made herself ignore the look. 'Hugh didn't say *anything* about it?' Yvonne shook her head. 'What *did* you talk about?'

'He just – he just came in, and – I was so surprised to see him I never thought about – I don't know, it was just such a relief, him here and everything like it used to be when David was there, not having to think about anyone noticing. I can't remember what – he got me laughing, remembering things, when David and I were little.'

'He didn't ask you what you'd been up to?'

She looked defensive again. 'I did tell him a bit. Things that happened the nights I had nowhere to go.' She broke off, the fear returning to her face. 'Aunt Anna, tell me what's happening.'

'No one speaks to him.'

'What do you *mean?*'

'Just that. They assume there was a man behind your disappearance, and there aren't many candidates they can think of. They know your dad doesn't have much to do with him any more, and that's enough for them. And you know what people are like, they'll never go to Hugh and say straight out, 'People are saying it's you.' They're just going cold on him, till the only people he'll have left to speak to are the tourists.'

Yvonne cried, 'Stop!'

But no way was she stopping now. She said, voice getting louder, 'I'm just telling you what no one else will, because they're all so concerned to be kind to you. What you do or don't do, what you say or don't say, has an effect on other people, and you can't hide away from it.'

'OK,' she shouted, 'I'll go and tell them, *now.*'

Anna let the words sink in through the pounding in her chest. Done. Thank God, it was done. Gradually the tension relaxed, enough for her to notice that Yvonne's eyes were wild, her breast heaving as if she had been running in fear. Anna said, smiling a little as she pointed out of the window where the light was beginning to fade, 'Maybe not now. It's a bit late. Tomorrow will be fine.'

But Yvonne was not ready for the smile. She glared at her and then suddenly shouted, 'Sometimes I really hate you.'

They faced each other through the silence that washed in after the shout. *Sometimes I hate you ...* And sometimes I hate you, Anna thought, for what you are doing to your mother. And you haven't the slimmest notion of it ... Let it be, let it be. It is over.

She went to sit next to Yvonne, her arm around her. 'As long as it's only sometimes,' she said, and began rocking her like the child she no longer was, and could never again retreat to.

It was dark when the girl finally stirred, dark outside and dark inside, for Anna hadn't moved to draw the curtains or turn on a light. She said gently, 'You slept.'

Yvonne said, 'I was dreaming about Jason.' Anna waited, but the girl said no more.

'Come,' Anna said. 'Bed.'

≈≈

Neville was sitting over a leisurely Saturday breakfast when Anna arrived. She joined him at the table and accepted some toast and marmalade. 'Vera's just popped out to the shops,' he said. 'She'll be sorry to have missed you.'

'She makes superb marmalade,' Anna said, mouth full and munching. 'Tell her I want the recipe.' Then, 'Yvonne's ready to talk.'

Neville put down his coffee cup. 'She's told you?'

'A headline only. I've reached the point where I don't want to know the rest. But she says she'll talk to you.'

He folded his napkin. 'I'll come as soon as you're ready.'

She said, 'I'm done. It was sheer greed anyway.'

They walked back together, Anna pushing her bike. When they got to the corner of her road she stopped and said, 'I'll leave you to it. I need to get out on my own.'

Anna kept herself away for an hour and a half. There must have been telepathy in the timing, for Neville was just coming out of the house as she got off her bike at the gate. He said, 'I'm going over to Thomas and Bella, give them some advance notice. She's ready to go back. I've suggested she has a quiet spell at home, find some practical things to help with, then start again at school after half-term. By then I devoutly hope everyone will have found something else to talk about.' He paused. 'I've said I'll take her over early evening, fewer people about. Unless you'd like to do it.'

'I'd be grateful if you would.'

He nodded. 'You've had enough, I imagine.'

'You've carried the worst of it, Neville.'

He half-smiled, acknowledging. 'There have been easier terms.'

Neither of them moved. They looked out over the bay, each following their own thoughts. The last time for this small ritual, standing at the gate to talk before he left. There are things I am going to miss after all, Anna realised. This, and Cari coming.

Neville's eyes had rested on a family group down on the beach. After a while he turned to Anna and said, 'And they build their sandcastles and think this is the place where life is simple.' Then he pulled himself back, to the step he was about to take, the task ahead. 'Well, there we are,' he said.

'Yes,' Anna said.

He moved to go. 'See you Tuesday night,' he said. 'Thank God life still has a few regularities about it.'

≈≈

The weekend hours stretched ahead, long and empty. Cari wandered about outside the cottage that was supposed to be her home, and made herself notice all she had been neglecting. The Tremain's flower fields were yellow again as they had been when she and Andrew first arrived, not with daffodils now but with marigolds, growing wild. Bothams, Mrs Tremain called them. Maybe they weren't wild, but planted to renew the soil? Cari didn't know. So much she still didn't know about the islands and her time was almost gone.

Ollie was in the yard, humping bales of straw, his body draped like a pile of clothes, no spine to him. 'How's it going?' she asked. He shrugged. How could he feel any enthusiasm? He had lost his job, had a court case pending for attempting to defraud the company by harbouring a stowaway, and here he was back on his mother's farm and she running him down with every sentence she spoke. Poor Ollie. Please God don't let Yvonne end up marrying him out of misplaced gratitude.

She went into the cottage. Her cottage and Andrew's. In six days he would be back to share it again. His files would sit again there, his books here, his papers spreading over the floor.

Stop it, she told herself. This is your life, you made it this way.

Anna looked around her house. Yvonne gone, empty spaces. Start again. Yet another new beginning; also a re-run of the old one, but subtly different.

Out on her bike she saw Cari walking, just as she had been in those first months when Anna had seen her and had to guess at the person behind those noticing eyes. Anna stopped, waited for Cari to get nearer. They smiled, acknowledging the sameness, the difference.

'What about some tea?' Anna said.

Same setting, Anna's kitchen, no one but them in the house, Cari watching as Anna got tea ready. And almost the same tentativeness – what to say, what not to say.

Anna started. 'I was about to start sorting out my paints.'

'Let me help you.'

They took their tea and moved upstairs. When they got there Anna said, 'I think as I go. I wouldn't know what to ask you to do.'

'Then I'll just watch,' Cari said, and settled herself with her mug on the window seat. Anna got busy, pulling things out of a low cupboard, spreading them on the floor, cleaning, grouping. After a while she looked up. 'I like having you there.'

'I like being here.'

'It's funny, some people definitely cut across aloneness, and others let you keep being yourself.'

'Yes.'

Beginning to pack things back, finding another stack at the very back. Kneeling down to stretch in and pull them out.

Cari's voice behind her. 'Anna.'

'Um huh?'

'Yvonne told me you were a doctor before you came here.'

'I was.'

'Why do you hide it?'

Anna pulled her head out of the cupboard and half-straightened up. 'I've got ridiculously stiff with all this being indoors.' She turned her head to Cari. 'Have you ever been on a plane?'

'Sorry?'

'A plane. When the air hostess asks is there a doctor on board? You ask any doctor, and the honest ones will tell you they have to struggle with themselves not to just lie low and hope someone else will answer first.'

'I don't understand.'

'I'm lying low. I spent most of my adult life trying to attend to the needs of others. I came here because I finally realised I could be no good to anyone until I had first attended to things in my own life. Which I had been grossly neglecting.'

'And now look at you.'

'What do you mean?'

'With Yvonne. You were scarcely letting someone else answer first. Even if you wanted to.'

Anna said, 'Cari my girl, you are too dangerous to be let loose.' And she put her head back into the cupboard.

Cari's voice reached her again. 'Anna, there's something I need to ask you.' Head slowly back out again. Cari said, 'I don't like to do this to you. I know you need a break.'

'Ask.'

'There are some things I don't understand, that I need to. And only you can help me.'

Anna looked at her without speaking, then closed the cupboard door and came to sit next to her on the window seat. 'What things?'

'About Hugh. Why you can't even talk about each other. And Sylvie. Why she left.'

A moment more to overcome her resistance. What to say?

'Please,' said Cari. 'It's really important.'

Anna said slowly, 'You have probably seen everything there is to see about Hugh. About the life he leads. About what moves him, and how he can't be moved. There's nothing more to say about Sylvie except that it all became too much for her. It's hard to keep your end up against that amount of life force.' She was watching Cari as she spoke, visualising her and Hugh together, compared to Sylvie and Hugh. Such different equations. She knew she had not answered Cari's question and made herself try again. 'Sylvie hasn't your intuition, or your resources. It's not easy trying to survive on St Martin's. Constant hard work, and lonely. She began to want something else to happen in her life.'

'Is she happy, with what she went to?'

'Happy?' Anna heard her own tone, sharper than she had intended. 'Now that's another question. What does being happy mean?' Then, softer, 'I really can't say, she's hardly kept in touch. A letter or two soon after she'd left, bits of news from Bella. And one phone call.' Then honesty compelled her, 'No, I don't think she's happy. But it's hard to expect that, so soon after a major upheaval.'

'And Hugh? I mean you and Hugh?'

'Cari, leave it now. It's not your story. Things happened that no one intended, and we got stuck with an unfortunate legacy. That's all. You have your own life to make, and it's got nothing to do with all of that.'

Cari turned to stare down at the bay. 'Everything else seemed to go into limbo the last couple of weeks. Now it's all back, pushing me somewhere, but I don't know where. I'm hopeless at decisions.'

'I'm not so sure,' Anna said. 'You were quite decisive in how you handled Yvonne.'

'Someone else's crisis I can manage. It's my own I get lost in.'

'That's normal.'

Cari turned, to look directly at her. Before she spoke again Anna realised something that she had been vaguely aware of, but not named. Cari's face was unusually pale, a pinched look around her cheeks. 'You're tired, my dear,' Anna said.

Cari said, 'I think I may be pregnant.'

≈≈

Yes, there was a child already forming. But so hard to see through to that child, that new miraculous being, for all the clutter of adult confusion that blocked one's sight.

'You weren't using contraception?' Anna asked, incredulous.

'I had a loop.'

No loop there now. Aborted itself, as they do occasionally, her body acting before her mind was ready. 'Did you *want* a child?'

'I hadn't got to thinking about it. There were so many other things to sort out first.'

A child conceived on the island. But which island? It could be either, it seemed. Little sexual activity for months with Andrew, but they had done it once in the critical period, the night before he left. An anxious love-making, Cari remembered unhappily, a trying-to-make-everything-OK love-making.

And with Hugh? No words offered. None needed, for it was obvious. The fruit of the desire of first real awakening.

What a choice to present to a child for its conception.

Anna sat sipping a whisky in the window ledge where Cari had sat a few hours earlier and observed the two possibilities, seeing them before her as if they had shape and size and texture. A child who might have light brown hair and a high forehead like Andrew, or an untameable dark mop and an obstinate jaw like Hugh. Who might grow up in Birmingham with a father rising to seniority in the university, earning a regular salary without his wife having to work herself to exhaustion point. Or a child whose earliest memories would be pottering about in the sands of St Martin's, handling boats at an age when other children can scarcely ride a bike; and who then would leave at sixteen for the mainland, there being no future for the young on the islands.

Thank God it's not me that has to decide.

They sang in the choir on Tuesday evenings Bach's Magnificat.

My soul doth magnify the Lord, sang Anna, contralto,

306

and my spirit hath rejoiced in God my saviour
for he hath regarded the lowliness of his handmaiden —

'There are women in your position,' Anna had said, 'who would say, this is too complicated, I'm having an abortion.'

'Oh I couldn't,' Cari said. 'I simply couldn't.' Then, 'It's a child.' And then, 'My child.'

My child. Yes, but never really yours. Given, to be cared-for, to learn love through; to learn to detach from; then to be taken away. Anna sat by the window after Cari had gone, watching the last strands of evening light fade on this scrap of land in the middle of an ocean, and felt for this young-girl-about to-be-a-mother a compassion that went far beyond the dilemma she faced now. She felt she was seeing a life stretch ahead of her, and then looking back over it, taking in the loss that would inevitably come with love. Seeing it all, and knowing there was no other way.

A quietness came over her about her own mothering, her lost child. She held Jason again as a new-born infant, and watched his mouth search for the breast and his hands move through the air, also searching. She watched the toddler peer intently at some stones he had stumbled on, touch them, turn them over. She saw the child, the boy, the young man; she held his hand and let it go so that he could move through the world on his own. I *didn't* want to hold on to you, she cried silently, I really *was* ready to let you go. I know you thought I followed you but I never had a chance to explain, that wasn't why I had come, I didn't even know you were here. It was something completely different, a crisis in my own life I had to get away from. I had faced the emptiness of the life I was supposed to be sharing with your father, and I knew that to stay alive I had to get out. I thought I had someone else to go to, and when I found I didn't, there was nothing — a cliff edge, and I was falling.

'Get away,' said Elaine, the only friend who knew. 'Anywhere. Climb a mountain. Join a tour, then you won't have to think. They just take you along, you just do whatever they've planned. And at least there will be other people.' But I couldn't cope with being sociable, having to pretend to feel normal. Then I thought – I could cope with Bella. Bella has never expected anything of me, she just takes me as I am. And it was only when I got to St Martin's that I found out, *that* was where you were sailing.

No one listening, no one there to listen. Anna looked down and saw that she was fingering the pile of stones that she had laid out in one corner of the window seat, feeling their smoothness. Stones collected from Jason's beach. At least stones last, they're solid. Foundations. Burial chambers. Stone circles. Carefully she let each stone slip from her fingers, moving her hand delicately to let them form a pattern on the window ledge. They had a surprising lightness, as if once broken off from the cliff face they could be whatever they chose. She watched the pattern they were forming, something coming through her, no decision of the mind. A spiral, moving ever outwards. They were the stones her grandfather had held onto in his last moments of life till he fell from the cliff face, the stones her father's child-hands had touched on that island now abandoned to the birds. They were fragments of Jason's spirit, broken loose. And now a touch of Cari's, hiding from the eyes of the world on that small beach that lay protected by the cliffs, the beach that had also been Jason's. And through both of them, Hugh's.

Just see, and accept what is.

It's their lives, good luck to them. There's nothing about it that can hurt me.

≈≈

'Andrew,' Cari practised as she cleared weeks-old ash from the cottage fireplace, 'there's a baby growing inside me.'

No, that sounded ridiculous, as if it were a tapeworm.

Andrew I'm pregnant.

Andrew we're pregnant.

Andrew I have to tell you, it's a bit complicated, I need you to listen quietly till I get to the end.

Andrew —

The whole trouble is, she told herself, as she tipped the half-dead geraniums out of the window boxes, the trouble is that none of this is Andrew's story. He isn't even a character in it anymore, I can't begin to imagine what any of it will look like from his side.

I have to start again, find his eyes to see it through.

OK, so I'm Andrew. Do I want a child? Have I ever even *thought* of having a child? No way. Like I never thought of getting married, till Cari started going on about it. Now here she is again, pushing me on to the next thing, and it's going to take a hell of a lot of time, I can see that already, and I need time to finish my thesis. Not to say peace. And the one thing I know about babies, they're not peaceful. What happened to science? I thought we were supposed to be able to control these things these days, choose our time? Really, Cari, how incredibly careless of you, I always said loops were unreliable, you should have gone on the pill.

This isn't working.

Andrew, I'm going to have a child and I'm not sure it's yours.

I'm really sorry Andrew, I never meant this to happen, it was all a huge mistake.

I should bloody well hope it was, what do you expect me to

309

do now? Ruin my peace for a child I don't even know is mine? We can talk about children later when the time comes but this certainly isn't the time and it certainly isn't the right way for it to happen. There's a perfectly simple solution, just go and have an abortion.

But there's a child already, Andrew. My child. And I'm having it. The choice for you is, do you want to do it with me? Because if you don't, I know someone who does.

No, that's wrong. Do that one again.

Because if you do, I'll be very happy.

Oh God, I want to cry.

Andrew a father. Think about it. Try and see it. Just *say* to yourself, it's Andrew's child, as if there is no doubt about it. Try that one. No mention of Hugh. Pointless trying to make him understand all that, he hasn't lived it, it's not his story. Pushing it on him now wouldn't be honesty, it would be oppression. Why should he have to deal with it? Isn't fatherhood enough new for him to come to terms with? And how can I give him a *choice?* Even I didn't choose it, why would he? Andrew, would you *prefer* to be woken three times every night, to have no time to yourself any more, to drag around all day half-awake and be left looking after a baby who cries with colic while I go somewhere for an hour and you can't even feed it because you're not equipped by nature?

Andrew, we're going to have a child.

That's it, nice and simple. Like women have been saying to their men since time began. I can't be the first one in history who had to say it even when she wasn't sure it was his. He'll be scared. It's OK to be scared, Andrew, I am too. You'll get used to the idea, just give it a couple of days. And when it gets nearer the time you'll be scared again, maybe, and stick your head deeper into your equations as if they can take you away from these complicated things that need dealing with. And I'm going to try not to panic when you do that, because once it comes you'll know it's something we have to be responsible for together. You'll be nervous about holding it, I know. You'll say, 'You're much better at this than me,' and hand it back too quickly. Don't worry, we can learn together, and if there are things that come more easily to me, I can wait while you learn –

I don't have to think about Hugh as a father. I know what he would be like.

Just stop it, Cari, that's *not* helpful. There are other things Hugh would be a disaster at, you know that. And probably even he had to be taught, you just weren't there to see Sylvie going through all that, Andrew can do it, with a bit of pushing. And maybe it will be the making of him. Maybe he needs something demanded of him, something personal and intimate that he simply can't say no to.

We're going to have a child, Andrew.

She stayed on in the classroom after school on Monday. Not ready to go back to face Hugh, no point going back to the cottage. Better to distract herself with work. All that marking she had left to pile up.

Gone six, and still hours of daylight ahead of her to fill. Almost, she wished for night. Her footsteps echoed in the empty school building. On her way out she looked in at the staff room, to check for post. What was she hoping for? A card from Robyn, maybe, something sane and neutral. Footsteps behind her. She turned. Neville.

'Thought I heard someone,' he said. 'I've just had the police in Plymouth on the phone. They've found Paul.'

She sat down, abruptly. Neville came to sit next to her. 'He's in Middlesbrough. He's been trying to sell his house, the one Yvonne tried to visit. The estate agent had his new address.' She stared at him blankly, hardly knowing what to feel. 'The police want to press charges, the family wants to drop it.'

'And you?'

'I want him taken off the books and never left in charge of children again. But police charges? I don't know. It can't be done without dragging Yvonne through the courts.'

They looked at each other, both weighed down. Cari was aware of that commonality of feeling and oddly comforted by it. She said, 'Do you never feel that you could have found yourself in his position?'

Neville stared at her. 'Now that's a surprising question.'

'I keep remembering his good qualities. Before all this. He *was* good for the kids, they really got a lot from him. It seems so – I don't know, Greek tragedy stuff. One moment of weakness and your life collapses around you.'

He said slowly, 'It depends on what you mean by the moment of weakness.'

'Desire. Giving in to it.'

'There was a lot more to it than that. Ignoring the fact that she was barely sixteen, that he had a position of trust to care for her. *In loco parentis*. And if you want to be less legalistic, that physical maturity does not necessarily go with emotional maturity. That is surely a level of judgement one has a right to expect of someone responsible for young people.' He paused, looked at her closely. 'Anyway, what matters more than the moment of weakness is how you handle the mess you've created.'

Cari said nothing.

'My dear,' he said, 'You're tired. You've taken more than your share of the strain. Do you need a couple of days off?'

She had a lump in her throat, as she now seemed to every

312

time anyone was kind to her. 'It's sweet of you, but I can't, you know I can't, we're too short-staffed.'

'Well tell me if you change your mind. I can ask Vera to come in again. I'd rather do that than have another crisis. Two is enough for one term.' She smiled but didn't feel capable of laughing with him. He said, 'There's something else I wanted to talk to you about. The applicants for Paul's replacement, they're none of them what we want. What would we have to do to persuade you to apply?'

Oh God, she said. Yes, she said. No, she said. Don't do this to me, she said. But she said none of them aloud because she was trying to get the lump in her throat to disappear so that she could speak at all.

She became aware of Neville's eyes on her, waiting. What matters more than the giving-in to desire is how you handle the mess you've created.

She found her voice. 'I would love to, Neville. I would love nothing more. But I can't.'

He said, regretfully, 'So you have other plans?'

And because there seemed nothing more to lose she said, 'I'm going to have a child. But I'd be grateful if you would keep it to yourself. Not even the father knows yet.'

≈≈

I need the weekend, she had said, but she might change her mind. Hugh worked close to his house, waiting for a phone call that did not come. The same on Monday. By Tuesday he had had enough of waiting and mid-afternoon set off down to his boat. A light wind streaked the sea with slowly shifting patterns of blue. Perfect sailing weather, he thought, and then was overtaken by a longing to be able to give the pleasure of that to Cari, just once, to take her out quietly past that obstinately lodged fear.

He beached the boat and climbed the steep cliff path, and for the first time made his way along the bracken track. He approached the Tremain farmhouse. He really didn't care if he was seen, but there was no one about. The cottage behind was empty. He wandered over to a gate and leaned up against it contemplating the state of Mrs Tremain's fields.

The bus arrived and Cari got off, humping her bag of books. A few yards short of the cottage she stopped, staring. She said, 'My God,' and then gave up, apparently unable to sort out which of many conflicting emotions to give expression to.

He saved her the trouble. 'The boat's waiting. Whatever happens later I can't let you waste these days.'

All the way over her eyes were glad. She had needed him to do for her what she couldn't do for herself. As they walked up his track she was touching him, small touches, to reassure. When they got inside they stood facing each other, uncertain. He knew from the settled sadness in her that she had made her decision, that even though she had come today and would maybe let herself stay tomorrow, and each tomorrow till Andrew returned, essentially this was the end.

'Come to bed,' he said. But she was afraid to let herself and he was afraid to press. He said, 'OK then, let's get out in the boat again. It helps, when things get stuck inside you.' The wind in your face, the sense of moving somewhere.

Again she let herself be led, too tired to think of a reason not to. They went back down to the beach, to his two boats pulled up on the sand, the everyday boat with its motor leaning into the earth, and the light dinghy, its mast tipped towards the sky. One for practicalities, one for joy. If he was ever to do it, it had to be now.

'Cari,' he said, 'what would you say to a sail? Just a little one?'

And one for joy, she smiled, and nodded. He was aware of her watching while he got the sails ready but he kept his eyes carefully away from hers so he couldn't see if she was changing her mind. He pulled out the life-jackets and so that she would not think he was treating her like a child he put one on himself before he passed one to her. She took it, half-laughing at herself, and then lost self-consciousness as she got absorbed in the remembered act of tying the straps. But she looked so ridiculously childlike in the clumsy orange thing that he started laughing and pulled her towards him to hug her, their life-jackets bumping – bumping her past nervousness, he realised, and felt like shouting in exultation. With energy surging through him he pushed out the dinghy and jumped in. 'Come,' he called, and she waded out to him. He gave her a hand in. She was like someone getting onto a bike for the first time in years, wondering if her body still knew how to balance. She sat tentatively opposite him as he got the sails up, the tiller in hand. He was content to let her sit there as a passenger as long as she needed, but within a minute or two of being out she said, 'Let me take the rope for a minute,' and he watched as her hands found their way again and her head tilted back to look up at the sail billowing in a perfect curve, and her eyes moved down again to take in the sea around them, docile as sleeping child. She glanced at him and they both started laughing again.

He took her over to Nornour, an island with no people. They beached and took off their life-jackets and began to walk slowly along the beach, saying little. A quiet joy at being together in this way again, but also an acceptance that there was nothing they could say that could change things. They wandered around the stone remains where thousands of years ago some man had built a home, had cut the rock and laid it and watched with pride as the walls rose under his hands, his own work. Then in that house that he had built he lay with his woman, and in love created children and together raised them here, teaching them to provide for themselves through knowing the tides, the movements of the fish. Just this one isolated household, alone on the island; till it fell to ruins and the Romans who came after them used it for a shrine.

Cari was trailing her hands over the stones, stopping at a collection of pennywort that grew out of the cracks in the broken down walls. He watched her fingers trace the leaves, small circles of life, the upright spikes of yellow-green flowers, and she waking to the pleasure of touch. He felt happy knowing that bringing her here had calmed her, even if it solved nothing.

Her eyes followed an oystercatcher down at the low tide mark, rapping away with its bright orange bill at a shell. Hugh said, for no reason he was aware of, 'They have interesting parenting habits.'

'Oh?'

'There's a ritual they go through. Groups of them form circles near the nests and run up and down in the sand going *kleep, kleep*.'

She asked, vaguely puzzled, 'The nests are in the ground?'

'They're just shallow scrapes in the earth, made by turning their breasts around to hollow it out a little.' They both watched the bird for a minute more. 'They make several nests. Then the female chooses the one she thinks best and lines it with shells and pebbles.'

She was staring at him, intense interest now. 'The female chooses the nest?'

'Yes. But they both incubate the eggs and tend the chicks.'

She turned back to watch the oystercatcher a few minutes more. Still looking at it, she said, 'Hugh, I have to tell you something.'

He had wanted to save her, to say, I know it already, you're

316

going to tell me this is our last time.

She said, 'I'm going to have a child.' And before he had time to feel, to think, 'Andrew's child.'

'How do you know?' he demanded

'The dates,' she said. 'It must have happened before.'

He heard and did not want to hear. He flailed against the knowledge, and all the time he was unable to speak, just seeing her sitting there looking wan and miserable. He wanted to fight off the world to take that sadness from her face, to see her run free again across the beach.

He dreamt that night, the last he would lie holding her, that he had taken her out in the dinghy again. They were in trouble, in seas far stormier than he had ever encountered, seas like those that had smashed Jason's young life. Cari was looking at him with eyes that were afraid but still trusting, expecting him to do something to save them. He held onto the ropes against the terrible pull of the wind and knew against all his desperation that it was useless. 'I don't know what to do,' he shouted, to himself as much as to her, 'I'm out of my own waters.'

≈≈

Time she got away, Anna decided, somewhere more simple, because anonymous. She dug out her address book that had lain unused for too long and worked her way through a list of possible friends she could land herself on. Someone who would be able to accept her brief return without needing to press her to talk about her transitions. Chichester friends – No, no, too many of them, too interconnected. If she stayed with one she would be repossessed by the whole lot, and much as they had meant to her, she was not ready for that. Or, for that matter, to revisit Chichester. Elaine, a few days in London – that might work. Elaine too had become single, shortly after Anna did, she too had moved away. She would understand more now about the need to start again. And being in London would mean Anna could see Gail and the children, without actually staying with them.

She phoned. 'Wonderful,' said Elaine. 'And about time. I'll take a couple of days' leave. We can do art galleries together.'

'I haven't been inside one since I started painting.'

'There you are then, a bit of culture to keep you going. When can you come?'

'Saturday?' Anna said. 'I know it's a bit sudden, but it's half-term next week and the island gets too crowded for my taste.'

Andrew coming back. A good time to be away.

She dropped in at Neville's to return the books Yvonne had been using. Neville said, 'London? Rather you than me.' She was grateful he didn't say, 'This is an unusual departure for you, Anna.' All he said was, 'While you're there can you get to a music shop?'

'Sure, give me your orders.'

Bella was over to do her shopping and they met for tea. It was the first time Bella had left Thomas and Yvonne alone together and she couldn't relax.

Anna said, 'How is it going?'

Bella shrugged. 'We're managing. No one's saying much.' Then, 'You know those clippers of Thomas's? No one in Penzance can fix them and he's so attached to them. If you're going to be in London maybe you could see if that shop he ordered them from is still there?'

'They've given up fixing things in London, they just throw things away and buy new ones.'

'Well even a new one would be OK, if it's exactly the same kind. It would be nice to find something to cheer Thomas up.'

It would indeed.

Noel and Penny's faces bobbed before her as she dialled. Gail said, 'Next week? That'll be wonderful, Mum. You'll be here for Penny's birthday.' Would she? How utterly negligent of her not to have realised. 'But come another day too, so it can be just us.'

'Lovely. Which day would suit?'

'Any day. We haven't got a lot planned. No wait, Tuesday's no good, I'm helping at the playgroup. And Friday's going to be a bit of a rush, getting ready for the party. Wednesday?'

'Wednesday it is,' Anna said. 'And I want to tell you, I gave Bella one of the photos you sent. She was very pleased.' Then she realised, Gail knows nothing about Yvonne. There's her life, almost too busy to fit me in, and here's my life, handling Yvonne, and neither of us need to know the details, we're both getting on fine.

'Mum,' Gail said, 'I wish you'd get a phone. What if something comes up at the last minute?'

'Leave a message with Elaine. I'll get it when I arrive.'

As she walked out of the phone booth she felt the wind lift her hair and was assailed by a memory of Cari saying, 'It shows, that feeling that you're becoming free.' Free she was not, for all the years of working at it. 'You're a fool, Anna,' she told herself, 'as foolish as Cari for not checking that her loop was still in place.' She too had thought she had protection but had let her guard slip, and here she was all over again facing almost certain loss. The girl had a sense of responsibility like an ogre, and a stupid one at that. She would do what she thought she ought to do regardless of how bad that would be for everyone, and then that baby would be born in Birmingham and all she, Anna, would ever see of it or of Cari would be an occasional half-term holiday on St Mary's, toes wiggling in the sand. With Andrew always there, needing her attention.

'I'll babysit,' Anna said out loud, getting her lines ready.

But it wasn't a lot of comfort.

Cari stood outside Anna's door. It was closed against her, no one in. She felt like a child denied. She was full of things she needed to say. Andrew's coming back and I need you to meet him. I need you to help me work out what I'm going to do.

The door made no answer. You have to deal with this yourself, it said, Anna's getting back to her own life.

Cari turned away. She could not go home, she did not know what home was any more. Scrapes in the earth from which she had to choose. She stood at the point where the steps led down to the beach, where three months ago she had stood with Karl and Eva, and they had looked down on two small children digging in the sand while two women watched. Sixteen years ago she and Robyn had dug in this same beach, had created worlds that the tides would wash away, but with the wisdom of childhood did not care, for they could build again. I wish Robyn were here, Cari thought suddenly, and uselessly. But Robyn was off on her own journey.

She started down the steps, slipping her shoes off to feel the wet grainy sand in her toes and the slippery seaweed that the receding tide had left exposed. Long brown ribbons with tough bubbles in them. Popweed, she and Robyn used to call it. 'Robyn,' she said, 'I'm going to have a child. A child of our island. Imagine.' No answer. Too far away.

Cari said, 'Hugh's child.'

I know it is. I've known all along, I know exactly when it

happened. It's funny how you can hide these things from yourself. I remember now, really clearly, waking up the morning after that first night we had together after Andrew had left. I woke to a feeling so free and full, that glow all over my body from hours of constant loving, thinking, *this* is what loving is meant to be like. And so obvious how that act of love can create new life. I felt it deep inside, something forming that I knew would keep growing, more and more lovely. And then I was afraid of what I heard myself thinking and I denied it, pushed down the knowledge, deep down.

She had reached the far end of the beach and climbed up onto the old harbour wall. Robyn used to put her flip-flops back on for the wall, Cari remembered, because the stones set in the concrete hurt her feet. Cari always carried hers. It scratched, but your feet got used to it. Jump off at the end of the wall and in at the churchyard gate now, and maybe she would find Anna there, sketching. But there was no one. She began to climb the line of stone steps that she had walked up with Yvonne, the day she had found a way to help Yvonne acknowledge what she was afraid to feel. She turned at the top, to sit and look down over the church below, the small enclosed bay with the tide even further out now. And beyond it, the sea. Quiet today, scarcely a ripple. She sat perfectly still and let her mind touch Hugh's name, letting the knowledge of his continuing existence seep into her and calm her. For so many days she had not been able to look at him straight, afraid of the pull. She had made herself say to him the words that had to be said, to put an end to the misery of indecision – for him. For her the words had changed nothing. Just words, against this continuing press of feeling, against the unavoidable fact of the child within her.

'I know you would love another child,' she told Hugh across that sea, speaking quietly now, no need to defend herself against feeling since he was not here. 'All that bottled-up love, no proper outlet. I want to share this child with you, I want you to have the joy of it, more than I can say. But I'm not sure I could manage life on St Martin's. Sylvie's life.'

'It wouldn't be Sylvie's life,' Hugh answered, 'it would be ours. Ours to create in our own way as we have created the child.'

She longed to listen, to give up fighting and be lulled by that quiet, beguiling sea. But the thought of trusting herself to it was too frightening. It would be like setting out across the Atlantic with someone she still hardly knew. And if she had to bail out half way as Sylvie had? To let him know he was a father again, and then take this one away from him too?

Let the words stand. Better that way.

≈≈

The truth was, Anna acknowledged, she was feeling slightly light-headed, not sure what was real. She was about to leave the islands, this time because she wanted to; and though it was only for a week, she did not quite trust that the life she had created here and that now sustained her would be here to come back to. It felt the end of an era, and she needed to do something to mark it. It was not, she realised, something she could do on St Mary's. It had to be St Martin's, a final goodbye to mourning for Jason.

She arrived at the pier only minutes before the boats were about to set off. Garth saw her and called out, 'Kingfisher for St Martin's, next one along.' The young man at the top of the stone stairs reached out his hand to guide her down. She sat squashed between holiday-makers.

They landed at the eastern quay. Hugh's end, she thought, and then pushed the thought away. She needed to escape from all that, from the thought of Cari and Hugh as much as from the company of Yvonne and Bella. She set off up the path that turned away from the houses, up onto Chapel Down. A slight drizzle, more like a snivelly cold than anything serious, hardly worth getting out a hanky for. For some reason that idea entertained her, the kind of silly joke she and her grandchildren got into together, and at the thought that she would be seeing them soon her stride got longer, more sure of itself. The power of grandchildren, she thought, though hardly anyone admits it, is that you get a chance to try again, and do it a whole lot better.

She imagined herself in another, calmer era, bringing them up here. Noel would run to the tall white daymark, stand up against its bulk, stretch his arms as if he could encircle its red and white stripes – Look Gran, look what I can do. Penny would stay nearer her, slower to react, wanting stories. She would show them the old boundaries still marked by turf covered stony banks, and the menhir, the Celtic standing stone. A mystery, this stone, like so much else. Almost a head-and-shoulders statue, but if it had been carved it had been done so sketchily as to leave almost everything to the imagination. Was this an object of nature then, yet so uncannily suggesting the human? She stared at the almost-head of stone, inclining hers to one side to match it. 'What do you think?' she asked the children. 'Do you think they were carving him and didn't finish? That a storm broke in the middle and they had to leave it half-done and run? And when it was over wouldn't touch it again in case the storm was the gods' displeasure?' She walked round it, tipped her head the other way and talked straight to the menhir now. 'You're an abstract artist's rendering, that's what you are. And highly symbolic. A half-finished person, as we all are.' The almost-man didn't answer.

She turned, to follow the northern fringe of the island,

looking out to the sea that Jason had sailed time out of number. Down a path to a small beach. The tide was going out, the sands still shining. Along the high tide mark was a low green plant that looked a bit like – She bent to examine it. Yes, sea sandwort. Early still, but its small white flowers were just opening. 'A line of sea sandwort' Jason had written, words in a diary she had never been meant to read. 'We beached in a small bay on the north west of St Martin's, with a line of sea sandwort following the high tide mark.' She sat down, legs stretched out, to get a closer view of the plant.

And only then did she become aware that she was not alone.

A man was standing a few yards away, his shadow falling over her as she sat on the sand. Then the shadow crouched into itself as he brought himself down to her level, and in that movement she knew who it was. For it was so that she remembered him going down on his haunches in Bella's yard, to take the child David onto his knee.

Hugh waited. Anna turned, stared.

He said, 'I startled you.'

'No, no,' she said, and went back to staring.

'I could go if you would prefer.'

'No, no,' she said again. Neither of them knew how to proceed. Eventually she asked, 'Were you following me?'

'I was out anyway. I happened to see you.' He paused, then, with a slight smile, 'I overheard your conversation.'

'Conversation?'

'With the Celtic Man.'

She said, offhand, 'It's encroaching age. You start talking to yourself.'

'I do it myself. It's not age, it's living alone.'

She checked, 'You saw me walking, and you decided –'

He nodded. 'I decided to days ago. But I didn't know how to. I get myself into traps and I can't find a way out of them.'

'Days ago,' she repeated, trying to make sense of it.

'Once I'd got inside your house. Things acquire a false power when you never see them.'

'*My house* had a false power?'

'The place where Sylvie spent Tuesday nights.'

'Of course. How stupid of me.' He took that in. How could she not have realised? She said, checking again, 'You blamed me for Sylvie leaving?'

'Not exactly. I knew she was unhappy. But she wasn't the kind of person who took large actions on her own. I thought –' He stopped himself. 'It doesn't matter what I thought.'

'Sylvie talked a lot. She needed to. I didn't ask to hear it, like I didn't ask to have Yvonne with me when Bella desperately needed her home.'

'Or Cari,' he said.

She looked cautious. 'I'm not sure about that.'

'When I saw Yvonne there, it became obvious. People use you when they're in trouble. Because you know about it.'

She shifted a few inches further away. From the safer distance she said, 'This is the kind of conversation people write for themselves in their heads, doing both parts so they can be sure it'll come out right.'

He sat down, overtaken by the need to move past the careful placing of statements to what he was really trying to say. 'I am sorry, Anna. I should have found a way much earlier to move on.'

'Forget it. I could have made the first move too but I was too much of a coward.' She searched for something safe to talk about. 'When does David come next?'

'July. For four weeks this time.'

'You lucky man.' His face showed instant defensiveness. 'Now

Hugh, don't be silly. I'm only saying you're lucky to have David in your life. Regardless of how much you see him.'

He shrugged, angry with himself for getting tripped again by feelings jumping out at him. He wanted to say, 'It's OK,' but he couldn't. He stared out to sea.

Anna said, 'And I gather Andrew's coming back.'

'Yes,' he said, warily.

'Luckily I won't be here to witness it.'

He looked up sharply. 'Have you met him?'

'No.'

'Do you know what she's going to say to him?'

'I don't. And I don't think she does either.'

'What would you want her to say?'

Anna turned to look at him, hard. 'That's not a fair question. I try not to have opinions about the viability of other people's marriages.' Including yours. They were glaring at each other, I'm-not-giving-in-first in both sets of eyes. Then quite suddenly they both let go and laughed at their own tension. Almost offhand now, Anna said, 'Of course, Andrew himself may have something to say.'

'Oh?'

'He's coming back to someone different from the one he first arrived with, and he may not feel comfortable with the changes in her. The island's had an effect on Cari. You're just the outward and visible manifestation.'

'Thanks, that makes me feel great.'

'Get used to the idea. It's no kindness to yourself to think differently.'

'You're a tough woman.'

'With myself. I'm paying you a compliment by extending it to you.' She watched his face. 'What do *you* think she'll do? You're in a better position to know than I am.'

I know nothing, he wanted to say, but he couldn't, too much going on in him. With difficulty he managed, 'I try to stop myself thinking about any kind of future with her because it's so unlikely to happen. But you can't stop yourself wanting.'

'No,' she said flatly. 'You can't.'

'And I've given up trying to work out the morality of it.' Then, bursting out of him, 'But I *definitely* don't want to meet Andrew.'

'No, that makes sense. I don't either.' They smiled, a touch of complicity. She said, 'He's probably a perfectly nice man. Just a bit ungrown up.'

'I really can't, Anna. Myself is enough to deal with right now.'

Incredible that he should be sitting here with Anna, laying his most vulnerable feelings before her. He felt comforted by the knowledge that it was Cari who had given him this, that in removing herself she had left him with a friend.

'You've heard about the child?' he asked Anna.

It was hardly a question, nor even asking for confirmation. It was plea, an irrational plea to some unknown power that might make itself manifest through this woman who understood loss. He became aware that she was watching his face intently. 'Yes,' she said eventually, 'Yes, I've heard.' And then she turned away.

For a while neither of them spoke. Hugh let his eyes follow the movement of her hands, trailing the sea sandwort, touching the about-to-be open flowers. Cari's flowers. They had walked to this beach, that first day she had come back to him. She had touched this same plant and said, 'I'm sure when I was a child it had flowers. Little, sort of creamy white.' It's a high summer flowerer, he had said. I don't know if I'll still be here then, she had said.

Anna's hand moved tensely away from the flowers, stirring the sand. 'I do have an opinion, actually, much as I try not to.' He looked up, taken aback by the sudden force. 'I think she's lashing herself to go back into something that has long lost any life, and it's not going to work. And I wish she would see it and save everyone the pain.'

He felt like crying. The fierceness in her voice, and for him. For what he longed for and could not have.

'Anna,' he said, 'There's something I've wanted to say to you. For a long time. About Jason.' The waves washed against the sand. 'I still grieve,' he said. 'I had no way to tell you.'

'It doesn't matter anymore,' she said, when she found the voice to do it with.

'I also loved him.'

'I know. I know more than I should. I read Jason's diaries. *It was impossible not to blame you —*' The words had come out like a cry, wrenched from her, and the harsh sound of it shocked her into silence again.

I blamed everyone. Max. Myself. Thinking, if I had never taken him to St Martin's, if he had never met Hugh.

You can't think that way, Anna. If you hadn't brought him, he would have found it some other way.

It was only when I read the diaries that I found out how powerful your influence was on him. All he wanted to do after he got to know you was get out on the sea, every weekend, every holiday. Pushing himself beyond what he could handle.

No, Anna, no. He was a fine yachtsman, he knew what he was doing. It was a freak storm, it could happen to anyone who spends a lot of time out there.

But he was obsessed, it wasn't normal.

The sea does that to some people. You can't stop it, like you can't stop sons growing up and going away. It was his life and he chose it, and if it ended too soon, at least you know he was doing what he loved.

I know, I know, I've said it to myself a thousand times, but it doesn't get inside me. Inside there's just a scream of Why? Why him? Why me?

Why? the scream raged like the storm let loose again. But gradually through its buffeting she began to be aware in a more profound way than before that she was not alone hearing that tearing sound of her own inner voice. He had come to kneel beside her, and his arm was around her heaving shoulder, holding her, comforting her against the sorrow that could not be taken away. It was so long since any man had touched her, since she had allowed herself to acknowledge that unmet need, that for the first instant it was a shock. But there was no ambiguity in the hold, simply a reaching out of shared humanity, deeper than any need of man or of woman. The strength in the hold was his own knowledge of suffering, the gentleness his understanding that only she could find her own capacity to survive. To be held changed nothing, yet it changed everything that she could now accept and be comforted by what he had once tried to offer and that she in her desolation had been unable to receive.

She rested in the arm, and waited for the rage to blow itself out.

The arm loosened. She moved her shoulders, to let the circulation get going again. The arm withdrew. He moved slightly away to sit on the sand near her but with space between them. They both sat looking out to sea, Jason's sea; and it was finished.

'The diaries,' she said quietly, 'I found them when I was turning out his room. For weeks they stared at me and I couldn't open them. Jason's words, Jason's thoughts, he hadn't meant them for anyone else. I've intruded enough, I thought, and I was afraid of his angry spirit coming to haunt me if I followed him again to a place where he wanted to be alone. But it became impossible not to open them, this bit of his spirit left to touch when there had been no body to mourn over. And when I read them I began to understand that his privacy meant something different from what I had always assumed. There wasn't anything in them that it mattered if other people saw, they were just sailing diaries. What the wind was like, how long they tacked for, where they landed. With vivid little descriptions, just a couple of phrases but enough for me to track the places by. It *did* bring his spirit back, but not angrily. It felt almost that he had written them knowing that one day I would find them. That he was shrugging in that off-hand way he had and saying, read them if you like, there's nothing much in them. But there was. There was the small boy who would confidentially tell me things. And the more I read the more I felt he was telling me he hadn't wanted to cut off for ever, it was just the way things had to be, until he got past proving his manhood.

And your name, more than any other. Quoting you, the final authority. Hugh said the wind is too unreliable to try Round Island today. Hugh said if we tried Great Gannick in the early morning we might see a shoal of pilchards. Hugh said. Hugh said.'

Hugh said, 'He was a fine boy, Anna. You were lucky to have him.'

≈≈

'You told Hugh it was Andrew's child?' Anna's voice was incredulous.

'Yes.'

'*Why?*'

'I wanted to make it simpler. For him. For everyone.'

'Cari, Cari –'

'Anna, *what?*'

But she just sat there with her head in her hands, rocking

330

herself, and wouldn't say what she was thinking.

She knows, Cari thought. She doesn't have to say it, I can hear it in her hands covering her face. The child will have Hugh's eyes, she is saying. You will know every time it smiles.

Yes. And I'll be happy every time.

And what about Andrew?

Andrew won't know.

Secrets can't be kept forever, Cari. It will come out one day when you're angry with him, something will trip-switch it out of you –

'Anna, *speak* to me,' Cari pleaded.

Slowly Anna looked up. Through the pressure of her own feelings Cari was shocked at Anna's face. It looked tired, with a tiredness of ages. Anna said, 'Do for yourself whatever you have to do. But don't take from Hugh what is his. If you think it's his child, tell him. Whatever you decide to do, he has a right to know.'

Cari was near to tears. Anna said, 'And now I need some time alone.'

'Anna, please. I need you not to be angry with me.'

'Come back tomorrow. We'll talk again when I'm not so tired.'

'Anna –'

'Cari my love, *go*.' And then, more gently, 'We're singing in the concert tonight. I need to get ready.'

OK I'm going – pulling on her anorak, out, pushing blindly through the gate, brushing the wet from her stupid eyes, oblivious of the quiet drizzle that had started up again, mixing with her tears. Running down the road, away from Anna's face that would not even look at her, away from the accusation in her voice that frightened her because she knew it was true. Run, run through the rain, anywhere, just away from this bottled up, useless emotion.

She stopped, dripping and panting, and realised she had arrived at the centre of the small town. The bus was parked, taking on passengers for its round-the-island journey, in the same place where years ago she and Robyn had climbed on board, two small girls who travelled the island alone. She stood next to the phone box and watched these latter-day Caris and Robyns climb on, and she felt lonely and confused, struggling to make sense of it all, of her whole life, the pattern of it from then to now. Of what coming back here had been for.

The bus set off, taking the children with it. She watched until it was out of sight and then went into the phone booth. She stared at the phone, trying to work out whose number she was meant to be dialling.

The through tone. Her mum's voice answered, slightly remote, her mind on other things. Cari was grateful. Too much emotion this side, she wanted to be shot of it.

'Is anything wrong?' her mum asked. 'We haven't heard much lately.'

'It's been a bit hectic,' Cari said. 'But I'll write soon, promise.' Mum must be about Anna's age, Cari thought. There I was watching Anna and her daughter, how come I never thought what my own mother might need of me? I'll try harder, she vowed, I really will. 'Did I tell you,' she said, 'Andrew's gone back to see his superviser?'

'No. So you're alone?'

'Not really. I've got good friends. Mum, where's Robyn?'

'On her way home from Italy. She's broken her ankle.'

'No! What was she doing?'

Her mum laughed. 'Stepping off a pavement.'

Cari joined the laugh and then heard it go on too long, in

relief at having something outside herself to react to. 'Oh God it's awful,' she said, 'why are we laughing?'

'She's OK,' her mum said, 'Just cross she didn't get it doing something more exciting. But she'll be in plaster for weeks so she thought she might as well come home and be looked after.'

Me too, please can I come and be looked after. But it's nothing as simple as a broken ankle. 'Mum, it's half-term next week. Can I come for a couple of days while she's there?'

Phone down, out again. She stared around her, taking in what she had just done. Her brain felt fogged with too much feeling, she couldn't work anything out any more, could only wait for things to surface. Something did. She went back in, to dial Andrew's number.

'How's it going?' she asked.

'Slower than I thought.'

I can't believe this, she thought. I could do his part of this conversation without even having bothered to phone.

'I was going to phone you,' he said. 'I'm not sure I can get there for your half-term.'

'Don't worry. I've decided I'll go home for a couple of days. I could come on to you after that.'

'Why the sudden change?'

She heard her voice trotting out inconsequentials. 'I'm getting island vision, like you said. A break might do me good.'

'Well, well. I hoped you'd get there on your own.'

The tone was so familiar – there's one right way and it's mine. You join me and things will be fine –

Revolt stirred. How will I put up with that again? I can't fight that tone, it's impregnable. *And I don't want to have to, ever again.*

Suddenly it was terribly easy. 'Andrew,' she said, 'I'm coming because there are things we need to talk about.'

Out of the phone booth, walking, anywhere. She felt an extraordinary lightness suddenly, a detachment from them all, from the holiday-makers, from Andrew, from Robyn and her mum, even from Anna's distressed face. She wanted just to be calm and look out over the sea and think about what was happening inside her. A new life, a child growing.

She looked down on the town beach at a young mother on her back in the sand, laughing as her child clambered over her, a little girl of maybe one-and-a-half or two, trailing sand over her mother's tummy. The mother playfully defended herself, the child gurgled wickedly as she scooped more sand and tipped it. Suddenly the mother's hands scooped her up and lifted her into the air, and she dangled there, wiggling and shrieking with delight.

A child like that, about to come into being. I'm carrying a miracle, nothing less. A-life-in-embryo, cradled in the water of the womb, its walls like the edges of the island, holding it safe. A child, not mine, not Hugh's, not anyone's, but itself, given to the world to laugh at the tickle and security of her mother's love, humanity renewing itself yet again.

Almost without being aware that she had made a decision she turned, walking back to the streets of the town, running now, running before that clarity could desert her again. The rain was back but she ignored it, just kept running through it to Neville's house because she could not possibly wait until tomorrow, running to knock on his door.

Vera opened the door.

'Good heavens,' she said, 'what is it?'

'I'm sorry to barge in,' Cari panted, 'but there was something I – Is Neville in?'

'There's the concert tonight. He's getting ready to leave.'

Neville appeared. 'Cari?' Surprised. Of course. But more;

concerned. Perhaps she looked wilder than she realised, running through the rain.

'Neville, I –' She didn't know how to go on. Vera there, expecting her to say, I'm sorry, I don't want to delay you, I'll talk to you at school tomorrow.

Neville said, 'How urgent is it?'

By what scale? Cari wanted to ask. It's not about Yvonne, not a crisis at the school. *Me,* said a voice inside her, coming up from who-knows-where – *it's desperately important to me.*

'I need to ask you something,' said her own voice, still breathless but definite. 'It won't take long, I promise.'

Neville hesitated only a moment, then said, 'Vera my dear, you go on ahead.' He took Cari's dripping anorak, hung it behind the door and led her into the living room. He motioned to her to sit down and sat opposite her, waiting.

Say it, Cari. He's here, giving you time. Ready to listen. Just say it – but no voice now. Just an echo in her ears of Neville saying, 'What matters more than the moment of weakness is how you handle the mess you've created.' The damage is done, no way of undoing it. Just start to clear up the mess. Her voice arrived. 'I've come to ask if I can stay after all.'

His eyebrows lifted. 'I thought I understood you to say –' He trailed off, waiting for her to finish it.

'I did. The baby. Nothing's changed. Except me. I've understood what I have to do.'

'And that is?'

'To stay. To take proper responsibility for what I've landed myself and other people in.' And suddenly it seemed simple to tell him, and it all came out in a rush. 'It's not my husband's baby. I can't be scientifically sure but I'm as sure as you can be any other way. And it's made me understand, I can't go back to him. I've been struggling with it, thinking it was what I owed him, that I had to make up to him for what I'd done. But I understand now that going back wouldn't make for up anything, it would make things worse, for him, for me, for the baby, for everyone. What's done is done, I have to stop pretending I can undo it.'

The flow of words had run itself out. No sign of how Neville was reacting. Slow down, slow down. More quietly now she said, 'I'm sorry to barge in at your home, to land all this on you. The thing is –'

'The thing is?'

'It's taken me ever so long but now I've realised what I need to do, I was so afraid you might already have –'

'My dear, just say what you have to say.'

'Can you delay advertising Paul's job? I'd like to stay until Christmas.'

'It's gone,' he said. 'I sent in the ad today.'

'Oh God.'

He was looking at her steadily, assessing. 'But it won't appear till Tuesday. It could still be cancelled.'

'Oh, *please*. That would be wonderful. I –'

'I said, Could be,' he said. 'I would need to think about it. And I would need to understand more about the whole situation.'

'Of course.' She felt suddenly deflated, seeing it from his point of view. So much better for him to get someone in who could stay.

'There are a number of questions,' he said. 'For instance, dates. The baby's due in –?'

'January. I could stay till Christmas. And after that – I don't know – it depends on – I don't know if you could bear to do another maternity cover – I don't how soon I'd be ready to come back. Maybe Janet might want to go on being half time and we could do a job share and then you could advertise the other

336

post.'

'Maybe. A lot of maybes.'

She nodded. How to deny it?

He said, 'Then there are the children. They can count backwards as well as anyone. Well before Christmas it's going to be obvious what's happening to you. I'd prefer not to have a lot of speculation about your private life filling their heads, about how it all came about. And it won't stop at the children. The islands don't easily pass up the opportunity to comment. I had rather hoped the school could now get on with normal life, free from drama.'

Of course. What could she say?

'You haven't said anything about the father. Presumably he's part of the equation.'

He had a right to ask, since she was asking him to fix things around her. Carefully she said, 'The father lives on the islands. I would like to be with him and he wants it too. But I'm married to Andrew. I can't unpick that fast enough to make the baby legitimate.' She paused, collected her thoughts. 'I can see I'm asking too much. I was only thinking of myself, what would work for me.'

He said, gently, 'No harm in that. But I don't see that staying till Christmas would solve much.'

It *would*. But how to explain? It would be safe. It would keep one thing at least unchanged. It would let me take it slowly, step by step. She said, 'I suppose I wanted to know I have a way to stay here myself, that I have a role other than just landing myself and a baby on him. He's a man who has to find his own way to things. I've made my choice, but I want him to know *he* has a choice. I don't want anyone to have to make decisions in a rush. I've made a mess of one marriage and I don't want there to be any more damage. I thought, if I can stay, we'll have time to think about it together. Really understand what we're taking on. I want something that will *work*. Long-term.' She paused and amended that to, 'Forever.'

Neville smiled. 'Forever. Don't we all.'

'*Yes*,' she said, refusing to be smiled at for wanting it. 'It *can* work, I'm that kind of person, I know I am. I just started before I was ready last time. And I'm ready now, to do it properly.'

For a few moments he said nothing, just stared out of the window. Eventually he said, 'Come and see me in the morning and I'll give you an answer.' He stood up. 'And now I do really have to go or I'll be late.'

She felt exhausted. Tomorrow seemed an interminably long way away. She had run miles, leaped continents, and she had still not arrived. She stood up, feeling it was an effort to stand steady on her feet. Neville saw, reached out to give her a hand. 'There,' he said gently. 'You go home now and take care of yourself.'

She nodded, let herself be led to the door. He handed her her anorak. 'Afraid this is still very wet.'

'It doesn't matter,' she said.

He took down his own coat, put it on. With his hand on the latch he stopped, turned to her again. 'And all this has been going on while you've been keeping Yvonne going.'

She nodded.

'Do you have any idea what that makes me feel?'

She shook her head, suddenly close to tears.

He said, suddenly brisk, 'You don't need to wait till tomorrow. The answer is Yes. We'll be lucky to have you.'

The rain had blown over, the evening air moist and gentle. Cari walked down the road a little way behind Neville, observing as if she were an outsider again, watching the gathering of people arriving at the church, shaking out umbrellas, going in. Door closed. She turned down towards the harbour where the last of the day was dribbling away. The debris of another day. An empty can of coke, one abandoned sandal, a child's bucket upside down in the sand.

An oystercatcher moved along the tide mark, its long orange beak pecking away looking for shells. Its red legs moved purposefully amongst the straggling lines of seaweed. 'They make several nests,' Hugh had said, 'then the female chooses the one she thinks best.' She had chosen. She could think of Andrew now, for the first time in all these weeks, without guilt. Why that was possible now when it had not been before, she could not say. Perhaps simply that she had come to the end of what she could feel. Perhaps she had already passed it earlier and been too afraid to realise it. But the lifting of guilt enabled her to feel compassion, for the man he was, for the man he would have to struggle to become. He isn't ready, she realised, for any of what I would have been landing on him. It wouldn't have helped him to force the pace.

A little way down the sand a man was bending over his boat. She watched him for a moment, and then the picture shifted, and in her mind's eye she saw instead Hugh with his dinghy, lying on its side on the beach below his house, a constant unstated invitation. A stillness began to settle on her spirit. She felt his presence as if it were there with her, not physical, but the indefinable composite of all his spiritual qualities. The obstinacy that caused him so much trouble; the life-energy that had to be engaged, but always in a way *he* discovered, driven by some inner purpose which no one but he could fathom. The love that made him stand quietly next to the boat, inviting her but not pressing, leaving her to take the step when she was ready. And her own remembered surprise, at letting herself be led beyond fear. At running free across the beach, Hugh chasing, both of them panting with laughter. 'Do you know about kittiwakes?' he had asked. Young kittiwakes calling, perched on their high narrow ledges, waiting till they are ready to fly.

'I think we'll manage,' she said, to the Hugh in her mind.

'We'll do more than manage,' he said.

Yes, it would be more. More everything. More joyous, more unpredictable, and probably also more perilous than anything she would have risked if she had been planning it herself. But worth it. Anyway, it was done. You don't choose the manner of your growing up but you can't turn back on it once it's happened.

The man she had been watching next to his boat stood up, and she saw wispy red hair, big shoulders – Hugh's friend, Garth, the boatman who had taken her over to St Martin's the day she went to be with Hugh, not being able to bear to think of him so alone. She remembered Hugh saying, 'You can ask him again, anytime you need to.' And here the man was, appearing exactly when she needed him. Her mind began to run picture stories again. She imagined herself walking down the beach to talk to Garth ... I'll say, 'I'm a friend of Hugh's.' And Garth will probably say, 'I know', because I'm sure he does. I'll say, 'There's something very important I need to tell Hugh. I was wondering if you could possibly take me over?' And he'll say, 'It's no problem.' And I'll climb into the boat, and make that short journey over the sea, our sea, Hugh's known waters, and now mine. And he'll open his door and see me there, and he'll know even before I tell him that this time I've come to stay.

She got up and started to walk down the beach towards him. From behind her came the sounds of the choir starting up. *My soul doth magnify the Lord.* She liked to think of Anna's voice being part of that sound, though lost among the others, losing itself to forget that other loss, those other failures, to accept the shape of her new life.

≈≈

Anna woke to a perfect May morning, the light sharp and clear, drops of moisture sparkling. It had rained in the night and the singing had washed her spirit clean. She ate breakfast slowly, then set out to cycle through town, going nowhere, thinking nothing. She weaved her way past the school, where Cari would be teaching, last day before the half-term. Out of town, past the furniture-maker who had designed her kitchen stools, past the small wooden gate where a father was leading two little girls to the start of the nature trail. Up the hill to the turnoff past the quarry garden, then down to Holy Vale where the wind soughed in the pines.

There was a house here, she had heard, where more than half a century ago there had been a scandal that had shaken the island, a story she hardly remembered but she thought incest came into it, and certainly murder. She cycled past the small group of houses now, wondering which one it was. Each stood quiet and picturesque in this sheltered dip in the land, gardens laden with exotic colour flowering over stone walls. Maybe in fifty years someone would cycle past her house and wonder which one it was where the St Martin's schoolgirl of long ago had taken refuge. But they wouldn't, because it hadn't come to anything the historians could make a story of. Just another life painfully moving itself onward, leaving behind as little trace as plants that return to the earth, as boats that sink below the waves.

On up the lane, to where it joined the road. She could turn left at this point and head north towards Jason's beach, or she could turn right, back home. She stood undecided, legs straddling her bike. Across the road a group of young people drifted back from Pelistry Bay, towels over their shoulders, flip-flops on their feet. They smiled at her as they grouped on the small scrap of grass opposite, waiting for the bus. She smiled back. They think I'm slightly crazy, she realised, just standing here over my bike, going nowhere. I'm probably an island feature, like the bus driver who knows everyone. One of the things they tell their friends about when they get back home. The woman on a bike, going nowhere.

The bus came. She waved to the bus driver, he waved back. The beach party climbed on, the bus trundled down hill. She got back on her bike and followed the bus.

Now for the first time today she let herself think about Cari again. She was sorry she had distressed the girl, but she did not ultimately regret it. What she had said had been jerked out her involuntarily by the intensity of the day, but Cari would survive it. And in a strange way it had been cathartic to allow herself to be angry. She felt, now, free of any need to feel further involved. Cari would decide one way or the other, and they would all simply try to make the best of it.

Inside her where her best conversations happened she heard Cari's voice saying, 'I don't feel grown up enough to have a child.'

'No one ever is,' Anna said.

And only now did she register the choice she had made as she had set off once more from that corner where she had paused. She was heading home. She couldn't remember any more why she would have wanted to go to Jason's beach. It was done, there was nothing more to feel.

The bike came over a rise to a view of the sea, a smooth expanse of benign blue. The birds circled over the cliff tops, *keeow keeow*, the sounds her grandma had been born to and Jason gone looking for, the sounds that Hugh knew as intimately as he knew the waters he sailed. Above her the clouds sailed, white and fluffy, in a sky without blemish. Really, she said to the sea, the sky,

342

who do you think you are fooling? The same sea that in other moods whipped up storms that battered the birds as they pulsed their way back from the cold north, that let loose waves as high as a house to sever boats on their moorings and smash against the rocks those who loved the sea and had learnt its ways. She held in her mind both the simple blue of days like today and the wild grey-green terror of the storm; the sea that sustained life, the sea that destroyed it.

She freewheeled down the hill, wind lifting her hair.